OTHER BOOKS BY VASSILY AKSYONOV

Half-way to the Moon (1965)

The Steel Bird and Other Stories (1979)

The Burn (forthcoming)

THE ISLAND
OF CRIMEA

POLAND

N

St. Petersburg

Moscow

U.S.S.R.

RUMANIA

BULGARIA

CRIMEA

Black Sea

TURKEY

SYRIA

IRAQ

IRAN

Caspian Sea

AFGHANISTAN

© 1983 A. Karl/J. Kemp

Miles
0 — 300
0 — 300
Kms.

U.S.S.R.

Black Sea

CRIMEA
Simferopol
Yalta
Sevastopol

Kms.
0 — 100
0 — 100
Miles

THE ISLAND OF
CRIMEA

THE ISLAND
OF CRIMEA

A Novel by

Vassily Aksyonov

Translated from the Russian by

Michael Henry Heim

Random House
New York

Library of Congress Cataloging in Publication Data
Aksenov, Vasiliĭ Pavlovich, 1932–
The island of Crimea.
Translation of: Ostrov Krym.
I. Title.
PG3478.K70813   1983   891.73′44   83–42756
ISBN 0–394–52431–4

Manufactured in the United States of America
9 8 7 6 5 4 3 2
Typography and binding design by J. K. Lambert
First American Edition

In memory of my mother,

EUGENIA GINZBURG

Preface

Every peninsula fancies itself an island. Conversely, there is no island that does not envy a peninsula. Every Russian schoolboy knows that Crimea is connected to mainland Russia by an isthmus, but not even every adult knows how flimsy an isthmus it is. When a Russian rides along it for the first time and sees it for its narrow, swampy self, he can't quite suppress a seditious "what if."

What if Crimea really were an island? What if, as a result, the White Army had been able to defend Crimea from the Reds in 1920? What if Crimea had developed as a Russian, yet Western, democracy alongside the totalitarian mainland?

The southern coast of Crimea is a subtropic zone protected from the fierce Russian winter by a range of mountains. During that winter the mountains are covered with black clouds seemingly fixed in time, while down below the sun is shining. If those isolating, doomful black clouds remind the Westerner of Stanley Kramer's film of *On the Beach*, the Russian can't help thinking that selfsame seditious "what if."

A month after I completed *The Island of Crimea*, the Soviets invaded Afghanistan. I must admit the invasion was not the only factor that made me wary of submitting the novel to a Soviet publisher. The Soviet authorities maintain a firm and realistic view of geography. They know that the world rests on three whales and two elephants.

Washington, D.C., 1983

Contents

THE ISLAND
OF CRIMEA

I

An Attack of Youth

Everyone knows the *Russian Courier* skyscraper, insolent in its pencil-point simplicity among the wild monuments to architectural self-expression in downtown Simferopol. As our story begins—at the end of a hard night at the teletype machines, a spring night late in the present decade or early in the decade to come (depending on when this book comes out)—we find the publisher-editor of the *Courier*, forty-six-year-old Andrei Arsenievich Luchnikov, in his suite atop the skyscraper. Although he prefers more modest names for it, it is in fact a playboy's penthouse.

Lying on a rug in the asana of perfect repose, Luchnikov tried to imagine himself as a feather, a cloud flying up out of his 175-pound body. It didn't work. His mind kept whirling with late news clutter, especially the conflicting reports from West Africa coming in on the United Press International and Russian Telegraph Agency wires: either Marxist tribesmen were making forays into Shaba or a band of European cutthroats was attacking Luanda. They had spent half the night working on it, talking long-distance to their Ivory Coast correspondent, but they never did make any sense of it and were forced to go with the bland "According to unconfirmed reports . . ."

Then, on top of it all, there was an unexpected phone call of a

3

personal nature: Andrei Arsenievich's father had asked him to come and see him immediately, that very day.

Luchnikov finally conceded that his meditation was going nowhere. He got up from the rug and began to shave, observing how (in accordance with the laws of contemporary architecture) the sun spread its strips of morning light and shadow across the Simfi cityscape.

Simfi had once been a sleepy little hamlet nestled in dreary gray hills, but after the economic boom of the early forties the municipal board declared open season for the world's most daring architects, and now the Crimean capital surpassed the tourist's wildest dreams.

Despite the early hour Baron Square was packed with expensive cars. Weekend traffic, Luchnikov said to himself, revving up his Peter Turbo and cutting off one car after another as he wove from lane to lane. At last he reached the back street he usually took to the Underground Knot, and crossed himself out of habit while waiting for a light. Suddenly he felt uncomfortable. Why had he crossed himself? The Church of All Saints Radiant in the Russian Land no longer stood at the end of the street, an oval traffic light having taken its place. Crossing yourself in front of traffic lights, eh, you imbecile? You're so wrapped up in the Idea and the newspaper you haven't been to see Father Leonid for a year now, and here you are crossing yourself at traffic lights.

Luchnikov's habit of going through the motions every time he saw an onion dome was the subject of great glee among his new friends in Moscow. The brightest of them, Marlen Kuzenkov, would even lecture him about it: "You're almost a Marxist, Andrei, and even from a purely existential standpoint it's ridiculous to indulge in such naïve symbols." Luchnikov's standard response was a slight and slightly ironic smile, and every time he saw a golden crucifix in the sky, he continued to make a quick cross "as a mere formality." But he'd been troubled lately by the formalities, the vanities of his life style, his distance from the Church, and here he was, to his horror, crossing himself at a traffic light.

A vague feeling of heartburn, the hangover from an all-night teletype session, had come over him. Simfi leaves no room for nostalgia. The light changed, and in a flash Luchnikov realized that the sphere shot through with light before him was in fact the

4

new, ultramodern All Saints Radiant, the swan song of the archi-
tect Hugo Van Plus.

Together with Luchnikov's Peter Turbo, the herd of cars was
drawn into the Underground Knot, wound through its maze of
tunnels, and spewed out at great speed onto one or another of
Crimea's state-of-the-art freeways. The idea was to enable the
underground traffic to pick up enough speed so that by the time a
car reached the entrance ramp of its choice, its needle had moved
over to the second half of the speedometer. As the years went by,
the idea became a more and more unrealizable ideal, especially on
weekends. In any case, entry speed was not so high as to keep
anyone from reading the strings of two-foot-tall letters on the cement wall above the tunnel's mouth. The youth organizations of
the capital took advantage of the situation, lowering their activists
on ropes to cover the wall with brightly painted slogans, symbols,
caricatures.

In fact, all along the walls of the Underground Knot the political
artwork had undergone an explosion lately as the myriad Island
parties began their campaigns in anticipation of the South Russia
Provisional State Duma elections still six months away. The evening rush hours often saw fistfights among representatives of the
various factions, the most virulent being those among the eight
"most progressive" parties, in other words, the various shades of
communism.

The Municipal Duma diehards called for an end to "the scoun-
drels' unbridled behavior" and demanded that the walls be painted
over, but the liberals—with the assistance of Luchnikov's paper, of
course—held sway, and since then the hundred-foot-high walls
leading in and out of the Knot, smeared top to bottom with all the
colors of the spectrum, had been considered more or less a tourist
attraction, a showcase, as it were, for the Island's democracy.
Then again, in Crimea every wall was a showcase for democracy.

Whizzing out of East Gate, Luchnikov smiled wryly at the sight
of a young enthusiast hanging like a spider in the middle of the
wall, putting the finishing touches on an enormous COMMUNISM IS
THE RADIANT FUTURE OF ALL MANKIND slogan that covered the poly-
chromatic revelations of the previous day with a band of pure red.
On the seat of his faded jeans the boy wore a spanking new
hammer-and-sickle patch. From time to time he showered the

stream of cars with what looked like small party favors, which exploded in the air and fluttered down in the form of propaganda confetti. The poor kid probably hadn't slept a wink all night, thought Luchnikov, and over the strident jumble of spray paint, over the gigantic slogans he imagined an overriding, overshouting SOS appearing one fine night, SOS, the Russian initials of the Common Fate League, the only conceivable future for Crimea, reunification with the Great Motherland, the only way to avoid the ultimate catastrophe. . . .

Luchnikov looked on either side of him. Most of the drivers and their passengers were totally oblivious to the enthusiast, though two lanes to the left some obviously tipsy British tourists in a Volkswagen van were waving their handkerchiefs at him and trying to take his picture while a middle-aged gentleman in the lane to his right frowned from behind the wheel of his shiny, luxurious Russo-Balt.

This exquisitely groomed, absolutely self-assured mastodon turned his head slightly and made a remark to his passengers, whereupon two female mastodons picked themselves up from the soft leather depths of the Russo-Balt and peered out the window. The two of them—one middle-aged, the other young, both beauties —showed great interest, but instead of squinting up at the spider in the sky, they squinted over at Luchnikov. White Guard trash. Must have recognized me. From that TV program the night before last. Anyway, all provacuees are acquainted in some form or other, and I bet those two bitches are trying to decide where they've met me—at the Beklemishevs' Tuesdays, the Obolenskys' Thursdays, or the Nesselrodes' Fridays. . . .

The windows of the Russo-Balt rolled down.

"Hello, Andrei Arsenievich!"

"*Mesdames,*" replied Luchnikov cordially. "How good it is to see you! And how well you're looking! On your way to the golf course, I presume? Tell me, how is the general's health?"

There was no risk involved in asking any provacuee about the general's health because every one of them was related to some doddering old general or another.

"You don't seem to recognize us, Andrei Arsenievich," the middle-aged beauty said sweetly. The young beauty smiled and added, "We are the Nesselrodes."

6

"But of course I recognize you," Luchnikov continued face-tiously. "We've met ever so many times: at the Beklemishevs' Tuesdays, the Obolenskys' Thursdays, the Nesselrodes' Fridays—"

"But *we* are the Nesselrodes!" said the middle-aged beauty. "This is Lidochka, and I am Varvara Alexandrovna."

"That's right, that's right," answered Luchnikov, nodding. "You are the Nesselrodes, and we meet at the Beklemishevs' Tuesdays, the Obolenskys' Thursdays, and the Nesselrodes' Fridays, *n'est-ce pas?*"

"An Ionesco dialogue if I ever heard one," said the young Lidochka.

Both women flashed him charming smiles.

Why are they being so nice to me, repaying my rudeness with smiles? Oh, of course. I'm the catch of the season. Leftist views notwithstanding, I'm an "eligible provacuee, a rarity in our times, my dear."

"I imagine you can't wait to sprint ahead of us in your Turbo," said Lidochka.

"Yes, ma'am," he replied in English. His slightly American intonation must have shocked the women's Russian ears.

"Our papa prefers Russo-Balts," said Lidochka, trying to keep up the "Ionesco dialogue." "They give a smooth, even ride, though they can give speed when speed is wanted."

"I could have told you right away your papa prefers Russo-Balts," said Luchnikov.

"Really, now," said Varvara Alexandrovna. "Is that because he is your political opponent?"

Aha! thought Luchnikov. My political opponent! But in response to her question he said aloud, "Why no, Varvara Alexandrovna, I realized your papa preferred Russo-Balts the moment I saw him behind the wheel of a Russo-Balt!"

Mr. Nesselrode turned his head slightly and said a few words. "Mikhail Mikhailovich was wondering about Arseny Nikolaevich's health" was how Varvara Alexandrovna rendered them.

Looking ahead to gauge the cruising speed of the cars and knowing that the gradient would soon rise and the herd thin out, Luchnikov gave his wheel a slight turn and, all but brushing up against the Russo-Balt, leaned over and whispered passionately into Varvara Alexandrovna's ear, "I'm on my way to my father's now. As soon as I have news of his health, I'll wire or phone. And let's see more of each other, shall we? I may not be young, but I'm available. Leftist views notwithstanding. What do you say?"

Then Luchnikov stepped down hard on the accelerator, and his bright-red twin-tailed sports beast roared its turboroar and shot forward, zigzagging in and out among the lanes until it left the herd behind and began tearing up the sun-drenched hump of the Eastern Freeway.

On its way out of Simfi the EF seems to follow a nearly vertical flight pattern. The light silvery viaduct with its lacework confluences and dispersions was one of the engineering miracles of the world. "Come to Crimea and See Eighteenth-Century Pastorals on a Backdrop of Twenty-first-Century Architecture!" proclaimed the tourist-board brochures. They weren't lying.

Where does all our wealth come from? Luchnikov asked himself for the thousandth time, looking down over the land-of-plenty landscape dotted with rectangular, triangular, oval, and kidney-shaped swimming pools and crisscrossed by winding back roads now bearing Cadillacs full of wealthy Yakis to their wealthy Yaki friends. Yes, an immorally rich country.

Luchnikov mentally compared it with the Southern Road up north in the Soviet Union. Not long ago he'd traveled it in a Volga with his old Moscow friend Vitaly Gangut, one-time film director.

What was the name of the town where we went shopping that day? Luchnikov thought. Fanezh? No. Fatezh. With its cracked-asphalt square and standard all-purpose Monument to the Unknown Soldier. Did it have an eternal flame? No, I don't think regulations allow eternal flames for monuments in towns smaller than district centers. That's right, no Eternal Flame in Fatezh. At least it had that going for it.

"And now for a display of Soviet abundance," Vitaly had said.

There were several women standing at the counter inside the shop. They turned and stared mutely at the intruders. Perhaps they took us for foreigners: strange bags over our shoulders, strange jackets. All the time we walked about looking at the goods the women followed us with their eyes, though if we looked over at them, they turned away.

Basically, there was nothing to be had. No, I don't want to

overestimate or rather underestimate the country's achievements. There were in fact a few things: one flavor of fruit drops, some soggy sugar wafers, one kind of packaged pastries, Tourist Breakfast–brand tinned fish. In what they called the delicatessen section, we found something truly frightening: a block of frozen deepwater fish, the gift of the murky depths to Fatezh. Compressed industrially into a hefty slab, the fish no longer resembled its genus at all except for a toothy maw visible here and there along the dirt-and-blood-caked surface of the ice.

"I see there are some gaps in your stock," said Gangut to the women with a vicious little smile.

"What are you looking for?" the women asked sullenly.

"Cheese," said Looch, half to himself. "We wanted to buy some cheese."

The second time he said the word "cheese" he used the diminutive, recalling that the Soviet populace was partial to diminutive names for food products. It worked. The women broke into smiles. The way Russian women could change in a split second from dark, sullen wariness to heartfelt warmth was a national treasure. An incomprehensible outsider naturally arouses suspicion, while a person who asks for a "cheeselet" immediately makes himself both clear and likable and earns a smile.

"Cheese? Why, you can get cheese most any time at the base," the women told him readily. "Eight miles down the road. A military base. You can't miss it."

"Fine, fine," said Looch. "We've got a car. No problem."

"What about butter?" asked Gangut, continuing the provocation. "And sausages?"

But the ice was broken, and the Moscow intellectual's bile was completely lost on its audience.

"Looks like you're going to have to drive all the way to Oryol," the women said. "Can't say we ever get much in the way of sausage around here. Now, butter they do bring in every once in a while, but not sausage, no, not sausage. You have to go to Oryol for sausage, and you have to get there early. It's all gone by now. And where would you happen to be going, friends?"

"Moscow."

"Oh. Moscow's got plenty of everything!" the women squealed joyfully.

"Tell me, which is more moral?" Gangut asked Luchnikov on their way back to the car. "Yeliseev and Hughes Supermarket or the delicatessen section in Fatezh?"

"I can't tell you which is more moral, but I can tell you Yeliseev and Hughes is more immoral," answered Looch with a frown.

"You mean, eternal taunts and eternal humility are less immoral? Then allow me to present you with a souvenir from the depths of Soviet Russia, a present to take back to your Island and regale your friends with."

Gangut handed Luchnikov a squat jar whose wraparound label described its contents appetizingly as HEADLESS SQUID IN NATURAL JUICES.

The memory of that jar, of the town of Fatezh, of that whole trip tended to lower Luchnikov's spirits, and although the Peter hummed contentedly along the steel-framed freeway, the sun flooded the prosperous countryside with its light, and the red mustache he'd always been so fond of shone up at him from the speedometer glass, he had been in decidedly low spirits the whole day and was still in a bad mood. Headless squid in natural juices? Those memories of the continent never seemed to leave him in peace. Conflicting reports from West Africa? The sign of the cross in front of a traffic light? The dizzy Nesselrodes? He must be getting old: things upset him more.

Annoying as they were, they were only common, everyday annoyances, and whatever was eating away at Luchnikov—now he was coming closer to the source—was an uncommon, extraordinary anxiety. There was something peculiar about the way his father had said, "No, come tomorrow. Tomorrow without fail." What was the matter? It was the imperative that did it. Imperatives were so unlike him. Even when Andrei was small, his father never seemed to say "Do this" or "Do that." The conditional was much more Arseny Nikolaevich's style. "You would do well to sit down with a book." "Might I suggest we take a drive to the seaside?" That was how the old Volunteer treated everyone around him. The clearly tortured imperative issuing from his father's lips was what had brought Luchnikov's spirits down and upset him so.

Actually, they saw quite a bit of each other; all that separated them was a quick hour on the EF plus thirty minutes of winding mountain roads. Arseny Nikolaevich lived in his country retreat on the slope of Suru-Kaya, and Andrei Arsenievich loved spending time there—climbing up on the flat roof in the morning, feeling the boundless fresh open space beneath him, taking bracing swan dives into the pool, then drinking coffee with his father, smoking, discussing politics, and following the movements of the brightly painted Greek and Turkish trawlers that ply their trade along the shore under the surveillance of a gray pike-shaped gunboat belonging to the Crimean navy. The Crimeans were guarding their oyster beds. Crimean oysters were flown daily to Paris, Nice, Rome, and London, but the pick of the catch ended up on the tables of Crimea's numerous intimate tourist-trade restaurants, and since the famous oyster tax went straight into the coffers of the Ministry of War, the gray pike-gunboat took its job very seriously.

Before he drove up the serpentine leading to Suru-Kaya, Luchnikov stopped by the side of the road. He always stopped there to prolong the magic moment—the appearance of his father's house on the slope. It was a spot that offered a sweeping panorama of Koktebel Bay, and towards the upper right-hand corner of that panorama, directly beneath the sheer rock walls of Sawtooth Mountain, lay the three white ledges that formed his father's house.

Nostalgia had nothing to do with his feeling for it. Arseny Nikolaevich had had it built there only eight or ten years before, when his stud farms began to boom. The sudden rise in his equine stock coincided with the phenomenal rise in Luchnikov senior's stock in Crimean society. There was even talk in certain circles of putting forward his name as a candidate for the chairmanship of the Provisional Duma—in other words, of making him for all practical purposes the president of Crimea. Arseny Luchnikov had all kinds of qualifications, said his backers: he was one of the few remaining participants in the Ice Campaign, a militant provacuee, a professor of history who "has made an enormous contribution to the preservation and development of Russian culture," a European with extensive connections in the Western world, and a millionaire horse breeder "who has done much to further the economic development of the Provisional Evacuation Zone," that is, the Island of Crimea.

The dailies had started running features on Luchnikov senior: his fantastic house built into an all-but-sheer cliff, his subsistence farm on the far side of Holy Mountain, the new breed of jumper developed on his stud farms. Soon a Luchnikov image, a Luchnikov look, began to take shape: a tall, thin man with laughing eyes, an elderly man, but dressed like the young in jeans and a leather jacket.

It was hard to say whether Arseny Nikolaevich was actively campaigning for the presidency or merely letting matters take their course. When asked during a television interview whether it didn't worry him to know that his spectacular house was in a seismically precarious zone, he replied, "It would be ridiculous to live on the Island of Crimea and fear earthquakes."

This statement occasioned a great wave of fatalistic mirth and an odd kind of resilience. Wasn't it in fact ridiculous to fear earthquakes under the radar, missiles, and satellites of—and fifty miles from the border of—the superpower, the much loved, much damned Historical Homeland, the USSR?

But the time was not yet ripe. Not even a man with an aphorism capable of rallying Simfi snobs and Yalta's cosmopolitan riffraff could lay claim to the president's armchair. The keys to Island politics belonged exclusively to the patriots, the true provacuees, the hereditary warrior class, still confident of its strength and its mission to watch over Crimea until the radiant day of the Spring Campaign, the Rebirth of the Homeland. "As for the Soviet leviathan, gentlemen, we . . . do not wish to gloat, of course, but neither can we forget our hero, Lieutenant Bailey-Land; and we should do well to call to mind the examples of Israel, of David and Goliath, and of our own glorious expedition, when Crimea's small but ultramodern forces overwhelmed the mammoth Turkish army in less than a week, forcing the present-day janissaries to accede to the terms of our peace treaty. Consequently, despite the clear and present danger—indeed, because of that danger—we cannot afford to elect a potential defeatist as president. Nor can we pass over the fact that his son Andrei is to all intents and purposes a communist, who runs off to Moscow at every opportunity." "Excuse me, gentlemen, but aren't things getting out of hand? If we go on like this, we won't be any better than the Central Committee or the KGB, and where will the sacred principles of our democracy be then? And anyway, Andrei's no communist. I've known him since he was a baby." "I see the time has come to bring our discussion to a close. We seem to have exhausted the topic at hand. . . ."

Such was Luchnikov's fantasy of how the upper echelons would greet his father's candidacy. It all came back to him now as he rounded the final curves of Suru-Kaya before Kakhovka.

As always, the thought of the upper echelons made his blood boil. Those clowns, those mastodons, those simple-minded shopkeepers sitting about discussing the rebirth of Russian culture, if you please! A pack of crooks and racketeers, and they dare to consider themselves the guardians of Russian civilization! From the day we're born they cram us full of "Bolshevik atrocities," as if they had none of their own. The Reds executed thousands of people; you hanged hundreds. No, that flag you brought to the Kremlin from the South and the East—it wasn't white; it was black, black and bloody. What moved your battalions onward if not the thirst for revenge? Liberals like my Cadet father or White General Denikin himself knew it was useless to bring up the word "republic" in your presence, to drop the merest hint about land reform. Just like the Reds, you had nothing but scorn for the Constituent Assembly, Russia's only chance for a popularly elected legislative body. Even after your defeat you went for Milyukov, murdered Nabokov senior. I hate to think of the witch hunt that would have followed your victory. For six whole decades you have basked in the freedom and comfort of your Provisional Evacuation Base, while our people sweated blood under Stalin's brutes, fought off arrogant foreign hordes with untold sacrifices, then stagnated in a state of lawlessness, spiritual torpor, poverty, and deception. And now that Russia is once more called upon to sacrifice her finest sons, now that she is beginning to undergo complex and dramatic change, what do you blabber about with your rebuilt jaws? The Spring Campaign . . .

The sudden wail of a siren up ahead tore Luchnikov away from his thoughts. Jamming on the brakes, he looked up to see a man in a faded blue work shirt who, half hidden by a luxuriant flowering dogwood, was waving at him and shouting. It was his father. Behind his father's back he noticed a small yellow bulldozer, which despite the bright sun had its headlights on. The bulldozer was evidently the source of the siren.

"Slow down, Andrei!" his father shouted.

Luchnikov took the curve at a leisurely speed. His father came up to him with a youthful gait, swinging his arms jauntily. "We had a bad rockslide here yesterday," he explained. "I've been clearing the road with the bulldozer, but it can wait till after lunch."

Arseny sat beside Andrei, and they made their way slowly through the dangerous stretch of road.

"All right," said Luchnikov senior with a smile. "Now you can go back to normal. You haven't lost the knack, have you?"

Until the age of thirty Luchnikov had been a semiprofessional racing driver, and though he was careful not to show off his skill on the freeway or in town, there were times on mountain roads when he would give vent to his puerile passion. He thought his father would enjoy seeing a bit of the little boy in the graying, wrinkling early-middle-aged specimen beside him and revved up his Peter Turbo. The motor roared, and the car lurched forward. Luchnikov loved to accelerate into curves as if he meant to take off over the precipice, but at the last moment the steering wheel would give a sharp turn, the backdrop would shift, and with a screech the two wheels still on the road would swing round the bend.

"Bravo!" cried Luchnikov senior as they sailed onto the Kakhovka grounds, stopping in the exact center of one of the rectangles in the parking area.

The Luchnikov estate was called Kakhovka for a very specific reason. Ten years before, Andrei had brought back some recordings of Soviet songs from Moscow. His father had listened to them condescendingly until one of them suddenly caused him to sit up and take notice.

> Kakhovka, Kakhovka!
> My rifle's no trifle.
> O fiery bullet, take flight!
>
> The battle was raging,
> The cartridges whistling,
> "Rat tat" went machine guns all night,
> And our favorite nurse roamed

Through flaming Kakhovka
In an army coat, aiding our fight.

Remember, dear Comrade,
The battles we fought there,
Remember the storm at its height,
And how through the smoke like
Two glittering beacons
Her eyes shone so blue and so bright.

Luchnikov senior played the recording several times over, then sat for a while in silence. "They're not what one would call the most literate of words," he finally said, "but strange as it may seem, their Komsomol romanticism reminds me of my own youth and our Cadet battalion. I was once under fire right there in Kakhovka. . . . And our own favorite nurse, Verochka, the Princess Volkonskaya, walked through flaming Kakhovka . . . in a long army greatcoat."

And so the Soviet song "Kakhovka" came to be the favorite of an old provacuee. Needless to say, Luchnikov junior was happy to make his father a present of the record. For him it was one more step on the road to the Idea of a Common Fate he so zealously advocated. Arseny Nikolaevich even made a tape of it for his comrades in arms now living in Paris: "Remember, dear comrade, the battles we fought there?" The response from Paris was ecstatic. It was then that Luchnikov senior hit upon the idea of naming his new Suru-Kaya residence Kakhovka.

"You haven't lost the knack, Andrei." Father and son stood silently in the sun for a minute, enjoying each other's presence. The walls around the courtyard were of different heights and belonged to different buildings; they were punctuated by balconies, spiral staircases, windows at various levels, potted trees, and sculptures.

"I see you've got a new piece," said Andrei. "Looks like a Neizvestny."

"I bought it from a catalogue," said Arseny. "My New York agent took care of the details." Then he added cautiously, "Neizvestny does live in New York now, doesn't he?"

"Alas." Andrei nodded, walking over to *Prometheus* and resting a hand on it. How many times had he seen and touched that very sculpture in Ernst's studio, first in Trubnaya Square, later on Gilyarovsky Street.

They went into the house, passing through a dark hall hung with African masks and into the multilevel southeast wing, the part that jutted out over the valley. Ancient Hua soon appeared with a teacart of beverages and fruit.

"You welcome, Andlei. Glad see you again, yes," he hissed through what was left of his teeth. His dentures looked like the rocks at the mouth of the Yangtze.

"Only forty years with us," said Arseny Nikolaevich, "and hear how good his Russian is."

Hua's blissful laughter took the form of an almost imperceptible quiver. Andrei kissed his brown cheek and picked up a hefty vodkatini.

"Make some coffee for us, Hua, will you?"

Arseny Nikolaevich went out onto the balcony and called his son over with a gesture that said, Come and have a look; I have something interesting to show you. When Andrei Arsenievich leaned over the railing, he nearly dropped his drink. There, standing by the pool, was his son, Anton Andreevich—with his grandfather's long slender frame, a shock of blond locks held in place with a leather headband, and a pair of bright American swimming trunks that reached down to his knees—the picture of laid-back insolence. Andrei Arsenievich had not heard from his only offspring for more than a year. It therefore took him some time to notice that he was not alone: there were two lissome girls swimming in the pool, both stark naked.

"They turned up yesterday evening on foot, with empty backpacks, filthy. . . ." said Luchnikov senior quickly, as if by way of apology.

"They look clean enough now," Luchnikov remarked dryly.

"Yes, and they've had a bite to eat." Luchnikov senior laughed. "They were as hungry as wolves. They sailed over from Turkey on a fishing boat. . . . Call him, Andrei. Give him a chance. . . ."

"Anton! Anto-o-o-shka!" shouted Andrei, the way he used to shout, the way he'd shouted not so long ago, almost yesterday, when his son would automatically respond by bounding up to him like a devoted pooch.

Contrary to his expectations, that is exactly what happened. Anton dived in, crossed the pool with a lightning crawl, jumped out the other side, and raced up the stairs, shouting, "Hi, Dad!"

It was as if nothing had ever come between them—none of those awful scenes connected with the divorce, the mutual accusations, the blows; it was as if the boy hadn't vanished for a year into heaven knows what dens of iniquity in heaven knows what corner of the globe.

After a long bear hug they went into their old routine of scuffling and sparring together. Out of the corner of his eye Luchnikov could see his father beaming. But he also watched the girls as they climbed out of the pool, pulling bright but skimpy bikini bottoms over their hips and making their leisurely way upstairs, lighting up and talking as they came. The idea of wearing the bikini tops never entered their heads, perhaps because they had none.

"Come and meet my father," Anton said to the girls in English. "Dad, this is Pamela, and this is Krystyna."

They were very pretty and very young—older than the nineteen-year-old Anton, but not by much. Pamela had a luxuriant mane of sun-bleached hair and firm breasts so perfect they looked almost sculptured. The California type, thought Luchnikov, à la Farrah Fawcett. Krystyna's hair was brown, and though her breasts (it is only natural Luchnikov's eyes went straight to the breasts; he wasn't used to hobnobbing with today's progressive youth) were not quite so perfectly formed as her friend's, their prominent pink nipples were provocative just the same.

The girls said their nice-to-meet-you's politely enough (Krystyna's betrayed a touch of Slavic) and shook Luchnikov's hand with a strong masculine grip. They made a point of ignoring their bouncing breasts and seemed to be bidding others to do the same; after all, what could be more natural than the human body? Perhaps it was their commitment, perhaps his own hunger, but suddenly Luchnikov felt his old friend stirring in his pants. Not that again, he thought, distressed. He was certain he'd kicked the habit by keeping up a mad pace.

"From the looks of things, you chicks are card-carrying libbers," he said with a malicious twinkle in his eye.

There was an immediate outburst of righteous indignation.

"We're nobody's chicks," growled Krystyna.

"Male chauvinist pig," snarled Pamela, and turning to her friend, she began an agitated tirade. "We might as well write off their generation. I mean, they'll never change. Did you hear the way he said that disgusting word? The way soldiers talked to prostitutes in those old fifties movies."

Luchnikov gave a relieved chuckle: the same old rattlebrains, after all! His friend calmed down as well.

"Oh, don't mind Pop," said Anton. "Sure, he's got some of the old-timer in him, but the truth of the matter is, you've thrown him for a loop with your tits."

"Sorry, gentlemen," said Luchnikov to the girls. "I suppose I did put my foot in my mouth. The sins of youth and all that. Memories of brothels past. You have me pegged, by the way. I *was* a soldier in the fifties."

"Time for lunch," said Arseny Nikolaevich. "Here or the dining room?"

"The dining room," said Anton. "That will get the women into some clothes. And if they don't put something on, Dad won't eat a thing."

"Or eat something he shouldn't," muttered Luchnikov.

Andrei and son lay down next to each other on chaise longues. "Where have you been all this time?" asked Luchnikov.

"Where haven't I been, you mean," he answered boyishly. He motioned to Hua, who brought over his ragged, threadbare jeans. Anton found the right pocket and took out a small metal box that had once held Willem II cigars and now held joints. He lit up. Smoking pot in front of your father—now there's real freedom! Could he really have thought I would hold him back, cramp him, bridle him in any way? Did he really consider me a relic of the fifties like those two minxes? Here I am, known throughout the world as a bellwether, a pacesetter, and my own son creates a generation gap between us. It's really too absurd. Every other family has its generation gap, so we have to have one, too. Maybe he's just not very bright. Or his taste isn't up to snuff. Where did he get that big brash nose of his? The low forehead and thick hair come from his mother, but whose nose is that? Wait a second. What am I thinking? The chin is all mine. And those mirror-image birthmarks: I have one over the left collarbone, he has one over the right; I have one to the right of my belly button, he has one to the left. And the build is pure Arseny.

"All right, then," said Luchnikov. "I'll ask where you haven't been. The States?"

"Coast to coast."

"India?"

"Forty days in an ashram. We even sneaked past the Chinese border guards into Tibet."

"Tell me, Antosha, what did you live on all year?"

"What do you mean?"

"I mean, how did you eat and drink? How did you pay for things?"

Anton chuckled a bit theatrically. "You've got to be kidding, Dad. Money's never a problem. Believe me. Not for . . . well, not for people like us. We live in communes, do some manual labor now and then, do the spare-change bit. And you may not believe this, but I'm getting to be a pretty good saxophonist."

"Where have you played?"

"Paris . . . The metro . . . You know—the Châtelet *correspondance* . . ."

"How about giving me a puff?" asked Luchnikov.

Suddenly Anton remembered what he was smoking, and he switched into that characteristic lazy, laid-back semi-out-of-it mode so popular among the young. "Like . . . it's the real thing," he mumbled to show the trouble his tongue was having. "From Morocco, you dig?"

So he's still just a kid after all.

"That's what I thought," said Luchnikov, taking the slobbery butt and inhaling its sweet smoke. "Great stuff. Strange, I've been talking to you in Russian, and you've been answering in Yaki." He looked over at his son. No doubt about it. A good-looking boy, very.

"Yaki is the language of my country!" Anton exclaimed with unexpected fervor. His good spirits had vanished. His eyes were burning. "I'm speaking the language of my country!"

"I see," said Luchnikov. "So that's what you're into these days."

"Listen, *atats*, don't start riding me again, okay? Sooner or later you're going to have to learn to take me seriously." The hostility in his voice was suddenly the same as it had been the year before. "When I want to speak Yaki, *atats*, I'll speak Yaki!"

The word "*atats*"—"father"—was a typical Yaki word, a mixture of Tatar and Russian.

Suddenly the figure of Luchnikov senior appeared below them in the doorway. "Soup's on, lads!" he called.

Anton picked himself up from the chaise longue and began hopping along the patio, pulling on his jeans as he went. "Oh, I almost forgot," he said, turning around. "I spent some time in Moscow, too."

"Well, well," said Luchnikov, standing up. "And what did you think of it?"

"Barfsville," said Anton with gusto, his spirits immediately rising. The dialogue had ended in his favor.

Luchnikov senior clearly adored the boy. Grandson gave grandfather a friendly butt in the shoulder as he passed into the dining room. Andrei stopped to have a word with Arseny. "Was Anton the reason you asked me to come today without fail? You didn't expect him to vanish by tomorrow, did you?"

"Of course not. Antoshka hasn't said a thing about his plans, but I don't imagine our threesome is in any hurry to leave. This is the first time the girls have been to the Island. Antoshka is looking forward to acting as their guide, showing them Russian mastodon mores and the new Yaki culture. And what with Koktebel and its haunts nearby, I think he can keep his American damsels busy for at least a week."

Though Arseny Nikolaevich was outwardly at his most jovial, Andrei Arsenievich could tell that his father was studying him seriously. The old man did not usually play games with him. He was worried. "Then what made you say 'without fail'? Nothing in particular? Just like that, eh?"

If he answers, "Just like that, nothing in particular," thought Andrei Arsenievich, something's really wrong.

"No, something quite particular," said his father, with a smile that seemed to indicate he had been reading his thoughts. "Freddy Buturlin is coming to lunch."

"But I see him nearly every day in Simfi!" said Luchnikov.

"Well, this evening we need to have a talk together, just the three of us," Luchnikov senior said in an unexpectedly harsh tone, the tone of a statesman in a tense moment of history.

They went into the dining room. One of the walls was all glass and offered a breathtaking view of the sea, Chameleon Rock, and Cape Crocodile. Pamela, Krystyna, Anton, and Freddy Buturlin had taken their places.

Buturlin was a member of the Cabinet, the Deputy Minister of Information, to be exact. A flourishing fifty-year-old scion of an old Russian line, Freddy to his friends and the electorate, Fyodor Borisovich to the provacuees, member in good standing of both the Cadet party and Russian Falcon Athletic Club, and more than anything a playboy without an idea in his head, Buturlin had at one time attended Arseny Nikolaevich's lectures and, at another, run after the ladies with Andrei Arsenievich; he accordingly considered the Luchnikovs his closest and dearest friends.

"Greetings, Andrew old bean," he said, giving him a big hug.

"*Privet*, Fedya!" answered Luchnikov, turning Freddy's dulcet Oxford into demotic Moscow.

Pamela and Krystyna—just look at them!—were transformed: both in dresses! True, the dresses were the latest style, all gauze and see-through and held up by the flimsiest of straps, but at least their budding nipples were covered with brightly colored appliqués. Antosha was still naked to the waist, but he'd combed his hair back into a ponytail.

The seventh place at the table was set for Majordomo Hua. Though he still directed the goings-on in the kitchen and gave constant orders to the waiter, he found time to sit with them, making a proud show of being one of the family, turning from one to another to follow the discussion, his deeply lined face beaming radiantly. At one point the conversation touched on him.

"Hua is an old Taiwanese spy," Anton was telling the girls. "It makes sense, after all. Crimea and Taiwan are kissing cousins. It's quite the thing for provacuee families to have a Chinese agent or two in the household. Hua's been keeping an eye on us for forty years now. He's one of us."

"What does 'provacuee' mean?" asked Pamela with an exquisite little twist of the nose.

"Starting in 1920, when the Bolsheviks ran my granddad and

his bright and shiny battalion off the continent, the White officers on the Island here took to calling themselves 'provisional evacuees,' and the contraction 'provacuees' caught on soon after. By the fifties, when the idea of the resurrection of Holy Russia had basically faded into oblivion, the provacuees had become something of a nation unto themselves."

Luchnikov senior and Luchnikov junior exchanged glances; Anton really is enjoying his new role. Freddy Buturlin let out a half-drunk guffaw. Either he actually had tanked up before he came or he thought his Athletic Club blazer and the presence of the pretty young things required him to act the part. "Really now, Tony!" he cried, threatening Anton with his finger. "You mustn't lead our charming visitors astray. The provacuees, my young ladies, are nothing at all like a nation. Our nationality is Russian. Indeed, *we* are the only true Russians, and not those . . ." At this point the valiant falcon faltered a bit, evidently recalling his position in the Cabinet, and completed his thought in a more diplomatic fashion, "and no one else."

"What you mean is that you are the elite, and your mission is to rule the Crimean people!" Anton fired across the table at Buturlin.

What makes his eyes pop out like that? wondered Luchnikov. Could it come from the pot?

"Not 'you'; 'we,' you and I," said Buturlin, pointing his fork—a spectacular shrimp perilously balanced on it—at Anton. "Don't tell me you wish to disassociate yourself from us, Tony."

"Anton considers himself a representative of the Yaki nation," said Luchnikov with a wry smile.

"The Yaki nation, yes!" shouted Anton. "Our country's future! And not your dead and buried provacuees or stuffed mullahs or shriveled-up Brits!" He shoved his plate away and turned to the girls. "Yaki is a combination of 'okay' and *'yahşi,'* a Turkish word for 'good.' It is a nation currently taking shape here on the Island of Crimea and includes the descendants of Tatars, Italians, Bulgarians, Greeks, and Turks, of the Russian army and the British navy. The Yaki nation is a nation of youth. Our goal is to make our own history, our own future. What do we care for Marxism or monarchism, the resurrection of Holy Russia or the Idea of a Common Fate?"

Anton's heated tirade gave way to an uneasy silence. The girls' faces seemed to have turned to stone, and Krystyna's right cheek was bulging with a choice morsel.

"Do try to excuse us, dear ladies," said Arseny Nikolaevich. "You may not quite understand the issues, but we Island Slavs are forever debating them."

"We don't give a damn about your problems," said Krystyna through the bulge in her cheek and then began to chew.

"Brava!" exclaimed Luchnikov senior. "And now may I propose that we all abandon the battleground of ideas for the groaning board of reality. If you look directly in front of you, where your shrimp cocktails were, you will each find a lobster and a dish of drawn butter. May I also call your attention to the paper-thin, almost transparent slices of Balaklava ham; I trust you'll find it in no way inferior to prosciutto. And next to it—in the crystal server, the jet-black mound adorned with lemon curlicues—is the pride of our Historical Homeland, caviar deluxe, also known as 'hard currency only.' The Nouveau Monde champagne needs no introduction. And now—go to it, one and all!"

What followed was a very pleasant, very normal meal during which the atmosphere was permeated with the heady vapor of alcohol, and soon they all began to ask one another questions without waiting for answers and answer one another's questions without waiting for them to be asked. After the coffee was served, Luchnikov felt Pamela's bare foot traveling up his leg. "You know who this guy reminds me of?" the girl of the Golden West asked, snatching the cigar from Freddy Buturlin's mouth and sticking it into Luchnikov's. "The Marlboro man."

"And do you know who *this* guy reminds me of?" asked Krystyna, hoisting her gauze dress up and plopping her bare bottom on Luchnikov senior's bony knees. "Our leader! The leader of our clan! A Moses in jeans!"

"Whoa, there, whoa!" cried out Anton. "Hands off the family tree, okay? Oh, and Dad, how about letting me take the Turbo out for a spin? No? What's that slang word I learned in Moscow? 'Zhmot,' that's right, skinflint. You're a real *zhmot*, Dad! You don't have any generous impulses. Granddad! Let me use your Rolls, okay? Just for an hour. A goddamned pack of *zhmots*, you provacuees! A Yaki would give you the shirt off his back."

"Let me give you the Land-Rover," said Arseny Nikolaevich.

"That way there's less chance of your plunging into the bay."

"Great! We're off." And off they went, singing, dancing, and clapping to the hit of the summer tourist season, "Town of Zaporozhye." On her way out of the room Pamela snatched the Minister of Information's stylish golf cap and pulled it down over her eyes.

> Town of Zaporozhye!
> Sanitation free!
> Oh, what faces! Nausea!
> Man, *je vous en prie*!

The Russo-Anglo-Franco-American hit faded away in the depths of the house, and the adults found themselves alone.

"Those girls will tear your dream house to pieces, Arseny," said Luchnikov. "Where did Anton pick them up?"

"He says he met them the day before yesterday in Istanbul."

"The day before yesterday? Fine! Great! And when did he become a raging Yaki nationalist?"

"This morning, I think. They spent an hour or two with Khairam, the man who takes care of my boats, down at the port this morning. He's an activist at the Yaki Future Center."

"You don't know how lucky you are, Andrei, old bean," mumbled a very drowsy Buturlin. "At least he's got some life in him, some girls around him. All my effete snobs are good for is hanging about provacuee salons with their string quartets and pianos. Every other word is Haydn or Stravinsky. The spiritual elite, if you please. . . . Disgusting! What do I hear when I go home? Rachmaninoff, Handel . . . Oh, the boredom of it all! They don't drink, don't loll about. . . ."

"That's enough, Freddy," said Luchnikov senior. "We're alone now."

Freddy Buturlin immediately ran a comb through his hair and straightened his jacket. "At your service, gentlemen."

"Disconnect the telephone, will you, Hua?" said Arseny Nikolaevich.

"I say, you mean you haven't had an isolator installed yet?" asked Freddy in amazement. "I highly recommend it. It may cost a bit, but it's guaranteed to take care of all bugs."

"What's going on here?" asked Luchnikov. He was beginning to lose his temper. When two people are in possession of a secret and haven't quite come round to letting a third person in on it, the third person can't help feeling exasperated.

Instead of responding directly, Arseny Nikolaevich took Andrei Arsenievich into his private quarters, the part of the house where he actually lived. The walls here were made of thick dark oak paneling and hung with centuries-old portraits of the Luchnikov line, some evacuated in 1920, others snatched from the claws of the Union of All Unions by hook or by crook. The room was crammed with bookcases, whose shelves were in turn crammed with books, atlases, albums, old maps, globes, telescopes, model ships, statuettes, and photographs of Arseny Nikolaevich's prize horses. A framed shot of his favorite hung over his desk. It was a five-year-old stallion of native Crimean Varyaga stock and had taken several firsts at important shows in Europe and America. In short, a superstar.

"I had a visitor from Moscow not too long ago," said Arseny Nikolaevich, "a man who knew horses inside out. A Jew he was, but extremely cultivated."

Andrei Arsenievich gave a wry smile. Nothing would ever cure the provacuees of their arrogance regarding the Jews. Even Papa, the great liberal, forgot himself on occasion.

"You know what he wanted to do? Start a 'Lives of Remarkable Horses' column in some journal of theirs. Odd idea, don't you think?"

"Well, and what came of it?" asked Buturlin, raising his aristocratic brow.

"I bet they ditched it," mumbled Andrei with a frown.

"Yes, that's the very word he used," said Arseny. "The editor 'ditched' the column."

"That's how they operate there now." Andrei laughed. "Jews do the thinking, Russians the ditching."

The three men sank into the leather armchairs encircling a low round table. Hua brought in some port and cigars and melted into the wall.

"Come on, out with it. What's happened?" asked Luchnikov, by now quite upset and annoyed.

"Your life is in danger, Andrei," said Arseny Nikolaevich. "They're out to get you."

Luchnikov gave a loud laugh of relief.

"Didn't I tell you he'd come out with that whinny of his?" said Arseny Nikolaevich, turning to Buturlin.

"I bet you've been getting calls from one of those senile Lupine Hordes people," said Luchnikov, laughing again. "There isn't a day that goes by at the *Courier* without a call from one or another of them. 'Commie bastard, Kremlin whore, Yid yes man . . .' The names they come up with. And the threats: 'We'll strangle you, drown you, string you up by the balls. . . .' "

"It's a good deal more serious this time, Andrew," said Buturlin, sounding a good deal more serious.

"We have it straight from the Homeland and Throne people," said Arseny Nikolaevich, and in a cold, almost distant voice he began to outline the information he had received from the heart of the League for the Rebirth of Homeland and Throne. "The right clandestine wing has resolved to remove you from the scene and thereby liquidate the *Courier* as it now exists. I have it on the authority of an old friend, one of the last surviving men of our battalion, and . . ."—here a corner of his mouth gave an all but imperceptible twitch—". . . and I can assure you he is by no means senile. You know very well that both your *Courier* and you personally do everything in your power to provoke the Island's rightist circles."

"Leftist circles as well, these days," inserted Freddy Buturlin.

"As I was saying, my old friend has always been unhappy with your general position and particularly with the Idea of a Common Fate, which he calls Sovietization pure and simple. But even he is troubled by the resolution of Homeland and Throne rightists. He doesn't like seeing them resort to the methods of the Reds and the Browns and menacing our democracy. That's the real reason he wants to stop them. Our friendship is merely incidental. Now please give the boy your thoughts on the matter, Fedya."

As soon as his speech was over, Arseny Nikolaevich jumped out of the armchair and began striding to and fro, his joints cracking ever so lightly as he went.

Luchnikov sat quietly with the unlit cigar still between his teeth. A pall of gloom began descending on him in soft folds.

"You are well aware that we are living on a powder keg, old bean," said Minister of Information Freddy Buturlin by way of introduction, "and you know what a sewer our Island has become. Thirty-nine officially registered political parties. Any number of extremist groups. And Marxism spreading like the flu. Rich Yaki businessmen decorate their ranch-house studies with Marx, Engels, and Lenin—the collected works, straight from Moscow. Provacuees read the brothers Medvedev. Mullahs read Enver Hoxha. In the house of an English couple not long ago I attended a poetry reading of the works of Mao Zedong. The Island is flooded with agents. The CIA and KGB operate quite out in the open and all but outnumber our OSVAG. Détente has turned us into a pack of softies. Endless friendship delegations. Cultural exchange. Scientific and technical cooperation. Relaxed visa restrictions. Duty-free trade. It will do wonders for our coffers, all right, but at the rate we're going, we'll end up more a den of international iniquity than Hong Kong itself. No one pays a whit of attention to the government any more. The democracy that Arseny Nikolaevich and his cohorts wrung from the baron in 1930 has run amok. The only one of our institutions that I feel retains its raison d'être is the armed forces, and even they have started coming apart at the seams. Why, just the other day I had to call an emergency meeting of the Cabinet; the missile crowd up at the North Buffer Zone has begun agitating for a union of military personnel! Think of it—an army calling a sit-down strike! Why have an army to begin with? According to figures provided by OSVAG—I'm sorry, Andrei, but an intelligence agency must gather domestic data—sixty percent of the officers subscribe to your *Courier*. In other words, sixty percent of the officers read a newspaper whose every page denigrates the very notion of a Crimean army. Don't misunderstand me, Andrei, old boy. If things were different, more normal, your Idea of a Common Fate would merely be one of the infinite number of ideas guaranteed freedom of expression by the Constitution of 1930. But given today's world, the Idea and its most active proponent, the *Courier*, represent a real danger—and not only to the ambitions of our mastodons, as you like to call them; they represent a danger to the very existence of our country, our democracy. You must realize that by promoting a common fate with our great homeland, by feeding the Crimean guilt complex vis-à-vis Russia, the guilt we feel at being spared Russia's sufferings and so-called great achievements, you are preaching capitulation to the Reds and the transformation of our banana republic into a Soviet socialist republic. How can you and all your classmates—fine provacuee lads like Petya Sabashnikov; Volodya, the Count Novosiltsev; Timosha Meshkov; Sasha Chernok—how can you limit our future to a union with the Reds? Must you really have communism on the shores of Crimea? I shudder to think of the regional committees, the district committees, the propaganda machine, the—"

"I fail to see your point, Fedya," interrupted Luchnikov. "What are you trying to do? Talk me into accepting my assassination? Show why it's historically necessary? There is a certain logic to it, I suppose."

Suddenly his body was suffused with a heavy weight. His body was a lead jungle, his soul a fox only one step ahead of the hounds. The pall of gloom now engulfed the entire room. Damn that Buturlin, going on and on about interests of state while Homeland and Throne refined its plot. Its plot against me. A living organism. A forty-six-year-old playboy, a Marlboro man, a lover of fast cars, all-night binges, and beautiful women. And a miserable loner soon to be mowed down by a single round of machine-gun fire. Poor little Andryushka. Mama! Papa! Why did you give me piano lessons, feed me Nestlé's baby food? The end is nigh.

"You ought to be ashamed of yourself, Andrei!" Buturlin exclaimed. "I was merely trying to give you the broad picture, make you understand the gravity of the situation."

He was aware of the gravity of the situation. Quite aware, thank you. And Father could save himself the trouble of naming names; he had guessed right away that the old friend in question was Lieutenant Colonel Boboryko, and that the man behind the assassination plot was Boboryko's nephew Yury, an old friend of Luchnikov's with the rather peculiar double-barreled family name of Ignatyev-Ignatyev.

That caricature of a type had been following Andrei all his life. Until Andrei went off to Oxford, they had been in the same class at school, and when, returning to the Island at the end of 1955, he bumped into him at one of the "welcome home" parties, Andrei was struck by the change for the worse in him. The dreamer, the draftsman of endless frigates and brigantines, the timid, pimply self-abuser had turned into a large, extraordinarily ungainly gelding, looking much older than his years, sporting a repulsive smile

—all gums and crooked yellow teeth—and a shock of constantly greasy hair, and spouting long, ranting monologues of ultrarightist propaganda.

In those days Andrei was completely indifferent to politics. He saw himself as a poet-playboy, singing the praises of the Island's cypresses and Yalta's newly introduced "climatic screens" and combing the nightspots in search of Anton's future mother, Marusya Germi. Whenever he ran across Yury, he would poke a little good-natured fun at him.

In fact, Andrei ran across him quite often, because Yury also gravitated to the exquisite Marusya. But Yury never said a word to her, never danced with her, never even came closer than ten feet. Most of the time he would simply slump down in a corner in his strange semimilitary Young Lupine Hordes uniform (complete with wolf tail) and stare at Marusya. After two cocktails he would smile a broad, cynical, slobbering smile, and after three cocktails launch into a stentorian rant, feigning utter indifference to her. His harangue always centered on one thing: now is the time, with Stalin gone and Khrushchev still floundering, now is the time to disembark on the continent, cut through that putrefying Soviet margarine with our Damascus swords, and on to Moscow and the New Monarchy!

Then the Hungarian revolution broke out, and while the Young Lupine Hordes went on ranting and raving in their cozy Crimean bars, a group of young liberals—beat poets, jazz musicians, the usual riffraff—had thrown together a barricade detachment, flown to Vienna, and made their way to Budapest along the caterpillar tracks of punitive tanks.

Andrei had been caught in the flaming Corvina Cinema, headquarters of the new revolutionary youth movement. It was a close shave, and he had a Soviet—that is, Russian—bullet in his shoulder to prove it. Badly shaken, badly burned, and deeply humiliated by the merciless diplomacy of his Historical Homeland, he returned to Crimea by the good graces of a Swedish relief organization. Of the three hundred volunteers fewer than fifty returned at all. Needless to say, they returned heroes. Andrei's picture appeared in all the newspapers. Marusya Germi stood watch over his bedside. When by the end of the year the freedom fighter's wounds had healed, he and Marusya staged a wedding long remembered by *le tout Simferopol.* Some even say it marked the dawn of the new youth subculture.

The otherwise perfect affair was marred by one incident: Ignatyev-Ignatyev had leaned across the table and shouted in Luchnikov's face, "Sure kicked the shit out of those Hungarian Jew bastards, didn't we!" Half the hall was ready to pounce on him, but the groom—the brilliant, urbane idol of his generation—decided to talk it out with him instead. Forgive me, Yury, but I've always felt there was something unsettled between us. Now I know what it is: you hate my guts. Later he found Ignatyev-Ignatyev in the white-tiled silence of the Blue Inn gent's retching, shivering, giving full vent to his inferiority complex. "You're right, I hate you, I've always hated you, you blue-blood turncoat! This is what I think of your wedding." And out it all poured.

Only then did Luchnikov realize he was face to face with his most dangerous enemy, dangerous because he could not treat him as a rival: Ignatyev-Ignatyev was clearly in love with him. As time went on, the hysterics increased: Ignatyev-Ignatyev would throw himself at Luchnikov's feet and make homosexual confessions, sob erotic sobs in Marusya's lap, smile insidiously from a distance, deliver threats through third parties. But after each flare-up Luchnikov would forget Ignatyev-Ignatyev, forget his very existence. And now this—an assassination plot! What was really behind it all—politics or glands?

"I'm perfectly aware of the gravity of the situation," said Luchnikov. "What of it?"

"The time has come to act," said Buturlin.

Luchnikov senior stood silent in the corner, looking out at the sea as it faded into the twilight.

"Report it to OSVAG," said Luchnikov.

"You're joking, I trust," said Buturlin with a chortle.

"Well, what do you expect me to do?" asked Luchnikov, shrugging his shoulders. "I never go anywhere without my Beretta as it is. Bond and I both."

"You could change the politics of the *Courier*."

Luchnikov looked up at his father, who walked over to the other window without returning his look or making a sound. The twilight sky above the hills looked like a sailboat regatta. Luchnikov stood up and, grabbing a bottle and a cigar or two, started for the door. Buturlin immediately blocked his path.

"Be reasonable, *mon cher*. I don't mean anything basic; I don't mean an about face. . . . Just a few negative fillers about the Soviet Union—disregard for human rights, strong-arm tactics in the arts. It's all true, after all. You won't have to lie. You print that kind of thing anyway. The trouble is, you always give an inside explanation, make it seem as though you were one of them, a liberal adviser. And yet—admit it, Andrei—every time you come back from *over there* you're shaking with disgust and indignation. Try to understand, Andrei. All it will take is a few short pieces and your friends will be able to defend you. Your friends will be able to say, 'The *Courier* is an independent newspaper of the Provisional Evacuation Zone. Hands off Luchnikov.' Forgive me for saying this, Andrei, but as things stand now"—and his voice suddenly swelled with the sonorous tones of History—"as things stand now, your friends are unable to make that statement."

Luchnikov moved Freddy gently aside and made his way to the door unimpeded. Leaving the room, he caught a glimpse of Buturlin throwing up his hands as if to say, Well, what did you expect? I've done what I could. Luchnikov senior stood immobile. He made no attempt to stop his son.

From his father's private rooms Andrei went straight to his own, in the Guest Tower. He opened the door to the suite that was always waiting for him and stood there in the dark, clutching bottle and cigars in the same hand. Then he slowly drew open the blinds on the regatta, in flames beyond the Valley of the Bible and its flat rocks. Luchnikov lay down on the day bed and absent-mindedly followed the meanderings of the deformed, blazing sails. Then his eyes fell on a pocket cassette recorder perched on the shelf above him. Seduced by the idea that he could touch it without changing his position, he reached up and pushed the ON button.

All at once the Black Sea calm was invaded by a burst of otherworldly sounds: the bustle of a strange crowd, the cries of unfamiliar birds, the far-off roar of poorly designed engines, a clanking noise, the pounding of a jackhammer, a silly tune—cold, foreign, distant as it was, it was the land of his forefathers, Russia, and there was nothing dearer to him.

31

The potpourri of sounds was abruptly cut off by the electric saw of a woman's voice, "Pray, dear people. Pray, good people. You say you've got no church? Stand in the corner and pray! You say you've got no holy image? Look to the heavens and pray! There's no better ikon than the sky!"

Last winter, while on business in London, Luchnikov had signed up for a cheap package tour with Magnolia Holidays and flown off to the Soviet Union. It was a spur-of-the-moment decision—he phoned none of his old Moscow friends and allowed himself to be shuttled about the ancient towns of Vladimir, Suzdal, Rostov the Great, and Yaroslavl with a group of middlebrow Brits—and he never regretted it for an instant: Intourist treated them like dirt, letting them "marinate" for hours in railway stations, sticking them in third-class hotels, making them eat in ordinary cafeterias; Luchnikov had never been so close to Soviet reality before.

The tape came about quite by chance. He had gone to see the Cathedral of the Assumption when he heard the woman calling out hysterically. The park next to the cathedral was dotted with run-down structures painted outlandish colors—a playground. It must have been a school holiday, because children were playing at rockets and spacemen. The house flanking the playground on the other side bore a stunningly obtuse slogan: WORKERS' GUARANTEE MEANS QUALITY FIVE-YEAR PLAN. Overcrowded trams and an endless stream of trucks—most of them, for some reason, empty—chugged past. And crowning it all—the great cast-iron claw of a crane surging upward, inspired.

Then out of nowhere a raging zealot. Turn away from healthy modern life for a moment and what do you find but a pack of never-changing Russian crones at the peeling wall of a church, flocks of grackles circling the cupolas, and a bloated hysteric with her forty-year-old son, Seryozha the Simpleton, Seryozha the Shaker, a fool in Christ if there ever was one.

"Look here at Seryozha, dear friends! He sleeps in the bed, I sleep on the floor, for he is a man of God. He eats with the dogs and the cats, for we are all God's creatures. And he has a lesson to teach us: do not go against nature, dear people!"

Luchnikov stood among the old women, his tape recorder hidden in his pocket, and watched them take out stale rolls and stuff them into Seryozha's bag. The bloated hysteric quickly made the sign of the cross over her benefactresses and shouted all the more shrilly, "Don't curse the Jews! The Jews are God's people! Your enemies tell you to curse the Jews, and you in your ignorance do their bidding. Our Lord was not sold by a Jew; he was sold by Man. All the apostles were Jews!"

Up came a policeman: What's that you're saying about Jews? Up came a group of little girls in fuzzy woolen hats: Look at the funny old woman! But neither the policeman nor the girls interfered in the least; they just stood there, shifting uncomfortably from one foot to the other and listening to what the woman had to say.

"Dear people! Good people! Don't curse the Jews!"

By now the regatta had faded, its sails smoldering like dying embers in the creeping darkness. A shadow crossed the wall, barely visible. It disappeared for a moment, then returned, striking an affable pose. Suddenly the door swung open and the shadow took flesh in the form of Krystyna. "Hi, there, Marlboro. This where you hang out?" As soon as her experienced hand found what it was after, she climbed aboard. All he could see in the dark was her shining eyes and the two strips of gleaming teeth bared by her smile. Then they, too, vanished, and Krystyna, concealed by her tresses, set to her maiden's feast. At the first touch of her mucous membrane Luchnikov felt an immediate, powerful rush.

"Thank you, dear ones! God have mercy on you! If any of you feel the need to see Yevdokia, take the bus to Kolyadino and walk the half mile to First Five-Year Plan. That's our village. We're the last house. God bless you all! God grant you peace and health! Holy Mother of God, soften our grief!"

Slush slurping underfoot. A song blaring out—"The farthest planet's not so far any more . . ."—then fading. Seryozha's belly laugh, an oligophrenic's delight: someone had given him a cigarette. Animal sounds. Luchnikov's own voice: "May I come with you?"

"And who might you be? You don't look like one of us." The woman's voice instantly drowned out all background noise. That's how they gathered together large crowds in the old days, before microphones. Fantastic vocal production they have, these Russian women zealots.

"Oh, I'm Russian, all right, but from Crimea."

33

"Good Lord in Heaven! Then what are you doing here?"

More slurping, followed by grunts and groans: they are climbing into a bus. A squeal of a voice, no weaker than the woman's (true, it is amplified), calls out, "Have your change ready, citizens!"

What language are they speaking anyway? Can it really be Russian?

Krystyna tried to dominate, but Luchnikov didn't care much for Amazons, and after a short battle the injustice of the ages triumphed once again: Krystyna was pinned under a mountain of muscle. The treacherous thought that so often accompanied his escapades—And if I don't last?—had popped into his head during the struggle, but she yielded in time with a thin, plaintive moan, giving herself up entirely to this member of the porcine fraternity she had so denigrated earlier Encouraged by her capitulation, Luchnikov began his ascent to the sweet, moist summit with exemplary vigor.

"Here, pass my fare up. Stop pushing, will you! What are people coming to these days? A pack of animals! This way, Seryozha! *Nga, nga, nga* . . . How'd you like a roll to suck on? Yes, you, stranger. Next stop, Main Bus Station! Where does he think he is, speeding like that? The roads are like ice. . . . I've been meaning to ask you, Mother Yevdokia— You'll get your chance, my boy, but first you tell me, what's the food situation like on your Crimea?"

A pneumatic hiss. The doors open. In flows the drone of the bus station. Loud curses. The battle for seats has begun.

"Could you tell me where you got those oranges?"

Luchnikov had forgotten his age and lost all his inhibitions with the frail but giving, moaning, mewing Krystyna. First he tortured her like a hot young soldier, pinning her down on the bed and against the wall; then he turned into a father figure, tenderly stroking her wet skin; next he played the infant to her all-embracing mother and sucked contentedly on her earlobes, gathering strength to grow back into the conquering soldier.

"I was on the train from Ryazan with my sister," said the colorless male voice on the bus, "when in come these drunks. 'You're coming with us,' they tell my sister and try to grab her. 'Cool it,' I tell them. 'Can't you see we're just minding our own business?' So they punch me in the eye and go away. And I just sit there, thinking how unfair it all is. But then my friend Kozlov comes along, and the two of us polish off a bottle or two and go and look for those guys. And when we found them, we said, 'Now let's have a real talk, man to man!' But one of them sticks his elbow through the window, through the glass—quick thinking, eh?—and starts stabbing us with this piece of glass while his pals keep us pinned to the seats. You can see the results for yourself. I didn't get out of the hospital till yesterday; Dima still has a long way to go."

The pitiful voice kept slipping away, overpowered by the rustle of a newspaper or a cough or a transistorized version of "The Dance of the Young Swans."

Luchnikov's own voice: "Are you a healer, Mother Yevdokia?"

Blood-curdling screams, squealing brakes, lesser screams, rumbling noises, muffled plaints, moans, gnashing of teeth. Damn-it-to-hell-that-mother-fucking-bastard-has-crippled-us-all-for-life-son-of-a-bitch-help-dear-people-help!

The moment of truth was approaching. Stifling his moans, he began preparing her for the final sprint through the barbed wire before the Pearly Gates. Now they are equal, no master, no slave, all differences gone, all barriers down, they cling together ready to erupt in rapture, they fly together, moving closer and closer and closer until finally they glimpse a fragment of something miraculous and, moving farther and farther and farther, fall away from each other.

It never ceased to amaze him that very soon—almost instantaneously—after making love his mind turned to other things: business, money, cars. . . . Now that he had fallen away from Krystyna and was worldlessly stroking her shoulder, he found himself back in the fields of grayish snow where the tape had originated and the Vladimir–Suzdal bus lay on its side in a bloated ditch.

No one was seriously injured in the fall. One passenger seemed to have broken an arm, another complained of a sprained ankle, but the rest had only minor bruises to show for it. Babies were wailing, women moaning, men cursing. A few of the latter managed to hoist themselves up and started helping the others. They all came out the doors on the left side, which were now above their heads. Luchnikov tried not to look at the old women's underwear. Yevdokia reeked of urine and the stable. Luchnikov and an artil-

35

leryman had scarcely set her down when she began to keen. "Seryozha! My darling Seryozha! Don't leave him behind, good people! My one and only, where are you? Where are you, my treasure?"

Seryozha the Fool was found in a back corner half covered with bundles and suitcases. His mangy head shook with excitement as he chewed through the net shopping bags in pursuit of oranges. He did not hear the calls at first—he was moaning loudly to himself— but when they did reach him, he leaped up and yelled, "Mama!" in a perfectly human voice.

Orange juice and bits of orange rind stuck to his unshaven cheeks.

When everyone had finally been removed from the bus, Luchnikov and his soldier friend jumped into the ditch. They sank up to their waists in burning cold muck. "Unreal," the soldier kept repeating. "This whole fucking thing is fucking unreal."

By now a number of trucks were standing by the roadside. An emergency vehicle pulled up, inched back along the icy crust of the asphalt, got caught in some bushes, and stopped. The bus coming in the other direction stopped, too. The crowd was growing fast.

"I told those bastards it was crazy to take the bus out with the roads in this condition," the driver of the overturned bus shouted over to his fellow driver. "Know what they said? 'You take out that bus or you hand over your Party card.'"

A mixture of rain and snow had begun to fall from the bleak early evening sky. Yevdokia sat at the side of the road cradling her enormous darling. Seryozha was sobbing, his head buried in her ample stomach. An ambulance came wailing up, accompanied by two yellow-and-blue police cars.

"Mother Yevdokia!" called Luchnikov.

At first the woman looked up at him with no recognition, but then she seemed to place him. "You be on your way now, stranger," she said in a hoarse voice he had not heard before. "I have no cures, no answers. Come back in summer when the birds sing and the grass is green. But now go your way."

"Give me your blessing, Mother Yevdokia," said Luchnikov.

She was about to raise her hand, but thought better of it. "Go back to your foreigners, your Crimea. You've got churches galore there. Ask them to bless you." And she turned away from

Luchnikov, her lower lip jutting out so far that there could be no doubt he no longer existed for her.

"Fucking unreal!" said the soldier, dragging a steel cable up from somewhere. "All we need now is some vodka."

Luchnikov began the walk back to town along the edge of the icy road. He raised the collar of his cashmere coat, the best the Left Bank had to offer, and crossed his arms over his ribs, but Russia's evil wet wind had pierced right through to his bones, his shivering bones, and dully watching the long, identical mechanized cow barns stretching one after the other, he felt how utterly unconnected he was with everything surrounding him, everything that had happened here, was happening, would ever happen. The last thing the tape picked up was the voice of the police captain barking at the bus driver: "Get a move on, there! Stop holding things up!"

While Luchnikov gave himself up to the tape and his memories, Krystyna slid from under his side, went over to the window sill, and picked up a tiny ball. With one shake it turned into a dress and in a trice she was sitting at the table, fully dressed and groomed, enjoying a smoke and a glass of sherry. "What are those weird noises?" she asked, pointing to the tape recorder with her chin.

"It's no concern of yours," said Luchnikov.

She nodded, stubbed out her cigarette, and stretched. "Well, I guess I'll be shoving off. Thank you very much, kind sir."

"Not at all. The pleasure was all mine."

She turned around in the doorway. "One question," she said. "Was it Pam you were expecting?"

"To tell the truth, I had no expectations whatever."

"Well, Pam's downstairs with Tony," she said. "See you, Mr. Marlboro."

"Good-by, Krystyna," said Luchnikov, bowing slightly. Alone, he poured himself a drink and lit a cigarette. True, he thought, it wouldn't take much to change the *Courier*'s politics. What could be easier than heaping scorn on that country, our country? As a matter of fact, the feature on Soviet roads will be running tomorrow. Right, how could I have let it slip my mind? Dissident material. Priceless. "Fast Food on the Road—Soviet Style" by Anonymous, Moscow. A clever Buchwald-type piece on the nightmares of the Soviet roadside café. Who knows? It may save my skin for a few more days.

Turning over, he picked up the telephone. In principle, he never had to leave his lair: the girls came to him, and he could dial anywhere in the world, including Russia. This time, however, he made a local call.

"*Courier*! Associate Editor Brook here." The voice was a bit too jaunty to be sober.

"Russian, Sasha, speak Russian! How many times must I tell you? This is a Russian newspaper, damn it!"

"Whoops, caught me again!" said Brook, this time in Russian, but cheerful and tipsy as ever. "It's you, isn't it, chief? No need to lose your cool. You know as well as I do that our subscribers are less than comfortable in spoken Russian. And since Yaki is Greek to me, I fall back on English."

"All right, all right. What's the news from Africa?"

"This'll cheer you up. Romka's got a real scoop from Kinshasa. There's heavy fighting going on between the Kikuyus and the Wiskruyus. Weapons on both sides, made in USSR. Ideology on both sides, Marxism. It's being set right now. Front-page stuff."

"Well, get it off the front page and onto the last. It will look a lot funnier that way."

"You think it's *funny*, chief?"

"I think it's a scream. And while you're at it, Sasha, ditch the Moscow feature."

Pause.

"You mean 'Fast Food on the Road,' Andrei?"

" 'Soviet Style.' "

"But . . ."

"But?"

Pause.

"Damn it, Sasha," shouted Luchnikov, "what's the problem? What are you hemming and hawing about?"

"I'm sorry, Andrei, but . . ." Brook's voice was suddenly stone sober. "But, well, you know. People have been waiting for that kind of thing from us for ages."

"What people?" roared Luchnikov. He could almost see his fury against the dark wall.

"What do I put in its place?" Brook asked coldly.

"Samsonov's interview with Sartre. That's it for now. I'll phone back in an hour and make sure you've done what you've promised!"

Luchnikov threw down the telephone, grabbed the bottle, took a few slugs, and threw it down, too. The crumpled blanket smelled of female secretions. Life and death. Even for blackmail those were pretty high stakes.

He picked up the telephone and dialed the same number.

"*Courier.* Associate Edi—"

"I apologize, Brook. My nerves got the better of me. I'll explain later."

"Don't worry. It was nothing," said Brook. "I've done everything you asked."

Luchnikov suddenly decided to get up and go.

Go where? I can decide that later. When you have a face like mine, you don't make plans in advance. Or when you're wearing slacks like mine, slacks that reek of prostitution. Male as well as female. Not political prostitution, at least. Oh, I suppose they're good enough for Koktebel night life. I'll just zip the fly up nice and tight. A tightly zipped fly—that will be a novelty for Koktebel. I'll need a wad of money. Where is my money anyway? Let's see. Here are the rubles, here are the dollars, and here is the official currency of the Bank of the Armed Forces of South Russia. The fact that its basic unit is officially the ruble doesn't seem to have hurt it. Of course, nowadays everyone uses "ticha" instead. That was the Yakis' doing: "ticha" was the way they pronounced "*tysyacha*," the Russian word for "thousand." Funny, the Foreign Exchange column in *Izvestia* had recently taken up the term: "Crimean tichas at so and so many rubles." Tichas were gladly accepted in all dollar shops, but the girls at the cash registers made believe that it wasn't Russian money, that they couldn't read the one, two, three "hundred thousand RUBLES, Bank of the Armed Forces of South Russia," printed on each note. It was an odd but universally accepted fact of life in contemporary Soviet Russia not to notice the obvious. All the so-called election ballots said, "Leave ONE candidate; cross out all the others," when there weren't any others—weren't and never would be. The whole thing was as fantastic as it was ridiculous, but no one noticed or cared to notice. People preferred to act like sheep; they liked the comfort of the

herd. The evening news on Soviet TV—"Time," they called it—
was like a daily lobotomy. Though I must say our mastodons are
on about the same level. Why did they insist on using the name
Bank of the Armed Forces? And of *South Russia* to boot! Why did
they still put that hideous baron on all our money? You call yourselves the guardians of our culture, yet you've never thought of
replacing the baron with Pushkin, Tolstoy, or Dostoevsky. A fine
hero you've picked for yourselves—Baron Wrangel, savior of "the
Homeland's final shore." A nonentity if there ever was one. Could
he have thought up the Chongar Straits maneuver? Was Bailey-
Land a figment of my imagination? Liars and dunces—the Russian
lands were ruled by liars and dunces. Why do they assign me an
interpreter every time I go to Moscow? I don't need an interpreter,
comrades. Do I sound as if I do? I feel ridiculous with an interpreter on my heels. Why spy on me? What's the point? You know I
have no secrets. "That's something at least." Why, then? "It's
simply the way we do things. Foreign bigwigs are assigned inter-
preters." You mean I'm considered a foreigner? "Look, Andrei,
when Stalin started toying with the idea of establishing relations
with Crimea, he decided that nobody there spoke Russian, nobody
there *was* Russian, that it was a bona-fide foreign nation, though at
the same time not really a nation, more of a geographical zone
populated by a 'people.' We like peoples; peoples are potential con-
sumers of Marxism." But isn't it true that neither Stalin nor
Khrushchev nor Brezhnev had ever given up the idea of reclaiming
Crimea as part of Russia? "Yes, it is," my clever apparatchik
friends respond. "Territorially we have never renounced our
claims to Crimea, nor shall we, and diplomatically we can never
recognize her; but culturally we consider her completely foreign, a
separate entity." I repeat: What's the point? "Is it really that
difficult to grasp, Andrei? Russia and everything Russian must be
unthinkable apart from socialism." Why, that's absurd! Everyone
knows that Russian is the official language of Crimea! "Everyone
may *know* it, but no one seems to *notice*. That's the point, Andrei." So that's the point? "Yes, the whole point. You know those
fools you talk about, Andrei? Well, we've got our fools too. Of
course our Crimean policy is crazy, of course it's an anachronism,
but it does have its uses: it holds us together. In that respect it's
like many other Stalinist anachronisms. And anyway, your Russian

could use a bit of modernizing, Sovietizing, now and then." *My* Russian? How can you say such a thing? My Russian is absolutely up-to-date. I can hold my own with the lowest of the low. "Fine, but do you know how to greet a television audience?" Nothing to it: "Good evening, Comrades!" "Sorry, but that won't do. In the first place, you've got to say, 'Good evening, dear Comrades,' and in the second place, your intonation is all off. We know, we know, you're a great patriot, and we have nothing but respect for your Idea of a Common Fate, your sins against the Homeland are forgiven, you're *ours*, Andrei, we trust you implicitly, but a Soviet cliché like 'Words fail to express my profound satisfaction' is quite simply beyond you."

Such were the quips Luchnikov was made to suffer in the company of his new friend, the extraordinarily bright, extraordinarily clever Marlen Kuzenkov, a hotshot in the Foreign Division of the Central Committee.

In other words, Moscow and Simferopol had something in common: a desire to ignore obvious but unpleasant facts, to cling to outmoded formulas—the countless fusty old "all-Russian organizations" on Crimea, the elitist attitude of the rulers towards the ruled, the provacuee mythology versus Moscow's refusal to recognize the presence of Russians on the Island, the hullabaloo about the First Cavalry without a peep about the Second, the TV documentaries commemorating every imaginable event, yet never mentioning Trotsky, Bukharin, Khrushchev (not even the relatively recent Nikita Sergeevich—who do they think welcomed Gagarin back to earth?) and any number of other tricks, but . . . but if we seem to lean in the same direction, could it be that totalitarianism is not the whole answer, that our national character had something to do with it as well? Ah, the Russian character. And a very distinct character it is, too. What other people has so fine a proverb as "Don't take your rubbish outside your hut"? The Celt, the Norman, the Saxon, the Gaul—each gave his hut a good cleaning. But not the proud Slav; no, he swept his dirt into a corner— anything but let the neighbors see. And if it all does boil down to the national character, then everything is justified. After all, we call ourselves shit, don't we? The English, now, they don't call themselves shit.

His long, convoluted ruminations having led him to this rather unappetizing conclusion, Andrei Arsenievich Luchnikov looked up to find himself in his Peter Turbo speeding down the serpentine and into Koktebel's main thoroughfare, lined on both sides with high-rise hotels. Little by little the sequence of events that had brought him there came back to him. He had left the Guest Tower brandishing a thick wad of tichas, slowed his energetic pace at the sight of Krystyna leaning against the balustrade at the edge of the terrace, immediately picked up speed, whistling "Sentimental Journey" and hoping she'd get the hint, slowed down again at the sight of his father standing silently by the library window, then vaulted into his Peter Turbo like a youth half his age. And hearing Freddy call out to him, "Give me a lift, will you?," he turned the key in the accelerator. He did not want Freddy to join him in his search for adventure.

Andrei Arsenievich was so surprised to discover himself approaching the golden haunts of his youth that he slammed on the brakes. Looking up, he contemplated the green sky through the skyscrapers, the sickle moon above the outline of Suru-Kaya. Reassured, he drove down a side street leading to the sea and sporting a brightly lit ball that turned slowly on its axis, the symbol of the Calypso Club. The wind blowing in from the Valley of the Bible ruffled the crowns of the cypresses, coated the plane-tree leaves with a silver lather, and perplexed and unsettled Luchnikov. What is it that makes my feelings so acute? Is it the danger, the threat? No, it was that something long forgotten had just returned —the open space and promise of a Koktebel night.

There were fifteen or so cars parked out in front. They were guarded by a couple of well-built Yakis doing steps to the music from within under the constantly changing light of the ball. At some point during the twenty years Luchnikov had been away from the club it had turned into a posh establishment. The cloakroom had once been decorated with a large painting that Luchnikov's crowd liked to call "artistic." It showed an ample-breasted Calypso with long Tatar braids taking mournful leave of a Tatar Odysseus about to brave the frothy billows. Now the same wall was covered with a highly sophisticated three-, perhaps even four-dimensional relief showing the adventures of a spermatoid Odysseus in the lap of a gigantic Calypso split into ten tantalizing pieces. It was all highly kinetic and lighted from below to emphasize every pulse and quiver. Luchnikov was certain one of the recent emigrants had had a hand in it. Nusberg perhaps?

The moment he started across to the bar, he heard raucous voices behind him.

"Well, look who's here!"

"If it isn't Mr. Courier in person!"

"Luchnikov at the Calypso! I wonder what's behind it."

They were speaking Russian and being loud about it; clearly they wanted him to turn and respond. He didn't. Leaning against the bar, he ordered a Manhattan and asked the bartender ("I bet they've played that idiotic 'Town of Zaporozhye' at least ten times this evening." "It seems like a hundred times to me, sir; my head is spinning from it") to have them put on "Serenade in Blue."

"Glenn Miller, the days of my youth."

"With pleasure, sir, the days of my youth, too."

"I had a feeling we were the same age."

"And I have a feeling we've met somewhere before."

"Only a feeling? It must have been in Yevpatoria."

"You wouldn't happen to own a hotel there, would you?"

"Oh, come off it, Faddeich."

"What's that you called me?"

"I said, come off it, Faddeich. Just because twenty years have passed and you're playing small-time bartender to my big-time editor, you can't tell me you don't recognize me, you son of a bitch you!"

"Andryushka!"

"Prickface!"

"Let's keep it clean now."

"Let me give you a hug, all right? Shed a few tears, all right?"

"Listen to those silver-throated trumpets! Glenn Miller and his band! 'Serenade in Blue,' 1950, our first raids on the Calypso. First kisses, first girls, free-for-alls with the American airmen. . . ."

Thumping Faddeich on the back and reveling in Glenn Miller's slide trombones, Luchnikov realized what had brought him here to the Calypso on this unusual night. In his youth this place had always had the heady air of danger about it. There was an American air base nearby, just beyond Cape Chameleon, and the men there never missed an opportunity for a brawl with the local Russian boys. Feeling younger than he had in years—it was the danger inherent in the word "assassination" that did it—he had naturally felt a desire to tempt fate, and where better to tempt fate than at the Calypso?

But how the joint had changed over the past two decades! It had turned into a highly respectable, extremely expensive gathering place for the cream of the upper-middle class. Besides, sex was no longer a giddy adventure, and the airmen had dismantled their base and were quietly growing old in their Milwaukees.

Only Faddeich was left. I'm glad he finally remembered me. As soon as I've finished my Manhattan, I'll drive back home to Simfi. Tomorrow I'll go to the office and a few days after that— Dakar, New York, Paris: an anti-apartheid conference, a session of the General Assembly, a meeting of the editors of leading world newspapers to discuss "Sports and Politics." And finally—Moscow.

Suddenly he saw his son peering out of the mirror behind the bar. He'd been so busy planning out his week he'd completely forgotten about the boy. Typical. The reason we lost each other is that we stopped looking for each other. Here I planned my whole week without a thought for my son, and I haven't seen him for a year.

Who else is with him? An unlikely assortment. Although Anton's table was wedged into an alcove at the far side of the room, Luchnikov could make out his long, pale face, Pamela's golden locks on his shoulder, and four hefty bruisers wearing expensive suits and gold bracelets. Oh, I know. They must be foreign workers at the Arabat plant.

"That's my son over there," he said to Faddeich.

"Your son? He's so tall."

"Who are those thugs sitting with him?"

"No idea. Never seen them before. Not your usual crowd."

Faddeich surveyed the room from behind the bar like a venerable potentate. Luchnikov waved to his son and called, "Antosha! Pamela! Come over here!"

"Bring on the champagne, Faddeich!" he added to his friend. With a snap of the fingers—Faddeich had three sprightly Italian waiters under him—a silver bucket with a bottle of Veuve-Cliquot materialized before him. But where was Antosha? It means a lot to me to introduce him to Faddeich. It's like passing on the baton to a new generation. Why doesn't he come? Is he trying to slight me?

Not that damn generation gap again. But when he looked up in the mirror, he saw that Anton was trying to get out from behind the table. He and Pamela were sitting with their backs to the wall, and the four flashy dressers were trying to keep them there.

"Those men at Antosha's table, they're not being very polite," said Luchnikov to Faddeich and watched as Faddeich pulled himself up—just the way he used to!—and squinted over at the guilty parties.

"Right," he said to Andrei with a familiar smile. "Not polite at all."

Excited by Faddeich's reaction, Luchnikov jumped off the barstool. "I think I'll go and teach them some manners," he said, starting out in the direction of the alcove to the tune of "Serenade in Blue" and immediately feeling the eyes of Simferopol's intellectual elite on him. When he reached the table, he grabbed the arm of one of the men and twisted it behind his back. It took no effort at all, because he wasn't expecting it. A brute like that couldn't possibly have such weak arms.

"What's the matter, Antosha?" he asked his son. "Who are these people?"

"God knows," Anton mumbled, embarrassed. Whenever he was embarrassed, he spoke Russian. "They came up to us, sat down, and told us we weren't going anywhere. I haven't the faintest idea what they want from us."

"We'll find out right away, right away," said Luchnikov, twisting the fat feeble arm a bit tighter with one hand and unbuttoning the man's jacket with the other. In the old days that gave them a big scare.

By this time a group of onlookers had gathered in the vicinity of the table, many of them Simfi people who knew Luchnikov well. A local policeman had suddenly appeared in the doorway and was keeping one eye on the happenings and the other on Faddeich, who was giving him signals.

The men were all over forty and spoke a heavily Tatarized Yaki, as was usually the case with the Arabat Oil Company's Turkish crew. "Give my arm, *aga*," begged Luchnikov's prisoner. "*Kaderler* very much, *pozhalsta, Luchnikov-aga.*"

Luchnikov let go of his arm and had them leave the alcove one by one, making sure his son had a good look at each of them. "See if you can come up with an explanation of why these gentlemen know our name."

The boy caught up with them when they were halfway across the room, and doubled the last of them over with a fierce karate chop. Luchnikov was thrilled. He saw the chop as an overture on Anton's part: they had taken karate lessons together a few years before.

"Where do you know my father from?" Anton asked his victim.

"TV . . . Yaki boy see TV," he groaned. *"Yuk mäşkel . . . Kaderler . . . Mayarta . . .* Sorry much."

"Let him go," said Andrei. Father gave son a slap on the back, son responded with an elbow in the ribs, and son's girl friend followed through laughingly with a few pats on the behind for each of them. The four Turks immediately made themselves scarce, and the policeman, hand on Colt, followed in hot pursuit. The Simfi crowd gave everyone a round of applause. After all, they had just been treated to a first-rate western. Faddeich's eyes were gleaming.

They all had some champagne. Pamela studied Luchnikov carefully, trying to tell whether Krystyna had gone to him and what had come of it. It could have turned out quite differently, Luchnikov realized. Meanwhile Anton had hypnotized Faddeich with his stories of how karate had come in handy in the most exotic places.

When the three of them went out into the street together, they found three of the tires on Luchnikov senior's Land-Rover neatly slashed. How can Homeland and Throne stoop so low? thought Luchnikov. I'll bet it's Ig-Ignatyev's doing. Yes, I wouldn't put it past him.

At this point the policeman came up in his best sheriff shuffle with the fearsome foursome in tow.

"See that, officer?" asked Luchnikov, pointing to the Land-Rover.

"Come over here," the policeman called to his captives, "and tell the gentleman all you know."

The four of them told their story by fits and starts, though willingly enough. As far as Luchnikov could make out, they had gone to the Calypso for a good time when an *aga* came up to them and offered them two hundred tichas—"Two hundred tichas?" "That's right, two hundred"—to rough up the Luchnikov brat. They were feeling their oats, and well, why not? The *aga*, it turned out, had actually been sitting in the Calypso the whole time, checking to see he got his money's worth. He'd slipped out just before them, slashed the tires, and made a swift getaway in his own car. "A bright yellow Ford, *aga*. Sorry *minga*. *Kaderler* very much."

"What did he look like, this *aga* of yours?" asked Luchnikov. "Like this?" And he did his best to imitate Ignatyev-Ignatyev: baring his teeth, drooling, popping his eyes as if in a stupor.

"That's him!" they cried in delight. "That's him, *aga!*"

"So you know who he is?" the policeman asked Luchnikov.

"No, no," said Luchnikov quickly. "How else could he look? Must have a screw loose somewhere. Forget about it, Officer."

"Those loonies can be real dangerous, let me tell you," said the policeman. "And they're bad for the tourists. Soviet tourists, they . . ." He was cut off by a squawk from the walkie-talkie on his chest, and while he reported the "loony's" appearance to headquarters, Luchnikov, Anton, and Pamela sneaked off round the corner, where they found Luchnikov's red Peter Turbo safe and sound.

"You take the car," said Luchnikov. "I feel like going for a little walk on my own."

"But why, Dad?" asked Anton.

Pamela stood there without a word, smiling peacefully and leaning her cheek on his shoulder. A perfectly viable wife for Antosha, thought Luchnikov. Yes, they should get married, the lucky fools!

"This is my night for nostalgia," he said. "I feel like walking through Koktebel by myself. Don't worry. I'm armed to the teeth." He patted the pocket of his safari jacket where he kept the Beretta.

But the charms of the night had slowly begun to fade, the malarioid attack of youth to pass. A ghastly recovery. His feet had touched ground again, and as he walked through Koktebel, he found nothing familiar, nothing but the landscape, that is. The landscape was truly unforgettable. The different facets of the mountains in sunlight and moonlight, the way they met and joined the sea, the lone olive tree trembling at the edge of a crag that marked the grave of his friend the Crimean poet Max Voloshin— it all pointed to an omnipresent Soul.

Then, abruptly, the landscape began to lose the contours he knew so well. It turned into a moonscape, crisscrossed with canyons and ravines. Unbelievable! Whole new configurations! A basalt boulder rising like an idol from behind a hill. Then two feet away—a completely uncharted hill sloping gently to the water, a grotto at its base . . . Only then did he remember. Of course! The municipal board had grown tired of having nothing to do and thought up a Disneyland for adults. Fantasy Arcades they called it, and it was totally obscene! No tourist could possibly distinguish between what was natural and what artificial; primeval nature made its appearance through skillfully masked openings in special prefabricated walls and was then complemented by remarkable imitations. Every step opened new vertiginous perspectives and vistas. The result in most visitors was a curious state of being, a kind of euphoria. And that's where business came in. Tucked away in the cozy little corners of this pseudoworld were elegant bistros, boutiques, even whole department stores. People didn't merely spend money in Fantasy Arcades; they threw it to the winds.

With the exception of "our Soviet Comrades," of course. Representatives of the highest stage of socialism had precious little to spend *or* throw; they were limited to a strict per diem. They, too, felt the Koktebel euphoria, but it had a different source—a common source of Soviet euphoria: Western shopwindows. Politely oohing and aahing at Koktebel's wonders when told to do so by their guide, trotting along in disciplined herds, they actually yearned much less for the arcades of fantasy than for the very real arcades of Fabergé, Testov, Jaeger, and Neiman-Marcus, and they ogled the displays as long as they could, counting and recounting whatever Western currency they might have smuggled out—francs, dollars, marks, tichas. . . .

Even at this ungodly hour Luchnikov saw a lone female figure in the distance. Soviet, no doubt. Who else would come out in the middle of the night to stand at the crossroads of the real and the artificial (symbolized by the real thunder of artificially produced surf) and stare, lost in reverie, at a perfume display?

Luchnikov decided not to embarrass her, and set off in the opposite direction along a walk with pseudo-timeworn pseudo-steps. When he reached the top, he found a picturesque miniature bay perfectly placed to receive the reflection of the moon through some gap-toothed rocks. But as it happened, he had not moved away from the woman at the perfume shop; he had moved towards her. Engrossed as she was in the attraction of Helena Rubinstein, she had no idea of his presence, and he could observe her at his ease. But one full-face glance and he began to reel. He took a few steps more and came up so close that he had to accept the evidence. He stared at her trench coat, tightly belted at the waist, at her dear sun-bleached hair, casually gathered at the back of the neck, at her pretty tanned face and the little rays of wrinkles leading to her ears, like reins to a horse. She had screwed up her eyes to read the labels on the flacons, tubes, jars, and boxes, and was silently trying to get her chapped lips around the English texts. No, she's one of a kind, said Luchnikov to himself. I'll have to believe my eyes and act accordingly.

"Tanya!" he called.

She gave a slight jump, straightened her back, and for some reason brought her hand up to her mouth. He must have sounded as if he were nearly on top of her, because she seemed to be looking for him within the radius of a few feet. "Andrei, is that you?" he heard her call from what sounded like a great distance. "Where are you?" she called again.

Slowly it dawned on him: this was Fantasy Arcades, and they'd done it all on purpose, the bastards. To her, he was merely a dot in the distance. He started waving wildly at her with both hands, and when that didn't work, he slipped off his jacket and waved it, too. Finally he saw the spark of recognition in her eyes. It made him want to rush up to her, give the belt of her trench coat a good tug, and tear her clothes off the way he used to do.

Now the real euphoria began. In the midst of this strange antiworld Andrei Arsenievich Luchnikov raised his hands to heaven and thanked God for making him deliriously happy. Trick mirrors, transistorized acoustics, and the resultant lack of physicality notwithstanding, I knew she was here, she knew I was here.

Father, son, love, past, and future all blended together into a vague feeling of expectation and hope. The Island and the continent. Russia. The center of life, the place where all roads converged . . .

"Tanya," he said, "let's get the hell out of this hellhole of a fun house!"

Needless to say, Arseny Nikolaevich did not sleep a wink. As soon as Andrei left, he started chain-smoking, which brought on first a coughing fit, then his loathsome bronchial whistle. By early dawn, when the worst had passed, he flung open the window of his study, put some Haydn on, took out a small anthology of Russian philosophy, and placed it under the reading lamp. He opened it at random. Father Pavel Florensky.

But before he could read a line, he looked up to see Antosha scrambling up the sun-porch railing and making his barefoot way to the open window. Straddling the window sill, he plonked one big, strong foot down on the table next to the anthology and heaved a sigh. Then gazing out over the rosy-fingered dawn, he dreamily asked, "Granddad, what was the most exciting sexual experience you ever had?"

"It happened when I was just about your age," said Grandfather Arseny.

"Where were you at the time?"

"In a train," said Grandfather Arseny with a smile and, completely forgetting his recent coughing fit, he lit a cigarette. "We were retreating, or to be more accurate, running for our lives. General Makhno had made a shambles of our rear guard; we had failed to take Moscow and were hightailing it south to the sea. Near Yelizavetgrad the remainder of our company—there were only about twenty-five of us by then—piled into a train that was packed full of former pupils of the exclusive Smolny Institute for Young Ladies. The poor things. To lose house and home and then be dragged from one battle to the next—you can imagine how tired and dirty they were. But they were our kind, the kind of girls we used to know, the kind we used to run after, waltz with—you know what I mean?—invite to skating parties. And they knew right away that we were their kind. But we frightened them, too— the civil war had taken its toll on everyone, after all—and they were primed to surrender without a fight. I pinpointed my girl immediately, in the very first compartment. That face, those angular shoulders—my head simply whirled at the thought that she would be mine. I have no idea where I got the nerve, but I went straight up to her and asked her out to the platform at the end of the corridor. She stood up on the spot and went with me. The platform was covered with sacks of coal. I lay my greatcoat over them and stood my rifle nearby. Then I helped her up onto the coat and she pulled up her dress. Never in my life had I felt physical love so keenly; never have I felt it so keenly since. In the middle of it all the train stopped at a tiny station and a gang of peasants tried to break into the train. I showed them my gun but kept up my primary activity. When they realized what was going on, they burst into laughter. Fortunately, she was facing the other way and the glass muffled their guffaws."

"And you never saw her after that?" asked Anton.

"Not for a long time," said Grandfather Arseny. "I did meet her again, though. It was in Nice, in 1931."

"Who is she?" asked Anton.

"There she is," said Grandfather Arseny, pointing to a picture of his late wife, Andrei's mother.

"Grandma?" shouted Anton. "Was she really my grandmother?"

"And why not?" said Grandfather Arseny. In English, to hide his embarrassment.

II

Time

Tatyana Lunina returned to Moscow the next morning. That very evening she was back on the television screen. In addition to her main job—she was a trainer for the junior all-star track-and-field team—she was one of the seven sportscasters on the evening news program "Time." In other words, our Tatyana was one of the most popular personalities in the land. A one-time undefeated hurdler—eighty meters of pure burst: eternally tanned legs racing ahead, shiny red locks streaming behind, perfectly shaped breasts straining towards the fatal finish—she not only won her race but set a record, and bound as she was to lose the title of champion to her successor the year after, her record had held for nearly ten years, until only a few months ago.

She returned to Moscow badly shaken by her unexpected encounter with Andrei (a whole year had passed since the mutual decision to cut off all relations had gone into effect, and now here it was, starting over again). She had spent the whole flight thinking about him; sitting there with her eyes closed, she would even feel an occasional shudder run through her, but nothing could have made her open her eyes: she had left the rest of the world behind, especially her legal spouse, hubby, or as she was wont to call him, the Hub. As usual, however, he had not forgotten her, and the first thing she saw in the crowd milling about on the other side of the customs gate was the hale and hearty figure of her decathlon champion (or the Champ, as Luchnikov was wont to call him). He had come to fetch her in his Volga and was decked out for the occasion with all the paraphernalia of the Moscow "in" crowd: a suede jacket, a Seiko watch, a supply of Winstons, a Ronson lighter, a combination-lock attaché case, and a small leather bag (hanging from his wrist) that several years before would have called his virility into question. Fiddling with the attaché case, glancing repeatedly at the watch, flicking the lighter on and off, and scanning the crowd with his dull, oxlike eyes, he seemed anxious to show the world—himself, too, perhaps—that he had only happened to be driving past and decided on the spur of the moment to see if his better half had come in. Tanya needed no more than a glance to tell what was going on in his mind or, rather, below his belt; she needed only a glance to bring back all their fifteen years of "relations": the slow, measured undressing, the exploration of the breasts and pelvic region, the increasing pressure, the quake of his overwhelming lust, and her own vile, voluptuous response. Fifteen years, day after day. It was all he needed.

"Anyway, Tanya, that's what's going on. That's what you've missed," he said on the way home from the airport, having tried to fill her in on recent events, but constantly losing track, repeating himself, talking nonsense: the anticipation was too much for him. Needless to say, it was raining in Moscow. The sun, a rare phenomenon these past few years, hung like a pig's snout in the invisible gruel above a mound of black clouds. The clouds, bearing down on the new high-rise developments, threatened the enormous letters marching from roof to roof: THE PARTY IS THE MIND, THE HONOR, THE CONSCIENCE OF OUR ERA! Tanya's first impulse was to turn away from it all—the gap between here and there was too great, so great as to be absurd—but there was nowhere to turn, and so, while watching the clouds, the mud flying up from under the wheels of the trucks, the pale snout, and the fiery letters, the oxlike profile of a husband permanently befuddled with anticipation, she thought of how depressing it was to feel the unsettling emotions Luchnikov had reawakened in her settle so soon, to feel Crimea's permanent carnival recede into the past, to feel her husband's anticipation reawaken in herself.

He tried to start in while they were in the elevator, then while they were on the landing, in the doorway, and he certainly had no intention of letting her go farther than the entrance hall, but all of a sudden Luchnikov flashed through her mind, a moonlit Luchnikov sitting across from her in bed, hands outstretched, and she froze, tore away from him, and raced back to the door.

"Oh, what a fool I am! How could I? This is awful—no, no, you'll have to wait, dear boy, no, really, I've really got to. I forgot the most important thing, would you please hold off for a second and let me go? Try to understand, I forgot to hand in my *foreign currency documents!*" What a brain, what instinct! With all the juices going, in the throes of a passionate embrace, she still found a way to get through to him. Foreign currency—a sacred concept if there ever was one!

He immediately let go. Tatyana ran out the door, jumped into the waiting elevator, and shot downstairs. Out in the street she flagged down a taxi, and, sinking into the back seat, she glanced up to see her Easter Island titan of a husband on the balcony, fairly bursting with desperation.

Although she had absolutely nothing to do at the Committee, she strode up and down the corridors looking very businesslike, even hurried, the way one was expected to act. Everyone stared at her: among the gray people who go to work every day for a living and have to come to terms with long stretches of rain and snow, Tatyana—tan, blue-eyed, and clad all in white, slacks, matching jacket, and cotton blouse (Andrei had bought it for her yesterday at Feodosia's most fashionable designer boutique)—Tatyana looked like a creature from another world. In fact, she *was* a creature from another world. Yesterday evening she had been speeding along in the Peter Turbo under starry skies, yesterday night she had been at the mercy of her lover in their Hilton suite, and yesterday in the wee hours she had been partaking of a light *souper* at a French restaurant on the coast, looking out at the cruise ships and yachts from all corners of the world, looking up at the Boeings taking off every quarter of an hour for Singapore, Sydney, Delhi. . . .

If I can hold out here long enough, something's bound to turn up, she thought. And sure enough, before long out came her close friend, the boss's secretary, Verulya, with wide eyes. "The top secret report they've just got in on you—all I can say is, I've never seen anything like it."

"How can it be ready so soon?"

"It just is, that's all."

"And the author is . . . ?"

"Can't you guess?"

She could guess, all right, but what difference did it make in the end? She knew perfectly well that her encounter with Luchnikov would find its way into a report. The only thing that surprised her was how well they had their operations down: the tattletale must have rushed straight from the airport to the KGB.

"You just won't believe what it says, Tanya dear. It says you spent two nights in a hotel with a White Russian! And not a word of it true, I bet!"

They had disappeared into a niche behind the typists' room, an out-of-the-way corner safe for smoking the Virginia Slims Tatyana had brought back with her. Verulya was a passionate smoker and willing to sell the most confidential state secret for a good foreign cigarette. "So it *is* true! Well, congratulations, Tanya. Give me just one night, half a night, a quarter of a night like that, and you know what you can do with this whole damn outfit, informers and all!"

Oddly enough, she found the hustle and bustle of all those former champions quite soothing, even invigorating. They themselves, athletes turned bureaucrats, were the regular heroes or authors of any number of secret reports—and sometimes both simultaneously. Now and then one of them would lose his privilege to travel abroad for a year or two, maybe three, but if, when the time was up, he hadn't gone to seed or drunk himself out of the picture, they would start sending him again, first to socialist countries, then to the West. It was scarcely worth batting an eyelash over.

Tatyana gave Verulya all the perfume articles she happened to have in her purse and told her about her new white suit, which nobody here in Moscow could possibly appreciate, while in the Feodosia branch of Muir and Merrilees it went for a good six hundred tichas and anyone in the West could tell at a glance where it came from. When she came to the end of her sentence, she heard her own name from around the corner. "Have you seen Tanya?" "I hear Tatyana Lunina is back." "Sergei Pavlovich has been asking for Comrade Lunina." Whenever that happened—and it happened quite often—she knew it was time to make herself scarce.

"Life is funny, you know?" said cross-eyed, pimply Verulya. "Nobody would give you twenty rubles for that outfit here, and jeans suits go for two hundred. How much is a jeans skirt with, say, a nice top?"

"Thirty-five tichas," said Tatyana with complete confidence. "Or as low as twenty on sale."

"Funny," whispered Verulya. "Strange."

Suddenly a stampede rose up out of nowhere, a flurry of loud voices and slamming doors, then, just as suddenly, silence: a meeting had been called to order. Tatyana jumped up, kissed Verulya (who was still lost in thought) on both cheeks, and flew down the corridor, down the stairs, into the street. The first thing she saw was a green Volga with her husband behind the wheel. He was looking positively emaciated from anticipation. Oh, I might as well, she thought, and made for the car. The secret report had served to reconcile her to her husband, and she no longer looked upon their imminent copulation as an unnatural act.

But once more the Hub's plans were foiled. A pack of evil spirits seemed intent on keeping him at full cock. For no sooner had they pulled up to the cement paws of their cooperative—their love palace, as the former decathlon champion called it diffidently in the depths of his soul—than his heart sank. Directly in front of them stood a microbus with TELEVISION printed along the sides and a couple of dandies from the news staff dangling their legs from the roof, just waiting to pounce on Tanya. Apparently there was no one to go on that evening. Of all the sportscasters, only Lunina was in Moscow. And what if the plane had been late? What would they have done then? "Oh, they'd have managed somehow without her. Now they can't." There was even a certain logic to what they said. But oh, those overtimes and overloads were hard to take! What kind of life was it when a man was prevented from making his legal claims on his legal spouse for an entire day? Where was law? Where was order?

Even Tatyana was a bit annoyed, and in her annoyance she recognized that good old Moscow malice. She had finally come home, back to the real world, and Andrei Luchnikov had—as so often before—drifted off into another, not quite substantive galaxy, the galaxy of Koktebel and Feodosia, of Crimea, of all the Western world.

Yet, appearing that evening on nationwide TV against the usual backdrop of Moscow's Luzhniki Stadium, she looked somehow out of place, ideologically questionable. Millions of men, watching her read out the idiotic scores, saw her as a private messenger of Eros. Her husband finally took her on the floor in front of the television set. He gave it his all and left her utterly exhausted. He was in love with every bone in her body and sensitive to them all in his lovemaking. Nor did he show any jealousy. You say you need a little romanticism? Be my guest. And if it ends up in bed, no harm done. As long as I get my share.

III

A Scumdrum Existence

Vitaly Gangut had found subtle signs of aging in himself a year ago and had been terribly upset by them. Now they didn't bother him at all. What difference did a gray hair make, a slight creak in the joints, a minor malfunction of the bladder? Biology was biology, after all. Besides, his one true-life companion, irony, was always there to help him out. How could anyone handle the day-to-day grind without it? I once had a bod that could sing, play, and dance, When it saw what it wanted, it jumped at the chance, When it saw what it wanted, it never lost hope. And now that poor bod's to be turned into soap. Thus, in his own Attic way, did Gangut, though still far from aged, greet the signs of aging in himself.

Then out of the blue he discovered something new and perplexing. Out of the blue he discovered a new drive in himself. But in point of fact, ladies and gentlemen, it was a drive to be home and seated in front of the TV set by nine o'clock every evening. Home by nine, and "Time." Old age was closing in. The imminent dissolution of the soul.

Abandoned by everyone in this musty flat, I, Vitaly Gangut, of small paunch and large screen, sit glued to "The Year of the

Shockworker." Statistics galore. Four million rubles in grain—is it a lot or not enough? "Readers from Across the Nation Meet in Moscow." Hands clap, faces impassive. "An Award for the Volgograd Region." Old men weighed down by decorations, banners raised. "The Year of the Shockworker, Continued." Bulldozers. "Human Rights Activists Increase Pressure on Western Governments." A band of long-haired capitalist slaves battle the police. "Israeli Warmongers Bomb Peace-Loving Arab Peasants." But now more news from home. Harp glissandos, bliss, stability, medals, children playing, tulips . . . What a humdrum, scumdrum existence . . . Gangut, the knee-jerk dissident, couldn't help grumbling sluggishly, but in fact he was completely lulled by the propaganda trance, completely relaxed, he felt as if someone were massaging the top of his head, and though of course he was also aware what was happening, he let it happen, let it pour over him, he actively looked forward to the evening massage. Having bumped its way down crisis-ridden slopes of Western reality and glided through the Elysian Fields of its Soviet counterpart, "Time" was ready for Gangut's favorite segment: sports. Gangut had read somewhere that although today's TV sports addict rarely leaves his armchair for the field, he still participates to some degree in the events he watches and his organism derives certain benefits from them. Utter nonsense, of course, but at least the kind he liked to hear. "Our sportscaster this evening will be . . ." There were seven or eight, all of whom Gangut treated as members of his family, something like the relatives in Bradbury's *Fahrenheit Four Fifty-one*. He had invented a nickname for each and enjoyed trying to guess which one would appear on a given day: the Pedant or Little Miss Komsomol or the Elephant Apparatchik, the Dormouse, the Frog, Blue Boy. . . . Today he was in for a rare treat: the Sex Bomb, a.k.a. Tatyana Lunina. He was bowled over by the way she looked—those shining blue eyes, that wonderful tan, the breathtakingly chic yet modest white jacket seemed a direct message to Gangut: you're coming apart at the seams, Vitaly; you're a bag of shit; you belong in the dump; you're done for.

They had known each other once upon a time. There had even been a certain something between them. He would get to the courts a few minutes early. . . . Tanya was practicing her serve. He would have a screening of a film he'd fought the bureaucrats tooth and

59

nail over. . . . Tanya was sitting front row, center. He would be out
with his pals drinking or eating, raising the roof. . . . Tanya was
waiting at the next table. Their eyes seemed to meet a lot, they
even exchanged wisecracks from time to time, but all that came of
it was a tacit agreement to the effect that "yes, this might develop
into something, yes, why not, though not right now, no, this isn't
the right moment, but maybe tomorrow, or the day after, or the
year after. . . ." Then one day when he was at an exhibit of underground—or rather, underroof—art in an artist friend's loft, he met
Tanya with Luchnikov, his overseas friend the Crimean magnate,
whose every visit caused a sensation in the lofts and basements of
Moscow: he always brought the latest jazz albums, the latest magazines, Levis and Adidases for our deprived youths; he threw lavish
(drunken) banquets, gadded about Moscow with a bevy of flooz-
ies, boozers, and stoolies in tow, then flew off to some fairy-tale
place like Buenos Aires and suddenly flew back from, say, Stockholm—more prosaic, perhaps, but for the common Muscovite
every bit as much a dream as Buenos Aires. At that party in the
loft it was absolutely clear—no psychologist needed—that Andrei
and Tatyana were a thing, a big thing, high-tension wires, the
works. Gangut's latest film, a two-year project, had just been rejected by the censors; he had just been hauled over the coals by the
Film Makers' Union; he had just been refused permission to go to
Cannes, his new script had just been cut to shreds; and Dina, his
wife at the time, had just made an ugly scene over the money he
was drinking away "while the family went hungry" and his frequent disappearances, "in other words, week-long orgies mas-
querading as flights of creativity." It was scarcely the time for
Gangut to revel in a friend's happiness. Like his fellows in misery,
he preferred guzzling rotgut, cursing the system, and keeping a low
profile.

And yet what wonderful times they had been. Despite all the
pressure from above—fantastic times. Where have they gone?
Where is that dissident artist? Where are two thirds of the people
at that party? Flown the coop. Tel Aviv, Paris, New York . . . Who
needed a telephone book any more? And Leningrad wasn't any
better than Moscow. How quickly they passed, these years, so-
called, and what vile, petty changes pile up in the absence of major

ones. The chain of years—a nightmare. The face of death—horrendous. The daily round—wild and immortal.

Vitaly Gangut tore himself out of his armchair and bent over the color image of Tatyana Lunina. She looked the same as she'd looked then. So we still have some decent material left, some live wires. And the Island of Crimea is still afloat.

"The junior all-stars outshone the Crimean locals in all events. The team's most dazzling success came when . . ."

What is she going on about? Why didn't I marry her? She would never have let me go to the dogs, go gray, go begging at the Popular Science studios. She's not one of your Dinas or Katyas or the rest of my idiotic retinue; she's . . . well, there she is. I wonder what Andrei's up to? It's been ages. Was it last year or the year before that we drove up to Moscow from the South in my jalopy? Arguing all the way like madmen. What we didn't go into: dissidents, the KGB, the gerontocracy, Czechoslovakia, Western leftists, the Russian national psychology, the new—and already tainted—messianic movement, that ridiculous Common Fate theory of his . . . When Luchnikov told him that he, his friends, and his paper were actively working for the reunification of Crimea and Russia, Gangut blew up. He called him a masochist, a suicidal shithead, a cock-sucking sucker, a schizoid degenerate, and an all-round prick. "You bourgeois bastards, you! You don't know when you're well off. What are you trying to do, anyway? Bring all our efforts to naught? Nip our hopes and dreams in the bud? You're just like your fathers, the top fucking brass that pissed away what was left of Russia and then turned tail and fled!" Gangut had to scream to be heard over the cracked piston of his Volga, but he would most likely have screamed it anyway.

"Wait a second, now, Vitaly," Luchnikov screamed back. "Wasn't your father a sailor on a Red destroyer? Didn't he risk his life to make Crimea Red? Why do you refuse to see farther than your nose? Is it because they won't let you make those shitty potboilers of yours? Yes, that's it, pure spite. You're a fucking reject of history, you know? Russia needs new sperm!"

In a filthy cafeteria just outside Moscow they more or less patched things up; they calmed down to the extent that in the spirit of their former friendship they began calling each other—with heavy irony—Comrade Luchnikov and Mr. Gangut and agreed on a time to go and hear the saxophonist Dim Shebeko together. But they both knew that they wouldn't meet again, that their lives would drift apart, that each could add the other to his list of losses.

What did Gangut's generation in the Soviet Union see in the curious political, historical, and geographical concept called the Island of Crimea? The hopes and dreams Gangut had shouted about to vent his fury? Everything they learned in school about Crimea was contained in a single all-embracing sentence: "Although the White Guard followers of the Black Baron Wrangel are temporarily entrenched on this tiny island, the Soviet people vow to continue their struggle against remnants of the White marauders and for the realization of the hopes and dreams of the territory's toiling masses, for the reunification of what once was Russian soil with the great Soviet Union." Since the author of those words was none other than a founding father of the nation, they were sacred, inviolate. In 1956, when the author himself was no longer quite so sacred, the youth of the nation began to take a special interest in the "tiny island," but if anyone then had tried to tell Vitaly Gangut that ten years later he would be close friends with one of the followers' followers, he would have considered it utter nonsense, a stupid joke, or perhaps even "bourgeois provocation." His father *had* actually been part of the expeditionary force sent to capture the island during the civil war and had been on the torpedo boat *Red Dawn* when it sank under heavy fire from a British battleship. Surfacing for a while, he took part in the period of reconstruction, then sank once more to emerge many years later from the gulag with a wealth of fascinating stories, some of which dealt with Crimea. "Our fleet was in pitiful condition," he told his son. "If Crimea had been attached to the mainland by the narrowest strip of land, if the Chongar hadn't been quite so deep, we would have crossed over on our own corpses." Excitement rose to fever pitch in those days.

Although during the early post-Stalin years the Island was no longer reduced to that one rigid, all-encompassing sentence, it did not thereby move any closer to Russia; in fact, it moved farther away. It gained the reputation of a den of iniquity, a suspicious international playground, an El Dorado of spies and adventurers.

With its American military bases and striptease joints, its jazz and boogie-woogie, it seemed another Hong Kong, Singapore, Honolulu, a symbol of Western decadence. And to a certain extent it was. Gangut once heard a drunken sailor tell his cronies about how the engine on their trawler had conked out and they'd bobbed up and down all night with an unobstructed view of the lights of Yalta. They'd even been able to make out a Cyrillic Coca-Cola sign through their binoculars. But Russian though the letters might be, Yalta was farther from Russia than, say, London, which Russian tourists had a vague chance of visiting, or Paris, which regularly came to Russia all by itself in the person of Yves Montand. Then one fine day, without offering his people much by way of explanation, Nikita Sergeevich Khrushchev signed a cultural exchange agreement with the Island. Enter peaceful coexistence. Crimea sent a colossally boring Tatar Folk Ensemble, but Moscow sent its circus, which made a colossal splash and was strewn with flowers and smothered with love. The sixties saw the first Islanders in Moscow and Leningrad, and it was then that Gangut and his generation first met their Crimean coevals. (Since the dyed-in-the-wool provacuees were afraid to go, most of the Crimean tourists were members of the younger generation.) That first group took their breath away. Imagine, you could be a Russian and still know two or three languages natively, travel all over the world, study at Oxford and the Sorbonne, and carry an American, British, or Swiss passport, do without internal passports altogether! The Crimeans thought of their country more as a way station than a political entity. Yet they were undeniably Russian. Not that they understood everything. They were completely in the dark, for instance, about the arguments raging at the time over jazz and abstract art. The most burning issues of Moscow life caused the strangest of reactions in them: an ironic smile, a shrug of the shoulders, a listless "Why not?" A generation raised on the assumption that every thought, every deed needed justification found it difficult to explain to the Islanders why jeans and haircuts and dances and the way paint is applied to a canvas and plays put on at the Contemporary or the Taganka were all burning issues. But a few of them did try to understand and immerse themselves in Soviet life, and the first was Andryushka Luchnikov.

Strange to say, Gangut met Luchnikov on the Island. Gangut

was one of the first specimens of *homo sovieticus* at the Yalta Film Festival. There had been an unprecedented lull in the screw-tightening process, and he was suddenly permitted to show his second film *hors concours*. The morning after he arrived he was greeted in the hotel lobby by a red-haired young man wearing a faded jeans jacket and a Rolex watch who introduced himself as a member of the editorial board of the *Russian Courier*—Andrei Arsenievich Luchnikov, at your service—handed him the Sunday edition, thick as a pillow, and showed him an article that began: "According to Vitaly Gangut, one of the leading directors of the New Wave in world cinema . . ." As if nothing could be more natural. Gangut right up there with Antonioni, Chabrol, Bergman, Buñuel. "One of the . . ." Needless to say, Gangut went gaga over Crimea. He gave in to every temptation and lost all his moral bearings. Most likely it was during this first stay that he began to see the Island of Crimea as the belated birthright of his entire generation, a dream come true, a model for Russia's future.

It was a time in which everything said, written, filmed, or staged was felt to be the expression of a generation. Where has it gone, our sixties' generation? How many of its members slipped through the chink in the wall and spread out from Israel all over the world? A question by no means rhetorical, thought Gangut. The very number is catastrophic. Emigration is a positive step, say some. All we are is putty in the gnarled fingers of the Soviet state. What kind of life is that? There are other possible steps, of course. The bravest among us are rotting in prison. Emigration is a climax, say others, and maybe that's closer to the truth. Those of us who are left behind talk about how catastrophic it is and buy flashy Zhigulis. And suddenly it transpires there is good money to be made in popular science films, so we kiss high ideals good-by and devote ourselves entirely to "self-improvement," which turns into nightly tea and TV sessions. Gangut's telephone almost never rang any more, he almost never went out any more, and he almost never had friends in. He had even begun losing friends— Luchnikov, for instance, though he was no Russian, just one of those crackpot leftists, good riddance—and women, and the little friend in his pants had been a good deal less demanding as of late.

All this was simmering in the back of Vitaly Gangut's mind as he stood there hunched over the television set, peering with great agitation at the face of sportscaster Tatyana Lunina on the screen. When, after flashing and sparkling for three or four minutes, she was replaced by the weather report, Gangut grabbed his jacket (a year ago it hugged his body snugly; now he couldn't begin to button it), glanced into his wallet (the piles he earned when he was hot never seemed to stay put; the piddling sums he got now by bowing and scraping were always there), and threaded his way through the flat past reflections in dirty windows and dusty mirrors, turning out lights (that is, disappearing as he went), and finally, stopping for a second at the front door, extinguishing his last reflection and heaving a sigh that said: This is it, damn it. Tomorrow morning I'm going to see about emigration forms. I've got to get out of here, I've got to get out. . . .

Suddenly, there on the landing, he was overcome by a fit of rapture, of what he called "youthful impetuosity." The thought of shedding all his burdens, making a clean break, washing his hands of the whole mess, burning his bridges behind him, call it what you will, was intoxicating to him. It would not be quite honest, however, to imply that the once-famous director had just experienced his first case of youthful impetuosity. Many were the evenings he dashed outside, wandered the streets in nervous exaltation, and ended up drinking himself silly; many were the mornings he forced three cups of coffee down his gullet and set off for the Pop Sci studios with a head full of vaguely renegade ideas on the male menopause, the goals of his generation, and man's lost connection with the soil. True, he also had to keep in mind that his name had come up in a survey article recently, which meant it was all right to mention him again, which meant he'd be given his own film to direct, and even the ever so slightly nonconformist film at home was worth more to the cause than ten or twenty Paris-based dissident journals, yet he had held on to the specious invitation to Israel acquired during his own flash-in-the-pan dissident period for just such future fits of youthful impetuosity.

And today's fit was no everyday fit; in fact, it was what might be called an attack of youth, the explosion of a secret arsenal, the sudden gush of a hormonal geyser. The first thing to do was to get hold of Tanya Lunina and find out what Andrei was up to. He had to look him up immediately. Crimea had a powerful film industry, and Andryusha wouldn't let an old pal down. After all, wasn't he, Vitaly, "one of the leading . . ."? After all, hadn't that fashion plate of a Hollywood director he'd plied with caviar the other day at the Film Makers' Union said to him, "You're right up there with the best of them"? And after all, wouldn't his decision to leave create a furor? So first he'd find Tanya and try to go to bed with her.

As the red eye of the elevator beamed dully down on Gangut's right shoulder blade, the stairwell of the fourteen-story cooperative roared like an air-raid warning and "Hey, Jude" came seeping out from under a nearby door. When the elevator finally arrived, out stepped Gangut's neighbor, a shifty-eyed middle-aged man with an enormous purebred Moscow mastiff. Not only did the man systematically refrain from greeting Gangut; he never responded to Gangut's greetings. One day it got to be too much for Gangut and he grabbed him by the lapel. Answer me! What? asked his neighbor. When someone says "Good morning," you answer. Oh, said his neighbor, shifting his eyes and walking on. Obviously the dialogue had taken place in the absence of the purebred Moscow mastiff. Gangut was certain he'd made a dent in the man, but no, his neighbor still walked past him as if he hadn't seen him or was seeing him for the first time.

"Oh, hello," the man said suddenly, straight to his face.

The dog swished its powerful tail.

Gangut was flabbergasted. "Hello, if you mean it," he answered, using a folksy cliché that for once actually fit the situation.

"The perfect response, and so Russian in spirit," said the man with a conspiratorial laugh. "What a mind!"

"I beg your pardon?"

"Our Russian people. So sharp, so astute." He held Gangut back by lifting his arm to his chest. The elevator went away. "How about coming in for a drink?" he said.

"I beg your pardon?"

"Yes, come in and have a drink," he said. Clearly he had something up his sleeve. "Here all this time we've been neighbors . . ." He was a bit tipsy.

"Normally I wouldn't dream of it," said Gangut, "but today I will."

"Yes, today's the day," said the man, laughing again. "It's a special day. I'm having a party. Join the crowd."

Gangut was led into a flat permeated with the smells of serious celebration: Yershov, for that was the name of Gangut's shifty-eyed neighbor, was celebrating his fiftieth birthday. The board was groaning appropriately, with Hungarian turkey legs sticking up at regular intervals and galantines glistening in unbroken marble slabs under a many-faceted chandelier. Glancing round the room, he knew immediately he should not have come.

"And this is our neighbor," the birthday boy announced. "Russian director Vitaly Semyonovich Gangut."

In the round of musical chairs that followed, Gangut found a seat near the end of a sofa between a woman in a resplendent wig and a fragile little schoolboy, the kind who rings the doorbell and puts the creative intelligentsia on the spot with questions like, "Excuse me, but would you have any old paper for our paper drive?"

Russian director . . . quite talented, actually . . . gifted, in fact . . . if possible, we would . . . you remember, that historical film about the motherland . . . set us back I don't know how many years . . . you know who I mean . . .

Faces turned towards him from all parts of the room. Bestial faces.

"What's all the Russian this, Russian that?" he asked the woman.

"Actually, for a long time we thought you were a kike," she said without blinking an eye, quite warmly, in fact, and smoothing down her wig and her bosom as she spoke.

"And how wrong we were," shouted a man's voice from across the table. They all had a good laugh. Then someone proposed a toast, and all the guests began drinking, eating, and talking to one another. Gangut was lost in the shuffle. It therefore took him quite some time to react, and his plate was overflowing with turkey, meat jelly, meat pie, herring, and Russian salad before he turned to the woman with the wig and asked in a loud voice, "And what is that supposed to mean?"

A strong arm suddenly reached across the table; a friendly hand seized Gangut's wrist. A virile, bearded face—a face he hadn't registered before—was smiling up at him with a smile that said, "You belong here, you're one of us now," a smile that used to be called "the smile of a generation."

"Avdotya is simplifying things as usual. Let's go out on the balcony, Vitaly, and have a smoke."

A large, athletically built man in a black leather jacket—the picture of a revolutionary commander—rose up over the table. Gangut decided to go with him if only to get off the sofa and away from the woman, still fussing with her polyester glad rags.

"Oleg Stepanov is my name," the powerful stranger said out on the balcony, producing a pack of Marlboros. "The domestic variety. See? Everything in Cyrillic. Made in Moscow."

"New to me," mumbled Gangut. "There's been a lot of talk about it, but this is the first I've tried." He inhaled. "The real thing!"

"Absolutely." Oleg Stepanov took a few steps across the spacious balcony, stopping a few feet from Gangut. "You may laugh, but until recently we often talked about you as if you were a Jew."

"May I ask a few questions?" said Gangut. "Why did you talk about me? Why often? And why as a Jew or Gentile, Tatar or Italian? What are you getting at?"

"This is a time when people are seeking their own kind," said Oleg Stepanov kindly and gently. "We are in a period of historical selection."

"So you're Slavophiles."

"Why, of course," he said with a smile. "You must admit the national genius needs a helping hand. The oppression it's suffered! And we especially need Russians in art. Take your work, now, your three pictures. True, they bear some superficial marks of the times, but down deep they seem quite Russian to me, quite healthy. The name Gangut does sound rather odd to the Russian ear, of course, and your patronymic is more than suspicious, but the main thing is the company you keep. How could we think otherwise? But after a little research I was proved right. And believe me, Vitaly, I'm glad, truly glad."

"Research?" Gangut looked at him questioningly.

"Why, yes." Oleg Stepanov nodded. "We've had a look at your roots. You yourself may not be aware of it, but the Ganguts entered Holy Rus on that glorious day when our forces took Hangö Point and a Swedish ship's boy came along as part of the booty. Hangö was Russified to Gangut, and from then on—pure Russian

68

blood. Anyway, Swedes, Varangians are quite acceptable. . . ."

"Are you serious?" asked Gangut.

They were on a tenth-story balcony of a fourteen-story building. Directly below was a road sign and a blinking traffic light. A huge stone colossus loomed in the distance beyond the thin, flat river—a new microregion merging with the night, turning into a city of caves. The once-rural sky could manage no more than a pitiful, lackluster sunset over the industrial swamps of the successor to ancient Rus. Gangut suddenly felt very low. It was the kind of feeling that takes over completely, robs you of your very self. He gave a sharp jerk of the head, as if struggling in a whirlpool, and rose quickly to the surface. Oleg Stepanov was resting his elbows on the railing, staring out into the green-gray abyss.

"The Jews," he said, completely motionless, "are merely accidental guests on our soil."

I've got to get out of here, thought Gangut. I've got to get out of this madhouse, and now. It was nearly morning by the time he left. He stuffed food down his throat from a plate that soon looked like a slop bucket, he drank everything that filled his glass, he listened on and on to Oleg Stepanov, who kept trying to make him promise he would phone a certain Dmitry Valentinovich and all his cares would be over. "Who is he, anyway?" he asked. "A minister? A secretary of the Central Committee? A general?"

"Oh, he's a rare species: the type of bird who's never seen but is heard in all the right places. Give him a call tomorrow and tell him who you are. Mark my words: your life will never be the same."

At dawn Stepanov dragged Gangut across the landing back to Gangut's flat. He laid him out on the day bed and even wiped away the remains of the last eruption.

For a while he waited beside the numb, unconscious body, trying to turn it over on its back or at least slide his hand under its stomach. But it was no use: the glob of Russian flesh responded with no more than a wheeze. In desperation Oleg Stepanov sat down in the chair at the desk, reached into his pants, and took off. His eyes fell on a picture standing on the desk, a shot of two naked men and a naked woman against a background of high surf, and he intensified his efforts. A few restrained moans and it was all over. He neatly wiped up after himself and, leaving a few pertinent telephone numbers on the desk, departed quietly.

IV

A Curious Incident

Marlen Mikhailovich Kuzenkov also watched sportscaster Tatyana Lunina on the television screen that evening, though she did not make quite the overwhelming impression on him she made on Vitaly Gangut. He simply enjoyed watching her again. It was gratifying to see a poised, nicely dressed woman on television, and Marlen Mikhailovich assumed the whole country shared his feeling, everyone but the moss-backed old guard, which opposed even television on principle. But what harm could there be in nice-looking faces? Times have changed. Now and again he would see a face in the street or on stage that was completely free of sociopolitical tics. If he were one of the television Comrades, he would bring in more of that sort of face, as much to make positive propaganda (which is how the more superficial Comrades might see it) as to point up the recent historic advances within the country. Year by year, decade by decade, faces like that can imperceptibly alter the psychological structure of the population.

All this went through Kuzenkov's mind while he was watching Tanya, and would be stored away in the secret archives of his brain, ready for retrieval when necessary. That was the way Marlen Mikhailovich operated: he never let anything go to waste.

He had, of course, been informed that morning that Tanya was due in from Crimea, and, of course, he knew that she had met Andrei Luchnikov in Koktebel and spent two days with him—two days and two nights, that is—in the Feodosia-Simferopol-Yalta triangle. It goes without saying that he was privy to the information even before the special report reached the First Division of the State Committee for Athletics and Physical Education. It was his job to know everything there was to know about Crimea. Not that he always wanted to know it all. There were times when, if the truth were told, he would rather have remained in the dark, but the material kept coming in, and he did know everything. Marlen Mikhailovich Kuzenkov was a one-man clearing house for information concerning the Eastern Mediterranean Region, better known as the Island of Crimea.

So she's back, and he's still in Simfi, thought Kuzenkov, leaving the room where his wife and children sat glued to the television set in anticipation of this year's song festival.

He ran through Luchnikov's itinerary in his mind: Paris, Dakar, New York, Geneva perhaps, then back to Paris—though it was impossible to predict where he would zig or zag next, and for all anyone knew, he could cancel all his appointments tomorrow and fly straight to Moscow to be with Tatyana. His multi-entrance visa was still valid, wasn't it? Marlen would have to check the details in the morning.

Can't you ever stop thinking about work? said Kuzenkov to himself reproachfully. Or at least look at it from another angle. Luchnikov is your friend as well as your subject. And OK—as they called the Island in private, OK being the initials for its Russian name, Ostrov Krym—OK was a miracle of nature as much as a political anachronism. You don't want to be like the moss-backed old guard that lived for work and got nothing in return but blood, sweat, and tears. You're a man of the present. Your name comes from Marx and Lenin, the two bright lights of the millennium.

But Marlen Mikhailovich was out of sorts. He had been involved in a curious incident in the streets of Moscow earlier in the day. Though his rank was such that he could easily avoid contact with the outside world (his colleagues never set foot in the streets of the capital, relying entirely on half-hearted glances at the bustling objects of their endeavors, glances shielded by the windows of chauffeur-driven Volgas as they made their way back and forth from dacha to Central Committee headquarters), Marlen Mikhailovich felt duty-bound to keep in touch with the populace. He maintained his own black Volga, fitted it out with all the Western gadgets he could find at GUM's "Special Section," and got a great kick out of driving it. He was a jaunty fifty-plus, played tennis regularly at the Dynamo courts, and wore English tweeds and fine shoes with intricate perforated patterns. That the upper echelons did not particularly approve of his tastes he knew quite well. Of course, he was sheltered by the fact that he worked with foreigners ("When in bourgeois Rome . . ."), but he was perfectly aware that on the floor below they never mentioned him, on his own floor someone would occasionally refer to him as the "tennis pro" and drop a sardonic remark about upholding the traditions of his "Christian" name, and on the floor above they never mentioned him either, though in a different way, a plus-or-minus kind of way, in which the promising little cross still prevailed over the destructive dash. It was the upstairs silence that encouraged Kuzenkov to stick to his guns, though every once in a while he would throw the comrades an external sop to remind them he was really one of the gang—say, use a dirty word or two in private, make a big thing out of going fishing, show a certain muted respect for Generalissimo Iosif S. (history is history, Comrades), comment favorably on recent village prose, cultivate a less-cultivated pronunciation, and naturally take part in the . . . um . . . you know what I mean, Comrades . . . the . . . the Finnish bath ritual. Which is not to say that Marlen Mikhailovich was not really one of the gang. He was completely at home with them, completely and utterly, more than most, perhaps. The psychologists upstairs were right about that. Yet Marlen had a secret, a secret he would rather have repressed, a little bubble of anxiety that kept forcing its way up to the surface. Inveterate dialectical materialist that he was, he explained it in terms of a point on his curriculum vitae, and if Marlen Mikhailovich kept it under his hat, well, no one actually asked him about it. He was left to guess whether the authorities knew what it was in fact their business to know. This said, we may finally turn from our necessarily shaky, provisional presentation of Marlen

Mikhailovich Kuzenkov to the "curious incident" that took place in the streets of Moscow.

After finishing his round of tennis with a general on the strategic aviation staff, Marlen Mikhailovich went out into Pushkin Street, where his shiny black Volga was parked directly under a NO PARKING sign. And though any policeman with the least bit of experience should have known that a car with that number plate was better left in peace, no sooner did he step up to his beauty— which for some reason he wouldn't have swapped for all the Mercedes, Porsches, or Russo-Balts in the world—than up stepped a policeman from the other side of the street. Kuzenkov smiled at the thought of how the rookie's overzealous jaw would drop when he had a look at his papers.

"Excuse me," said the servant of the law, a boy scarcely twenty, with sergeant's stripes, "but would you have two or three extra liters of gas? Enough to get me back to headquarters."

"Be my guest, be my guest," said Marlen Mikhailovich. "The tank is full. But you take care of it, will you, Sergeant? I don't have a siphon in the car."

This insignificant bit of contact with the real Moscow or, rather, with a bona-fide representative in uniform gave Marlen Mikhailovich a great deal of pleasure. He could just imagine how his floormates' faces would drop if they saw a person of their rank and station offering his tank to a puny local police sergeant. Ah yes, a bunch of apparatchiks, that's what we've become; ah yes, our loss of contact with the streets, that's what we need to change first and foremost. Lenin knew it long ago.

The sergeant brought over a jerry can and a piece of hose with a bulb at one end to create the proper suction. He fussed and fidgeted for a while, but made no headway whatsoever: either the hose had a hole in it or the sergeant was doing something wrong, but he coaxed out no more than a trickle.

"Don't worry. Don't worry," said Marlen Mikhailovich to the young centurion. "Take your time. How about trying your mouth?"

Meanwhile the crowds kept sailing past, and Kuzenkov, not to waste time, began to observe them. He had not been at it for long when an odd couple entered his field of view. They were two eras personified, one hanging on to the other. A pale, disheveled old man, his threadbare jacket trimmed with the bars of several war medals, was trailing behind a long-haired boy in jeans. His right hand clutched a net bag with a few pitiful-looking groceries in it, his left clutched the boy's sleeve. "Forty years!" screamed the old man, his face hideously distorted. "Forty years I've slaved for socialism! And you think you can get away with it? Not on your life! You're coming with me!"

"Shove off, you old goat!" said the boy in a low voice. "Leave me alone, will you?" He was obviously trying to avoid a scene and free his sleeve as unobtrusively as possible. He could tell that any show of force on his part would only bring on more ranting and lead them to the brink of catastrophe, but he also seemed to realize his exhortations were futile, the catastrophe inevitable. In other words, a typical Muscovite of the older generation was hassling a typical Muscovite of the younger generation.

"I will *not* let you alone!" screamed the old man. "I have *never* let the enemy alone! I'm taking you straight to the police. They'll teach you a thing or two."

Catching a Moscow crowd's attention is no mean feat. Furrowed brow after furrowed brow hurried past, giving no evidence of noticing either the humiliating position of the young man or the old man's raucous offensives. But the latter finally grew so vociferous that finally heads began to turn and feet slow their pace.

As if in deference to an inner voice, a signal vaguely connected with his secret, Kuzenkov went over and planted himself in front of the pair. "What's going on here?" he asked the old man in his most official voice. "Why are you preventing this young man from going about his business?" He sounded so much like a character out of Zoshchenko he had to smile.

The old man was taken aback. He stopped in the middle of a sentence, looking first at the black Volga, then at the police sergeant squatting beside it, and finally at the cold sarcasm in the eyes of the man in the street who was clearly more than a man in the street. Confronted simultaneously with so many symbols of power, he lost his bearings for a moment and dropped the boy's sleeve. But immediately he rallied his wits. "I was waiting to pay for my groceries, and this hooligan here started walking through the shop hissing at everything."

"You're the one who's hissing," retorted the jeans era rather lamely.

"Why do you keep pestering him?" Marlen Mikhailovich asked the old man, trying to sound both stern and avuncular at once.

"Hissing at everything. Carrying that attaché case and hissing at everything. We went without shoes, and he's got an attaché case. Walking through the shop and hissing."

"That's no excuse," said Marlen Mikhailovich in the same tone.

"But Comrade, you don't understand!" the old man wailed in desperation. "He did it to show there was nothing to buy!" By now he was trembling all over. The pitiful old fool. Besides the jacket he wore a checked grease-stained shirt under his trousers and a pair of worn-out sandals over his bare feet. Though he smelled slightly of wine, he reeked of acetone and decay, of premature decomposition. His pasty face twitched spasmodically: What can you do if the Comrades refuse to understand? "He even said it straight out: 'There's nothing to buy.'" Whereupon he swirled around to recapture the enemy, but the enemy—long hair, jeans, attaché case, and all—had in the interim flown the coop. Even Marlen Mikhailovich had failed to notice his departure.

"Do you mean to say we can buy anything we want?" asked Marlen Mikhailovich by way of provocation.

"Anything we *need*," the man snapped back, still searching for the enemy, burning for retribution. But once he realized his quest was in vain, he turned back to the matter at hand and held his net bag up to Marlen Mikhailovich's face, which, after the injustice he had condoned, was itself beginning to look suspiciously like the face of an enemy. "Anything we simple people need is readily available. Look: macaroni, groats, butter, macaroni . . . and some nice white bread rolls. You know who hisses? Gluttons, that's who! We slave our lives away, but no, they're not satisfied!"

"What about you?" asked Kuzenkov coldly. "Are you satisfied? Satisfied with everything?" The stringent tone was a way of convincing himself his concerns were purely sociological, but something very different had taken shape beneath the surface: a violent gut reaction to this aggressive protoplasm, this self-appointed informer.

"Yes, I'm satisfied with everything." His trembling hands began to reach out for Kuzenkov's tweed jacket. "I've slaved forty years for the cause! Without shoes . . . without shoes . . . And these attaché-case know-it-alls . . ."

"Move along, move along," said Marlen Mikhailovich, turning away from the old man.

When he got back to the car, he found the police sergeant still fiddling with the hose. Even if he'd never so much as raised his head, he couldn't have helped hearing the rumpus the old man had made.

"How's it going?" asked Kuzenkov in a businesslike, automobile-like voice. "Coming through?"

The policeman was quite embarrassed. He put the hose in his mouth, sucked up some gas, and, spitting it out, transferred the hose to the jerry can. A few drops did trickle through, but nothing like the stream he needed. Kuzenkov leaned over both to have a look and to recover from his confrontation with history. Then he felt something spongy against his side. It was the old man's stomach.

"You seem to have missed my point, Comrade," he said softly, and squinting down at Marlen Mikhailovich, added, "Who are you, anyway?"

The corners of his mouth were caked with dried spit, the edges of his eyes with a puslike discharge. The squint and the now quite sober intonation told Marlen Mikhailovich that he was not dealing with a simple fool, that the old man might well have been one of Stalin's falcons, an insider, a camp soldier at the very least. "Look," he said with a combination of disgust and pity, "don't you think it's time you calmed down? You're satisfied with everything; the young man wasn't. People are different. You can accept that, can't you?"

The old man took in every word while scrutinizing his face. "Of course. People are different, very different. And who are you? Sergeant, what is this Comrade doing here?"

By now the policeman was engulfed in fumes, and, without even looking up, barked a standard, "Drunk, eh? Get going."

The old man flinched and retreated slightly. The policeman represented power and was automatically in the right; besides, he *had* had a few drinks. Still, he didn't do as he was told; he kept staring at Kuzenkov. And though he couldn't possibly have guessed the provenance of Kuzenkov's jacket, the glower on his face made his thought processes clear. Who is this man? Why did he let my enemy go? Is he really on our side? He doesn't act like one of us, Comrades. Could he be on their side? Could there be a group of them?

Marlen Mikhailovich read that face like a book, and it made him furious. But on another, deeper level, in his heart of hearts, a tiny fountain of fear had sprouted.

The old man's hands reached out to his chest, and the slobbery lips began moving in a delirious monologue. "Well, and if I have had a few . . . so you have the upper hand . . . forty years I've slaved . . . without shoes . . . damn attaché cases . . . nothing to buy . . . we feed half the world . . . papers . . . how are you . . . know me here . . . hey, Sergeant . . ."

Marlen Mikhailovich was angry with himself for being afraid. Here he had all but reached the top, and he still couldn't squeeze the slave out of himself. How simple it would have been to cut the Stalinist pig short ("Stalinist pig"), shove him out of the way, and speed off in his Volga—if not for that imbecile of a cop with his imbecilic siphon. What's there for me to be afraid of anyway? Even if he did make a fuss, I could smooth it over in no time flat. Half an hour at the local police station. Less. A call to Shcholokov and they'd all be quaking in their boots. Then again, nobody wants another ridiculous scandal, and it just might go upstairs. They're very sensitive to these old dodderers nowadays, and there are those who consider them the backbone of our society (pity the society with such a backbone). In other words . . . But how can I get rid of him? If I don't act right away, he'll grab hold of my jacket, go into convulsions, and bring the whole street running. We dearly love our epileptics, we do. . . .

Then in the nick of time a perky woman of about forty swooped down on the old man, her breasts all but tumbling out of a cheap black T-shirt with GRAND PRIX written boldly across the front. "Time to go, Uncle Kolya. What are you up to, anyway? Come on, come on! Quickly, or Aunt Lyalya will be after you. We've been looking all over for you!"

Tearing himself away from her with a grunt, the old man started waving his net bag in Kuzenkov's face. Long strands of pasta came slithering through the holes. "It's all his fault!" he cried. "Won't show his papers! And the sergeant here, he won't do his duty! Help me, Comrades!"

"Come on, Uncle Kolya, come on! Get his number and you can write a complaint," she said, stuffing her breasts back into the shirt and her feet back into a pair of floppy slippers—she had obviously run out as she was—and somehow managing to give Marlen Mikhailovich a wink at the same time, a wink and a pucker of her intoxicated lips.

The idea of writing a complaint so appealed to the old man that he allowed himself to be dragged away, though not without turning back and yelling threats, the more drastic and garbled the farther he got.

"How does it look, Sergeant?" asked Marlen Mikhailovich, peering into the jerry can, upset. The bottom was scarcely covered. What began as a pleasant and informative escapade into the life of the streets had turned into a grotesque joke. Kuzenkov was extremely disturbed by that flash of fear. Did it really live on in him? How repulsive!

He snatched the siphon from the sergeant's hands and examined it carefully. Just as he thought: a hole. With a sharp curse he opened his trunk and pulled out a tube. He stuck one end in the tank, the other in his mouth, and by the time he had coughed the viscous liquid out of his system, it was flowing out of the tube in a steady stream. The sergeant soon had more than enough to get his mini-Moskvich back to the station.

"The fruits of noninterference," said Marlen Mikhailovich sarcastically. "No oil embargo for us."

The sergeant looked up at him with the makings of fear in his eyes. He, too, must have begun to wonder who this Comrade was. In any case, he did not fall over himself with gratitude.

Kuzenkov was already behind the wheel when in the rear-view mirror he noticed Uncle Kolya racing back to the ideological front, jacket in the wind, paunch-filled shirt three-quarters open. This time he had left his net bag at home and in its stead was waving a small red book above his head like a signal. All Marlen Mikhailovich had to do was to perform a few simple operations and he would be on his way and out of the ridiculous mess. All he had to do was to turn the key, shift into first, and switch on the left traffic indicator. If he had done everything a shade faster than usual, he would have made a clean getaway. But he did not want it to look like a getaway, and did everything more deliberately than usual. As a result, Uncle Kolya had time to run up to the car, stick his head through the window, and shove the little book in Kuzenkov's face. "See this Party card? Here, read it! It's mine. And show me yours! Now!"

"Informer!" Marlen Mikhailovich said suddenly and pushed his face out of the car with one smooth motion. "Don't you dare spy on anyone again, you dirty stool pigeon!" And with those words he took off. The old man ran after him for a few feet spouting foul language. Waiting for a light a block away, Marlen Mikhailovich glanced in the side mirror and saw Uncle Kolya waving his little red book in the police sergeant's frowning face with one hand and gesticulating towards the car with the other. The sergeant took the old man by the shoulder and pointed with his chin to the police car as if to say, "In you go." But the old man lost his balance and fell down in the road. The last thing Kuzenkov saw was a pair of legs in baggy blue trousers struggling for equilibrium. The light turned green.

The first thing Marlen Mikhailovich did when he got home was to give his hands a good wash; he could still feel the old man's sticky imprint on them. Then he took off his clothes; what he really needed was a shower. Undressing, he examined himself in the mirror. Graying, but tan, and still full of get-up-and-go. It wasn't wise of you to lay yourself bare like that, Marlen, he said to himself. It was wrong, all wrong, and not at all in keeping with your position. Position nothing; it was not at all in keeping with your duty, with your responsibility to—why mince words?—to history. You behaved—it suddenly hit him—you behaved like a dissident. You behaved like a dissident and felt like a dissident. No, that has to be stopped.

Putting himself in the old buzzard's shoes, he tried to picture what it would be like to have the logical world he had constructed with the meager resources of his brain crumble beneath him, to have the police, the black Volga, the squint in the eye—hard and fast symbols of the power he had guarded all his life like a watchdog—blow up in his face, turn against him. A major catastrophe. No, getting rid of these old fogies, eliminating them—and they are legion—would be a tragic mistake for the state; it would be tantamount to dismissing an entire era; it would be antipolitical and antihistorical.

He spent the rest of the day mulling over the "curious incident" (that was how he decided to present it to his wife when the whispering hour came—"a curious incident"). He thought about it at his desk, reading the Crimean papers. He had been asked to prepare a brief survey of current events on the Island for one of the members of the Politburo. Surveys were one of his pet projects, and he took them very seriously, but now that damned curious incident was making it hard for him to concentrate. He kept wishing the evening would fly and he could be alone with his wife and share his feelings and impressions with her.

Tanya Lunina's face on the TV screen provided a bit of relief: she reminded him of Andrei Luchnikov, the problems relating to him and, by association, Luchnikov's Moscow friend, the director Vitaly Gangut, and he wondered how Gangut would have reacted to the silly little Pushkin Street squabble. Substituting Gangut for himself, he found that everything turned out naturally, as expected. Putting himself back into the picture, he watched everything go sour.

As usual when night was about to fall, and yet as unexpectedly as usual, Dmitry, his son from his first marriage, rang him up. The twenty-five-year-old Dmitry hadn't lived at home for years and considered himself a free agent: he was saxophone soloist with a semiunderground jazz-rock band called C_2H_5OH. He answered only to his stage name, Dim Shebeko, Shebeko being his mother's name and Dim his Americanization of Dmitry. He considered all politics "a load of shit," though he was a full-fledged dissident, since dissidence means iconoclasm. Marlen Mikhailovich had the feeling that Dim Shebeko was ashamed of being related to a Party bigwig like himself and kept it a secret from his pals. Nor was Marlen Mikhailovich in a position to boast of his little boy's achievements to the Comrades at work, his floormates. Besides, their relationship had been very much on-again off-again for years because of the boy's mother, whose fury at being cast off by Marlen had never abated. Lately the boy seemed to have gone downhill: he'd stopped seeing the mother he so adored, loafed about town with an I-don't-give-a-damn grin plastered over his brazenly handsome face, and reestablished normal—in other words, financial—relations with his father, cadging cash or Stolichnaya (which, because it was available only to high officials, was often worth more). But this time he had phoned to find out when their common friend Andrei was due in. Andrei had promised him the latest recordings of John Klemmer and Keith Jarrett; of the Sex Pistols, too, though Dim Shebeko didn't think they or the whole punk craze had much of a future. Still, he had to keep up.

When the call was over, Marlen Mikhailovich went back to the curious incident. That long-haired boy could just as well have been Dim Shebeko, though even vigilant Uncle Kolya would have second thoughts about accosting a mug like his son's. "Those people are dangerous, Dad," Dim Shebeko would have said. "If I were you, I'd have run over the old fart."

At last Marlen Mikhailovich pushed away the typewriter and began the long wait till the end of the next TV program. Shortly after eleven he heard Vera Pavlovna sending the children off to bed. The moment he so longed for was nigh. Here it was, almost their silver anniversary, and they were still as smitten as ever. Every evening, no matter how tired he was, Marlen Mikhailovich looked forward ardently to the soft, gentle body of the ever-fragrant Vera Pavlovna.

"Was that Dim Shebeko on the phone, dearest?" she asked, a bit breathless after his greeting.

Marlen Mikhailovich's head lay on her faithful shoulder. Here was a world of peace and quiet, a world familiar to the last square inch of skin, the world of his wife, of her glorious hills and dales. If only he could spend all his life there and never return to the muddy waters of foreign policy.

"I was involved in a curious incident in town today, darling," he whispered almost inaudibly. She immediately grasped the gravity of the matter and dropped her question about the phone call.

"I see," she said after Marlen Mikhailovich had told his tale or, rather, analyzed the feelings the ridiculous little episode had called forth in him. "Well, here's what I think, Marlen. A:"—whenever she bent down the little finger of her left hand like that, Marlen had the feeling it was no longer the little finger of her left hand but a highly serious A, the forerunner of B, C, D . . . , all equally serious and concrete—"A: You shouldn't have got involved in the first place. It was none of your business. B: Once you were involved, you had to take a stand, which you did. C: The stand you took amply demonstrated your superior moral fiber, though I wonder whether it was wise to have called the old man a 'dirty stool pigeon.' And finally D: The most important thing of all, the vague fear you felt under Uncle Kolya's scrutiny. I interpret the whole affair as a subconscious protest against the fear still alive in you and me and our whole generation—in other words, as something completely positive and natural. As for the possibility that the old epileptic will file charges against you . . ." She completed her sentence with a wave of the hand so airy as to dismiss the very idea and close the discussion once and for all. What depth she has and what insight, thought Marlen Mikhailovich, stroking her shoulder with gratitude. How perfectly she understands me. What logic and strength of purpose.

Vera Pavlovna was an instructor at Moscow University, the assistant secretary of her department's Party Bureau, a member of the Executive Committee of the Society for Cultural Ties with the Eastern Mediterranean Region, and everything her husband thought she was.

Relieved, he put his arms around her, and the two of them fell asleep as one, the picture, none too frequent nowadays, of connubial bliss. Early the next morning they were awakened by a call from Paris. It was Andrei Luchnikov. "My visa's expired, Marlen. Could you give the embassy here a call? I have to leave for Moscow immediately."

V

Those Damned Foreigners

It's the Stone Age all over again, thought Luchnikov. They put
men on the moon, but just try to put a call through from Paris: the
wait, the operators. It's worse than what we had to put up with in
the fifties. And getting through to the provinces from Moscow is
harder than getting through to Paris. Nothing was ever nearly so
bad as that on the Island.

Luchnikov went over to the window. The Boulevard Raspail
was unusually quiet. The cars were parked bumper to bumper,
with an occasional tree wedged in between. A sorrowful-looking
Moroccan with a broom was sweeping his way along the asphalt
strip next to them. Traffic would not begin for another hour.
Luchnikov closed the shutters to keep out the noise, jumped back
into bed, and fell asleep immediately. He woke up three hours
later, at seven o'clock sharp. He had a hard day ahead of him, but
now at least he could relax for a few hours. Arriving in Paris and
not having to rush off somewhere—what a luxury!

A leisurely yoga session. A leisurely shower and shave. Then to
Montparnasse to the Dôme for breakfast. Everything was just the
way it had always been: the old man with *Le Figaro*, the old
man with the *Times*, the old man with *Il Messaggero*, all three

smoking cigars; a lone woman *d'un certain âge* and as white as porcelain; and—who else?—oh yes, a fair-haired young man with a dark-haired young woman or a dark-haired young man with a fair-haired young woman or a fair-haired young man with a fair-haired young man or a dark-haired young man with a dark-haired young man (the single-sex couples seem to go in for less mixing); and, of course, a young American family with mother sitting sideways, her baby strapped to her back. There was room for one and all, both physically and psychologically, on the Dôme's spacious terrace; even at breakfast it upheld the foremost commandment of the Renaissance. Two of the usual waiters, men who had never been young and would never be old, distributed coffee, cream, and *croissants* with great dignity. Next door the local *fruits de mer*-monger was laying out his oysters for display. Rarely, which meant not *quite* every day, a new arrival from a nearby hotel, a young gentleman getting on in years, would make his appearance, trying to look as though he had all the time in the world and invariably carrying a newspaper. It was the invariability of Parisian breakfasts that made them so wonderful. Yes, Paris was still Paris.

At the kiosk on the corner of the Boulevard du Montparnasse and the Boulevard Raspail, Luchnikov bought a *Herald Tribune* and the bilingual edition of his own *Courier*. After his first sip of coffee he imagined Tatyana Lunina sitting opposite him. So much for private life, he said to himself with a smile and turned to the papers. First the *Courier* and the weather report at the lower right-hand corner of the front page: Simfi $+78°$, Paris $+82°$, London $+82°$, New York $+87°$, Moscow $+44°$ . . . Once more Moscow comes in last. Even the climate seemed to be getting worse. For several years in a row anticyclones had been giving Russia the slip—poor Russia, so low on everything as it was—and regaling rusty old Europe with good weather and all that goes with it. The *Courier*'s main story was the launching of a Soviet space vehicle manned by a Russian and a Pole (or, as they put it, "a citizen of the Polish People's Republic"). Large helmeted heads with high cheekbones and broad, official smiles. On the lower left-hand side of the front page he found Andrei Sakharov's latest statement headed by a small picture. And what's wrong with that, gentlemen? Isn't the Pole the *first* Polish cosmonaut? And hasn't Mr. Sakharov, quite apart from the debt of respect we all owe him, issued any number of statements? In the *Trib* things were the other way round: the Sakharov picture was much larger, the article more prominently placed, while the cosmonauts looked out from the bottom of the page like two worn coins. Yet one way or another, Russia—decayed, demoralized Russia—continued to give the world its headlines. Who was the true hero of today's Russia, who was braver—the cosmonaut or the dissident? A childish question, perhaps, but worthy of serious consideration.

On the sunny side of the Boulevard du Montparnasse, Luchnikov spied the lean figure of Colonel Chernok. Funny, he was wearing nearly the same-colored suit as Luchnikov. Nearly the same blue shirt. Funny, he, too, stopped at the corner kiosk and bought the *Courier* and the *Trib*, though he also lingered over the July issue of *Playboy*. He then went into the Rotonde and ordered breakfast, though he also asked for a small glass of Martell on the side. He seemed aware of the presence of his friend sitting on the shopwindowlike terrace of the Dôme. But though aware of his presence, he did not acknowledge it. Nor did Luchnikov acknowledge his. They had arranged to meet at another nearby café, the Sélect, an hour from then, but both dearly cherished that hour and enjoyed making believe—as they luxuriated in the sun, looking through the papers and savoring the coffee—that they had nothing else to do all day.

And so on they went, item by item. Crimean politics. "The Yaki nationalist faction in the Provisional Duma has launched a new series of attacks on the provacuees, demanding the immediate formation of a discrete and independent state with all the appropriate institutions. The group has met with the strong opposition of the League for the Rebirth of Homeland and Throne, the Communists, the Social Democrats, the Constitutional Democrats, the Laborites, and the Friends of Islam." And each for its own reason. But paradoxical as it may seem, the whole motley cast of characters—ravings, drivel all—was closer to us than the eminently likable Yaki nationalists. Yes, these vibrant, energetic grassroots proponents of a new nation represented a greater threat to the Idea of a Common Fate than all the monarchists and liberals put together, to say nothing of the Island pinkos and reds and every shade in between. The Moscow commies spouted Moscow's slogans, the Beijing commies Beijing's, and the Eurocommies sat calmly in their university offices while their guerrilla students played at revolution according to 1905 rules: "Eat the bread, burn the bakery." It was a noxious, senile idea, its only saving grace being the recent healthy Moscow offshoot that the Idea of a Common Fate was banking on. Often over morning coffee Andrei Arsenievich Luchnikov prided himself on being a sensible, sensitive, and wholly unbiased analyst of the fate of his nation, of the fate of the human race.

One last sip and he dug into his pocket for yesterday's messages. A squad of loudly sirening police cars raced along the Boulevard du Montparnasse in the direction of the Boulevard Saint-Michel. Nine forty a.m. The Paris day of the editor-in-chief of the *Russian Courier*, one of the most puzzling journalistic enterprises of our times, had officially begun.

Most of the messages turned out to be confirmations of previously made appointments, but there was one unexpected piece of news. Mr. J. P. Halloway of Paramount Pictures had phoned yesterday at noon and asked Monsieur Loutchnikoff to contact him at such-and-such a number. Later that afternoon, Mr. Halloway (Mr. Halloway—ha! J. P. Scumbag, alias Octopus, and dear old friend), obviously drunk out of his mind, had apparently come to the hotel in person and dropped off the following note:

Andrei Luchnikov,
Lay down your arms and come to a surrender party tomorrow at one p.m., Brasserie Lipp, Saint-Germain-des-Prés.

Octopus

Well, he'd work it in somehow. Lunch with Octopus and Co. at one. He couldn't stand up an old pal like Octopus. How many years had it been since he'd seen him last? Four? Five? Actually he fitted into the schedule perfectly. In fifteen minutes, the meeting with Chernok. At eleven, UNESCO and Petya Sabashnikov. He'd take Sabashnikov along with him to lunch at one. Then after lunch, a quick call to the Soviet embassy to find out whether they'd prolonged the multi-entrance visa. At five, to von Witte's with Sabashnikov. At half past six, the ABC interview. Then over to PEN club headquarters for a reception in honor of a recently depatriated dissident, a half-hour latitude in arrival time. I'll just about make it. The rest of the evening I'm on my own. Alone. At last. I can take in the latest Bertolucci. Or check out that new jazz club in the Quartier Latin. Then settle down with Plato. I won't drink a drop. In fact, I won't go to the Bertolucci or the jazz joint at all. I'll go straight back to the hotel and to Plato, the dialogue about tyranny and freedom. . . .

Andrei Luchnikov paid for his breakfast, picked up his papers, and left. His friend across the street, Colonel Chernok, commander in chief of the Island's North Buffer Zone, did the same. They both then made their way to the Sélect, mirror images of each other.

They were actually quite similar anyway: born in the same year and into the same provacuee elite; one a bit stockier, the other more slender; one a military pilot, the other a journalist and politician.

"You made it very hard for me to read my papers in your Rotonde," said Luchnikov.

"And you made it very hard for me to drink my coffee in your Dôme," said Chernok.

"The Dôme is better," said Luchnikov.

"But my suit is better," said Chernok.

"You win," said Luchnikov.

"Of course," said Chernok.

Shades of the Tsar Alexander II (Liberator) Classical School for Boys in Simferopol.

"Have you read the latest from Simfi?" asked Luchnikov as their beers arrived.

"The Yaki business?"

"The same. The latest polls show their popularity up three points. Now it will shoot up astronomically. The idea of a new nation is catching. It's like the New World all over again. In one day on the Island my Antoshka turned into a raving Yaki nationalist. With Duma elections coming up this winter we'd better do some fancy campaigning, or we can forget about reunification."

"Right." The colonel was a man of few words.

Their most urgent concern was to form a party with mass appeal. There was great support for the Idea of a Common Fate among all levels of society. Immediate reunification with the homeland was the editorial policy of dozens of papers besides the *Courier*. Luchnikov proposed they call the party SOS, the Russian initials for the Common Fate League.

As soon as the SOS catches on, the other parties will start losing membership. The name itself—who can resist a party called SOS? —is half the battle. We'll announce it as soon as possible, pull out all the stops. This is no hush-hush affair. Why hush it up? Even the mullahs are for autonomy within the boundaries of the USSR. The military? Why, of course they'll be allowed to join. We just won't register it as a political party. What? Oh, it can still take part in the elections. We'll just have other candidates endorse us. No, I don't see a trace of demagogy in it. Well, maybe a trace, but no more than the Soviets use or our own mastodons. We're for détente, but we need more propaganda; we're not a state, but we are independent; we're not a party, but we do take part in elections. . . . No, demagogy isn't for us. Our ruse is no ruse. We . . . Who are we, anyway?

That's a moot question, old man, and we're interested in something completely different. It's not Crimea we want to save. You know that. If we're going to have any influence on Russia's bloodstream, we've got to inject ourselves into it. Think how everything's changed during our own lifetime. When we were young, your fathers still dreamed of the Spring Campaign, Russia liberated from the Bolsheviks, new elections to the Provisional Assembly. . . . Then came the war. Remember how everyone rushed to the front—Leningrad, Stalingrad—to fight the Germans? True, Stalin refused to acknowledge our troops, but our elder brothers, no matter which of the Allies they joined, still fought for Russia, for Russia alone. . . . And now that the post-Stalin hopes for democratization, "the adventure of our generation," are dashed once and for all, now that Russia is hurtling full steam ahead towards 1984, our generation has only one more chance: to join hands with Russia under the banner of SOS. What else can we do? Time is wasting. Another generation and it will be too late. The Russian dream will die. . . .

Not once during his harangue did Luchnikov look up at Chernok. He played with his glass, lit a cigarette, twirled his lighter in his fingers. But when he finally did raise his eyes, they were met serenely by his friend's. "Good," he said, "let's get down to practical matters."

They talked about "practical matters" for a while, but broke off suddenly when they noticed two girls looking in at them through the glass.

The two Montparnasse regulars were terribly snobbish: faded tunics, unbrushed hair, painted faces. A little soap and they might turn out attractive. Chernok and Luchnikov exchanged amused glances. The girls cuddled up to the glass, curving their bodies in a "What do you say, big boys?" pose. Luchnikov pointed to his watch, meaning "So sorry, *mesdemoiselles*, but we're on a terribly tight schedule; our time is not our own; you know how it is nowadays." They nodded, laughing, and went on their way blowing kisses at them. One of them had a violin case tucked under her arm.

"I met the most charming woman yesterday," said Chernok dreamily. For some reason he cultivated the old-fashioned genteel approach with women when, in fact, he was as dissolute as they come. "She was thrilled to learn I was Russian—'*Ce que j'adore les hommes soviétiques!*'—and desolate when I explained about Crimea. '*Alors, monsieur,*' she said, '*vous n'êtes pas russe, mais criméen?*' It took me a long time to convince her I was the *crème des Criméens* and a hundred percent Russian to boot."

"How is your Mirage venture coming along?" asked Luchnikov.

The colonel had been in Paris for almost a month to purchase a fleet of the famous bombers for the Crimean air force. "They'll have the contract ready any day now. We're down for fifty." Chernok sniggered at the thought. "The whole thing's absurd. What in the world are we going to do with them? Our Sikorskys are perfectly serviceable for the time being, and before long we'll be switching over to Migs." Suddenly he looked Luchnikov straight in the eye. "Sometimes I wonder whether they'll need any pilots . . . like me."

Luchnikov turned away. "You know how hazy everything is there," he said after a long pause. "I sometimes have the feeling that they themselves don't know what they want. But we must be clear about what we want. I want to be Russian, and I don't care if they send us to Siberia. . . ."

"Of course," said Chernok. "There's no turning back now."

Luchnikov looked at his watch again. Time to move on to the Place de Fontenoy.

"Not just yet, Andrei," Chernok said in a different tone of voice. "I have one more question."

The Boulevard du Montparnasse suddenly began to sway, to ripple, to break up into long, thin lines, like jets of rain: there was something out of the ordinary in Chernok's voice, something personal. The recent interest in his private life, his life outside the "movement," had put a damper on that life as he enjoyed living it.

"Say the word, Andrei, and I'll change the subject, but . . . has it ever occurred to you"—the gentle, considerate voice he reserved for women and the infirm suddenly cracked, and he bolted through the rest of the sentence—"that you need a bodyguard?"

So that's it, thought Luchnikov. The assassination. No, the threat. No, the hint of a threat. Funny, I'd completely forgotten about it. Too busy thinking about Tanya, I suppose. It's embarrassing to be pitied by everybody, pitied as a condemned man. Chernok should know that. A veteran of Sinop. No one is more surely condemned than a soldier. . . .

"Look, Andrei," Chernok went on after a short pause, "I have a special squad at my disposal. The men are trained to be highly discreet, and you would be absolutely safe. Why let the Lupine Hordes take pot shots at the best the Island has to offer? What do you say? You're putting me in a tough spot, you know?"

Luchnikov made a fist and dusted Chernok's jaw with it. "Let's change the subject, okay, Sasha?"

"Okay," said the colonel without missing a beat, and stood up. That was the end of their talk.

Ten minutes later Luchnikov was offensive-driving his rented Renault 5 through one long traffic jam. He had decided to take a sentimental detour, and since at the intersection of the Boulevard Saint-Germain and the Rue du Bac even Luchnikov had to surrender to the snail's pace anyway, he was able to concentrate wholly on his daydreams. Three years had passed since he flew in to meet Tanya and took a room at the Pont-Royal, which he was now inching past. She was in Paris with her crew to cover some Communist sports event—the *Fête de l'Humanité* or *Cross de l'Humanité*—and could get away for two hours and not a second more. Right here, on the third floor, Tanya smothered him with Moscow tenderness. "You mean you flew all that distance for just one little roll in the hay, my sweet, my darling, my own!" He would have flown five times round the world for that "little roll in the hay," that *piston, pistonchik,* as current Soviet slang put it. Once again the blissful thought of Tanya had taken his mind off the threat of assassination. In fact, whenever he thought of her, his worries seemed to vanish. So if for no other reason than to put himself in a good mood . . .

He was in an excellent mood by the time he had made his way along the Rue du Bac to the Seine and then left to the Quai d'Orsay—the Right Bank was bathed in sun—and up past the Invalides. The detour had been worth it.

Inside the Maison de l'UNESCO he was immediately greeted by music. The United Nations Educational, Scientific, and Cultural Organization did not want people bored for an instant. It seemed the main goal of the powerful Institution of International Freeloaders was to ensure that no one be bored for an instant.

In the exquisite oval auditorium with its Chagall-like (or authentic Chagall) murals a subcommittee (or semicommittee) was holding a hearing on statistics. Luchnikov was lucky; he arrived just in time for the regular—almost daily—show of the Crimean representative, Pyotr Sabashnikov, another classmate and old friend. Needless to say, Crimea was not a member of the United Nations—the USSR would never stand for such heresy—but it did take an active part in UNESCO. Serious international activity in the area of UNESCO's mandate would have been unthinkable without the aggressively active Crimea. As a result of Soviet pressure, the Island could not be referred to publicly by the name it chose to use: Crimea-Russia. Not a single subdivision of the Organization had dared confront the Giant, and the only countries that had protested were ones no one ever listens to, like Chile, the UAR, Israel, and—for some reason—Gabon. Official UNESCO documents always used "Island of Crimea," but every day Pyotr Sabashnikov brought a Crimea-Russia sign with him, and his first item of business was to substitute it for the humiliating reminder of geographical capitulation. At the close of each session he would take it with him to keep it from being tossed out.

"I give the floor to the representative of the Island of Crimea,

Mr. Sabashnikov," said the chairman of the semicommittee (or demisemicommittee) just as Luchnikov entered the absolutely empty press box.

Petya Sabashnikov ambled leisurely down the aisle to the podium, a leather portfolio under his arm. The newer delegates and the delegates from the newer nations followed him every step of the way, stunned. What is so special about an orator making his way to a podium? The fact was that this orator made a farce out of everything. He pursed his lips, he wrinkled his brow, he thrust his jaw forward in a caricature of determination and puffed out his jowls in a caricature of either Soviet Minister of Foreign Affairs Gromyko or the well-known Moscow actor Oleg Tabakov. Luchnikov chuckled mutely into his hand. Good old Petya. Hadn't changed a bit: the actor in him kept finding new roles to play.

He mounted the podium. One hilarious imitation after another. First he flashed a broad toothy grin (President Carter) and stood there with it glued on his face for an inordinately long minute. Then he coughed, smacked his lips, cleared his throat, rinsed his palate (General Secretary Brezhnev), and removed a pair of spectacles from his breast pocket. Finally, cocking his head and staring off into the distance, he launched into a speech in the grand old manner of Kublitsky-Piottukh, prime minsiter of the Provisional Government of Crimea: "Honored chairman, ladies and gentlemen, dear Comrades. Before I begin, I should like to introduce a correction into the minutes of our august proceedings. When giving me the floor, our honored chairman committed a *lapsus linguae*: he referred to me as the representative of the Island of Crimea, while in actuality I am the representative of an entity officially called Crimea-Russia. I respectfully request the honored chairman and assembled delegates to take note of this fact and to do everything in their power to prevent the above-mentioned slip from recurring." His traditional preamble out of the way, Pyotr Sabashnikov made a deep bow to the hall, with special emphasis on the Soviet delegation, thereby making it clear that he, Pyotr Sabashnikov, was above all this nonsense, that is, both his own protest and the Soviet protest to come.

Luchnikov looked out over the floor for the Soviet delegation. He spotted it with ease: a very smooth-looking gentleman—the commies now cultivated a more bourgeois look than the cappies—

stood up and made a sign to the chairman. The latter gave his habitual nod. Everything was proceeding according to habit; immediately following every remark by the representative of Crimea-Russia the Soviet Union lodged a formal protest. The seasoned delegates were so used to it they treated it as an all but canonized part of UNESCO protocol. Now Sabashnikov could begin.

"Gentlemen, in the highly demoralized society in which we live, the social sciences have undergone significant moral corrosion. The field of statistics has perhaps suffered more than most. It is our duty as members of the most humanistic branch of the international sodality of nations"—Luchnikov had the feeling he was either just about to or wanted to look as if he were just about to burst out laughing—"it is our duty to help an ailing discipline to reinstate its good name and serve once more as an impartial indicator of the health of the planet. But alas, gentlemen, as representative of Crimea-Russia and therefore a product of our contradictory times, I must pour oil on the flames. Here in my hands I hold a recent issue of *Time* magazine. It contains a detailed statistical map of the world with data culled from numerous respected sources, including UNESCO itself. The very fact that I value *Time* so greatly as a forum for the independent American press entitles me to the privilege of taking exception to the biased manner in which certain of the data are presented. First, what do the 'levels of freedom' expressed in percentages mean? What is *Time*'s point of reference? And what right has *Time* to translate the sacred philosophical concept of freedom into figures? Second, the figures themselves—the Russian figures, at least—are highly inaccurate. Crimea-Russia is naturally flattered that *Time* sees fit to award it a hundred percent rating, and it is equally chagrined to find that the Soviet Union must make do with a mere eight percent; however, that is not the point. As we have stated many times before, we demand that all statistical data touching on Crimea-Russia and the Soviet Union be averaged together, with the necessary adjustments for difference in population. Let me give you an example. According to *Time*'s figures the Soviet Union has 18.5 passenger vehicles per every thousand inhabitants; Crimea-Russia, which the magazine, taking its cue from the tourist trade, vulgarly calls OK, has 605.8 passenger vehicles per thousand inhabitants. Using the only valid method—that is, combining the data for the Soviet Union and Crimea-Russia—we find that at the present time Russia has 25.3 passenger vehicles per thousand inhabitants and a freedom rate of sixteen percent. That is all I have to say for the moment. Thank you."

The picture of modesty, Sabashnikov gathered up his papers and started back along the aisle to his place. Again he looked ready to explode into hilarity. As he went, he signaled to Luchnikov up in the press box, moving his eyebrow towards the exit. At the same time, his fantastically supple body expressed the most profound respect for his Soviet counterpart, who strutted past him angrily on his way to the podium as if protesting the clownish provocations of the representative from an obscure and fusty political entity that had wormed its way into the international forum of nations despite the will of the most progressive of those nations.

Leaving the press box, Luchnikov noticed that the Soviet and American delegations had registered his presence and were looking up at him and whispering to one another: "The editor of the *Courier!*" He met Sabashnikov in the doorway to the auditorium listening to a thunderous voice declaim from the podium, "The Soviet people condemns the pseudoscientific provocations of the bourgeois press, to say nothing of the impudent buffoon tactics of obscure and fusty political entities that worm their way into the international forum of nations despite the will of the most progressive of those nations!"

"Giving it all he's got, is Valentin," said Sabashnikov, shaking his head. "I wish he'd be more aggressive where it counts."

"Where it counts?" asked Luchnikov, looking over his shoulder at the hulking machine spitting out assembly-line abuse. Amazing, an item like that with a normal name like Valentin.

"We played doubles this morning with a Uruguayan and an Irishman," Sabashnikov explained. "Lost our shirts."

They went outside. Everything was quivering in the sun.

"How wonderful life on earth would be without ridiculous petty passions to contend with," sighed Sabashnikov. "It's been downhill ever since the Fall."

"Great spiritual renascence you've got going here at UNESCO," said Luchnikov with a snort.

"Go ahead and laugh, Andrei, but I'm thinking seriously of becoming a monk."

"I'm sorry, but that reminds me of a joke."

"I can just imagine what kind," sighed the Crimean diplomat, "and I'd rather not hear it."

Whereupon they climbed into Luchnikov's Renault and set out for Saint-Germain-des-Prés.

As they drove along, Luchnikov was able to break through Petya's constant clowning long enough to establish that he had actually completed a mammoth project: a comparative study of Soviet versus American views on Crimea. In the Kremlin heavy fog prevailed as usual, while the White House was calling for cloudless skies of geopolitical stability à la Kissinger—you know him, Andrei, don't you?—in other words, they don't give a flying fuck about us. And for all his "scholarly" endeavors Sabashnikov had not forgotten to arrange the meeting with von Witte; the general would see them at five sharp.

General von Witte was a distant relative of the statesman Witte, but a very distant one. Evacuated from the mainland with the rank of first lieutenant, he stuck with the army and the army stuck with him. By 1927 he was one of the youngest and most dashing generals on the Island. The baron worshiped him. "It is a well-known fact, after all, that for all the Orthodox borscht he consumed he could never quite give up his taste for those Ostsee wursts. Another year or two and young General von Witte would doubtless have been named commander in chief of the armed forces of South Russia, but the devil got there first, the same devil that tempts us all, Andrei: love, love for the glorious, the pitiful, the powerful, the vulnerable, the one-and-only motherland and what a—you'll excuse the expression—what a mother she is, our Mother Russia. Why he took it into his sensible German noggin to go and join the blacklisted Young Russian League and take part in the infamous Yevpatorian Guards incident I'll never understand. Counterespionage really had it in for him. He barely escaped to Paris. But when our parents set up the Democracy of 1930 and forced the baron to retire, von Witte chose not to return. He's been languishing in his Paris exile ever since. My feeling is that he went through what I've been going through lately, Andrei: a spiritual rebirth, a purification process by which the sinner comes to know the Unknowable. . . ." Having reached stentorian magnitude, Sabashnikov's voice suddenly broke off into an aesthetically effective series of sobs. He turned his blond, balding head to the Renault's open window, letting the wind fan his locks and Luchnikov picture tears of quiet joy and profound devotion running down his cheeks.

"Encore! Encore!" shouted Luchnikov. "You've come a long way!"

"Laugh if you like," said Sabashnikov in a thin voice, his shoulders quivering. It was impossible to tell whether he was laughing or crying.

"You know why I think von Witte never went back to the Island? Because he knew our papas were against him. All I want to find out is whether he really did meet Stalin, and if so, what old Comrade Cockroach thought about reunification."

"All right, but let me warn you. The old bloke is almost totally cuckoo."

Luchnikov zoomed into the Saint-Germain-des-Prés parking lot and found a space almost immediately, on the third level. The Mercedes that had been on his tail since the Place de Fontenoy was not quite so lucky. Just as he drove up, a black jack-in-the-box popped out of his booth, hung a chain with a COMPLET sign across the entrance, and popped back. The driver of the Mercedes was very upset. He was about to abandon the car and already had one foot out the door when he saw the two Simferopol dandies emerge from the bowels of the structure. The leg remained suspended in air. But when the driver saw them turn into the Brasserie Lipp and fall into the arms of a big, strapping American, he retracted his leg and heaved a sigh of relief.

Jack Halloway did actually look like an octopus when greeting friends: the number of his outspread limbs seemed to double as they opened and closed, pulling people in, sucking them in. Everyone looked like a miniature of himself in the clutches of the former discus thrower. Even the broad-shouldered Luchnikov felt as fragile as a ballerina when Octopus's arms clapped him in their steel vise. At one or another of the Olympics—history glosses over the date in silence—Halloway won either a gold or a silver or a bronze medal for the discus throw, or nearly did, was only a hair's-breath away; in any case he was on the American Olympic team, or was a strong candidate for the team, or people thought he'd make a strong candidate, or at least they knew he had thrown the discus at one time or another. Ask any of the regulars down at Santa Monica Beach or Zuma, Big Sur or Carmel. They'd all tell you, Sure, Jack's great with the discus, once won a gold medal or something, that spare tire around his waist, it don't make no difference, man, he can still throw that thing farther than any one of your college boys. But what's a little medal here or there when today the name of Halloway calls up another kind of gold, heavier gold, Hollywood gold? He had produced three blockbusters in as many years. Starting from the very bottom with a minuscule budget of not quite honest money and a couple of New York unknowns, Francis Bukniewski and Irving Stokes, as writer and director, he had managed to put together a supergalactic package. His biggest coup was to sign that star of the first magnitude Lucia Clark, who went along with him basically for old times' sake; she "would have done anything for that playboy, romantic, gourmet, polyglot, erotic guerrilla of an Octopus." Nor did the generosity of "Crimea's hottest export" go unrewarded. The first film, *The Hint*, grossed a fortune, paid back the investors in spades, and won Lucia rave reviews. The next two, *Leprosy* and *Eurydice/Registered Trade Mark*, fared even better. Halloway was riding the crest of the wave.

"Andrei! Pete!" he cried, hugging his Crimean pals. "You don't know how glad I am to see you ugly sinners! Especially here in the dappled shade of Saint-Germain-des-Prés! How did I know you were here? I could recognize your halitosis across half of Paris! God damn, this calls for a celebration! Makes me feel like sitting down at the fucking piano and tickling the fucking ivories!"

Halloway's welcome speech was a good indication of how far gone he was and how much farther he envisioned going.

Upstairs they made their way to a large table. The gang was all there: in the center, of course, the incomparable Lucia; to her right (and therefore her current partner) Irving Stokes, to her left (and therefore yesterday's partner) Francis Bukniewski; in the outer orbit, Chris Hansen, her cohort in wide-screen love and his "husband," the balding, thick-lipped Rolf Ruthen; Volodya Gusakov, cameraman and recent Soviet émigré, and Mirra Lunz, artist, imposing matron, and Gusakov's wife; and finally, "the mystery girl," a must at all Octopus get-togethers.

"*Privet*, guys!" Lucia Clark called out, glad for the chance to speak some Russian again. Born Galya Burkina, she received the "great and mighty, free and truthful" Russian language Luchnikov so often apostrophized in his campaigns as a gift from her Yalta provacuee parents. From her parents' temporary refuge, in other words, from the Island of Crimea, she also received high Tatar cheekbones and an ever so slightly Tatar slant to her blue, Novgorodian eyes. But what could a poor woman like Mrs. Burkina do when Karim the gardener kept staring at her through the speckled grape leaves on those long, hot summer days? Aren't gardeners' thoughts known to travel practically unimpeded to languishing ladies of leisure?

According to a by now well-established battle of wits, the New York intellectuals greeted the Crimean intellectuals with exaggerated nonchalance and a snicker or two, while the Crimeans, secure in their feeling of cultural superiority, were as open and warm with the New Yorkers as anthropologists with their aborigines. Halloway was engrossed in an enormous wine list, scratching his head and consulting the highly officious (like all high priests of French *haute cuisine*) sommelier.

How picturesque, thought Luchnikov, watching Octopus. He had always been the perfect exemplar of whatever group of bipeds he happened to represent. In the fifties (when he and Luchnikov had first met in England) he was GI Joe, white socks, crew cut, and all. In the early sixties he sprouted a beard à la Thelonious Monk and took on all the mannerisms of a jazz musician. As the sixties shaded into the seventies, he let his graying curls straggle down over his shoulders and donned a multicolored, paunch-hugging T-shirt and shaggy hippie-style vest to become the image of the Beverly Hills millionaire eccentric. Now with the end of the seventies and uncertainty ahead, he was putting his bet on short, well-groomed hair and a snazzy white linen suit.

Meanwhile conversation at the table had ground to a halt: the New Yorkers had got their digs in at the Crimeans and needed time to regroup after the Crimeans' kindhearted response. Lucia Clark flashed an absolutely unambiguous smile across the table at Luchnikov, Chris and Rolf were whispering to each other heatedly, more like business partners than husband and wife. Volodya Gusakov, like any recent Soviet arrival, was doing his best to fade into the background, while his wife, Mirra of the stone bosom, sat over him, chin in air, daring anyone to touch a hair of her husband's head. Luchnikov tried hard not to look at the New York contingent, afraid he would lose his temper, and turned instead to Lucia, with a smile that said, Down, girl, down. We're just old friends, remember? Bukniewski and Stokes, casually sprawled out in their chairs, were, for all their winking and smirking, put out at something, pissed off. The mystery girl looked as though she would have given anything to split. Only Pyotr Sabashnikov felt completely at home. His actor's instinct had taken him right to the heart of the situation, and he was having a high old time portraying "embarrassed silence"—wheezing timidly, sending shivers through his shoulders, catching a neighbor's eye and then turning away immediately, even blushing, the rat.

"What the hell is taking you so long, Jack?" said Luchnikov to break the silence.

Halloway came back to the table. "The correct wine is extremely important. If I ruin the meal by choosing the wrong wine, in a couple of hours you'll all look like a pig farm."

Everyone laughed. The ice was broken. That enormous bulk at the head of the table—those pudgy, good-natured cheeks and keen, intelligent eyes—had restored harmony. Everyone agreed the wines were well chosen, and the meal was a huge success: avocados stuffed with crabmeat, mock turtle soup, kidneys provençale, and chateaubriand. The Lipp kitchen under Octopus's creative baton scarcely gave them time to come up for air.

Luchnikov told Lucia and Jack about Petya's diplomatic high jinks at the UNESCO meeting. Petya protested vigorously—"How dare you mock my diplomatic mission!"—and Lucia laughed uproariously. When the New Yorkers saw how little the Russians made of their blue blood, they jettisoned their Manhattan snobbism once and for all. The conversation being in English, Luchnikov looked over at Volodya Gusakov to see how much he had caught.

"I don't think I understand too well," he said, before Luchnikov had had a chance to ask. "You seem to be talking about percentages of freedom." His face was a network of wrinkles. He was confused and on his guard. Perhaps he understood more than he thought, more than was said.

"Mr. Luchnikov is making fun of us," his wife said in a brittle voice, lifting her chin even higher. "Our pain is nothing to him but an excuse to show off his wit."

The Americans did not understand her Russian, but laughed at her theatricality. "Mirra of Moscow," said Bukniewski, "of the Moscow Art Theater."

The discus thrower leaned across the table and put his hand on Gusakov's shoulder. Suddenly Luchnikov realized that Jack's small eyes had an unusual hard, cold glare to them; they seemed illuminated by W-shaped filaments. And suddenly he realized that the meal was more than a friendly get-together, more than the start of a typical Halloway spree: Octopus had something serious on his mind. He looked back and forth between Jack and Volodya Gusakov.

The new wave of émigrés represented a kind of riddle to the earlier waves, but to Luchnikov they represented much more. They were essentially the people he went to Moscow all the time to see, and he identified with them, felt he shared their lives and struggles. Now there were fewer and fewer of them in Moscow and more and more in Paris cafés and on American campuses. They visited Crimea only on holiday or on business. Not a single one had settled there: we didn't break loose from Mother Russia's embrace to huddle under her skirts, they told him.

He was just about to say something to Volodya Gusakov, something like, Don't be insulted; I'm making fun of myself, not you. But then it occurred to him that neither he nor his wife would understand anything he said. He could say it in Russian, he could say it in purest Moscow, but the gap would remain, the sixty-year-old schism, rift, fault in the bedrock of a common Russian fate.

"You Russians are a bunch of masochists, you know?" Jack laughed. "What you need, Andrei and Volodya, is a ten-minute private session with Dr. J. P. Halloway, specialist in the Russian soul. Right this way, please." He stood up and put his hand on the mystery girl's shoulder. "You, too, pussycat," he said to her with a time-for-some-action wink at Luchnikov. But Luchnikov knew they would talk about something else altogether.

Of course, the ten minutes in the bar downstairs stretched into thirty. There were no fewer than three friends of Halloway's in the bar: the only three customers in the bar at the time. One of them, a former Prix Goncourt winner who looked more like a drunken watchmaker than a paragon of French literary taste, turned out to be his *best* friend, but that didn't mean too much: of any three of Octopus's friends one was always his best friend. Halloway also appeared to have things to reminisce about with the bartender, a complex affair dating back to his last stay in Paris and involving a complaint lodged by a certain Monsieur Delaroche and the visits of a Monsieur le Commissaire Privé, who turned out quite a good chap in the end, Monsieur Halloway was wrong about him, but in any case you don't have to worry about any trouble in the *Sixième* now, because Monsieur le Commissaire is as good as his name, *vieille France*, that's what he represents, the good old days when people could look each other in the eye, when they had never even heard of socialism and the computer society, evils that come from America, yes, America, not Russia, the way some people think, it's those monster socialist computers that will get us in the end, they remember everything, every little sin you commit, every table you kick over in a café, every bastard you punch, every damn towel they find missing in your hotel room, at least that's what happened to a Polish professor not too long ago, and here, too, here in the *Sixième*, but you don't have to worry, Monsieur, because Monsieur le Commissaire knows who's who. . . . Just then the mystery girl began making signs in the direction of the window, and they turned to see a strikingly beautiful girl motioning back. Halloway quickly held her down by the derrière, subjecting her to a long tirade in Spanish about the *absurdidad* and *insipidez* of lesbian love.

"Listen, Octopus, I'm getting a little fed up," Luchnikov said finally. He had been glancing repeatedly at his watch, not wanting to be late for the general.

Jack immediately let go of the girl, covered the ear his literary friend had been mumbling into, turned away from the bartender, cursed foully in a few of his ten or so languages, and, putting his arm around Luchnikov's shoulders in the style of Richard M. Nixon, launched into a business proposition that knocked even the ultrablasé Luchnikov for a loop. "Now you listen to me old buddy old pal I'm the one who's fed up fed up with raking in the dough I raise my right hand and swear the hand I use for everything important the hand I use to open my fly swear it's not the big bucks that keep me going in this whorebound business of flickering pictures oh I know what you're thinking behind that snide smile of yours here it comes old Octopus on Art well you're wrong though I do have my ideas on the subject and someday I'll make you listen if only to show your blue blood how far a kid from the Philadelphia slums can go that's right I grew up in the slums of Philadelphia didn't know that did you well let me tell you it was no picnic and if you don't believe me I'll prod you off the barstool and call Monsieur le Commissaire and he'll feed you into his socialist computer and you'll be banned from Paris forever and you'll wander for thousands of years around the outskirts but they'll never let you in you'll never live down your scandalous behavior chez Lipp they may even send you back to OK under Island arrest until your friends the Reds come and liberate you but to get back to what I was saying I don't turn the crank for myself I do it to feed the hungry bastards who follow me around I do it for the pleasure of the thankless dregs of international society otherwise known as my friends and if that's too much for you to accept then I swear by my fifth and favorite extremity to have you ridden out of Paris before dark and chained to the grandest statue of Marx in Moscow where you can sit at the Master's feet until your darling Common Fate goes into effect and your friends show their gratitude by shoving a dietetic salami up your ass, lighting the other end, and blasting you nonstop to the permafrost of Yoshkar Ola though I hope it never comes to that because I love you you're my best no honest injun my very best friend in the whole world and I am your slave. . . ."

At this point Halloway's drunken ravings segued without warning into serious talk.

"You know, I've just finished your book, the latest one, *Are We Really Russian?* Mind-boggling! The psychological ins and outs of it all—they're so typically Russian. We Americans demanded independence from the motherland, while you dream of reunification, the bear hug of the most progressive people in history perhaps, but also the most thick-skulled. To us it sounds like a combination of moral degradation and the suicide instinct, but how it all comes together in your book! Bravo, Andrei! You're as good a mystic as you are a journalist. That Tatar sperm did a job on the Russian aristocracy! But there's one thing I want you to tell me. The reunification idea, the idea of handing Crimea to Moscow on a silver platter—is it for real? Or is it . . . is it part of some political deal you're in on? We've been out of touch for so long now I don't know what you're into."

Halloway seemed to be staring into Luchnikov's brain. Those two filaments of his were white-hot and so strong they completely eclipsed the colorful collection of bottles along the bar wall and the windows opening onto Saint-Germain-des-Prés. The world was suddenly black and white, stark, high-contrast black and white, and darkness descended on him in soft folds. He felt his muscles go flaccid, out of control. "We've never talked about serious things before, Jack," he said, "and I'd prefer we didn't start now. I want to keep thinking of you as my good friend Octopus."

Halloway's reaction was so condescending that Luchnikov couldn't help wondering whether he was actually the Octopus he had once known. "It really has been too long, Andrei. Don't you see what I'm getting at? Don't you see that any other political commentator in the world would give his eye teeth to be having a talk like this with me? Don't you see, you idiot, that I'm about to make you a proposition? A proposition you can't refuse?"

"On what basis? What do we have in common?" Luchnikov closed his eyes and pressed his fingers against his eyeballs, but the colors refused to return. Then he tossed down a double cognac. That did the trick immediately. "If it's publicity you're after, you don't even have to ask. The *Courier* always plays your pictures up big. Lucia finds her way into practically every issue—'our Island pearl.' What is it you want, anyway?"

"What an idiot! My proposition is worth infinitely more than any two-bit Lucia! You and me, Andrei, we can reunify the Island with Russia!"

"What do you mean?" Suddenly Luchnikov was tight as a spring. He grabbed Octopus's wrist and looked him straight in the eye. "What kind of crap are you handing me?"

"Monsieur Gobineau, your right ear has suddenly grown inordinately long," said Halloway to the bartender, who was doing his accounts at the other end of the counter. "What do you say we get some air, Andrei? I can't stand seeing a man turn into an ass in my presence."

Out on the boulevard the Hollywood mogul took over, giving Luchnikov's arm a friendly twist and gesturing animatedly with his free hand as he dragged him along expounding his idea.

"A blockbuster. A good old-fashioned sweeping epic about the reunification of Crimea and Russia. Tragic, lyric, ironic, dramatic, realistic, surrealistic—a sure winner. The totalitarian colossus devours the carefree bunny rabbit at the latter's request. You'll do the screenplay, Looch. Well, actually, the screenplay's nearly done. Lots of crowd scenes. You know, the role of the masses. I'll bring in Vitaly Gangut to direct. Stokes has been getting too big for his breeches lately. So what if he's in Moscow? We'll spring him loose. No problem. Well, what do you say, old buddy, old pal?"

"Let go of my arm," said Luchnikov.

"What's the matter?" asked Halloway, amazed at the request but not heeding it.

"I feel like a cigarette," said Luchnikov. "And what the hell do you want with my arm? I'm not your date."

"You're a real character, you know?" He still held Luchnikov's arm fast. "Here I offer you millions, and you—"

"Sorry," interrupted Luchnikov, giving his friend a quick punch in the stomach and pulling his left arm free.

Amazed again, Halloway stopped short in the middle of the crowd. People looked up at him.

Luchnikov walked a few steps farther, lit a cigarette, and only then turned and asked, "Who's putting you up to it?"

"Bastard!" Octopus yelled back over the heads of the bustling Parisians and started off again. But after a few feet he spun round and shouted, "I treat you like a friend, and you treat me like shit!" Then a few more steps, seething, and in a clarion voice: "I never want to see you again!"

Luchnikov stayed put.

Halloway dropped into a chair at the Deux Magots, shook his fist at Luchnikov, then opened it to call a waiter.

Luchnikov noticed Sabashnikov coming out of Lipp, motioning to him. They both converged on the entrance to the underground parking structure. Sabashnikov, playing the role of Virtue Wounded, filled Luchnikov in on the last half hour of the lunch. The American contingent had finally got round to calling him a degenerate aristocrat, while Volodya Gusakov managed to spit out "White Guard relic" and "dirty commie flunky" in the same breath. And all the time Lucia was busy with his fly. "It got to be too much, Andrei, even for an old UNESCO veteran like me, so I upped and left without a word."

"Except to say that . . ."

"Well, except to say that they reminded me of characters out of a Grand Guignol. That's all. Then I left without another word. Except to say that . . . In a word, it was a nightmare. The world is going down the tubes, Andrei. We're in for another holocaust. I'm going to find me a monastery before it's too late. Somewhere on Malta, or the Tristan da Cunha Islands . . . You wouldn't happen to know where the most remote, most poverty-stricken Orthodox monastery is, would you?"

They crawled out from underground into the satanic stop-and-go traffic. Their goal was the Rue de la Bienfaisance on the Right Bank, where another passionate champion of the Russian idea had lived for fifty years. Luchnikov decided not to mention Halloway's proposition to Sabashnikov; in fact, he tried not to think about it himself. He wanted to be level-headed for his meeting with General von Witte, and he knew that any attempt on his part to penetrate more deeply into the sacrilegious and typically venal, typically Hollywood proposition would make him fly off the handle. Instead, he ran through his jam-packed schedule from the beginning and realized he still needed to phone the Soviet embassy.

"Hello! Comrade Tarasov? Andrei Luchnikov."

"Oh, hello, Mr. Luchnikov," answered a most obliging voice. "Myasnichenko here."

"It's about my visa," said Luchnikov, noticing from the booth how exquisite the play of the sun was on the Church of Saint-Germain-des-Prés. "Has there been any action on it?" Luchnikov used the current Soviet expression to emphasize the miracle that never failed to amaze him: a Mr. and a Comr. speaking the same language. Wondrous are Thy ways, O Lord!

"Everything is ready for you, Mr. Luchnikov," said Comrade Myasnichenko, sounding like a *perpetuum mobile* of good cheer.

"Is that possible?"

"More than possible, Andrei Arsenievich. True, one hundred percent true. All we have to do is to put our stamp in your passport. You may drop by whenever you like."

"Yes, well, to tell the truth, I didn't expect you to be so efficient. The thing is, I'm terribly rushed—"

"If you will be good enough to come in immediately, Andrei Arsenievich, I can assure you you will be out in ten minutes."

Comrade Myasnichenko was giving Luchnikov tit for tat: Luchnikov imitated Soviet bureaucratese ("Has there been any action . . ."), Myasnichenko Russian aristocratese ("If you will be good enough to . . ."). If that is how they spoke in Tolstoy, he reasoned, that is how their relic descendants must speak on the Island of Crimea.

True to Myasnichenko's word, the stop at the Rue de Grenelle took no time at all. Myasnichenko himself turned out to be a young Soviet of the new breed: a casual, easygoing way of moving, the latest in tinted lenses, a pleasant but slightly crooked smile.

Luchnikov slid the passport into his pocket and headed back, reassured, to the Boulevard Raspail, where Sabashnikov was waiting for him in the Renault. As soon as they started off, Petya started up again. "Look, Andryushka, why don't the two of us say good riddance to all this mess and go to New Zealand? We can buy some land, set up a Russian farm, persuade a few friends to join us; Father Leonid, too. Raise vegetables. Read the Scriptures. Grow old peacefully. . . . You must be as sick of it all as I am. What? Everything: Paris, New York, Simfi, Moscow. Politicians, police, *putains*. Take the Place de la Concorde here; it's faster. If only we could gather together, say, fifteen or twenty good friends. Then I wouldn't feel the need to leave the world and join a monastery. When you come to the Avenue Washington, start looking for a parking space."

Luchnikov had expected the general's town house to be all fust and must, a conglomeration of semisenile quiddities, a haven for alley cats or talking birds, a repository of peeling wallpaper, the epitome of decay. Of course, he might just as well have pictured the opposite, a neat, cozy refuge of ripe old age. What he was totally unprepared for was the office of an active politician: a massive, finely ornamented door with a brass plaque announcing, in French and Russian, the general's long title; a spacious antechamber decorated with old maps of Russia and portraits of a number of important public figures, including Lavr Kornilov, commander in chief of the White Army, and the chairman of the Council of People's Commissars, V. I. Lenin; a young man in a gray flannel suit, the picture of the up-and-coming French diplomat, who greeted them and asked them to follow him: His Excellency the Baron von Witte was expecting them.

The general was sitting at an enormous desk and dashing something off (a bit too quickly). During the several seconds it took for the general to look up (a second too long) Luchnikov compared him with his own father. Luchnikov senior clearly came out on top: the general had nothing of his style and grace and, though far from a ruin himself, lacked Arseny Nikolaevich's youthful, rugged look. He still had a firm grasp, though, and held on to Andrei's hand longer than usual, his eyes overflowing with good will (all overplayed).

"Take a seat, my boys! Devilishly glad to see you, you know. Always glad to welcome guests from Russia, particularly you young chaps. True, I've lived away from home for almost fifty years now, but my heart is there still—in its mountains, on its plains, on its rivers, seas, and *islands* [he laid special stress on the latter. A sharp, questioning look (or the imitation of a sharp look or at least a lively pale blue shine) emerged from his eroded clay face.] Why, not a half hour ago I received the secretary of the Komsomol organization of a Sverdlovsk tractor plant [the right eyelid made an imposing descent, then returned to its original position]. Quite a clever young batch of fellows we've got in the Urals. Interesting ideas, strength, determination. And how are things in the south? What can you tell me about Crimea? Yes, how is Arseny Nikolaevich getting on? Do give him my very best! We were comrades in arms, you know. Kakhovka, Kakhovka, and all that . . . You don't realize what it means, my boys, to fight a fratricidal war. Well, and what about yourselves? How do you keep yourselves busy? Sports? Sex?"

Here the general broke off. He must have realized he had gone too far. Through all the blather he never once looked up at Luchnikov, not even when giving his best to Luchnikov senior. The whole time he kept his eyes trained on Sabashnikov, whom he knew and who played up to him, cleverly acting out the "young chap" role, complete with blushes, giggles, and even a fit of nail-biting, the clown. When he finally did venture a glance at Luchnikov, he got a mean scare. For Luchnikov met his glance straight on, and the figure flicking ashes from his cigarillo into the Kremlin tower ashtray was no "young chap" by any means.

"Is it true, Vitold Yakovlevich, that in 1936 you had a meeting with Stalin?" he asked.

"Now, now, boys," said von Witte, shaking a reproachful finger out of inertia, but clearly frightened.

"I am the editor and publisher of the *Russian Courier*, the newspaper you have lying there on your desk."

"Come, come, Andrei Arsenievich!" said the old man, flinging up his arms. He seemed to have regained his political savvy in a flash. "Do you really think we don't appreciate you? You can't imagine how important the native tongue is for us abroad, be it *Pravda* from Moscow or your Simferopol *Courier*. We Russians—"

"There's something I would like to ask you. . . ." Despite both conditional and dots, Luchnikov's request sounded like the height of insolence, and underpinned by Luchnikov's unexpected follow-up—he took the old man's wrist between his thumb and middle finger and gave it a firm pinch—it took on the force of an ultimatum along the lines of "Cut the crap."

Once more the general made an about-face. A quick and energetic change of glasses. Strong, clear lenses replacing the blue, smoky variety. Full and undivided attention. "You may proceed, Mr. Luchnikov."

The brisk dialogue that followed also transformed Petya Sabashnikov, who provided a running commentary in mime, raising his brows or frowning, vigorously nodding or shaking his frail aristocratic head.

LUCHNIKOV: We stand for the Idea of a Common Fate.

VON WITTE: And whom do you represent?

LUCHNIKOV: A specific intellectual tendency.

VON WITTE: Namely?

LUCHNIKOV: Namely the Union of a Common Fate. SOS.

VON WITTE: Bravo! SOS! Quite clever, actually. But whom do you—

LUCHNIKOV: We have no backing from any intelligence service whatsoever, Your Excellency.

(VON WITTE does not respond. His eyes grow nonsensically large behind the lenses.)

LUCHNIKOV: You seem to have trouble accepting the idea.

(VON WITTE does not respond. His eyes contract to normal size and sense.)

LUCHNIKOV: Our strength derives from our willingness to act in the open and . . .

VON WITTE: Why do you hesitate?

LUCHNIKOV: . . . and our ability to adapt to any circumstances.

VON WITTE: Don't you really mean it derives from your feeling of doom?

LUCHNIKOV: Now it's my turn to congratulate you. Bravo, General! Quite clever, actually.

(The two men exchange ironic smiles. They are now, as the saying goes, quits.)

Pyotr Sabashnikov, seeing that the buffonery had run its course, went over to a corner of the room where decorative fish had been eying the goings-on from their aquarium and some Russian birds, doubtless the gift of the Urals Komsomol leader, were chirping in a cage.

"Perhaps my question about Stalin seems more to the point now, Your Excellency," said Luchnikov. "I am interested to know how the leader of progressive mankind reacted to the idea of reunification."

"Your question may be to the point, but the irony in your reference to Iosif Vissarionovich most certainly is not," said von Witte with a frown.

"If you refuse to answer my question, General, you are a first-class shit," said Luchnikov with a smile.

For the time being the general chose to interpret the four-letter word as a joke. His face froze in a broad smile. But his right knee also gave a few odd twitches. I wonder how long it will take, thought Luchnikov.

It did not take long. The door of the office flew open: the secretary in the gray flannel suit flanked by two bruisers in checked jackets.

"Tsk, tsk, tsk, Vitold Yakovlevich," said Sabashnikov, shaking his head. "And I thought you had style."

"Your Komsomol friends from the Urals, I presume," said Luchnikov, looking the strong men up and down.

"Let me confront your question with one of my own, if I may, Mr. Luchnikov. Why are you so interested in Stalin?" The general looked at his guest with an amiability that could not quite veil the threat behind it.

"It is our lot to deal with the Generalissimo's descendants," Luchnikov replied.

"Vitold Yakovlevich, Vitold Yakovlevich," said Sabashnikov, scolding the general as if he had just done something naughty. "Scaring us with your homo muscle boys. And I thought you had style."

"What are you talking about, Petya?" Von Witte did have a certain naughty-boy quality to his voice. "They're fine young men, devoted to me."

"Would you like to know why I consider you a first-class shit, General?" Luchnikov inquired in his most urbane manner, and launched into an exposition of his most urbane views. As he talked, he paced the room, now noticing clearly the signs of dissolution and decay that a hasty tidy-up had kept from him at first: the mousy smell along the walls, the outdated, broken-knobbed radio equipment, the finger-length triangle of dust left on a map by a careless rag and newly illuminated by the sun as it edged towards the frozen wastes of Greenland. "I consider you a first-class shit because you gave up your ideals too early. Yes, you fought for them, but no longer than Dubček fought for his. And at least Dubček didn't sell himself, which you did, right away. That's why you're infinitely more of a shit than he is. You know what else raises your shit quotient, Your Excellency? When you sold those ideals of yours, you priced them too low. At bargain rates like that you had to peddle them to both sides, Right and Left. And what do you see when you look in the mirror now that you're getting on in years? A pitiful petty official of three or four intelligence services—that is, a bag of shit. By the way, you know that sardonic smile you put on as soon as I mentioned ideals? Well, that smile is doing great things for your shit quotient at this very moment."

Throughout Luchnikov's monologue the thugs threw questioning glances at their boss. They obviously did not understand a word of Russian. The general paid no attention; he had deteriorated fast. Gone was all the political panache. The tension was too much for him. His jaw was slack, his eyes glassy.

Luchnikov and Sabashnikov turned on their heels and left unimpeded. A few minutes later they were sitting in an outdoor café on the Champs-Elysées.

"I'm a little ashamed," said Luchnikov.

"Well, you shouldn't be," grumbled Sabashnikov, fussing nervously with his Campari-and-soda. "He had it coming to him, the old bastard. Trying to impress us with that guard of honor! No matter how afraid he is of *you*, he knows *I* wouldn't hurt a fly. The days I've wasted playing cards with him in that hole! And then he goes and pulls a Goldfinger on us." It was no act this time; Sabashnikov was extremely agitated.

Meanwhile evening was approaching—Paris at its most bewitching: the sun still shining in the mansard windows, the shopwindows down below newly bathed in shade, and in between, the half-opened mouth of Sylvia Kristel beckoning to the multilingual crowd ambling along the electrified Elysian slabs.

"I hate to say it, Andrei," Sabashnikov blurted out after several moments of silence, "but you have something coming to you, too. Remember our 'ratfink' phase in school?"

"Of course. What of it?" said Luchnikov with a frown. "Ratfink" was the name they used to give all the swots and teacher's pets, sons of low-ranking officers for the most part.

"This Common Fate business of yours—it's turning you into one."

"You really mean that, don't you?" said Luchnikov, surprised at how deeply hurt he felt.

"I really mean it. I don't often mean what I say, but this time I do. This time I'm being very serious. My old friend—a ratfink! Do you have to go at it with such fervor, Andrei? With such ferocious tenacity? With the ideological fanaticism of a Bolshevik novitiate? That's not the Looch I once knew. What happens to life in your Idea? Our life, for instance."

"I've always assumed we have the same way of looking at things, Sabasha," said Luchnikov.

"And we do!" Sabashnikov exclaimed. "You and I are comrades in high spirits. Even in Budapest it was one laugh after another. The gibes we make at the mastodons' expense would fall flat without a sense of humor. I know your Idea is serious, I don't deny that. But . . . but even so . . . isn't there . . . can't you see a touch of, well, levity in it?" He stopped and waited expectantly; he even tried to stare him into acquiescence, but Luchnikov would not be outstared. Schoolboy sentimentality was giving way to mature anger.

"No, I see no levity in it at all."

"You've been poisoned," said Sabashnikov softly.

Suddenly Luchnikov's anger flared up full force. "Degenerates!" he shouted, as if the word could order Sabashnikov's lowered eyes back up to his. "You and your high spirits! Congenital syphilis is more like it! Do you have any idea what our sophisticated word games have cost the Russian people? Eternal butterflies flitting in the lap of nature! You can go fuck yourselves, the lot of you!"

As his fury reached its crest, he stood up and lurched away from his friend, kicking the wrought-iron table when it tried to stop him, then turning and shaking his fist in the direction of an electronic flash—so they've recognized me, the bastards—but not finding anyone who looked like a reporter, just a crowd of twenty or so multifarious faces attracted—just for the fun of it—by the prospect of a bit of scandal *à la russe*, he set off towards the Place de la Concorde, away from the Arc de Triomphe, and pushing his way through the high-spirited, electrified crowd, past the trivial commercial strongholds of trivial Western civilization, he felt his fury subside, he felt less and less sure of himself, more and more ashamed. How could he have been so crass and vicious to his all but blood brother? How many boyhood provacuee friends did he have? The Tsar Alexander II (Liberator) Classical School for Boys may have had its ratfinks, but he had made ten or twelve true-blue friends there. . . .

Then he disappeared from sight. Only the man tailing him knew where he was. Another flash. The picture shows a long parking lot: scores of cars and ten times as many shadows. The important part of the picture would be enlarged later. Someone was at work reconstructing his life. Every bit and piece helped. The time was not far off. Though he saw himself as performing a historical mission, he lived each minute as it came, oblivious of its value, wearing himself out as they ticked past, trying to get out into the street, for instance, first, reverse, wheel all-the-way-to-the-left, then all-the-way-to-the-right, bloody frogs, all they care about is sneaking their way in, nobody gives a hoot that there's a car waiting to get out, no, if they just go on sipping their apéritifs long enough, everything will take care of itself . . . screech, one of those squat little Citroën DS's . . . I bet I have a scratch there . . . what a bore, what a waste of time . . . a bad dent in the right door . . . render unto Hertz till it hurts . . . here I go again with that crazy feeling that nothing I do is worth it, up to snuff . . . something essential is missing, I've forgotten the heart of the matter . . . what is it? . . . why can't I get over that worthless feeling? . . . and now on top of it all that idiotic interview at ABC, the dissident reception . . . it's not for myself, it's for the Idea . . . my raison d'être. . . . How dare you call me a ratfink, you prick! You poor fool, we'll always be friends, always. Is there anything more tragic than the fate of Crimea's boy provacuees!

In this minor mode—the anger had long since played itself out —he bumped along the cobbled streets of the Right Bank when suddenly he was thrown into a terrible panic: I'm flying to Moscow tomorrow, and I haven't gone shopping yet.

I haven't bought double-edged razor blades, Tri-X and high-speed Ektachrome, flash cubes, jazz records, shaving cream, long stockings, jeans (the perennial Moscow curse), more jeans (corduroy), T-shirts with English lettering, running shoes, women's boots, downhill skis, hearing aids, turtlenecks, pantyhose, teddies, bobby pins, angora sweaters, cashmere sweaters, Alka-Seltzer, current transformers, paper napkins, talcum powder for private parts, Scotch tape and Scotch whisky, tonic water, gin, vermouth, Parker and Montblanc ink, leather jackets, tape cassettes, woolen underwear, sheepskin coats, winter shoes, folding umbrellas, gloves, dried spices, kitchen calendars, Tampax, felt pens, colored thread, lipstick, stereo components, nail polish and nail polish remover (they always make a point of the remover!), hair bands, birth control pills and baby food, condoms and pacifiers, three-in-one vaccinations for dogs, flea collars, Mace, Monopoly, rheostat switches, coffee grinders, coffee makers, tinted glasses, wall bottle-openers, plastic tablecloths, Polaroids, car fire extinguishers, car cassette players, STP motor oil supplement, lighter oil, lighters, shower curtains (with rings!), quartz watches, batteries, yellow headlights, knitted neckties, suede purses, the latest issues of *Vogue, Playboy,* and *Downbeat,* even a salami or two to help someone through the latest shortage. . . .

Anyone who arrives in Moscow empty-handed will be misunderstood. Misunderstood by everyone. Not even the most intellectual, the most spiritual Muscovite can help but wonder "What has he brought?" at the sight of a Western tourist, especially a tourist from Crimea. Any little trinket does wonders for morale; it is a sign that another kind of life exists in nature, a sign that the realm of "economic democracy" is alive and well. You can't go to Moscow empty-handed. It's a crime. Rush hour, no place to leave the car, no one has ever come out of the Galeries Lafayette in less than a half-hour, and in a half-hour the TV gang will be waiting, you can do anything to those bastards but keep them waiting . . . and I haven't bought a thing for Tatyana!

When Luchnikov came out of his funk long enough to see where he was, he found himself driving along the Faubourg Saint-Honoré. Suddenly it hit him: Saint-Laurent had a branch close by. Comrade Lunina was in luck!

Ah, the joys of bourgeois living! You enter a cool, private salon lulled by soft, soothing music. From its mirrored depths comes a breathtaking creature, all green eyelashes and chiffon. He, she, it does not say a word, yet a world of wondrous possibilities opens before your eyes.

Bonjour . . . Madame? Monsieur? . . . Oh, I'm sorry, Mademoiselle. What a pleasant surprise. What I'm looking for is a complete outfit for a young lady, blond, about your size, but with more definite contours, so to speak. I need everything, from bra to wrap, and a matching set of earrings, necklace, and bracelet. Use your imagination, but not to the detriment of common sense, please. No, no, money is no object, I just want to see a measure of traditional sexual identity: it's for a woman. Is that a gleam of understanding I catch in your eyes? Congratulations! I know how hard it must be for someone of your way of life. Oh, and one more thing. I have only fifteen minutes at my disposal. The girl's superior, dressed in a communist-looking boiler suit, hurried out to precipitate matters.

Though it was more like a half-hour by the time Luchnikov left the shop followed by three Saint-Laurentiennes juggling twelve boxes, he was exuberant. The nearest Simfi Card office, on the Avenue de l'Opéra, had authorized him to charge 15,899 francs to his account, that is two and a half thousand tichas, that is two and a half million Russian wartime rubles. Plus the ticket he found under the wiper of his Renault. My compliments to the *aubergine*! Brava, Madame! Five hundred francs! You, too, I see, have a wild imagination! Thank you, girls. Just shove it all in the back seat. And here's a hundred each for toothpaste, Mesdemoiselles, and for you, Madame, the Party handshake. Lenin's teaching is invincible, Comrade Madame, because it is true. *Au revoir*, girls. Should by any chance the whim strike you to come and visit your generous benefactor in the middle of the night, you'll find him—that's right, me—at the Savoy, Boulevard Raspail. The invitation applies equally to you, of course, Comrade.

Before we begin, I want you all to know—announcers, gaffers, cameramen, everybody—I want you all to know that Andrei Luchnikov is no ratfink. He's Looch, that's who; Looch the basketball star, Looch the racing star; Looch the youth leader of the fifties, jet-set leader of the sixties, political leader of the seventies— Looch the leader. Now let's get on with the show.

"Tonight we have with us in our Paris studios the famous newsman and news-maker Andrei Luchnikov, better known to his friends as Looch."

Luchnikov had a good time with the interview. Walter Gesundheit, the program's bore of a host, had his heart set on a serious discussion of the problems of publishing one of the world's most influential newspapers on a tiny out-of-the-way island and was not beyond hinting here and there at the doom he saw in store for the paper and the island itself if Luchnikov's Idea ever held sway. In the end, he came out and asked point-blank, "Can you picture your newspaper coming out in the Soviet Union?"

"We Russians are known for our imagination," Luchnikov responded. "Those endless pages of propaganda in the Party press are as much the product of our imagination as everything else Russian. Take our all but imaginary island, for example. A UFO if there ever was one, but a UFO with a difference—an Unidentified *Floating* Object. Our whole world is built on fantasy, on the free play of the imagination. And so I answer your question in the affirmative: Yes, I can picture the *Courier* on Moscow newsstands every morning, though it's much easier to imagine it shut down on account of the chronic Soviet paper shortage. I can also picture

Russia reunited, though again it's much easier to imagine the country with the greatest forest reserves in the world suffering from a chronic paper shortage."

Slightly stunned by the slalom of Luchnikov's exposition, Gesundheit barely had time to turn his hanging jaw into the lower half of a grin before the camera flashed on him again. Unidentified Floating Object, wonderful! Bravo, Mr. Luchnikov . . . er, Looch. And thank you. I hope that you'll . . . You betcha, Walt. Wouldn't miss it for the world! And now . . . He saw the camera rolling toward him and flashed a sexy, toothpaste-ad smile. "And now in the name of our transcontinental TV friendship may I invite you to visit OK? It's a wonderful place. You can read all about it in the *Courier*. Good night, everybody!"

Click. The spotlights went out. A great closing shot. What have you got to drink, Walt? I'm sorry, Mr. Luchnikov, I don't drink. A ratfink of the first magnitude. Excuse me? Well, I'll be off! See you soon!

He could just picture the *New York Times Magazine*: the white outline of Crimea against a black background with "UFO?" (the question mark was absolutely essential) in red. A clever journalistic metaphor . . . And suddenly there it was again. It wouldn't leave him alone today for some reason. The feeling that he was nothing more than a frenzied, sweaty old international gossip-monger. Why do I keep rushing from one place to another? Why can't I stay put? What is the vital point I'm missing? Why does it escape me? Where do these spasms of shame come from?

The "sweaty old" feeling was the least metaphorical of the lot: his blue Oxford shirt was black around the armpits, and his morning get-up-and-go had long since departed. In fact, he was suddenly unable to move. It was not the first time he had experienced his forty-six years as a series of dumbbells weighing him down from shoulder to heel. He even lacked the strength to turn his head and follow the Mercedes that seemed to have been tailing him. By an ironic quirk of fate he had landed on the Rue Cognacq-Jay. Why, of course. That's what I need. A double cognac, and pronto. Then Plato's analysis of tyranny. Time to myself.

You look a lot better now than when you came in, Monsieur, said the bartender. Had a rough day? Opening his wallet to pay for the cognac, Luchnikov came across a small card: the invitation to the cocktail party in honor of the newly arrived dissident. Rue des Saints-Pères. I suppose I've got to go. Another double, *s'il vous plaît*.

A three-story flat in a sixteenth-century house, slightly warped but highly polished parquet floors, rheumatically misshapen staircases of powerful French oak—a stronghold of common sense in its day, a hotbed of sedition in ours.

The guests had draped themselves gracefully over all three stories and along the staircases. Conversations in French, English, Russian, Polish, German. The guest of honor, a middle-aged Soviet-looking intellectual, was talking to his host (gray-haired, gray suit, ironic) and hostess (tall, lavender dress, goggle-eyed). The guests—journalists, publishers, translators, writers, actors, politicians, all either ultraconservative or superradical—ran the usual Paris gamut from Adidas to alligator, from outrageous message buttons to outrageous diamond necklaces. There was also a bona-fide rock star—Carleton Peters, or was it Peter Carleton?— with stick-figure arms protruding from a gold lamé vest over a bare chest. The inscrutable convolutions of his marijuana psychology had recently wrested him from the European Khmer Rouge League and dropped him in the lap of the Society for the Promotion of the Democratic Process in Russia.

Luchnikov had known the dissident, a mild-mannered Muscovite, since the mid-sixties. Stifling his queasy reaction to chopped herring and chopped eggplant, he had spent hours on end in his kitchen discussing philosophy and politics. He could never get over the way the man used the pronoun "we." He was not a dissident then—the concept had not yet emerged—he simply said what he thought, like thousands of other Moscow intellectuals in their kitchens at the time. "We never stop lying, you know what I mean? We're constantly distorting history: the Katyn Forest incident— we're completely to blame. And look how we fell on our face with those tungsten experiments; we're so far behind in technology it's pathetic. We're fooling ourselves when we try to fool the world." Like all foreigners, Luchnikov was struck by the degree to which everyone in the USSR identified with the regime.

Here, in this new context, Luchnikov kept out of his sight. When the time was right, he would go up and shake his hand, hug him, perhaps, but he was ashamed to push his way up through the crowd. Leaning on a deep cherry railing, sipping the finest champagne, and exchanging pleasantries with the latest flame of one of his French writer friends, a modestly dressed Ms. Vanderbilt, Luchnikov kept glancing over to the corner where a broad soap-colored face would now and then peek desperately through the heads and shoulders assembled in his honor. The attentions of the Free World were obviously beginning to wear on him.

What the dissident needed most of all was a three-week retreat in a good hotel on the Normandy coast. He had never been to the West before, and it had been only a week since his plane set down in Vienna. He should have been making the rounds of the department stores, finding something to replace the rags he was in, and not holding forth as the invincible Russian intellect personified. He was dizzy from culture shock. Yesterday the KGB had been squinting at him, today it was the celebrities of the Western world (Brigitte Bardot was not able to make it, but Senator Moynihan was there). You all know about his "bold statements on behalf of human rights," thought Luchnikov, but can you even begin to picture his tiny flat, the telephone wire yanked out of the wall, house arrests during every national holiday, constant summonses to the public prosecutor's office, hints at the necessity for psychiatric treatment . . . ? I can't, and I know Moscow backwards.

For a while he was so caught up in his friend's puffy face and principled smile that he did not notice he himself was under observation. Slightly off to the side stood a man whose beard went up to his cheekbones and hair down past his shoulders: a Charles Manson with KGB eyes. Look what you've got yourself into, Looch! First Ignatyev-Ignatyev and his boys, now the Kremlin.

Instinctively, he led Ms. Vanderbilt to the security of a large group that had gathered round a carved bird and were eating, talking, and gesticulating wildly.

"What are *they* talking about?" she asked, intrigued by a contingent of Russians. Three men, two women. He didn't know any of them. Or did he? That good-looking blond chap on the left, the one with the elegant frames. Could it be? Slava! Slava the jazz pianist! A friend from his first visit to Moscow. The Youth Café, Gorky Street. Then Simfi. I arranged some concerts for him. Nineteen sixty-nine, I think. Missed most of them, he was so plastered.

Spent all his time running naked through the halls of the hotel, yelling, "Pussy, Madame? May I wipe your pussy?" The next thing Luchnikov heard, he had defected to the States. Slava!

Don't you Slava me, you fucking traitor, you Bolshevik pimp you! How much are they paying you for Crimea? I ought to beat the shit out of you, you dirty cocksucker, you fucking commie bastard!

You try to keep your European cool, your tolerance, even with a Moscow scandal in the air. The stream of obscenities does not disturb your smile, your superior smile, not at first. But it goes on a bit too long. Poor pretty-boy Slava. So he hasn't made it. So he's not the combination Dave Brubeck–Oscar Peterson–Errol Garner he thought he was. Nor will he ever be, because you are now about to fracture his right hand. The West, tainted with the microbes of Bolshevism, will fail to react. So will the brave freedom fighters who only yesterday worked overtime for the cause in the Moscow of the Ilyich boys (Vladimir and Leonid)—they're too afraid of what their elegant new benefactors will think. So bid your right hand farewell, Slava. No more tickling the ivories, no more tickling the tarts.

Using what he called his Chinese hold (he had learned it on Taiwan from a major in the Special Forces), he twisted the aggressive pianist's hand behind his back and turned in the direction of the bar. This called for a celebration, didn't he think? Slava's mouth dropped into an O, his eyes rolled wildly, he looked ready to faint. He obediently turned towards the bar. When his friends began whispering among themselves, Luchnikov recalled another of them, a scrimy little Jewish photojournalist known for playing up to his anti-Semitic editor. "Let's have a drink, Slava. We each have one hand free. How about some Hennessy? Off the bottle, eh? On to stronger stuff, I suppose. Look, you poor bastard, you've been in the West a long time now. You ought to know better. You ought to know that 'Anyone who's not with us is against us' holds only in Mafia circles here. Civilized society has a different view of life. Your kind has to learn it the hard way, I see. And now let me introduce you to Count Basie. Oh, Count! Need a one-handed pianist?"

Luchnikov took a little of this and a little of that, a delicious filo dough hors d'oeuvre, a few shrimp; he nodded graciously when bigwigs stopped to chat; he was the editor of the powerful *Courier*, after all, and had to make appointments, promise interviews, give his views on the SALT talks, wink at the beauties. And all the while the ill-starred Slava, hoping to save his means of production, trailed along docilely: any attempt to release the pressure could lead to permanent damage.

Wedged tightly among *le tout Paris*, they listened to the dissident's formal presentation: ". . . so you see, Comrades, we have nothing left to believe in. You can't believe a word we say. . . ." The interpreter, a third-generation Franco-Russian aristocrat, was at a complete loss. After a moment's embarrassed silence he began trying to explain what his charge *really* meant, but a good number of those present had caught the word *tovarishchi*, "comrades," and were having a loud laugh over it.

Suddenly the dissident's face lit up. Everyone turned to see what had caused the change. When they saw the face of the popular editor, they all beamed, too. Our hero was reminded of the studio lights at ABC.

"Andryusha!"

Although he had to release friend Slava, he gave him a precautionary knee in the groin as he turned to meet the dissident's embrace. Despite the latter's seven whole days of *la dolce vita* the odor of chopped herring exuded from the folds of his face, but Luchnikov was touched by the ball bearings of salty liquid rolling down its crevices. It seems like only yesterday! What a surprise! Remember the old flat in the Old Arbat? Remember the all-night kitchen talks? And now look at me! I'm in Paris. Can you believe it?

The idea that an ordinary mortal could actually be in Paris was too much for him, and his good, kind face was seized by a convulsion. But then an even more inconceivable idea took hold. What? You're on your way to Moscow? Tomorrow? Moscow? For several days? Unbelievable!

The famous dissident immediately released Luchnikov from his clinch and began searching through his pockets. I have it here somewhere. . . . If only I'd known, Andryusha. . . . Yes, here it is. . . . The number is 151–oo–88. . . . Tamara Fyodorovna . . . and her son Vitya . . . Oh, if only I'd known, Andryushka. . . . The things I would have sent you. . . . Here, take this at least. . . . Promise you'll deliver it?

The correspondent for *L'Express*, the president of a prestigious American publishing concern, and the wife of the Minister of Overseas Territories all looked on disconcertedly while the guest of honor transferred several packets of chewing gum from his pockets into Luchnikov's. You promise, now, you promise to pass them on to Tamara Fyodorovna for little Vitya. And make sure you tell her (the rest he said in an eggplant whisper) . . . she's the only . . . ever and ever . . . waiting . . . exit visa . . . work out in the end. There, did you get it all, Andryusha? And when you come through again, be sure to look me up. . . .

A volley of electronic flashes. Who let in those *paparazzi*? Islands of panic. Who is shooting? Who's being shot? Neither hunter nor prey was discovered.

Luchnikov walked out into the courtyard, enjoying the feel of the priceless medieval cobblestones through his shoes. One wall of the enclosed rectangle shone resplendently on all three floors, while in the other walls, much as during the Middle Ages, there was only a tiny light or two flickering. A massive cloud was moving across the sky. Did our clouds differ from the clouds of the sixteenth century? Most probably, with the difference in the earth's atmosphere. . . . Did I exist in the sixteenth century? Does it exist in me? Something glimmered inside him, a soul in flight. A fleeting impression that instantly turned to torpor.

Suddenly, the remote-control medieval gate creaked open, and Octopus's noisy band—the mighty figure himself in the lead— burst onto the scene. Luchnikov flattened himself against the nearest dark wall, then sneaked into the Street of the Holy Fathers, covered by the rasp of a car starting up nearby. He took a few steps along the narrow sidewalk. A dark mass, a monster of a car, sped by. Through the restrained roar of its engine came two sharp reports: a sudden increased pressure in the temples, a ringing sensation; two tiles—one just ahead of him, the other just behind him—crashed to the ground. A passer-by let out a blood-curdling scream and ducked into the nearest doorway. Luchnikov quickly drew his pistol from its hidden holster and dropped to one knee. Two hundred and fifty feet ahead of him the car braked at the corner of the quay. The stoplights flashed an obedient red. Luchnikov put his pistol away. The car swerved around the corner, offering itself up to the constant stream of speed demons.

Luchnikov's head was spinning slightly, the way it did when he took a deep dive. A minor concussion, perhaps. Firing at short range in a narrow Paris street. How could they have missed? No, they were just giving him a scare.

"You can come out now, Monsieur!" he called to the man who was still cowering in his doorway. "The danger is past."

A pale face appeared. "So it's you they were after, Monsieur. I've never seen anything like it in my life! Just like in the *films noirs!*"

"*C'est la vie*," said Luchnikov only half ironically.

"Damned foreigners," said the Frenchman, still shaken.

Luchnikov fully agreed. "Though in this case I'm afraid I belong to the category myself. And even when I'm at home, when I'm not a foreigner, I have to put up with that rabble. If people stopped gadding about so much, the world would be a safer place, don't you agree, Monsieur?"

A lock in the Renault-5 had been picked and all the packages slashed open. Fortunately, the gifts seemed unharmed. Perhaps the culprit set too great a store by material wealth to bring himself to destroy such an opulent show of it. In any case, Tanya was in luck again.

Flee with her. Take her away once and for all from her joke of a jock, marry her, go off to Australia, or even better, New Zealand. Forget about all things Russian—island or mainland—and do some writing, set up a farm, open a bed-and-breakfast place. . . . Why do we let ourselves get fired up so easily? What is the Idea of a Common Fate to me, personally? Is it really an issue at all? And if so, am I on the right side? Tonight's not the first time I've been called a traitor, but it is the first time I've had bullets spit at me through a silencer. I don't give a damn if that gorilla Ignatyev-Ignatyev or a twerp like Slava turns his nose up at me, but when people I respect, people I love, start looking askance . . . All anyone seems to care about is ideology. The fate of a nation is at stake, a nation abandoned by its intelligentsia again and again, and all people care about is isms.

With heavy heart and aching head he drove along the Boulevard Saint-Germain. Despite the late hour it was packed with people. He glimpsed a fire-eater and two graceful mimes, then sped on to the hotel. Pulling up, he noticed an old man sitting outside the café next door. The man stood up as Luchnikov got out of the car. It was General von Witte in person. With his collar up and his hat pulled down he looked the very picture of a *clochard*. "This is the first time in many years I have ventured outside my arrondissement," said the old man, coming up to Luchnikov. "I have been in an agony of remorse since you left."

Unexpectedly Luchnikov felt an impulsive affection for the general. The bags under his eyes, the twitching veins, the fat yellow Boyard butt in the corner of his mouth, the rolled-up newspapers sticking out of a pocket of his baggy old cashmere coat—it no longer seemed the least bit phony; his was an honest old age and quite daring in its own way.

"Come in with me," he said.

A sad smile appeard on von Witte's face. "I don't believe this is the time," he said. "You have visitors. They're waiting in the lobby."

"Visitors? In the lobby?" Luchnikov turned abruptly towards the entrance. Through the glass door he could see the dozing night porter, a patch of the carpet, half of one of the pictures decorating the wall, an empty armchair. The curtains on the windows were all drawn.

"Pleasant visitors," said von Witte. "Besides, there's no reason for me to go in with you. I simply wanted to answer your question, and that will take but a minute or two." He took out another Boyard, lit it, and plunged into reverie. He seemed to be retreating into that far-off time when Stalin had received him. Luchnikov leaned back against the Renault. The engine was warm, like a rock near the sea, on a Greek island. His thoughts turned to the "pleasant visitors." Who can they be? he wondered with neither fear nor bravado. The best thing to do is shoot first and ask questions later. He stifled a yawn.

"Here is what Stalin told me, word for word. 'The Soviet people despise your White Guard enclave in the Black Sea, but for the time being they do not object to its existence. You must wait fifty years or so. Now go back to Paris, General, and fight for the Cause.'" Needless to say, von Witte could not restrain himself from imitating the famous Georgian accent.

"Just as I thought," said Luchnikov. "The only thing that does surprise me somewhat is the concrete estimate he gave. Fifty years. Still quite far off, isn't it?"

But von Witte was still lost in his memories. "It was my last visit to Moscow. That evening I saw *Swan Lake* at the Bolshoi. Divine!"

"Thank you, Vitold Yakovlevich," said Luchnikov, forcing himself to sound appreciative of the moment's historical significance. Then, shaking the general's large soft hand, he added, "And please forgive me if I was rude, but I hope you'll believe me when I say . . . how much I value . . . and I was certain that in the end . . ." At this point he dried up completely.

The old man stamped out his cigarette and immediately took out another. "You were right, Andrei Arsenievich," he blurted out hoarsely. "I *have* lived a terrible, pitiful, completely despicable life." And he turned, walked slowly across the street, a funnel of smoke rising from his left shoulder, and lifted his walking stick to call a cab.

In the lobby of the Savoy he found the three beauties from the Saint-Laurent boutique draped over the rest of the green leather armchairs. Well, what do you know! Maybe the times they really are a-changing. You make a little "Why don't you come up and see me sometime" kind of joke, and to your great surprise they come up and see you. Look, I can barely move, I'm so tired. Whoops! I take it back. Something is moving all by itself. Unexpected reserves of the organism. After you, Mesdemoiselles. Your arm, Madame. The straps of your gown and the fur thrown casually round your swanlike neck inspire me with a great deal more optimism than the Antonio Gramsci revolutionary étude you had on earlier in the day. I am greatly flattered by your attentions, Monsieur le Russe, but we are not alone. *Soyez sans inquiétude, Madame.* We shall make a merry foursome. . . .

All around Luchnikov, in the strips of light shining through the louvered window, there was something wonderfully aromatic, quivering, elastic going on. His hands slid through it all until one of them came up against a hard pulsating pillar similar to his own.

And whose peter is this, might I ask? Not yours, I trust, Madame? Oh, no, Monsieur. Juliette's. She's from Corsica, you see. That's the way they are. Aha. Now I understand. My role is to light the fire. Very well then. Please come this way, Madame, and leave your girls—I include, of course, Juliette and her *corsaire* in that category—to their own devices. You and I shall enter the tropics as the missionaries were wont to do. Welcome, Monsieur, to the Mekong Delta. . . .

Thank you very much, Madame. The pleasure was all mine, Monsieur. Many heartfelt and sincere thanks from my girls and from me. Come and thank the gentleman, girls.

As he fell asleep, he could still feel the rustling, the kissing, the nipping, the sighing, the happy laughs and gentle growls. Blissful sleep. Plato, an airplane, the dawn of civilization . . .

VI

The Decadent Life

Sheremetyevo Airport looked like an open-air market: it was being completely rebuilt for the Olympics extravaganza. Originally designed for seven flights a day, it handled upwards of a hundred. You couldn't get away from those damned foreigners nowadays.

Waiting for the border police to scrutinize him, Luchnikov spent his time, as usual, scrutinizing the border police. For the second visit in a row he had the feeling that beneath the impassive, almost mongoloid, faces of these boys, the ironic superiority they used to feel towards foreigners—that part of mankind they had been taught to call the enemy—had given way to a kind of perplexity.

It was a clear autumn day. Marlen came up to him, beaming. He was accompanied by a high-ranking customs official who took Luchnikov away from the crowd and went off with his documents. Across the road a stand of birch trees was waving in the wind as if the airport had never existed. When High Rank returned with his passport, they walked out to Marlen's Volga, trailed discreetly by a cart carrying the two gigantic suitcases Luchnikov had bought at the last minute in Le Bourget's duty-free shop. The wind was from the northwest, wafting the scents of the lake country—Pskov and Novgorod; the sky was alive with the soundless peal of freedom.

THE SOVIET PEOPLE KNOW—THE PARTY MEANS SUCCESS AND VICTORY proclaimed a mammoth sign at the entrance to the main road. The message was illustrated by a portrait of its author, who on that day in that wind looked like a Pecheneg wandering through pre-Tatar Rus. It was a clear autumn day. GLORY TO OUR COMMUNIST PARTY! To the left of the road a row of cubes belonging to some research or engineering institute, to the right—off in the limpid distance—the freshly polished cross of a country church. In red letters on a cement overpass: WE PLEDGE TO FULFILL THE RESOLUTIONS OF THE TWENTY-FIFTH PARTY CONGRESS! The gardens of lopsided country estates preserved along the Leningrad Road. Elders, broken dahlia stalks, puddles, and the clayey strip between asphalt and garden fence. The sun peeking out after an ordinary spell of Moscow's finest. THE PEOPLE AND THE PARTY ARE ONE! From the hump of a bridge the two arms of the Moscow River and the steep bank of a flaming red island topped by a tuft of evergreens. WORKERS' GUARANTEE MEANS QUALITY FIVE-YEAR PLAN! Beyond the bridge the impregnable fortresses of new high-rise developments with thousands of glittering windows, the invisible activity of the bells of Novgorod hovering inaudible among the buildings, recalling the joys of the Hanseatic League, and letters of fire marching from roof to roof proclaiming THE PARTY IS THE MIND, THE HONOR, THE CONSCIENCE OF OUR ERA!

The farther they went, the faster they came. WE SHALL WITNESS THE VICTORY OF COMMUNIST LABOR! THE PLANS OF THE PARTY ARE THE PLANS OF THE PEOPLE! KEEP UP THE TEMPO OF THE SPECIAL QUALITY FIVE-YEAR PLAN! GLORY TO THE GREAT SOVIET PEOPLE AND ITS CREATIVE TALENT! ART BELONGS TO THE PEOPLE! LONG LIVE LENIN'S KOMSOMOL, THE PARTY'S FAITHFUL PARTNER! MAKE MOSCOW A MODEL COMMUNIST CITY! THE USSR IS THE STRONGHOLD OF WORLD PEACE! LENIN'S IDEAS ARE ETERNAL! THE CONSTITUTION IS THE BASIC LAW OF OUR LIFE! A decorated Pecheneg raising a hand in salute, a bespectacled Pecheneg reading a newspaper, Pechenegs multiplying by the minute as the center of town came nearer, each more confident, less lost, more the symbol of all the beloved symbols, less like a Pecheneg, more like Big Brother, large-scale, stable, one and only . . . At last they came to the Byelorussian Station and Luchnikov's favorite Pecheneg apothegm, an object of true nostalgia, the one he always looked forward to, had always looked forward to since his first visit, when, wrapped around the entire square and outlined in neon (it was night), it bowled him over with its daring concatenation of words, its seemingly inscrutable message: A NEWS-PAPER IS NOT ONLY A COLLECTIVE PROPAGANDIST AND A COLLECTIVE AGITATOR—IT IS ALSO A COLLECTIVE ORGANIZER!

Actually the message was quite straightforward. It enlightened the benighted masses who assumed that a newspaper was no more than a collective propagandist; it edified even those who knew that a newspaper was both a collective propagandist and a collective agitator, but were unable to proceed any further; it proclaimed to all Moscow and her throngs of visitors that a newspaper was collective propagandist, agitator, *and* organizer!

"Well, now you're back in the swing of things." Kuzenkov smiled.

"Yes, I feel the chill of recognition," said Luchnikov, nodding.

The Intourist Hotel. A group of Frenchmen near the entrance was observing the strange crowd tripping past: curious phenomenon, these Russians—white-skinned, yes, but how unlike Europeans they were.

Arguing with Kuzenkov in a loud and strident voice, Luchnikov headed straight for the two strapping doormen. The sound of native Russian put the gallooned bouncers on their guard, and they exchanged smiles in anticipation of the impending power play. And where might you be going, my fine feathered Comrades? asked the veterans of the invisible front. Then with a flick of the wrist the tables were turned. One of them suspicious Russians holds up—get this—a Central Committee ID between his thumb and middle finger. Next he points back over his shoulder with the index finger and says, Take care of the visitor's luggage. And sure enough, a couple of goons from the Moscow Soviet pull up and start unloading these fancy foreign bags. The other guy, the "visitor," you know what he does? He pulls out this alligator wallet and hands us ten rubles, but with a two-headed eagle on it—ten tichas! That's right, one of them Crimeans. They're the pick of the bunch, let me tell you. First of all, they speak the language, and then, those rubles of theirs are hot stuff now that the dollar is in the dumps.

"What jackals!" said Luchnikov. "Where do you dig them up?"

"Where do you think?" Kuzenkov smiled. He smiled whenever

he spoke to Luchnikov. He had the smile of a man who takes his superiority for granted, who is privy to certain basic truths that his companion cannot possibly understand. Luchnikov found this infuriating.

"Why do you always have that superior smile plastered on your face, Marlen? What makes you so superior anyway? Your economy's falling apart, your politics are a pack of lies, your ideology's at a dead end. . . ."

"Take it easy, Andrei. Take it easy."

They were in the elevator, riding up to the fifteenth floor, and the other passengers, West Germans, were giving them strange looks.

"The shops sell nothing but rotten junk, the people are gloomy, morose. And you wear a condescending grin from ear to ear." By now they had reached the fifteenth floor. "Wipe it off," he ordered. "No more smiling till you go abroad. You have no right to smile here."

"The reason I'm smiling," replied Kuzenkov, "is that I'm looking forward to a fine meal and some fine vodka. And the reason you're on edge"—Kuzenkov threw open the door to the luxury suite with a specially broad smile—"is that you have a fierce hangover."

"Why must you always put me in these double-decker palaces?" shouted Luchnikov. "What do you think I am, an African Marxist prince or something?"

"Playing the dissident again, I see." Kuzenkov smiled. "All you have to do is set foot in Sheremetyevo and out comes the dissident in you. Oh, I almost forgot. They're very happy with you here. You know. The new direction the *Courier* is taking."

Luchnikov stiffened. "Happy with the *Courier*'s new direction?" He was ready to explode. But then he realized, Well yes, I suppose you could consider it a new direction. After the threats it was only natural for them to assume . . .

The table in the Millionaire's Suite had been set for their arrival. It was groaning with all the delicacies Moscow brings out to turn the heads of visiting dignitaries: the finest of salmon, caviar, ham, crab, vodka in crystal decanters, and several dusty bottles of Luchnikov's favorite red wine, the Georgian Akhasheni.

"So this is what I get for my 'new direction'?" Luchnikov inquired venomously.

When Kuzenkov sat down across from him, he had stopped smiling, a clear sign he thought Luchnikov was going too far with his cheap gibes. Luchnikov decided Kuzenkov was right: he had gone overboard; he had overstepped the bounds of taste.

After the first glass of vodka the atmosphere changed completely. Moscow comfort. He never could quite understand how it worked. Here you were, primed to feel the prying eye of the KGB on your back, aware of the most heinous form of lawlessness going on all around you, and suddenly you were in bliss. Moscow comfort. It was one thing when it came over you in the Old Arbat—you could still find side streets there where nothing the least bit Soviet met the eye, where you could easily imagine, say, the young Arseny in his Cadet uniform—but even here in the lower reaches of notorious Gorky Street—where a look out the window gave you an unobstructed view of the stone giants of Stalinist decadence—even here after the first swallow of vodka you immediately forgot your Paris night fever and sank into it ecstatically: Moscow comfort. It was like the old family nurse massaging their heads: Go to sleep, Arsyushenka. Sleep tight, Andryushenka. Nighty night, Antoshenka.

With a vigorous shake of the head he grabbed the phone and dialed Tatyana's number. What if the Champ answers? The damn sluggard. Loafing away his time, waiting for Tanya to come home from work. A wild combination of roofs out there. A Novgorod cloud floating by. So many styles one on top of the other! Hello, hello . . . There's something wrong with the connection. Hang up and dial again. He hung up and gave a sigh of relief. Home again. Everything is part of it: the vodka, the smoke . . . "The very smoke of the Fatherland smells sweet," says the poet. "Russia is my home. My only home . . ."

"There's a new political force on the Island," he said to Kuzenkov.

Marlen Mikhailovich nodded pleasantly. Very interesting. He put some salmon, caviar, and crab on a plate for Luchnikov and pushed the salad in his direction.

"It's called the SOS, the Common Fate League," said Luchnikov.

Marlen Mikhailovich ran his eyes over the walls of the luxury suite and looked at Luchnikov with a cocked head, meaning, Are you sure you want to talk about it here? Luchnikov dismissed the unspoken question with a wave of the hand. Just then Luchnikov's metal-edged bags arrived. The Moscow Soviet boys showed due respect for the foreign quality workmanship.

"I've got nothing to hide. That's our main ruse. We're completely aboveboard."

"Have something to eat now, Andrei. I apologize for not asking you home, but Vera's busy with meetings today." He smiled. "She's been more and more active lately. . . ."

Except for an occasional toast they said almost nothing while eating. The main course, fresh sturgeon fried *à la moscovite*, came just in time and piping hot, and for dessert—for dessert Marlen Mikhailovich began to talk about Paris, about how much he loved the city; he even quoted Ehrenburg's lines:

> Forgive my having lived here in these woods,
> Having lived through and outlived all of you.
> Forgive my having brought here to the grave
> The wondrous twilights of my Paris days.

He hinted at a romantic involvement connected with the city, which is of course in some sense native to every member of the Russian intelligentsia ("if you are willing to include an apparatchik like me in that category"), and admitted a certain jealously of Andrei's cosmopolitan life style and the stories *he* could tell of Paris.

"I'm sorry, Marlen, but I just can't figure you out," was Luchnikov's cold reply. "You are Mr. Crimea here in Moscow. No individual has more stake in Crimean affairs than you. Yet here I hand you a bombshell, the formation of a Common Fate League, and you hardly react. Maybe it's time I reminded you I don't like playing games."

Kuzenkov mopped his forehead with a napkin and lit a cigar. "Forgive me, Andrei. I'm not playing games. It's just the way I am. I'm really quite reserved, Andrei, reserved and slow on the uptake. Of course I'm interested in SOS; of course it's important. But to tell the truth, I'm a good deal more concerned about your Colonel Chernok's hesitations."

Now it was Luchnikov's turn to show "the way he was," that is, to cover up his surprise or, rather, amazement. Marlen Mikhailovich's revelation left him completely groggy. To give Luchnikov time to regain his bearings, Kuzenkov gave him a rundown of his conversation with Chernok at the Sélect on the Boulevard du Montparnasse. "You see the problem, don't you, Andrei? We know Chernok is a selfless Russian patriot; we know he's every bit as dedicated to the Common Fate Idea as you. Yet even he has his doubts about going over from Mirages to Migs. If *he* is worried about whether the Soviet Union will find a use for him, how can we help but wonder what's going on in the minds of other Islanders, Islanders who lack his commitment?"

Luchnikov poured himself a cognac. The hand that raised the glass was still unsteady; the hand that set it down was absolutely firm. The grogginess had passed. "Big Brother watches us everywhere, doesn't he?" he said in English to make sure the reference came across.

Mr. Crimea's eyes shone with their usual gentle smile. All condescension was gone from them. "Now at least you understand how important we consider your ideas."

Luchnikov stood up and walked over to the window. The sun had started to sink. The silhouettes of the proletarians of all nations were fading. Down below—but above PERFUMES, above RUSSIAN WINES, above GIFTS—he saw a neon garland of flowers in the folk style. Who had overstepped the bounds of taste now? "First you tail me, then you bug me, then you throw in a bit of scare tactics."

"Scare tactics?" Kuzenkov reacted so fast that Luchnikov looked over his shoulder. Kuzenkov was standing next to the television set. A color cartoon was winking and blinking across the screen, accompanied by high-pitched laughter.

"So your boys weren't in on the shoot fest," said Luchnikov sarcastically.

"Shoot fest?" Marlen Kuzenkov was suddenly a taut spring.

"Two bullets," said Luchnikov gleefully. "First this ear, then the other," he pointed as he spoke. "Now there's a reaction! At last I've caught you off guard."

"I'll look into it immediately, though I'm ninety-nine percent sure that . . . Unless you acted in a way so as to . . ."

"Bastard," said Luchnikov affectionately. "Kremlin-bought bastard. So I'm supposed to act like a good little boy while your hit men breathe down my neck!"

"Really, Andrei, that's not what I meant at all. I meant that even the best operatives lose control sometimes, go against orders. And if that's the way it was, they'll pay dearly for it. Can't you see that . . . ? I'm sorry, Andrei. I'm not at leave to go into it any further. I'm sure the Lupine Hordes were behind it."

Silence reigned for the next few minutes in the luxury suite. Luchnikov went into the bedroom, opened one of the bags, and took out the gifts he had brought for the Kuzenkov clan: a micro-cassette recorder for Marlen, a bracelet watch for Vera Pavlovna, cashmere sweaters for the children. He decided to give Dim Shebeko his records personally. What a different world Dim Shebeko lived in, a healthy world. That was the word: healthy.

He went back and put the gifts down in front of Marlen Mikhailovich. "Forgive me, Marlen. I lost my head. No matter what happens, I know the two of us are friends. Here is . . . a token . . . of our friendship. For you, for Vera, for the kids. I hope you like them. I don't think you'll find anything similar here"—he could not hold back a smile—"not even in GUM's 'Special Section.'"

"I'm touched at the care you've taken in reconnoitering our lines of supply."

For the first time in all the years they had known each other, Luchnikov saw Kuzenkov truly wounded. His "Kremlin-bought bastard" and "GUM's 'Special Section'" had hit the progressive ideologue below the belt, a moral analogue to the shots fired at him in Paris. Kuzenkov seemed the victim of a mild concussion.

"But thank you. They're beautiful gifts, just what one would expect from a rich representative of a rich country. Beautiful, elegant, expensive. Vera has asked me to invite you to lunch tomorrow. 'Special Section' lunch. Your interpreter will drop by in the morning and arrange your schedule with you. You can count on first-class treatment all the way, of course—especially now." Luchnikov could feel the sting across the room. "You will have your own car. Well, I must be going."

His delivery was calm and, if Luchnikov was not mistaken,

rather despondent. As he spoke, he put on his hat and coat and loaded the gifts in his attaché case. He held out his hand. His eyes were brimming with intelligence and grief. How the inexorable laws of history could dwarf the individual!

"I have several requests, Marlen," said Luchnikov, taking his hand. "Coming from a persona grata, they should present no problem. One, I have no need for an interpreter. My interpreter is Tatyana Lunina. She takes care of my every need. Two, I have no need for a chauffeur-driven limousine. I am perfectly happy with Avis, which, I note, has invaded our"—he laid special emphasis on the word "our"—"capital. Three, I wish to make a private trip with the following itinerary: Penza, Tambov, Saratov, Kazan, Omsk, and the new Baikal–Amur Railway. Please have your friends ventilate"—special emphasis again to allow the Soviet word to sink in—"the idea. And four—I'm absolutely serious about this, it's no joke—I want very much to visit the Masonic lodge with you."

They looked up at each other and burst out laughing. All the nasty hints and innuendos had gone up in smoke.

"Do you mean what I think you mean?" Kuzenkov could scarcely talk he was laughing so hard. "Do you mean . . ."

"That's just what I mean," nodded Luchnikov. "The Finnish bath. It's an absolute must. The bathhouse period of the Socialist Empire. Rome. Decadence. You understand, don't you?"

"Bravo, Andrei! Of course I understand!" Kuzenkov gave him a good slap on the back. "That's the Andrei I know and love! I've never met another foreigner like you!"

"No bravos for you, Marlen," said Luchnikov jokingly. "How many times must I tell you I'm no foreigner!"

Sparring at each other down the corridor, they rang for the elevator. The arrow moved down; the door opened. The cabin was empty. Luchnikov followed Kuzenkov inside. "Just tell me one thing before you go, Marlen. Have you an answer to Chernok's question?"

"No," said Marlen very definitely. "No one heard the question, and there is no answer."

Gorky Street that same evening. After Kuzenkov left, Luchnikov walked slowly up to the main post office. Straight ahead, boldly writ in blue fire against the golden sunset and stretched across the roof of a building that had survived its bourgeois "Sytinsky House" past, was the word LABOR. Traffic obediently funneled itself off into the correct lanes. An outsize thermometer gave the modest reading of +8°C for the surrounding area. As always, the post office had its blue globe out, proclaiming defiantly to the world that the earth does in fact turn on its axis, though surrounded by a cluster of lobster claws or ears of corn, depending on how you interpreted the sculptor's intention. It was all highly normal and highly improbable. Up and down the steps sat large numbers of young men, many of whom seemed of the southern persuasion and all of whom were awaiting adventure. The amazing thing is that it came to them. After all the years people have tried to squeeze the adventure out of Moscow, it lives—crawling along the streets, sticking to the windows, getting into the hair of the police; it still finds those who seek it out.

Luchnikov leaned against the nearby entrance to an underground passage and lit a cigarette. The black-market crowd immediately picked up on the smooth Virginia smoke. "Shit, man! There's a Kent in the neighborhood!" "But that ain't no jeans suit he got on." "Shit, man! Can't you see? That's the real thing, man. This guy's *class*. Time for your English lesson, okay? Excuse me, mister, what time is it? Where are you from? Can I bum a cigarette off you? You looking for girls? You got greenbacks? What have you got? You mean you're from Crimea? Hey guys, a Comrade from Crimea! Say, man, do they really speak Russian there?"

Laughing, Luchnikov passed out all his Camels to the crowd surrounding him. A puny, dark-haired hustler kept trying to push his way through the shoulders of his taller brethren. He wore a look of unmitigated despair: he had to get through to the foreigner, he had to. "Hey, friend! Hey, look here! Listen!" But the others kept pushing him back. Then suddenly he leaped onto somebody's back and shouted out in unbearable anguish, "I'll buy everything you got! Everything!"

Now it was their turn to laugh, and Luchnikov joined in wholeheartedly. He had never felt disdainful of black marketeers. On the contrary, he saw them as self-appointed outcasts from monolithic Soviet collectivism, elemental rebels against totalitarianism, no less courageous—maybe even more so—than the protest generation in the West.

"Does any of you happen to know Dim Shebeko?"

"C_2H_5OH? Sure, everybody knows Dim Shebeko!" they answered with respect.

"Well, would you tell him Looch is in town?" He made it sound top secret. "I'm at the Intourist."

They were thrilled at the inside dope. Big things are happening, guys. Looch is in town. Better get the word to Dim Shebeko on the double!

Luchnikov clapped a few of them on the back and threaded his way through the tightly knit group to the post office steps. And who should be coming down them but Vitaly Gangut. No, I don't believe it! Gangut, the dyed-in-the-wool sit-at-home, here in the heart of Moscow, my very first night! And that look in his eyes! There's life in the old cockroach yet! Luchnikov had not seen him so excited in a long time. Suddenly he felt a little alarmed. What if he's so high he starts going through the old Moscow routine and accuses me of betraying the ideals of my youth and so on and so forth?

They hugged.

"Andryushka!"

"Vitasya!"

Wonder of wonders! The smell he gave off was neither vodka nor puke, but eau de Cologne. Fabergé, no less. Underarms dry, too.

"Am I glad to see you, Looch! Just the person I wanted to see. Everything's coming together so well I can't believe it!"

"Begin at the beginning. What shall I congratulate you on first?"

"Guess who I've just talked to on the phone. You'll never guess."

"Emma? Milka? Viktoria Pavlovna?"

"Hell no! Fuck them! I'm through with sexual slavery. Octopus, that's who! This morning I got an international telegram. I'm lying in bed with a splitting headache thinking how life's not worth living, and suddenly I get an international telegram!" Trembling all over, he handed Luchnikov his morning manna. GANGUT OLD BUDDY CALL SOON AS POSSIBLE PARIS HOTEL PLAZA ATHENEE TELEPHONE 359.85.23 OCTOPUS. So old J.P. was really on the ball. He wasn't kidding about Gangut.

As soon as Luchnikov looked up from the telegram, Gangut

ripped it out of his hand. Then he folded it carefully and tucked it away in the safest place he knew: the back pocket of his jeans. "Well, what do you think? You're the one who introduced me to him. Remember? The time we went skinny dipping in the pond at Arkhangelsk. Crazy guy. Mythological in scope almost. He's a big producer now. Anyway, I spent the whole day lying on my fucking bed trying to put the fucking call through to Paris. Each time I dialed the fucking international operator, they fucking cut off my phone for the next ten minutes! Fucking bastards! Scared shitless the minute they think you're trying to stick your prick through their bloody iron curtain. All right, then, I said, if that's the way you want it. And I marched myself down here to the Main Post Office and said to the Comrade at the window, 'Parizhsk, please. Parizhsk Region. French Soviet Socialist Republic.' And before you know it, I'm talking to Octopus. To Octopus in Paris! I've been waiting for your call all day, haven't left my bed. And then the proposition he made me! Man, can he talk! He said he was having a contract drawn up. The pay is fantastic, the whole thing's fantastic. So I said to him, I said—"

"In what language, if I may ask?"

Gangut ran his hand through his luxuriant mane for time and inspiration, then looked up at Luchnikov and said, "You know, that's a good question. My English is, well, a bit rusty, and his Russian is nonexistent. What difference does it make, anyway? We understood each other. That's all that counts. I know enough English to say 'I agree.'"

"What kind of picture does he have in mind?" asked Luchnikov cautiously.

"What do I know? What do I care? None of that shit about the problems of youth at technical colleges or the Baikal–Amur Railway or the Siberian pipeline. You wouldn't believe the juices I've stored up lying on my back all these years. See that horse?" They were passing the equestrian statue of Yury Dolgoruky, legendary founder of Moscow. "Well, I could fuck the hell out of it. Octopus knows that. He knows I wasn't wallowing in my own filth. No, when a real artist takes time off to recharge, the world doesn't forget him. So here I am, all recharged and raring to go."

"And you think they'll let you?"

Gangut burst into a paroxysm of rage. "You mean those cowards, liars, demagogues, nitwits, bribe-taking hypocrites, those self-righteous self-seekers, the dregs of society, Stalin's stoolie stooges!" By the time he ran out of breath, he seemed in a trance, but then he filled his lungs with air again and said almost caressingly, "I can handle those fuckers."

At that moment they were standing in front of the historic headquarters of the Moscow Soviet, a policeman was eying them from a distance. Luchnikov, in turn, was eying a sign that stood out among all the neon artwork for its constant flicker. FISH it said, and a gargantuan, four-story, oddly pulsating FISH it was.

"So you're planning to fly the coop, are you?"

Gangut zipped up his jacket and took a cap out of one pocket, a scarf out of the other. "Have you ever stopped to ask yourself why you can flit off to America or Africa, while I, in other respects quite similar to you, am chained to the land like a serf?"

"It's a question I ask myself every day," said Luchnikov. "That and many others like it."

"Swap your Swiss passport for the bright red variety and you'll have a simple answer to all of them."

"Look at that powerful fish," said Luchnikov, pointing to the sign. "Look at it flopping about in the midst of Moscow's stately splendor. A pity I've never noticed it before. O wonderful, marvelous, invincible fish!"

"There's the Looch I love." Gangut laughed. "What do you say we forget we're forty-five? Just for tonight. What do you say?"

"I've been thirty since morning," said Luchnikov.

Whereupon Gangut sauntered up to the policeman and said, "Excuse me, Your Excellency, but you didn't happen to see a pair of dark-eyed beauties pass by here this morning, did you?"

He was prepared for one vast bomb site, the smoky remains of a series of trumped-up trials and expulsions: the Guardians of the Future dispose of everyone in their path, and the rejects sit, swill, diddle, and bad-mouth the Mother of All Mothers. Instead he found an uncanny gaiety: loft parties all over town, amateur theatricals in private flats, concerts at scientific institutes and outlying clubs by Dim Shebeko, Kozlov, Zubov, poetry readings by the young and struggling, meetings of the Metropol group, all-night philosophy discussions over tea, samizdat discoveries, basement exhibits, get-togethers with local bards to sing underground songs . . .

There were times he felt they were doing it all for him, putting a bold face on things. See, Looch? There's life in the old Moscow underground yet. But then he changed his mind. Maybe it was barely dragging along, but it could drag on indefinitely. For it is like a field, which shall never be barren.

Sitting next to Tatyana on a sway-backed sofa, picking through the usual assortment of food and drink, and listening to the latest genius hold forth, he looked around from face to face. He was amazed to find so many new deviations from the ideal citizen. Where did they all come from? They themselves sang Bulat Okudzhava's mournful:

> Scattered are my friends to the end of the earth.
> Even Neizvestny has opted for rebirth.
> Now Yura Vasilyev and Borya Messerer
> Are all I've got left in the USSR.

Yet here they were, living proof that life went on, a whole new hive of worker bees having nothing in common with the devotees of physical culture who parade up and down before the Mausoleum. And when you got right down to it, quite a few old-timers had stuck it out, too. All you had to do was look a little harder.

"Decadence is an integral part of our country; it cannot be eradicated." Thus spake the young jeans-clad dancer Antinoy after a concert of the Studio for Experimental Ballet in the cultural activities room of a Mosstroy factory dormitory. He was quite proud of having said it, and to a foreigner, a foreign journalist. The dressing room was piled high with coats and props, and everyone was drinking tea and an extraordinarily vile Rumanian champagne.

Suddenly the props jiggled a bit and out came a most insignificant-looking gray-haired little man, all bits and pieces, who turned out to be the director, who turned out to be Garik Paul, who turned out to be more than another guzzler from the All-Russian Theater Society restaurant; in fact, he was a genius when it came to dance and quite a philosopher. Butting like a goat and gesturing like a penguin, he entered into a polemic with the youthful Antinoy.

"On Decadence" (Transcribed from Tapes Made in the Soviet Union)
"Decadence is my life, my art. . . ."

"I'm sorry, but what you call decadence—the kind of thing we do—isn't decadent at all. It's as healthy as it can be, living art. . . ."

"Yes, but it's not at all realistic, what we do. . . ."

"I'm sorry, but you've got it all wrong, you've got it backwards. What is decadence, after all, but complete and utter cultural demoralization, degeneration, decay, aesthetic syphilis, and what have I just described if not, you'll excuse the expression, socialist realism? There's no degeneration or decay in modernism, in any avant-garde art. The whole point of the avant-garde is to shake things up, put new blood into circulation. If what you want is honest-to-goodness decadence, then try socialist petrified realism. . . ."

"Yes, but that goes against our whole way of looking at things, because we've always thought of ourselves as representatives of the twilight, and if we represent the twilight, then they represent the dawn, and much as their dawn turns our stomachs, it's still the dawn of a new society, which means their art is healthy by definition, 'pro-,' and ours is 'anti-': antiprogressive, antisocial, antirevolutionary, lacking in mass appeal and therefore unhealthy. While the rest of the country marches off to the Radiant Future, we sit behind, nursing our hangovers. . . ."

"I'm sorry, but you've got it backwards again. It is my firm conviction that the health of a society is directly proportional to its liberalism and that revolution equals degeneration. Blood-and-iron tactics block all new paths of thought and action and inevitably lead back to the old ruts, further decay, general ossification, rigor mortis. . . ."

"And I'm sorry, but the aesthetic of revolutionary societies with its fear of change, all change, everything new, with its periodic orgies of dreary propaganda—listless flags, endless waves of identically dressed athletes, speeches stupefyingly uniform year in and year out, the ceremonious pose of an entire nation—is an aesthetic of degeneration. Think of the late Byzantine period, of heavy gold brocade covering layer upon layer of filth and putrefaction. . . ."

"And I'm sorry, but this is nothing recent, no 'twilight of the Revolution'; it goes back to the roots of revolution in general, because revolution is a twilight phenomenon to begin with, a giant step back to primordial gloom and the glory of bloodlust, because what could be more degenerate than the most ancient form of interpersonal relations, by which I mean violence, the attack of a majestically festering monster on the last outposts of liberalism, renewal: on dance, on music, on the divine afflatus in man. . . ."

"Yes, but I refuse to give it up. I like the word 'decadence.' . . ."

"I'm sorry, but if you're going to use it—and be my guest—you ought to know what it means. . . ."

Luchnikov led a parallel, more official, Moscow existence as the editor of the *Courier* and a leading figure in the world press community. The *Courier* had an office on Kutuzovsky Prospect. It occupied most of a floor and was perfect for receptions. Of the three Crimean correspondents, one was definitely a KGB agent, one a CIA agent; the third, however, Vadim Beklemishev, was completely trustworthy: like Chernok and Sabashnikov, he was an old classmate.

Both Beklemishev and Luchnikov liked to think of the *Courier* as a Moscow paper and lovingly referred to the Moscow office as the city desk. Half a dozen young Moscow journalists worked together with the Crimeans. They received half their salary in Red rubles, half in White or Russian rubles, that is, tichas. They spent all day in the large, sunny office—three bonny lads and three bonny lasses—chatting among themselves in a mixture of English, French, and Russian (in that order), smoking, drinking endless cups of coffee, and cooking up "human interest stories" about Moscow celebrities to make up for the lack of scandal sheets in the USSR. They all regarded their jobs at the *Courier* as incredible sinecures, adored Crimea, and worshiped their boss and jumped for joy whenever he came to Moscow for a visit. Gazing into their bright and eager faces, Luchnikov found it hard to believe they were employees of the KGB, yet there could be no doubt. One way or another, they were reporting on me, thought Luchnikov. On the paper, on the Idea. But if they're doing a job *on* me, they're also doing a job *for* me, and if they have to do the former to do the latter, well, so be it.

While the boss was in Moscow, the office threw a champagne brunch. The menu was modest: steaming loaves of white bread with black caviar and an incomparable brut called Nouveau Monde from the Crimean cellars of Prince Golitsyn. The guest list included a number of prominent diplomats and, of course, the Eastern Mediterranean Region director of the Cultural Relations

Commission, that is, the de facto ambassador of Crimea in Moscow, Boris Teodorovich Wrangel, the infamous Black Baron's great-nephew, who had blushed so red over his background that he was suspected, not without foundation, of holding membership in one or two of the five Crimean communist parties. The Crimean diplomatic corps—or, rather, the conglomeration of missions, observation points, and commissions that served instead of formal embassies—was forbidden by the constitution to accept communists, but since the constitution was as provisional as everything else on the Island, everyone was accustomed to turning a blind eye to petty violations. The secret was to avoid calling a spade a spade.

Also included on the guest list were the usual cultural figures, many of whom Luchnikov knew personally from former sprees, and a sprinkling of the *haute bureaucratie*. Though Crimea-watcher Marlen Mikhailovich Kuzenkov was already on hand, they were expecting an unidentified notable from—according to people in the know—"the stratosphere." The strange contemporary ritual was in its second hour, however, and despite the periodic caravans of militia Mercedeses speeding by below, no dignitary had yet appeared. All receptions at the Moscow *Courier* desk/office also featured a bevy of local beauties hand-picked through the years by the boss. Though strictly nonmembers, nonrepresentatives, they tended to be a bit past their prime, and while some still got by on part-time posing and modeling and others had claimed foreign husbands for their skill at musical beds, most had sunk into semi-whoredom. At *Courier* functions they all basically played the role of walking nosegays. Beklemishev's lads would even phone ahead and coordinate their colors. The beauties did not mind it a bit. They were glad to be of use for a change.

Tatyana Lunina in her three-piece tweed suit from the Faubourg Saint-Honoré was, of course, in a different class altogether. The role she played highly gratified her self-image. To the casual onlooker she was just another pretty face, but at *Courier* functions no one was a casual onlooker: everyone knew perfectly well what Lunina was doing here, where the suit had come from, and who had given it to her—in other words, everyone knew she was the First Lady. Yet it titillated her to think of herself as one of the girls. In the middle of a conversation with a Brazilian diplomat she started scanning the room for her regular check on Andrei's whereabouts, but stopped short when she caught a stranger's sharp, penetrating gaze trained on her. It somehow made her feel that her present exhilarating, seemingly secure position was in fact tenuous and transitory, ephemeral, that she could expect major changes—and soon. Luchnikov was busy with someone, someone else was busy with her husband, the man who had been staring at her put on a pair of tinted glasses, and the Latin lover found himself talking to a frightened little Russian provincial instead of a suave international whore.

Just then the room came alive with excitement. He's here! He's here! The Mercedeses must have been clearing a path for him! Which one? Protopopov! Protopopov himself! Who would have guessed! What an honor! The only one of his superannuated colleagues with a bit of pep in him. Everyone was speculating wildly about the significance of the visit. First the bodyguards made their entrance and quickly mingled with the crowd. Boris Teodorovich Wrangel ran up to greet him, as smarmy as any local Party official. Protopopov carried his undersized chin in the air as a sign of class consciousness. According to the hierarchy of Party etiquette, he extended his hand vaguely in Wrangel's direction without looking at him, but honored the editor of the *Courier*, representative of the provisionally independent "progressive forces of mankind," with a smile and a meaningful handshake.

"I've managed to break away, but for ten little minutes only." The inhabitants of Moscow's Olympus were apparently as partial to diminutives as the Soviet population as a whole. "We're extremely busy now with the upcoming . . ." "What? What? The upcoming what?" The crowd was all astir. ". . . the upcoming anniversary." The crowd immediately calmed down: an anniversary—no matter which one—is never news. "But I feel it my duty to inform you that I read your paper now and again. . . . You'll forgive me if I point out that the quality is rather uneven. . . . Nonetheless, I find it quite interesting. . . . Several recent articles in particular. . . ." Pause. Smile. Take it as you like. "We have always welcomed the development of progressive thought in . . ." Don't tell me he's going to utter the word "Crimea"! Maybe something really is going on up there. ". . . the Eastern Mediterranean Region. . . ." That's the end of that. What do you mean? He's here, isn't he? Doesn't that count for something?

Champagne was served, Nouveau Monde, the limpid color of the sky preparing for sunset. Comrade Protopopov took a sip and clicked his tongue. He liked it! Rumor had it that brut was what They drank when They drank at all. He declined the caviar with an expression of mock horror: he was on a diet. No, something must be going on up there. He's acting so human!

"We dream of the day, Timofei Lukich, when the *Courier* will be sold in Moscow next to *Pravda* and *Izvestia*," proclaimed Luchnikov.

Everyone froze. Even the nosegays. Only the Security wolf-hounds were true to their mission and continued eying people with suspicion. Comrade Protopopov took another sip. All he had to do was to pay a compliment to the champagne and Luchnikov's effrontery would be consigned to the annals of political gaffes. Everyone held his breath, listening for the tick of history.

"That all depends on . . ." Comrade Protopopov smiled. ". . . on give and take, Mr. Luchnikov." The room swelled with excited but reserved whispers. "I've made it clear, I believe, that I find the quality uneven." He's a sly one, that Protopopov. You don't catch him napping. "Well, from now on everything will depend on give and take, mutual understanding." The nosegays perked up, sensing imminent exaltation. "We share a planet; we share a sea. There is much we have in common, friends . . ." Instantly everyone wore a broad, open smile. ". . . but much that divides us as well." The smile disappeared; it couldn't last forever, after all. "And so I lift my glass to mutual understanding!"

A farewell handshake to the provisionally independent forces of mankind, a cold but approving glance in Wrangel's direction, and—bearing in mind the necessity for Security to take the proper precautions and for himself to maintain the proper class dignity—a leisurely exit.

After Protopopov's departure the life seemed to go out of the party. The official guests began whispering among themselves. The semiofficial and unofficial cultural figures (they included some rather down-and-out characters) began giggling among themselves: none of them had ever dreamed of seeing one of the "portraits" come to life. Wouldn't you know the *Courier* would be behind it? Verily I say unto you, brethren, we live in an age of miracles. The diplomats, smiling mysteriously, turned immediately to the ballet, sports, Russian champagne—and thence to the door. It was all in a day's work. The journalists gathered round Luchnikov, chattering about everything under the sun, but in reality stalking him for a statement.

"Ladies and gentlemen! The editorial board of the *Courier* finds the give-and-take formula as set forth by Timofei Lukich an eminently viable proposition."

Scratch, scratch, scratch went the *style rétro* Montblanc fountain pens of UPI, AP, Reuters, the Russian Telegraph Agency, Agence France Presse, and three Japanese free lances.

The reception was coming to an end.

"I never thought you'd sink so low, Andrei," said Gangut on his way out. "It makes me sick to look at you. Congratulations on your new progressive partners."

"Off for the Island soon, Andrei Arsenievich?" asked a *Pravda* foreign correspondent on his way out. "It's high time," he added quickly with a sneer and slipped away.

"Well, what do you think?" Luchnikov asked Kuzenkov on his way out. Kuzenkov's only response was a farewell smile, but a commendatory one.

"Why don't you ever give me a ring, Andryusha?" asked one of the nosegays on her way out. "You really ought to, you know. We could have a few drinks, a few laughs, reminisce about the good old days. . . ."

The room was emptying fast. The window showed signs of a drizzle. The view of Kutuzovsky Prospect was depressing. A feeling of the inanity, inconsequence, complete irrelevancy, and senselessness of a common cause, common idea, common fate, of any activity or attempt at activity, a feeling of anguish and of shame, filled Luchnikov as he stood looking out of the window. Empty bottles and scraps of bread with lipstick stains looking like used sanitary napkins—these were the only tangible results of the silly champagne brunch. New Zealand, here I come.

"Bye-bye, Andrei!" It was Tatyana.

He flinched and turned away from the window. For the first time he had failed to connect the idea of the New Zealand farm with Tanya. It gave him pause.

By now the room was nearly empty. In a far corner one last drunken nosegay (it looked like Lora, one-time music-hall dancer) was laughing provocatively while three young men earnestly discussed the issue of which of them would take on the gentlemanly responsibility of escorting her home.

Tanya was standing in the doorway. The Champ had her by the arm. She could not quite look Luchnikov in the eye, and her whole manner felt forced, unnatural. She could easily have left without saying good-by, but no, she thought, I'll let him know. Good-by. That's all. She could tell he had completely forgotten about her. She was supernaturally sensitive to that sort of thing.

The Champ gave a polite, half-diplomatic, half-friendly smile. Luchnikov had the feeling that deep down inside the handsome athlete's body was an aging, sickly soul yearning to be free. Perhaps the feeling came from an inordinately bull-like stance exaggerated by the official responsibility of representing the Soviet sports establishment. Can he really suspect nothing? wondered Luchnikov.

"How would you like to come to our place for tea?" said Tatyana.

The Champ turned his monumental face and frozen smile in her direction, not quite certain how to react to the invitation. The editor of a bourgeois newspaper for tea?

"Tea? Your place?" Even Luchnikov was a bit nonplused.

"And why not? We have some wonderful English tea. We can sit and chat. . . ." The daring and completely unpremeditated move had worked a sea change on Tatyana. Suddenly Luchnikov saw before him the spirited Moscow filly who had so attracted him ten years before, who could bestow favors indiscriminately in a bathtub or inspire the love of a lifetime.

"How nice of you to think of me," he said, still feeling his way. "It might not be a bad idea. My stomach is a little queasy, and—"

"And tea would be just the thing for it," said Tatyana, beaming.

"I always feel depressed after a party."

"I know," Tatyana said to him with her lips only.

"Well then, it's settled. You're coming to our place for tea," the Champ finally said. He looked over at his wife as if to say, "Have you gone out of your mind?" And received a "Get a move on, mate!" look in return.

Luchnikov kept a supply of foreign liquor and cigarettes in his rented Zhiguli just in case. Piling the lot of it on the table in Tatyana's entrance hall, he heard the sound of high-pitched voices and realized with a start that he had forgotten all about the children. He was totally unprepared: no chewing gum, no Coke, no matchbox cars. He somehow never gave her children any thought, nor did she seem to have much to say about twelve-year-old Milka or ten-year-old Sasha.

The children came out to meet the foreigner. Milka was a perfect nymphet. How could Tanya's daughter be otherwise? As for Sasha, the strangest image popped into his head: Arsyusha, Andryusha, Antosha, and Sasha. Could it be? A thin, sad-looking boy with a high forehead. It's been ten years since we met. I remember dragging her off from a wild party and . . . no pretensions on either side. Could it really be? He has gray eyes, so have I. So has the Champ. He has a strong jaw, so have I. The Champ has a jaw like iron. Luchnikov was so distracted he gave the boy his Montblanc with the gold nib.

"Getting friendly in there?" Tatyana asked cheerfully, sticking her head out from the kitchen. Luchnikov questioned her about Sasha with his eyes. She gave him a comic "Who knows?" shrug and a silly, guilty, monkeylike grin. They all laughed—both Luchnikov and the children—and Tanya did an impromptu little dance in place.

Meanwhile the Champ had gone off to what he called the bar and returned with two bottles of French cognac, his way of saying, "Anything you can do we can do better."

The incredible falsity of it all! The Champ sat down across the polished table from Luchnikov and filled the crystal cognac glasses —you see, we have crystal, too—as if the curious foreigner had come to see him for a man-to-man talk.

"To our meeting," he said. "Tatyana, are you joining us?"

"I'll be right there!" she called from the kitchen.

"Tell me, where do you work?" asked Luchnikov.

"What do you mean?"

"I mean, have you got a job or are you"—after searching for the word in Russian for a moment, Luchnikov gave up and said it in English—"free-lance?"

"What was that?" the Champ asked, pricking up his ears.

Tatyana shouted in the Russian equivalent from the kitchen.

"Actually, I'm chief assistant to the assistant chief of the Main Division of Single Combat Events."

Luchnikov had a good laugh. Maybe this guy wasn't so thick after all. At least he had a sense of humor.

"What are you laughing at?" Tatyana asked, carrying in a tray.

"You husband's joke. Chief assistant to the assistant chief of the Main Division of Single Combat Events. Priceless!"

"What's so funny?" asked the Champ.

"He really is, you know," said Tanya.

Every time Soviet reality surpassed his parodic fantasies he felt a bit inadequate. No matter how hard he tried, he seemed unable to get to the bottom of it.

"Even so, don't you see the humor of it?" He tried not to look at Tatyana. "I mean, chief assistant to the assistant chief."

"So what?" asked the Champ.

Tatyana burst out laughing. She had downed a large jigger of cognac by then. "You know, it never occurred to me. Pretty funny, eh?" Her laughter betrayed a tinge of alarm.

"While we're on the subject, I think you ought to know that we look after our own," said the Champ. "Look over here and you can follow my career. For eight years I was in the top ten. . . ." The sideboard, made in Yugoslavia, was lined with cups and bronze figures. Luchnikov was somewhat chagrined at the pedestrian style of the furnishings. Insofar as he had pictured Tatyana's living conditions at all, he had pictured them differently.

They were on their second round of cognac. Tea was the last thing on anyone's mind.

"That's why I'm so well taken care of now," said the Champ. "You see what I mean?"

Luchnikov looked over at Tatyana. How shall I behave? But she was not about to spoil her fun. Luchnikov had to bumble on by himself.

"You see what I mean? I'm asking you!" The Champ was boring his eyes into Luchnikov's over their fourth cognac.

"Yes, I see."

"You don't see a thing. As soon as your athletes are over the hill, you drop them, you turn your backs. Well, we take care of our own. Now do you see?"

"Now I see."

"You know, somehow I have the feeling you don't see at all. It's that face of yours."

"Oh, I can't stand it!" Tatyana was laughing so hard she seemed about ready to fall off her chair. "Try to look a trifle more intelligent, please, Andryushka!"

"This is no laughing matter," said the Champ, taking his wife by the shoulders. "They have their way, we have ours. Your friend Luchnikov here will tell you that, propaganda or no propaganda."

"It's true we lack the machinery to carry out programs like yours on a large scale." He glanced furtively at Sasha, who was sitting on a day bed with one leg tucked under him. "We have no Sports Commission whatsoever. We let things take their course. Many sports fare quite poorly."

"You see?" the Champ exclaimed, looking over at his wife, who was in turn looking over at their foreign guest with a shame-on-you pout on her lips. "You see? I couldn't have put it better myself." Cognac number four disappeared into his bottomless pit. "Now I bet you're going to tell me all Soviet athletes are professionals!"

"It will never pass my lips," said Luchnikov staunchly.

"Go on, say it, say it! You think we don't know how to handle it?"

"He took part in an antipropaganda seminar a few weeks ago," Tatyana put in by way of explanation.

Enter Milka, parading across the room in jacket and cap, a bag slung over one shoulder; exit Milka, slamming the door in protest against her parents' disgusting drunken orgies.

"Figure skating," said the Champ, pointing in the general direction of the door. "How many artificial skating-rinks have you got in your White Guard paradise down there?"

"Three," said Luchnikov.

"Well, we've got a hundred and three!"

Exit Sasha, removing his leg from under him, making his way to the door (My walk or his? Luchnikov wondered), and slamming it, his proud Luchnikov-like nose held high. Obviously the children were not happy with their parents' drinking.

"Hockey," said the Champ, nodding towards the door again. "Great future!"

"Well, now we're alone," said Tatyana with a giggle.

"If you won't ask me, then I'll ask you," said the Champ, moving his chair closer to Luchnikov's and filling the glasses again. "Are we professionals or are we amateurs?"

"Neither," said Luchnikov.

"Neither?"

"Soviet athletes are government employees."

Glass number six stopped in midair. The Champ's mouth fell open. Tatyana was in ecstasy. "Bravo, Andryushka, bravo! You're done for, Hub. He's got you where he wants you. That's one they didn't touch on at the seminar!" She swung her chair over to Luchnikov and planted a kiss on his cheek. The chair slipped out from under her, but instead of falling (she had the reflexes of an athlete), she flew into Luchnikov's lap and gave him another kiss, this time on the lips.

"Really, Tatyana," muttered the Champ. "Kissing a stranger on the lips. . . ."

"Andrei's no stranger," she said, tickling him and laughing. "He's not even a foreigner. He may be a bit deviant ideologically, but not in any other way. What I mean is, he's as Russian as we are."

"Really?"

Luchnikov was amazed to catch a glimpse of himself in the mirror: his face was livid with rage, his arm draped with proprietary solicitude over Tatyana's shoulders.

"A hundred times more Russian than you, Comrade Hub! We trace our line back to Rurik of Novgorod, the Viking Prince!"

"Well, I don't give a damn where you or your ancestors came from. All that counts with me is whether you're honest and have good progressive ideas. Come with me." And he grabbed Luchnikov by the arm with one of his iron claws. Tanya, still laughing, tripped along behind them, pushing the ON button of the stereo system as she went. "The Ballad of John and Yoko" filled the room just as they left it for the dark room next door. There in the flicker of a street lamp, like a huge gravestone, stood the conjugal bed.

"I want to go home, to the enormous space of my melancholy room," the Champ suddenly said in a perfectly human tone of voice.

Luchnikov could not believe his ears. "What's that?" he said. "I can't believe my ears."

"The Hub here is a poetry freak," said Tanya. "Who is it this time, Hub?"

"Boris Mandelstam."

"You see!" said Tanya gleefully, bouncing up and down on the bed. "He even keeps a notebook of his favorite poems and aphorisms. No slouch he! He takes the title of intellectual seriously."

"Look over here," said the Champ quite ominously. "The rest of my career. Wasn't enough room out there." The street lamp lit up a shelf of cups and statuettes running along the entire wall.

"Hub is a good name for him, you know, Tanya? He thinks he's the hub of the universe."

"You think you're pretty hot stuff yourself. Especially when it comes to my wife." He closed his hand into a mighty fist and swung a hook through the air.

"Why waste a powerful stroke like that?" said Luchnikov. "Punch me in the chest!"

"Ha! Ha!" said the Champ. "Now you're talking like a man. None of that nobility crap."

'Two ideologies!" Tanya cried, plopping down on the bed. "Two ideologies in a single combat!" Here in this room lit only by streetlight she seemed an honest-to-goodness tart, a bitch in heat just waiting for the first stud to come along.

Animal lust rushed through Luchnikov's body like a shot of adrenaline. "Come on, Hubby," he said, taking his Taiwan stance, "give us a punch!"

It was a knock-down-drag-out fight in the finest tradition. At first the Champ did not know what hit him: no matter how well he placed his blows, Luchnikov parried them effortlessly. But true sportsman that he was, he valued a challenging partner and was soon letting out enthusiastic whoops.

"Cut it out, Andrei," Tanya suddenly said in a sober voice. "This is ridiculous. Cut it out right now."

"And why, may I ask? I'm no Tolstoyan. I stand up for myself when I'm attacked, that's all. Besides, I've shown admirable restraint: the Hub is still in one piece, isn't he?"

Suddenly his head exploded, and the next thing he knew he was sitting on the floor in a litter of broken glass and a cloud of cognac fumes. His face was dripping with a strange combination of liquids.

"Is he alive?" he heard the Champ say up on the bed.

So he's smashed a bottle of Courvoisier over my head. My pate. My skull. My noodle, noggin, nob, bean, and whatever else they call it here. "Tanya," Luchnikov called out.

Tanya did not respond.

He realized he was beaten, and, grabbing hold of whatever he could, pulled himself to his feet. "Congratulations, Hub," he said. "You win. It was an honest fight, and the best man won."

"Now scram, do you hear me? Get out. I want to make love to my wife."

Tanya was lying face down on the pillow. Luchnikov could see the right half of his face dimly in the mirror. It was covered with blood.

"The lady is coming with me," he said. "My skull is split open, and the fair sex has a well-developed sense of pity."

Tanya did not respond.

"I'm glad I didn't kill you, though," said the Hub. "I don't think they would have been too happy with me for killing the editor of the *Courier*."

"Tanya!" Luchnikov called out again.

Tanya did not respond.

"Have a heart, will you?" said the Hub. "We've been living in blissful matrimony for fifteen years."

"Come with me, Tatyana," shouted Luchnikov. "What are you waiting for?"

"Listen, Mr. White Guard, screwing my wife isn't the same as owning her. She's mine, do you hear? So get out. Get out while the getting's good. You have harems waiting for you back there on your Island. Tanya's all I've got."

"Tell him you're mine, Tanya," begged Luchnikov. "At least get up and wipe off my face. I'm bleeding."

Tanya did not respond.

The Hub hunched over her, slipped his hand under her stomach, and began struggling with her buttons. His body looked grotesque next to her fragile frame.

"Hasn't it occurred to you, Hub, that I could bash you on the head with something, too? One of your trophies, say. The Winged Victory of Samothrace over there."

"Yes, but what good would it do you?" He laughed hoarsely.

"You're right. You know, you're not nearly so simple as you look. Carry on, then, if you must. My own true love."

"Want to watch?" asked the Hub. "Want to see how we do it? Be my guest! Be my guest!"

Tanya's shoulders twitched and her head tore away from the pillow.

"Tanya!" Luchnikov called softly. "Wake up!"

"Now you'll see. . . . Now you'll see," muttered the Hub, hulking over his wife. "Now you'll see how we . . . what we . . . Hit me. . . . Go on. . . . Nothing will pry us apart. . . . She's all I have left. . . . Squeezed dry, sucked dry by the Motherland . . . Only Tanya . . . Nothing without her . . ."

"Please go, Andrei," said an unknown voice. It was Tanya.

He stood for a long time in front of the building, feeling the right side of his face swell up. What nonsense! Bells in my head! Excruciating pain! Behind every door of that fifteen-story monster, lights on and lights off, the Hub was legally fucking my own illegal love. My own true love, aglow under the Crimean moon. Crimea is my only home, my pride, my joy. The Island of Crimea floating free among the waves. We shall never merge with you, you lawabiding, monumental, hulking, northern, Russian swine, you! We're not Russian by ideology, we're not communist by nationality; we're Yaki Islanders, we have a fate of our own. Our fate is the carnival of freedom, and it makes us stronger, no matter how thick the glass you bastards hurl at our heads!

It began to snow.

September, when all over the Northern Hemisphere people sat under chestnut trees listening to music, when in Yalta nymphs with barely covered labia emerged from waves to sand . . . Oh, the hopeless, dank, and dreary Russian September . . . Damn the whole country! Damn my doomed Russian love! . . . Taxi! Taxi!

The rented Zhiguli with the reversible English raglan thrown over the seat stayed behind, forgotten.

———

Three days later Tatyana Lunina was invited to appear at the Sports Commission's KGB office, or the First Division as it was euphemistically called. With your husband, please." "What's he got to do with it?" "I don't believe we need to go into detail over the telephone, Tatyana Nikitichna. I will only say it is a matter of grave importance to both you and your husband."

They arrived on time. She was not surprised to see the man who had tried to hypnotize her at the *Courier* reception. The latest model werewolf, complete with scraggly beard and tinted glasses. A charming specimen! He even took off his glasses when shaking hands to show her how clear and honest his eyes were. No digs, no innuendos: you can trust me, I'm a friend. The head of the division introduced him as Comrade Sergeev, a foreign correspondent. He will be present for our little talk.

Tanya looked over at the Hub. He was sitting at attention, his gleaming white shirt and sleeves protruding a bit too far from the rather tight-fitting blazer. He was so nervous he looked years younger; there was something boyish about a pair of frightened little eyes peering out of so huge a frame. She could never get over how Soviet supermen—boxers, wrestlers, weightlifters—turned into helpless ninnies when faced with First Division brass or "correspondents" like Comrade Sergeev. It made her hackles rise. "I don't see why we need a correspondent here. I don't plan to give a statement to the press."

"Tatyana Nikitichna . . ." Comrade Sergeev began with a friendly smile.

She broke him off. "Which reminds me, what right had you to come up and make eyes at me like that at the *Courier* reception? Showing off the latest in psychological pressure techniques?"

"Not in the least. I was simply enjoying the view." And he leaned back in his chair as if to admire it again.

"Well, let me tell you, you were taking a big risk." She grabbed her handbag and pulled out a cigarette.

Two fists with tongues of flame immediately hovered at her face.

"Tanya, Tanya," muttered the Hub almost inaudibly. He was completely immobile, ready to burst at the slightest move.

"There's no need for you to be so upset," said Comrade Sergeev. "We merely want to have a friendly chat about—"

"About Mr. Luchnikov," the head of the division chimed in, glowering.

At this point the time-honored tradition of friendly chats called for a ritual of stupefication, qualification, and capitulation. But Tatyana's hackles were still up, and the ritual broke down.

"All the more reason to do without correspondents. What's he here for, anyway? Look, go and tell your boss to put you on another assignment, all right?"

"Quiet, Lunina!" commanded the division head, punctuating his words with a solid fist against the desk top. "You know perfectly well what's wanted of you. Stop playing the fool!"

"No, *you* stop playing the fool!" she shouted and even shot out of her chair. "Correspondents! If you want me to be open, you've got to be open yourselves! I have a right to know who I'm talking to!"

"You're acting like a real dissident," boomed the division head, sounding simultaneously indignant and paternal. In the old days he had been one of the trainers on the air force soccer team, an intimate of Stalin's son.

"Where do you pick up these ideas of yours, this talk about 'rights'? You ought to be more careful, Tatyana."

Seeing Comrade Sergeev uncomfortably grasping at straws bucked Tatyana up considerably. She calmly returned to her seat, clearly master of the situation. Well? Frowning, Comrade Sergeev took out his telltale identity papers.

"I assumed, Tatyana Nikitichna, that we understood each other and might therefore avoid dealing with certain aspects of the case head-on." He threw a significant glance in the direction of the Hub.

The Hub's eyes were half-closed. He was all but comatose.

"Since you insist, however . . ."

"Come on, out with it" said Tanya. "Now that we've gone this far, we might as well tackle it head-on. I don't like the idea of creeping up from behind, anyway. It smacks of treachery."

"Allow me to express my admiration for your—"

"Thank you, I can do without it," she snapped back.

Funny. His papers identified him as Sergeev, but instead of correspondent they called him Colonel.

"As you wish," the colonel said in English.

"What was that, Comrade Colonel?" Tatyana opened her eyes wide as if to say, "Was that English?" For suddenly she understood intellectually what she had intuited all along: Sergeev really was attracted to her, and she could get away with murder by playing up to him.

"I'm sorry." He smiled. "It's an old habit. Hard to break."

She had guessed right. He was actually quite grateful for the question. It gave him a chance to make an oblique but transparent reference to a mysterious foreign—and from his point of view at least, romantic—past.

Then he got down to brass tacks. He began by stating he had nothing but respect for Mr. Luchnikov, both as one of the most influential journalists in the world and as a human being. He even hinted he was on first-name terms with him. . . . "Yes, yes. That's right. And to make a long story short, a number of high-level organizations in our country attach considerable importance to him. We—you don't mind if I simplify matters by saying 'we,' do you?—we are of the opinion that in certain historical situations a man like Luchnikov has a decisive role to play. Our historians can belittle the role of the individual in history as much as they please. We know better. And so . . . And so, Tatyana Nikitichna, we have a very real interest in keeping close tabs on him. For one thing, as anyone who has studied his biography can tell you, Andrei Arsenievich's development has been full of twists and turns, much like his psychological development, for that matter. To be blunt, we are afraid that at a critical moment he will make a totally unpredictable move on the basis of what we might call his creative reflexes, thereby injecting an element of subjectivity, of the absurd, into the objective historical situation. It is therefore very much in our interest to ensure that Luchnikov have a proud, devoted, intelligent, and outspoken friend at his side at all times. . . ." He looked over at the Hub again, then turned—questioningly, confidentially (they're all ours now)—to Tatyana.

Tatyana did not bat an eyelid. She was fury etched in stone.

The "correspondent" was forced to go on. "But this is all just a preamble to our main concern, Tatyana Nikitichna, and our main concern is Andrei Arsenievich himself, his personal safety. The truth of the matter is . . . The truth of the matter is, Tatyana . . ." Comrade Sergeev was so deeply agitated that he inadvertently called her by her first name alone. He then stood up and paced the office several times, trying to pull himself together. "The truth of the matter is that Mr. Luchnikov is the object of a sophisticated assassination plot. Reactionary forces on the Island—" He stopped short in a corner of the room and fixed his eyes on Tanya.

"Yes, I know," she said with all the nonchalance she could muster.

"What's going on here?" the Champ asked suddenly, for the first time looking from one to the next with an expression approaching comprehension.

"Why don't *you* explain the situation to your husband?" Comrade Sergeev suggested cautiously.

Tanya's lips formed a crooked smile. "First tell me why you had to have him here with me."

"To dot the *i*'s and cross the *t*'s," said the head of the division with a frown.

"All right, then." She turned to her husband. "Though I'm sure it comes as no surprise, Luchnikov has been my lover for years."

The Hub did not look up at her. He repeated his deceptively simple question. "What's going on here?"

The division head said not a word. He sat there shifting something from one cheek to the other, massaging the folds in his face, and doodling on one of bureau-socialism's endless cryptograms. Evidently he was displeased—either by the tone of the "chat" or by the turn it had taken.

Sergeev started pacing again. Tanya could not help thinking that the whole thing was proceeding like a badly padded TV melodrama: slow cross to other side of office, sharp turn in far corner, monologue in far corner.

"Given the gravity of the situation, friends, we must take certain extraordinary measures. I certainly hope you don't think of me as a monster or a cog in the state machine. . . ." Sergeev lit another cigarette. He was so nervous he waved the lighter as if it were a match. "Though I don't suppose you believe me," he added bitterly. "What can I do to make you see? Let's think things through together, shall we? You, Gleb"—he smiled at the Hub—"were our idol. The day you went over the eight-thousand-point mark was a holiday for us all. You're a giant, Gleb, really, the ideal of Slav or, if you like, Varangian manhood. The reason I asked you here with

Tanya is that I admire you too much to do anything behind your back. Of course I hope you are strong and understanding enough to help us, but if we, shall we say, fail to find a common language, if you tell me to go to blazes, I'll understand, believe me. And that will be that." Suddenly he snuffed his burning cigarette out in his fist and lit another. His expression never changed. "Isn't it ridiculous how things turn out? You and I, we ought to be sitting down having a cognac somewhere or . . . or . . ." Sergeev took a deep breath. The time had come. "To be brief, it is our belief that crucial matters of state make it desirable for Tatyana Nikitichna Lunina and Andrei Arsenievich Luchnikov to live together as man and wife. Whether they go through with a legal ceremony or not is up to you; all that matters is that they never leave each other's side."

End of monologue. The vacuum it left was almost physical. The oxygen level seemed to have dropped abruptly. Each of those present reacted in his own distracted manner. The head of the division stood up and opened the window, though the street noise would play havoc with his hidden taping devices; Comrade Sergeev gulped down two glasses of soda water one right after the other; Tatyana opened her bag and rummaged through the miniature bottles and boxes, the change, and the keys until she realized she was not looking for anything; the Hub peered into her bag, then took off his tie and wound it round his left fist. . . .

"I have been asked to inform you of the following," said Comrade Sergeev with great effort. "Whatever decision you may come to, it will have no effect on your jobs, your . . . h'm"—here a note of scorn crept into his voice—"your privilege to travel abroad. In other words, you can expect no repercussions of any kind. It is my duty to inform you of all this and to take personal responsibility—" Again he broke off as if overcome by emotion, though an impartial observer could not help noticing that the emotional attacks occurred only after the point that needed making had been made.

Tanya regained her impartiality that evening when she went over all the details in her mind, but at the time she had not noticed a thing, at the time she had focused all her attention on Gleb, whose turn it was now to pace the room. Mesmerized by the tie fluttering behind him, she recalled the day they first met and how he had bowled her over with his strength, youth, and freedom of movement. He was practicing the pole vault; she was working on the curve for the two-hundred-meter dash. She kept running past him, head down, making believe that she did not notice him, that she was completely involved in the curve and the progress her splendid airborne limbs were making, until finally the young giant flung down the pole and began running alongside her, laughing and looking into her face. This was the first time in years she had thought back on that evening in Luzhniki Stadium; it was the first time in years vigorous, victorious young Gleb had peeked through the shell of stodgy, puffy old Hub. At first he had scored less in bed than on the field—either he put his all into the ten events or simply lacked experience—but she had eyes only for him. She herself was still a little wet behind the ears and admired him unabashedly, and when they walked along together, shyly beaming at each other, everybody would stop and say, "Don't they make a nice-looking couple?" What a laugh!

Yes, gallant young Gleb, ready for the foe, born to win, had peeked through, but he pulled back right away, back into the cumbersome, bull-like, everyday, homespun Hub: titanic sex machine, bloated boozer, groveling bureaucrat, totally helpless—and mine, all mine. There he stood in the middle of the room, moving his bovine eyes back and forth between the division head and Comrade Sergeev, not even acknowledging his wife's presence. Then suddenly he opened his fist, dropped the tie, and stalked out, clumsy, sweaty, and breathing heavily.

"I accept," said Tanya to Comrade Sergeev.

The old Stalinist division head narrowed his eyes in scorn. Strategy is strategy, they seemed to say, but a White Guard's bed is no place for a nice Soviet girl.

Sergeev gave a businesslike nod and held out his hand to her. Instead of taking it, she waved her hand in his face. If they're going to cast me as a bitch, I might as well play the part: a cynical, arrogant, brazen hussy, the kind who'll stop at nothing, the perfect agent.

"Congratulations," she said to Sergeev.

"On what?"

"On an operation well begun. Now all you have to do is to deliver Luchnikov, and we're off and running."

"So you don't know his whereabouts?" Sergeev asked cautiously.

"Haven't seen hide nor hair of him for three days. Don't tell me *you* don't know, Sergeev!"

Sergeev smiled his usual we-know-everything smile, but Tatyana saw right through it. "Naughty, naughty," she said, shaking her finger at him. "Slipped up, eh?"

He was close to the cracking point and even glanced tentatively at the telephone. "Don't push me too far, Tatyana," he said in a sharp voice. "You can't expect me to believe you have no idea where your lover is. You meet every day. I can give you a list of the addresses, I can—"

"You can show me the pictures, is that it? What kind of operation are you running anyway, if you lose sight of your object for three whole days?"

"His car has been parked in front of your place for those three days," said Sergeev quickly.

"But he hasn't been near it."

"He hasn't given up his room at the Intourist."

"But he hasn't been near it."

"He's phoned Beklemishev twice."

"From where?" she cried, suddenly hysterical.

So she had cracked first. She jumped up and started flailing out at both of them. By the time they had calmed her down, Sergeev knew for certain she was all his. The big boss poured her a glass of whiskey and started acting paternal. But no sooner was the signature ceremony out of the way than Sergeev began to worry about Luchnikov again. We'll find him, of course; of course we'll find him; we'll ferret him out no matter where he's hiding. But how could the impossible have happened? How could he have vanished, poof, into thin air? And for three whole days!

It was either Volgogradsky Prospect or the Enthusiasts' Highway or Sevastopolsky Boulevard or Profsoyuznaya—one of those broad, many-laned thoroughfares with identical gray blocks of flats stretching along either side, with enormous slogans framed in red, with flowers and bushes arranged to highlight one or another powerful symbol (the hammer, the sickle, the five-pointed star, and, more recently, the rocket—all poorly riveted and welded, but made of the highest-quality metal), and with gigantic faces of Lenin peering out from the most unexpected places—in short, it may have been any number of places that provided the backdrop for three rather inebriated individuals straggling along at four o'clock in the morning.

Luchnikov had his arm around the unprotected shoulders of Lora Lerova, one of the fading nosegays who had adorned the *Courier* brunch. Ten or twelve years ago—the toast of Moscow, star model for the Ministry of Light Industry, mistress of a dozen geniuses; now—Miss Passée. True, she still wore the latest in everything (which now meant floppy, Paris, violet), but the everything no longer came from selfless Moscow geniuses; it came from self-styled musician and artist types, or to be precise, underworld and undercover agents.

Racked with sobs, she leaned all her weight on Luchnikov's chest. She seemed about to collapse: it was the d.t.'s, the beginning of the end. In the old days nothing could daunt her. After a night of sin she would take a douche, freshen her make-up, take a good stretch, and in no time she'd be eager for the fray again. Now she was desperate for something to drink, anything, the most disgusting rotgut. "They've all abandoned me, every last one of them," she wailed, smearing her evening scent all over Luchnikov's unshaven cheeks. "Irka's in Paris. Opened her own boutique. . . . Alka's finally married her Brazilian millionaire. . . . Lenka's got a job at Ted Lapidus in New York. . . . Even Vera's in London, barely eking out a living as a typist, maybe, but happy, devoting her whole life to Lev—Lev, who always loved me more. I'd be the one devoting my life to him, Andrei, if it hadn't been for that damn Serb. . . . Lev, Oskar, Ernst, Yura, Dima—every last one of them, my boys. . . . There's no one to talk to on the phone any more, no one to invite me to Pitsunda, to the south. I just sit at home and stare at the slush. . . . Oh, now and then some punk or other will stop by for a quickie, for a *piston*, but everyone who is anyone has gone, gone, gone. . . ."

Luchnikov kept squeezing her shoulders and mopping her puffy, wet, once-beautiful face with a handkerchief, which he would then roll up in a ball and stick in his jacket pocket. After three days of Moscow low life he had lost so much weight that his jacket hung on him as if on a hanger. He felt great pity for the poor lost Moscow souls he met; he identified with them wholly. He was quite fond of himself as he was now: thin and full of pity.

His friend Vitaly Gangut, on the other hand, looked bloated, round, as if abnormally full of himself. He was apparently less than fond of himself as he was now, and was therefore out to get the world.

The predawn socialist thoroughfare was completely empty. The only sound came from flapping flags—big flags, small flags, medium-sized flags.

"Don't cry, Lora," said Luchnikov. "We'll find you a rich husband, you'll see, an Italian Communist. I'll send you a whole drawerful of the latest fashions."

Gangut was several steps ahead of them—collar up over his neck, fedora down over his ears, his back expressing utter scorn for sufferer and comforter alike.

"Take me away to your Island, Andryusha," she bawled. "I'm so afraid. I'm afraid of America, afraid of France. At least there are Russians on your Island. You have room for a poor little lush on your Island, Andryusha, haven't you? She'll dry out there and stop her whoring. . . ."

"Of course we have, Lora," said Luchnikov comfortingly. "You've been victimized, understand? We've used you, sucked all the beauty out of you. But don't worry, we won't throw you on the dump. We'll—"

"Why don't you ask her how much she sucked out of Vakhtang Charkviani?" said Gangut without turning his head. "Some victim! The genes she's sucked out of our generation!"

"Beast!" screamed Lora.

"Yes, Vitaly is a beast." Luchnikov nodded drunkenly. "He doesn't know the meaning of the word 'pity,' that wanton wizard of the silver screen. But when he's rotting in Hollywood, we'll still have our pity and our Island."

"Not if you give it away to the Comrades, you dirty quisling," grumbled Gangut. "You know what you can do with your fucking Idea. . . ." All at once he stopped and pointed to a group of people queuing up before a closed door. They were all quite elderly, all dressed in black, and all covered with medals and ribbons.

"Well?" asked Luchnikov, ready for another of Gangut's antipatriotic tirades.

"So you love Mother Russia, do you, and you know her inside and out? You're Russian yourself, as Soviet as the rest of us, right?

Well, then, tell me what those people are standing there for, O creator of a Common Fate!"

"For fruit, maybe, or—I don't know—to order a rug. It could be almost anything, there are so many shortages."

"Ha!" Gangut exclaimed triumphantly. "Those people are waiting for the polls to open. They've arrived two hours early to be the first to cast their votes for the only candidates on the ballot: the Bloc of Communists and the Unaffiliated. Today is Election Day, the day we elect representatives to the Supreme Soviet."

Until the arrival of the "foreigners," the pensioners had been conversing quietly among themselves in front of the monumental columns of the Palace of Culture. Now they looked up hostilely at the two degenerates and that shameless creature, the cause of all our woes.

"They all live in my house," said Lora. "Heroes of the First Five-Year Plan."

"What a find!" said Luchnikov. "Perfect interview material."

"And if they turn you in?" asked Gangut.

"Taking risks is part of being a journalist. I took plenty of risks in Vietnam and Lebanon, I can take a few more here."

"I thought we were going up to your place for a drink," said Gangut, sorry he had started it all in the first place.

"If I'm a quisling," said Luchnikov, "you're a coward, a deserter. Go and beg a drink from your fat-cat friends. Go and file your bloody emigration papers. We'll sober up right here at the polls." And putting his arm around the faded nosegay's waist, he helped her to hobble on precarious heels to the vigilant stalwarts of the First Five-Year Plan.

From then on, everything went according to Gangut's scenario. While Luchnikov tried to encourage the early risers to give him an interview, Lora tried to find out whether any of them had a quarter liter of vodka stashed away in a pocket, pledging her diamond ring in exchange. She also kept trying to go down on her knees to show her appreciation for all that surrounded them: the posters, notice boards, wall newspapers, sculptures. Luchnikov tried to learn whether the older generation saw itself more as hangman or victim —but could not stop himself from expounding his own incurable guilt complex vis-à-vis the lacerated populace of the Historical Homeland. Gangut tried to hail a taxi so they could make a run for it when the time came, but could not stop himself from inserting snide remarks about the servile nature of the old-timers' enthusiasm and the absurdity of elections without choice.

The brigade from the Militant Komsomol Voluntary Patrol, summoned by one of the old-time enthusiasts, arrived in plenty of time. The detachment that night happened to consist of the cream of the crop: it was made up entirely of jeans-clad students at the Institute of International Relations, diplomats' offspring. They immediately went through their paces, tying the troublemakers' hands behind them, throwing them into the van, and planting well-developed posterior muscles squarely on their backs.

At the last moment Lora was saved. One of the old women—now an elevator operator, once the first volunteer to go to Komsomolsk on the Amur River in Siberia—claimed her as her niece. In this act of solidarity Luchnikov saw a sign that the spirit of the people was still alive, indomitable. It gave him food for thought all the way to headquarters, even after one of the future diplomats, whom he had managed to zap in the ribs with his Taiwan special, gave him a kick or two in the stomach with the steel-edged heel of his imported shoe.

At Patrol headquarters they sat the two firebrands on chairs in the middle of an office decorated with no more than a portrait of Dzerzhinsky, and tied their hands to the chair backs. The future diplomat with the black-and-blue mark just below his ribs spat in his palm, brought his open hand up to Luchnikov's mouth, and offered him the spittle. Lick it off and you're completely demoralized. Result: leniency. Refuse to lick it off and watch out. Before the handsome, clean-cut, sedulous future diplomat knew what had hit him, he was removed from play by a swift, well-placed kick. After that, his colleagues tied Luchnikov's legs to the chair as well.

Meanwhile, Colonel Sergeev was coming out of his second sleepless night. Needless to say, none of his men—two lieutenant colonels, three majors, and four captains—had had a wink of sleep either. From the moment their main object—the be-all and end-all of their existence, the *reason* for their existence—had disappeared, Colonel Sergeev began looking at them with a different eye. Suddenly they all seemed first-rate shirkers. He kept making the rounds of the three offices allotted them, flinging open doors and expecting to catch the buggers reading Crimean pornography. You had to try pretty hard to lose someone like Luchnikov in Moscow. Pretty hard.

Then he caught himself at the intersection of two suspicious pairs of eyes (belonging to his most trusted assistant and the latest rookie) and realized they had their doubts about him as well: Sergeev's gone soft now that he's back in Moscow.

Not that there wasn't some truth to the matter, he thought in a self-critical vein. After ten years of service abroad I've grown accustomed to capitalism and forgotten what things are like here at home—all the searches and friskings and such. And now, like it or not, I'm back in the rut of making sure I get my special provisions and reestablishing connections for goods not available in shops, tickets to the in theaters, decent books, that kind of thing. . . . I catch myself falling back on the old Russian saw "Work is no wolf; it won't run into the woods." Our job is much too risky for that: one false move and they string you up by your balls.

For the last three days Sergeev's agents had been combing Moscow—visiting all Luchnikov's haunts, tapping phones, installing bugs under cars, tailing any number of individuals—and all in vain. They did make one important discovery, however: the reason the bugs were less than fifty percent efficient was that more than every other one had disappeared into the pockets of the secret lab staff, to be disassembled and resold as replacement parts for foreign audio equipment.

In short, the situation was critical. The head of the division, a full-fledged general, was shaking in his boots and had refrained so far from reporting to his superiors. But now there were intimations of unrest on high, and an aide had even phoned and asked straight out whether everything was okay with object OK. Sergeev had managed to put him off with a detailed account of the successful encounter with Lunina, but after two nights without sleep, after a thermos of vile coffee, after the ritual pinches to get the circulation going and a wave of nausea at the thought of his men's faces and even the faces in the official portraits on the walls, he could feel it in his bones: any minute now the aide would phone again and force him to tell the whole truth—they had bungled it, they had lost him on their own turf, the editor of one of the major newspapers of the world, wavering liberal, fitful ally, history maker, and quite a likable chap, actually.

But things turned out worse than Sergeev had expected, for at the very moment that Luchnikov and Gangut were being untied from their chairs and taken in to the chief of the Komsomol Patrol for questioning, at that very moment he received a call not from any piddling aide but from across the square, from the Big House, from the Big Man himself, Marlen Mikhailovich Kuzenkov, who wished to learn where Andrei Arsenievich might be reached. That evening Kuzenkov was to have a strictly confidential meeting in one of the most secret saunas with a person so important he could not be named. That's it. The End. Fuck off, Comrade Sergeev.

Both of the *agents provocateurs* caught trying to undermine the electoral process were thoroughly searched. One of them was relieved of a pass to the Mosfilm motion picture studios and eleven rubles in Soviet currency, the other of a wallet containing a considerable sum in dollars and tichas, the cards of numerous foreign journalists, and a pocket diary with telephone numbers in Simferopol, New York, Paris, and other foreign cities.

Stunned by the report, the chief of the Voluntary Patrol immediately disappeared, either to consult with a superior or simply to catch his breath. The troublemakers were sitting, arms untied, at a table with a phone on it. A single guard stood watch from the door.

"Give your pal Marlen a call, will you?" said Gangut with a pout. "I'm getting tired of this."

"Well, I wouldn't miss it for the world."

"Look, I've had enough of your fucking games. The next thing you know they'll be hauling us off to the KGB, and where will my plans be then?"

"That's your business."

"I'm growing less fond of you by the minute, you know that, Andrei?"

"Then that's the way it's got to be."

"All right. I'll make my own call." He picked up the receiver.

"Put down that phone!" barked the guard, but his bark turned out worse than his bite: Luchnikov had no trouble arranging for Gangut to put a call through to a certain Dmitry Valentinovich.

The young demigod, the self-assured hero in the imminent space wars for the triumph of socialism, was writhing on the floor in pain and disgrace when the chief came puffing in with the rest of the future Soviet diplomatic corps in tow. "Hands off!" he roared when the youths quite naturally tried to stand up for their Comrade's honor.

Just then the two telephones beneath the portrait of Dzerzhinsky rang simultaneously. In the scramble to answer them a heavy velvet flag fell over with a crash. That crash marked the beginning of what in the current Russian vernacular is referred to as an extraordinary procedure, or EP, in the course of which the fate of our heroes shifted from one scene to the next at a feverish pace. First they were dragged to a dark cell reeking of disinfectant and hurled on the slimy floor, then they were invited next door, seated in comfortable armchairs, and served coffee. Then a twitchy-lipped neurasthenic appeared out of nowhere and started cross-examining them coarsely, only to be replaced by a pleasant, athletic-looking globe-trotter type who offered them Marlboros and went on endlessly about possible routes of the great migration of nations, about papyrus boats and rafts of palm bark, about visitors from other planets. Then the criminology people arrived and took a series of mug shots: full-face, three-quarters, and profile. Then some girls with flowing tresses brought in plates of evil-smelling meat patties and bottles of Czech beer. And all the time they heard music— now patriotic, now light and airy—coming from the depths of the building: the elections to the Supreme Soviet were going on as usual.

Then in walked a hale-and-hearty specimen wearing a leather trench coat. His face was adorned with a droopy moustache and long, pencil-thin sideburns; his eyes were wild but streaked with intelligence. He held out both hands to Gangut and, receiving not one in exchange, put his arm around Gangut's shoulders. "So you see, Vitaly," he intoned unctuously, "our fine feathered friend did the trick. Everything is taken care of, my boy. You're free. Let's go now. Let's go. . . ."

Some savior he's got there, thought Luchnikov.

The savior clearly read his thoughts. "Oleg Stepanov," he said, holding out his hand and looking him over carefully, as if comparing him to a mental standard.

"Andrei Luchnikov."

The savior seemed pleased. He smiled and asked the two ex-firebrands to follow him. The chief hurried along beside them, mumbling apologetically about "a terrible mistake," and "hot-headed youth," and "thickheaded old geezers." He obviously had not quite grasped what was happening.

In the car—there was a black car with an antenna on the roof waiting for them outside the door—Oleg Stepanov subjected Luchnikov to another careful scrutiny and said, "Your name is mellifluous to the Russian ear."

"And what about my name is so mellifluous to the Russian ear, if I may ask?"

Gangut did not attempt to intervene. Beneath his sullen exterior he was ashamed.

"The Luchnikovs are an ancient Russian line and served brilliantly in many wars for the fatherland."

"Including the civil war."

"Including the civil war," said Stepanov with great respect. "How could it be otherwise? They harkened to their country's call. Tell me, are you by any chance related to the Crimean Luchnikovs? I hear they're flourishing down there. One has a seat in the Duma, another owns a newspaper. . . . Please don't think I'm trying to pump you for information. Vitaly will tell you. That's not my style. . . . I'd be proud to be a Luchnikov."

Luchnikov and Gangut exchanged glances.

Stepanov was sitting in the front, but had turned to face them, giving them a close-up of the two large yellow teeth that peeked out from under his mustache with every patronizing smile. A driver with no marked features in a car marked by an antenna on the roof and a telephone. Doing pretty well for themselves are the Slavophiles, thought Gangut. "It so happens," he said out loud, "it so happens Andrei *is* the newspaper owner you mentioned."

The well-trained driver barely twitched, but Oleg Stepanov's whole face lit up. Aladdin could scarcely have beamed more brightly as he entered the cave.

From that point on, the EP grew more and more turbulent. First they went up to the flat where a group of guests was waiting to have brunch with Vitaly Gangut, Russian director. But within a minute or two of their arrival, everything turned topsy-turvy. The scope of the enterprise changed from one minute to the next. The brunch was suddenly in honor of that Crimean celebrity Andrei Luchnikov, creator of the Idea of a Common Fate, an idea much bandied about in Moscow's neonationalist circles. This was history in the making, fellow patriots, this was the real thing, the soft caviar of history. Suddenly the brunch no longer seemed important; it became very much secondary, as did all the guests, including Dmitry Valentinovich—a repulsive-looking character sporting a crocodile, symbol of the all-powerful satirical magazine, in his buttonhole—who minutes before had been considered all-powerful himself and whose stature Oleg Stepanov was now quietly pooh-poohing to the honored guest. Through it all the phone kept ringing urgently, and soon a whole new group of people crowded into the entrance hall. Excited voices boomed louder and louder, until all at once Luchnikov and Gangut found themselves whisked off from brunch to lunch, lunch in the stratosphere.

The lunch was held high above the roofs of old Moscow in a banquet hall decorated with ikons in rich silver settings and Glazunov's ikonlike portraits. The menu included Russian pancakes with caviar, sturgeon pie, suckling pig, and buckwheat groats —more a nineteenth-century merchants' feast than a top-level meeting of twentieth-century communists. There were no more than twenty at table. Only Dmitry Valentinovich and Oleg Stepanov were left from the brunch crowd, and they were clearly no more than tolerated. The others introduced themselves by first name and patronymic: Ivan Ilyich, Ilya Ivanovich, Fyodor Vasilyevich, Vasily Fyodorovich—there was even an Aron Izrailevich and a Fattakh Gainulovich, token representatives of the national minorities.

We provide all our peoples with everything they need, Andrei Arsenievich, said Ilya Ivanovich in a gentle, quiet voice. He was the one who seemed to carry the most weight. He realized that the minorities still lacked a great deal, even after six decades of Soviet rule, but the first to receive what it needs, Andrei Arsenievich, will be the long-suffering Russian majority. That is only just, don't you agree?

All of them were in the prime of life, between fifty and sixty. No mention was made of official ranks or responsibilities, but their manner, appearance, and intonation clearly obviated the need to do so.

Over and over they raised their glasses to loyalty: loyalty to the land, to the people, to the flag; loyalty to duty, to friends. Fyodor Vasilyevich proposed a toast to Russians abroad who have retained their loyalty to history, and they all stood and clinked glasses with Luchnikov.

Only Gangut remained slumped in his seat, playing drunk. Not that anyone cared: What can you expect from an artist type?

Throughout the meal Gangut flashed significant glances at his friend: Let's split while the splitting's good. But Luchnikov had no intention of "splitting." Ace journalist that he was, he was bound to milk the opportunity for all it was worth, and it was worth a great deal: here he had stumbled into the sanctuary of Moscow's Russian Club. Not only that, here was a direct connection with the guiding light of his life. For where would he find support for the Idea of a Common Fate if not with these patriots? And who says they're anti-Semites and chauvinists? Look at Aron Izrailevich. Look at Fattakh Gainulovich. Besides, the notion of the Russians as a sacrificial people dovetailed quite well with the Common Fate ideology, and if I could tactfully bring things out into the open, bring the conversation round to reunification and life in a unified Russia . . .

Meanwhile—unbeknownst to Luchnikov, of course—the EP was moving forward in full swing.

The telephones in Colonel Sergeev's Special Division, which kept track of all foreigners in Moscow, were jumping with EP business. It fact, it was this Special Division that the modest crocodile, Dmitry Valentinovich, had approached and this Special Division that had sent out the car with the antenna and given the chief of the Voluntary Patrol his instructions. And it was here the hurly-burly began in earnest when word came through that one of the two men detained by those Komsomol idiots (and released—let's be honest—by connections, pull pure and simple) was a hotshot foreigner.

What made the whole thing so piquant was that the office that received word about the foreigner never passed it on to Sergeev's office, though they were located on the same floor, in the same corridor—indeed, directly across from each other.

Sergeev's office had spent the entire day racing through Moscow and the environs following the slightest leads and trembling all the while lest Marlen Mikhailovich Kuzenkov phone again, while across the way their colleagues were effectively directing the object of the hunt from brunch to lunch and beyond, keeping track of his every mood, movement, and glance—and number of glasses downed. Apparently it can't be helped. Oversights of this nature are endemic to contemporary administrative structures requiring a high degree of division of labor.

True, for a single moment communication was at least theoretically possible. During lunch break a typist from Sergeev's office happened to sit at the same table as the secretary of the office across the way. They've all gone crackers in our office today, said the typist. They've all gone crackers in *our* office. Do you know where I can find that new washable wallpaper? asked the typist. The two stray lights veered apart.

Evening. Crosses blazing out over Moscow, the crosses of restored churches. Time for a new phase in the EP: the journey into the womb.

"Don't worry, Andrei Arsenievich. We're not going to abandon you. Maybe you've caught a touch of the English reserve down there on your Island, but here in Metropolitan Russia hospitality is alive and well. We keep up our traditions, revitalize them. Where is it we're going, you ask? To the womb!" they answered, winking and chuckling and rubbing their hands. "To the womb! To the womb!"

"You mean you're really going to the womb with this posse?" Gangut whispered to Luchnikov. "What is the womb, anyway?" "It's a State-owned dacha with a Finnish bath run by fat-assed sluts." "Then you bet I'm going, wouldn't miss it for the world. What about you, Vitasya? Your friends have been awfully good to you, after all." "*My* friends? What the fuck have I got in common with that fucking oligarchy! I'm getting the hell out of here. You make me want to puke, you know?"

The Russian director had no trouble slipping away. No one even noticed his absence. They were all quite far gone and completely involved with the miracle millionaire from that Russian pearl, the Island of Crimea.

They set off in a caravan of cars. Luchnikov ended up on the soft cushions of a new Mercedes. After passing through three carefully guarded checkpoints, they came upon a wondrous landscape of rolling green hills lit by the setting sun, crisscrossed by paths of bright-red brick, and dotted by inviting pavilions in the traditional style but with all modern conveniences—including, of course, a Finnish bath. The twilight of the Third Rome: Finnish baths under lock and key.

Disrobed, they were even more friendly, more cordial, not only to their guest but to one another as well. See how well our socialist economy is doing, said one of them, patting another on his jiggling flanks. Have a look at Andrei Arsenievich over there. That's the Western look for you. Not an ounce of fat. They keep in shape. They're blue bloods, after all, and we're just your run-of-the-mill peasants. Our ancestors filled up on bread and kvass, while the Luchnikovs—what do you think? How many generations of Luchnikovs have dined on the finest cuts of meat?

"Tell me," said Luchnikov, "where's Aron Izrailevich?"

By now all the Ilya Ivanoviches, Vasily Fyodoroviches, and Dmitry Valentinoviches had turned a rosy pink in the dry Finnish steam. Their pores were open, their chests heaved freely, their eyes glistened.

From the steam room they moved directly to the pool, from the pool to a row of tables spread with Russian generosity. Each session in the steam room revived their appetite, rewhetted their thirst, and even provoked some interest in the nimble waitresses in their short terry-cloth robes.

"Tell me," said Luchnikov, "where is Fattakh Gainulovich?"

What's your favorite sport, Andrei Arsenievich? they asked him. Whatever happens to turn up. His lascivious eyes could not help following the comings and going of the nimble waitresses. I can take them or leave them. Ha! Ha! Ha! He can take them or leave them. Yes, we can see that. Hey, Lyuda, come over and meet our guest. He can take you or leave you. Really, Vasily Spiridonovich! You've got a one-track mind! By the way, you'll notice our guest has a cross round his neck. They've spent so much energy on their economy down there they've had to let philosophy slide.

Luchnikov was observing his hosts as carefully as they were observing him. They represented real power, he could see that. They were at least a cut above the middle level and might well go much higher. By maintaining both an affable exterior and a low profile (they were all impressed with how little he spoke), he tried to catch scraps of the conversations they held among themselves as they sat there full of their own importance, yet aware of the gray fluff of their exposed genitals. The main topic of those conversations, it turned out, was levels: he's at the same level as Mikhail Alexeevich; no, he's more at Felix Filimonovich's level; perhaps, but that kind of issue is decided at a much higher level, at the level of, say, Kiril Kireevich. . . .

Climbing out of the pool, he had a chance to see them at a remove. From that perspective they reminded him of something, but he could not quite put his finger on it. Eight men with towels carelessly draped over them sitting at a long, artificially roughed table of expensive wood, one leisurely pouring his friends some Gordon's gin, another pouring himself a Tuborg, a third winding a slice of smoked salmon onto his fork, a fourth giving Lyuda's terried behind a hug as she sat down a tray of tropical fruit, and all taking part in a slow and easy conversation, which, as soon as "our dear guest" walked into earshot, came to an abrupt end. No, not Roman senators. Why, of course! The Mafia! That's it. Chicago, the roaring twenties, a Hollywood B-movie, the *nouveau riche* combination of ferocity and flab, the sense of power usurped . . .

"Where is Aron Izrailevich?"

On the way back to the steam room Oleg Stepanov came up to him. Beyond all doubt this was the first time the enormous stallion of a man had been in such exalted society. He was slightly shy, slightly uneasy, like a boy first admitted to the company of men; he seemed embarrassed by his size, stooped a bit, and kept his loins covered with a towel; but oh, how happy he was, how happy! His eyes, otherwise gloomy and shifty, shone with joy, servility, and a kind of inspiration. This was his big chance, and who did he owe it to? Gangut! Yes, thanks to that pitiful souse of a Gangut, here he was hobnobbing with the cream of Russian aristocracy and chiefs of the Party, the army, the leading trade organizations. Today he was just a rank-and-file member of the national movement, but tomorrow . . .

"I know why you keep asking about Aron Izrailevich and Fattakh Gainulovich," he said. "You wonder whether non-Russians are allowed in here. You have the reflexes of a Western journalist, Luchnikov. You'll have to do something about that if you want to be one of us." At first he seemed to be having a private chat, a chat with Luchnikov and Luchnikov alone, but his voice grew louder as they came closer to the steam room, and a few of the less talkative members of the group turned and looked his way. When Stepanov dropped his towel before going in, Luchnikov was surprised to see his long, thin penis not quite at attention, but definitely not at ease.

They all took their places in the miniature amphitheater of finely polished wooden tiers, and the image of the Roman senate came back to Luchnikov. Again they began the process of sweating out the old wastes to make room for the new, the ones they intended to acquire momentarily. Didn't Lucullus have a vomitorium for his guests so they could return to the table many times over?

"We are no primitive chauvinists," said Oleg Stepanov, his voice increasing in volume even more. "All we want is to set a limit to Jewish influence in the country. The country is ours, after all; we are the masters here. But Jews stick together; they look out for one another and exclude the rest. Take my case, for example. Three times I was refused my university degree, and why? Because I'm Russian. I would never have made it through if I hadn't picked up some friends along the way. No one will touch the Jews once they learn their place. We are the masters here, and we have granted them proletarian asylum. . . ."

"What was that again?" asked Luchnikov. " 'Proletarian asylum'?"

"That's right. That's what I meant to say. Don't think our ideology will die out with the rebirth of the national spirit. Are you interested in the transformation that the Russian historical triad is currently undergoing?"

"I am."

Gradually the levels talks faded away, and Oleg Stepanov's

voice rang out. He had slipped down off the bench and was facing the amphitheater in all his gangling majesty, half man, half horse —much like Orwell's horse, in fact, but with eyes shining at the thought of his incredible stroke of luck. "Orthodoxy, autocracy, and nationality! The historical Russian triad lives on, but transformed, transformed to incorporate our one and only future— communism!"

"Who is this fellow?" asked a man behind Luchnikov in a lazy voice.

Someone quickly whispered something in his ear.

"Quite a speech he's making," came the reply, not quite laudatory, not quite portentous.

Oleg Stepanov unquestionably heard these remarks, but, undaunted, brushed his dark Mayakovsky-like locks from his eyes and went on, determined not to muff the opportunity. He would do anything rather than leave the baths unnoticed. "Christianity is a Jewish invention, and Orthodoxy—a particularly clever ruse concocted by the wise men of Zion to confound the Russian giant. But when the time came, the turning point in history, our people readily cast off the Christian myths and reverted to their own primordial wisdom—the ideology of the commune, the ideology of communism!

"Autocracy, all things being equal, is the ideal form of power, but given a number of unfortunate marriages and births, its Russian element was much diluted towards the end. Our last ruler had no more than one sixty-fourth Russian blood. So in its infinite wisdom our people combined ideology and power, faith and a strong hand, and astounded the whole world with a new form of power: the soviet! And here we have it, the Russian triad of our times: communism, Soviet power, and nationality! Only nationality remains untouched, for nationality is our blood, our spirit, our strength, our mystery!"

"Will you look at that!" said the lazy voice in back of Luchnikov. "It's about to take off with him! Look at it go! Didn't know you had it in you, Stepanov!"

In the first flush of inspiration Stepanov himself had not noticed his penis rising, and now with a gasp he tried to cover it with his hands. But the erection was so powerful that the little red head on the end kept peeping out triumphantly through his fingers.

The Finnish bath rocked with laughter. Quite a cudgel he's got on him for a theorist! Quick, quick, Stepanov! Lyuda will take care of it! Don't be silly! He hasn't got it up for Lyuda; he's got it up for the triad! He's really something, that Stepanov! You're really something, Stepanov!

The "theorist" looked up at the laughing faces, mortified, until finally it got through to him: the laughter was friendly, he had made a lasting impression on them, he was one of them! And he, too, began to laugh, laugh and shake his head, laugh, shake his head, and gallop about holding on to his mischievous organ for dear life.

In the midst of it all the door to the steam room opened and a newcomer appeared, a strong, athletic figure of a man.

The laughter died down.

"Just who we needed," muttered someone under his breath. "Aron Izrailevich."

Luchnikov looked up to find his friend Marlen Mikhailovich Kuzenkov. There was a snicker behind him. He quickly turned and glanced over at the lot of them, but they were all smiling pleasantly at their colleague. Evidently he was tolerated among them, but not quite at home.

His eyes trained on the top bench, Marlen Mikhailovich approached sheepishly, shrugging his shoulders and smiling a guilty smile. Something was clearly bothering him. Even more embarrassed by the lack of response, he dropped his eyes and saw—Luchnikov!

"Andrei!" he cried out, flabbergasted. "I can't believe it. How is it possible? You here? Magic. It must be magic. There's no other explanation. A *deus ex machina*. What a surprise."

"What's the surprise?" asked Luchnikov with a smile.

Not until they had left the steam room and were paddling in the pool did Marlen tell Andrei the story of the three-day EP: how the "appropriate governmental organs" had lost track of him, how they'd looked all over Moscow for him, how he'd given them hell over the phone that very afternoon, yes, he used their services, too. You've got to be realistic, Andrei, a person of your caliber can't help attracting the attention of the appropriate governmental organs, and when you disappeared without a sign, without a call, I had to request their assistance, remember we had unfinished business to attend to, and besides, we're friends, aren't we? I phoned Tatyana, I phoned the *Courier* office, I even phoned Dim Shebeko, nobody knew where you were—it's all somehow related to you and Tatyana, isn't it?—so I phoned the appropriate governmental organs, you know today was the day you were supposed to have an appointment with an extremely important person, you were the one who brought up the Masonic lodge, after all, so I arranged clearance for you, and you disappear, well, let me tell you, our seniority system knows no greater breach of etiquette, which is why I had no choice but to go to the appropriate governmental organs, and then it turned out they didn't know where you were either, isn't that something? I don't imagine they know where you are now, that you're here swimming in this pool with me, ha! ha! ha! what a farce!

"And I thought every chair in this country was directly connected with the appropriate governmental organs," said Luchnikov. "I was certain this pool flowed directly into the appropriate governmental organs."

"Andrei in Wonderland," said Marlen Mikhailovich, raising his arms helplessly and sinking a foot or two into the transparent, green, potassium-enriched water.

"So I've missed my chance to meet your panjandrum?"

"Unfortunately for me, you *have* met him." He went down again. "Unfortunately for me, because I was not in control. The fact that you made it here on your own steam today will have wide-ranging ramifications. . . ."

"You mean the panjandrum . . ."

"Of course he's in there!"

Luchnikov climbed out of the pool. Marlen scrambled up after him.

"Look, Marlen, I haven't changed my shirt in three days. Could you lend me one? I have . . . I have . . . well, a reception to go to at the British embassy, and there's no time for me to stop at the hotel."

"Yes, of course." Kuzenkov looked deep into his eyes.

"One more thing." He put his hand on the shoulder of the man who had just called himself his friend. "Would you drive me back to town? I've completely lost my sense of direction."

Kuzenkov looked even deeper into his eyes.

The door to the steam room opened, and out stepped Oleg Stepanov, girding his loins with a towel. At the other end of the pool in the shade of the sheltering potted palms three waitresses were nimbly resetting the tables. On the other side of the glass wall in the shade of real fir trees a gaggle of secret service men were idling, waiting for action. Oleg Stepanov stood stock still, his face distorted by a grimace of perfect bliss.

"All right, Andrei, let's go," Kuzenkov said peremptorily.

It was hard to tell whether the original team was still on the job or Sergeev's men had taken over, but Kuzenkov's Volga was skillfully tailed all the way back to Moscow, and at a tactical distance. Now and then Kuzenkov glanced up at the rear-view mirror and frowned. Far from trying to hide his dissatisfaction from Luchnikov, he played it up, as if trying to show him how distasteful he found the whole thing.

"Your itinerary has been almost entirely approved, Andrei," said Kuzenkov as they drove along, "but don't count on going it alone. Foreigners of your stature simply must have an interpreter along. I'll do my best to have them give you a decent fellow. . . ." He looked over at Luchnikov apprehensively, but found him nodding amiably. Luchnikov willing to have an interpreter? What is going on? "I might even request a decent girl," he added with a smile. "It's up to you. By the way, how are things between you and Tanya?"

"Oh, nothing special," mumbled Luchnikov. "It's just that her husband—"

"A real case, isn't he?" Kuzenkov quickly inserted.

"No, perfectly normal. He's just . . . how shall I put it . . . well, he's a touch psychotic when it comes to his wife. . . ."

"Are you disappointed in her?" asked Marlen.

"Not in the slightest. I don't know whether she needs me. That's the problem."

"Would you like me to have a talk with her? Or Vera? Yes, Vera's the one. They're very close."

"Maybe the appropriate governmental organs will have a talk with her," Luchnikov suggested innocently.

Kuzenkov practically choked with indignation. "Really, Andrei, there are times when you make me furious! You and your Orwell!

You talk like a complete outsider! Don't forget the strides we've made since Stalin. Don't forget what it's cost us, people like me, like you . . . And don't forget the Idea!"

"Forgive me, Marlen." Luchnikov did in fact feel pangs of conscience. He knew that by asking Kuzenkov to aid and abet him in his getaway he was asking him to violate Mafia ethics. In other words, Kuzenkov was taking a big risk. "We need to have a heart-to-heart talk one of these days, Marlen. No holds barred and no joking allowed. There's a great deal riding on it, more than just our friendship."

Kuzenkov looked over at him gratefully.

"As for the bathhouse episode," Luchnikov went on, "I'm actually quite glad I missed the chance to meet the grand panjandrum formally. If he surrounds himself with the types I saw today, I don't want to have anything to do with him. They're not my style, you know? Not my style at all."

Kuzenkov looked over at him again and smiled.

"Stop the car, will you, Marlen? As soon as you see a taxi stand."

They were driving along Kutuzovsky Prospect. The Volga tailing them kept the same distance as before, which posed no problem, since at that time of day there was almost no traffic apart from taxis and an occasional diplomat.

The moment Kuzenkov slammed on the brakes and Luchnikov jumped out he experienced it again, that fleeting rush of youth. It was a combination of the scarlet light breaking through the clouds beyond the spire of the Hotel Ukraina and the excitement he always felt when a new adventure, no matter how petty, was in store.

The second Volga flew past, then screeched to a dazed halt on the bridge over the Moscow River as Kuzenkov flew past it. Luchnikov jumped into a taxi and gave the driver Tatyana's address.

When the taxi passed the tail car, its three occupants feigned indifference. The taxi crossed the bridge and took advantage of a green light to zoom past the Comecon Building. The light changed immediately, however, and Luchnikov saw the cross traffic begin to pick up speed. All at once he spied the Volga emerging on two wheels from behind an enormous Intourist bus, breaking every rule in the book. From then on it was completely on top of things, making all the lights and keeping the sputtering little taxi well in sight.

When the time came to pay the driver, Luchnikov realized he had not a kopek in Soviet currency. "Senk you, senk you," said the driver, thrilled with the ten-dollar bill.

Luchnikov walked inside and pressed the elevator button. He made no attempt to hurry. The door of the main entrance remained open. He could see most of the courtyard—closed in by high walls—reflected in its glass, and had no trouble following the black Volga as it reconnoitered the terrain for a favorable lookout point. Creeping along the asphalt past a playground, it came to rest opposite the entrance. The driver switched on his lights and—immediately catching Luchnikov in them—switched them off again.

Just then a bread van drove into the courtyard and, stopping at the rear entrance to the bakery on the ground floor, hemmed the Volga in between some bushes and the playground. Luchnikov could not believe his luck. Without thinking twice, he raced across the playground to the van. The ignition key was safe in his pocket by the time the agents piled out of the Volga.

The van's long-haired driver stood by dumfounded as the vigilantes and Fancy Dan played out a classic cops-and-robbers scene before his very eyes. First Fancy Dan scooted into the archway leading out to the street and ducked out of sight. Then two of the vigilantes, setting new hurdling records, raced across the playground and ducked out of sight. Then the Volga raced across the playground, mowing down an elephant and the swings and finally coming a cropper between the merry-go-round and the wall bars. Then the bread man ran into the archway to watch Fancy Dan get caught—who could escape the pros?—and to reclaim his key—why the hell did he make off with it, anyway?

But here the plot took an unexpected turn: Fancy Dan turned out to have a Zhiguli (number plate TUR-00-77) waiting for him, and he jumped in and sailed past the vigilantes with a wave and a smile, slowing down just long enough to throw the bread man back his key and shout "Thanks, pal!"

Immediately the vigilantes grabbed the long-haired bread man by the shirt and dragged him back into the courtyard. Get that fucking tub out of here! Blocking a black Volga! Now a dangerous criminal is on the loose, and it's all your fault! The bread man was understandably indignant. Just watch what you call a tub, okay? That "tub" is full of bread, the staff of life, our country's greatest treasure. They gave him a quick rabbit punch, grabbed the key, ran to the van themselves, and plunged through the archway with it, overturning a news kiosk as they went. By the time the Volga was ready to go, the Zhiguli was nowhere to be seen. Oh, well, said one of them, he won't get far. But are we going to get it, said another, and right in the balls. How about some of that staff of life? said the third. Why not? said the bread man, handing them three warm rolls. You'll need all the strength you can get when you show up empty-handed.

Luchnikov parked the Zhiguli in the Old Arbat section of town, slipped on the reversible raglan waiting for him in the back seat, and, feeling better than he had in days, set off through the back streets that always evoked in him a deceptive sense of the normalcy, sanity, sagacity of Russian life.

On the corner of Sivtsev-Vrazhek and Starokonyushenny (what could be more normal than Sivtsev-Vrazhek and Starokonyushenny?) stood an old building in whose courtyard stood an older building in whose courtyard—in other words, twice removed from the street—stood a dilapidated six-story remnant of the Silver Age. And on the top floor lived a musician, one Dim Shebeko by name, in a flat endearingly known as the "communal refuge," comfuge for short.

It was two in the morning, the rest of the building was asleep, but the comfuge was alive with voices and laughter. The story of its metamorphosis into the lair of Moscow rock was a curious one. Long ago little Dmitry Shebeko and his mother occupied two rooms in the large communal flat with its feuds, squabbles, and kitchen altercations. By the time he had grown into Dim Shebeko, his friends in the various rooms that made up the flat had also grown into rock musicians or at least rock fanatics, and they all got together and decided to get rid of the deadwood (the older generation). After a highly complex system of exchanges, personally engineered by Dim Shebeko himself, they proclaimed the

"Free Territory of the Arbat." The local authorities, though deeply chagrined, were powerless to stop them: the paperwork was impeccable and completely aboveboard.

The comfuge door was always open, but Luchnikov found it impossible to make headway inside: the entrance hall was jammed with equipment, backpacks, and suitcases—C_2H_5OH was obviously about to go on the road—and band members were dragging more and more from their rooms. Luchnikov could make out a shiny pair of Premier drums and three Gibson guitars. They'd done well for themselves this past year! "Where's Dim Shebeko?" he asked a girl he had never seen before. She was wearing a T-shirt with DIRTY BUT HONEST on it.

"He's in there." She moved her head in the direction of a brightly lit door. "Drinking tea."

Dim Shebeko was more than the musical leader of the group; he was its spiritual leader, its guru. He was sitting at the head of a table drinking Uzbek tea from a large, handleless mug. Everyone else in the room was drinking tea as well. The irony of the situation lay in the fact that although the group bore the name of the ethyl alcohol molecule, it had recently gone "dry" on principle. The idea was Dim Shebeko's: no highs outside the music itself.

Many of the musicians knew Luchnikov. For several years now he had brought in all the important latest releases plus full runs of *Downbeat*. Soon the whole band had dropped its preparations and crowded around the table. To the new members he was introduced simply as Looch, "the Ray" in Russian, or—as Dim liked to call him—a ray of light in the kingdom of darkness.

"We're going off on a gig, Looch," said Dim Shebeko not without a touch of pride.

"Where to?" asked Luchnikov.

"Kovrov. A motorcycle factory. Oh, it's nothing special, but they pay good money and provide transportation. And they're dying to hear jazz rock. Hicksville, USSR, and they're dying to hear jazz rock."

"Will you take me with you? I have to go underground for a while. It's the KGB."

"What do you say, guys?" asked Dim Shebeko.

"Sure! Welcome aboard!" they all cried, beaming. "We'll hide you!"

"What do they want from you?" asked Dim Shebeko.

"Nothing in particular," Luchnikov answered, shrugging his shoulders. "They won't let me alone, have to be in on every little thing. All I want is to take a private jaunt across my own country."

"Looch is a real Russian," Dim Shebeko explained to the new members. "He's the editor of a Russian paper in Simfi."

"Far out!" they said, wide-eyed. "Hey, like, we hear the whole Island's far out. That true?"

"To a certain extent." He was about to plunge mentally into all the problems he had left behind when a beautiful sweet young thing came up and kissed him on the lips. "And what does that mean?" asked Luchnikov.

"Yes, what's that supposed to mean, Galka?" asked Dim Shebeko, raising his eyebrows.

"It's a sign of national solidarity," she explained with an inscrutable smile.

"Do you really think you can get away from the KGB?" asked a boy with a leather band around his forehead.

"You've got to be kidding." Dim Shebeko laughed. "Ask Ben-Ivan what he thinks. How many times have you crossed into the West, Ben-Ivan?"

Everyone turned to look at the short, dark, and hairy trombonist perched on the edge of the table and nibbling at a piece of black bread. "Twice," he said quietly. "Twice so far. I may try again this autumn."

"You don't really mean that," said Luchnikov.

"Sure I do. I've got some Hungarian smuggler friends. We slip back and forth across the Carpathians all the time. They've taken me along to Munich as a reward."

Benjamin Ivanov was born in 1952 at the height of the campaign against "rootless cosmopolitans." Strange parents he had: their response was to give their son a Biblical name in its English form.

Ben-Ivan went on to explain quite self-effacingly that crossing the border was difficult but not impossible. His Hungarian friends had gone to Munich on business, but he had gone along for the ride. When the band came back, he was thinking of going to Stockholm. A Swedish friend had offered to fly a Cessna into Karelia. . . .

"But what about the radar!" said Luchnikov.

"It's always on the blink. Sure they could shoot us down—nothing's foolproof. But the Swede's done it three or four times: dissidents. All you need is the guts to take a few risks and"—by now he had almost effaced himself completely into his army shirt—"and a little experience with the occult."

"The occult?" said Luchnikov. "I must have heard wrong."

Ben-Ivan shrugged his shoulders, and everyone stood up. The time had come to drag the equipment down to the gigantic Ikarus bus sent by the motorcycle factory. It was parked downstairs near the Canadian embassy.

"Everybody here?" asked Dim Shebeko. "Brass section? Give Looch a little breathing space, Galka, will you? Okay! We're on our way!"

The narrow strip of asphalt lit up by the Ikarus's powerful headlights was lined with woods and an occasional mammoth long-distance hauler waiting out the night.

Luchnikov and Dim Shebeko sat in the back talking. Everyone else was sprawled out asleep.

"I've been meaning to ask you," said Luchnikov. "You didn't happen to meet my son last year, did you? Anton."

Dim Shebeko gave himself a slap on the forehead. "And I've been meaning to ask you how Antoshka's getting along!"

"So you did meet!"

"Spent two whole weeks together. Did he have a high time here!"

"Then why did he call Moscow 'barfsville'?"

"Simple. That's what we call it."

"Now I see." Luchnikov laughed.

"He played his sax with us. I gave him a few pointers. He's got a natural feel for it."

"Your pointers came in handy." Luchnikov told Dim Shebeko about the Paris street musicians and the Châtelet metro station where his friend had earned a living wage thanks to his Moscow lessons.

"How great it must be!" whispered Dim Shebeko, smiling like a child at the thought of the Paris he had never seen. "How great it must be out in the real world, and how shitty it is here. . . ." He paused for a second, then shook his head. "Still, I'll never leave. Some American jazzmen heard me play a while back. Guaranteed me all kinds of gigs over there. But I won't go, and I tell the guys in the band not to."

"Why?" asked Luchnikov.

"Because Russia needs Russians playing here in Russia," he said with great conviction. "You know who I wish would get the hell out of Russia?"

"Who?"

"All those filthy informers, that's who." He smiled bitterly.

"Tell me, who do you think does the informing for the band?"

"We have no informers!"

"But that's impossible!"

"Impossible?"

"Absolutely. Twenty people working together without an informer? I'll bet there's more than one."

Dim Shebeko put his hand over his eyes and thought awhile. "You're right, Looch." When he took his hand from his eyes, he looked dazed. "It's impossible. A collective of twenty without an informer—impossible. It makes me sick just to think of it. I wonder who it is."

"What about the guy who's been to Munich? What's his name? Ben-Ivan."

"Ben? You must be off your gourd! Though why not?"

"Or Galya. Galya of the sweet and easy kiss."

"Galka? We sleep together sometimes. She's completely open in sex."

"That's just the kind they use." Was he pushing the cruel game too far? he wondered.

"Gerka, Vitya, Izva, Askar, Nina . . ." Dim whispered, running through his closest friends. "Of course. They go after the ones you expect the least. Now that I think of it, they tried to recruit me once. It was at the Bomb Shelter—you know the bar in Stoleshnikov Lane? From what I hear they've got a special division for hippies and rock and jazz musicians there. With hippie colonels and everything. They closed down a commune last month in Leningrad on Krestovsky Island. I wonder how many informers they had working on that job. Who would have suspected it? It's not like my dad, after all."

"So you consider Marlen an informer?"

"If he's not, then who is? Vera Pavlovna, too. International informers of the highest order. Tell me, what about you? Are you one, Looch?"

Luchnikov laughed. "In this crazy country of yours, I mean, of ours, a person can't help wondering sooner or later, Am I an informer or not? How can I be an informer if informers are informing on me? Though maybe in some indirect way I am."

"You know what's just occurred to me, Looch?" Dim Shebeko had held up his hand to his mouth and was whispering into Luchnikov's ear. "Maybe in some indirect way every Soviet citizen is an informer. We all do and say things they don't like, and they always find out about them. . . ."

"Which makes you one, too, Dim Shebeko."

"Indirectly, yes, right," he said, still whispering, still shocked by his discovery. "Take our band. The music we play is anti-Soviet, and foreigners flock to hear it, so in a sense we're, like, pulling the wool over their eyes, making them think how groovy and free everything is here. Or, like, in Kovrov, the place we're going to, we get these motorcycle guys all hepped up, they start shooting their mouths off about something, and the next thing you know they're in deep trouble. Yes, there's no two ways about it: every man, woman, and child in Russia today is a direct or indirect informer!"

"Now you're going a bit too far, don't you think?" said Luchnikov, alarmed by Dim's triumphant tone. "Look, I owe you an apology, Dim Shebeko. I planted that idea in your head on purpose. I needed a control to test my own thoughts on the matter, and I used you. Forgive me."

"What do you mean!" said Dim Shebeko, brushing off Luchnikov's apologies. "It's true! We *are* all informers! Every last one of us!" Suddenly he broke off, thought for a minute, and said in a scarcely audible whisper, "No, there's one exception."

"Who?" asked Luchnikov, putting his hand on Dim Shebeko's shoulder.

"My mother. My mother is no informer, direct or indirect."

The lights of a village flashed by. A drunk was walking his moped along a lighted shop front that said GENERAL STORES. Then the bus plunged back into the woods.

"Can you fork up a hundred rubles?" asked Luchnikov. "I'll give you the *Izvestia* rate of exchange."

"I don't need your damn dollars," muttered Dim Shebeko. "I can make you a gift of any amount—two hundred, three hundred. We're rolling in dough, Looch. They just keep peeling it off. Talk about irony! We play what they hate: they pay us a fortune. Crazy, eh? We go off in the other direction; they run after us and stuff bread in our pockets. What do we do now, Looch? Tell me. Where do we go from here?"

Luchnikov took a package of ten-ruble notes from Dim Shebeko and asked him to stop the bus. They reeled their way up front.

"Got to take a leak?" asked the driver. His radio was playing softly: Pugachova, a top-notch pop singer.

One of the musicians raised his head when the bus stopped. Hey, are we there?

"Where do we go from here, Looch?" asked Dim Shebeko in a voice that sounded drunk.

"The only place you can go—farther into your music, deeper. I envy you, Dim Shebeko. I've always envied musicians. Musicians always have a place to escape to. Go deep enough and they won't catch you."

"You think so? Really? And where are *you* going?"

Luchnikov felt drunk himself. Dead drunk. Even after the bus door opened and let in the damp, dark Russian air, he felt they were both drunk, two old soaks exchanging muddled confessions at the tavern gate. "I'm just going to follow my nose. I'd follow my eyes, Dim Shebeko, but I seem to be going a little blind here in my Historical Homeland. Well, I'm off." And, parodying Lenin's classic stance, he raised his right arm into the darkness. "The loneliness of the long-distance runner. Good-by!"

He jumped down. The bus pulled off immediately. Relieving himself into a ditch, he watched it go. The oversized suitcase of a bus was ridiculously out of place on the narrow road with its cracked edges and primitive asphalt patches, yet it immediately scooted off, and within seconds its back lights disappeared and utter silence settled in.

Though damp, the Russian air proved a good deal less than dark: it was full moon. The road had a silver tinge to it, and the winding river below was bright silver. To one side was a steep hill covered with grain and, in the distance, a village with the ruins of a church.

After walking for a while, he detected a small campfire up ahead. Several figures flickered in the flames. Coming closer, he saw three men wearing coarse-cotton caps with celluloid peaks, open shirts, and track-suit trousers so baggy that even their protuberant behinds could not begin to fill them. They were trying to push some sort of vehicle out of the ditch, and a very fat young woman, her flower-print dress tucked way up, was laying branches under the wheels. "Hey there, Comrade!" she called out, the first of them to notice Luchnikov.

He walked up to them and saw a van that seemed to have collapsed into the ditch. The windows were shattered, the roof badly beaten in. "Just what we needed," said one of the men. "We're one man short. Give us a hand, will you, pal?"

The second he stepped off the road his shoes weighed a ton: they had instantly filled with wet clay. All five of them heaved to. For a time the wheels would only spin, then suddenly they caught, and the van began to move. They all let out a cheer. "Just what I fucking said," panted the man next to Luchnikov. "One more fucking guy would fucking do the trick."

"A few words with you and I'll need a chaser!" said Luchnikov with a smile.

"You've had a nip or two yourself, pal. High-quality stuff, too. Am I right or am I right?"

"You guessed it." Luchnikov nodded.

The van was up on the road by now. The man pointed to the roof and said, "Bloody idiot! Hauling pipes at night in a fucking trailer. Didn't even bother to tie them down, the cocksucker. Suddenly I see one of them fucking pipes sticking out in my lane, and before I know it—bam!"

"At least we're alive, thank God!" the woman squealed, crossing herself and pulling her dress down over her stomach.

"Thanks be to God," said Luchnikov, going down on his knees and making a large, slow cross.

VII

OK

For several years now, Yalta's beach-front Lieutenant Bailey-Land Square had been closed to traffic and turned into a gigantic, world-famous outdoor café. Every inch of space from the stylish old Oreanda to the angular glass-and-steel Yalta Hilton was covered with white wrought-iron tables and brightly colored canvas umbrellas. Five gigantic plane trees spread their ever-fluttering shade over tables and tiles, over swift-footed young waiters, the stripped-down international holiday set, and the local "cadres" (as they liked to call themselves, Soviet-style), that is, the breathtaking sun-and-sand-bred Yalta girls. Stripped down was not the term for them; they were purely and simply naked—the pastel gauze over their nipples and pubes turned the most daring bikini into a nun's habit.

"The sexual revolution has put an end to prostitution." Arseny Nikolaevich Luchnikov was enjoying a chat with his old friend Fred Baxter, a New York banker. "Who would have expected it? Look at the new generation—these girls, for example. They bowl me over each time I come down here to Yalta. So fresh and vital. Well brought up, but ready for a good time. They talk about sex as if it were nothing more than a dance. My grandson tells me you can go up to any of them and say, 'May I have the next *piston.*' '*Piston*' is this season's Soviet slang. By the way, they go up to men, too. Remember 'ladies' choice' at the *thés dansants* of our youth?"

Baxter chuckled, disappearing, wrinkles and all, under his Panama hat. "But old farts like you and me, Arsy, we couldn't even get a jitterbug out of them."

"I still prefer the tango," said Arseny Nikolaevich with a twinkle in his eye.

"But you do tango." Baxter replied in kind.

"Rarely. All too rarely."

"So you get your kicks at the stables."

"You know, Bax? I'm beginning to think you're a sexual counterrevolutionary."

"And proud of it. I'm an all-around counterrevolutionary, and if I take it into my addled pate to do a little dancing, I pay hard cash on the line. Though I must admit, my expenses in that area have been nosediving year by year, inflation notwithstanding."

The two tall elderly gentlemen—one in his usual faded jeans, the other in the latest Parisian designer overalls—found a table in the shade of the trees and ordered the local specialty, water from the nearby waterfall of Uchan-Su.

The sun had almost completed its daily arc above the daily carnival of Yalta. It was nearing the dark-blue side of the mountains and Yalta's glistening climatic screens at their crest.

"What do they put in this water?" asked Baxter. "What makes it so lively?"

"Not a thing. It's completely natural."

"This place bugs the hell out of me," mumbled Baxter. "Every time I come to visit you, I catch myself falling for all the old advertising gimmicks, the 'Yalta miracle' crap. It's hypnotic. I really do feel younger. Say, is it true that the Oreanda is the setting for that Chekhov story? You know the one I mean. 'The Lady with the Dog.' That's it. What kind of dog did she have—a Pekingese?"

"Don't tell me you've started reading Chekhov in your old age!"

"Everybody's reading Russian literature nowadays," grumbled Baxter. "And the only thing anybody talks about any more is the goddamn Russian question. You'd think everything else was just hunky-dory: oil, the ayatollah, gold . . ." Suddenly he pulled his glasses out of their case, set them on his fleshy nose, and peered through them at a woman sitting several tables away. "There she is," he said. "Look, Arsy, the prototype of Chekhov's lady! Minus the Pekingese, of course."

Unlike the tactless banker, Arseny Nikolaevich refrained from sticking out his neck and gawking; he waited a few moments and then turned as if by chance. What he saw was a pleasant-looking young woman sporting a beautiful mane of hair and wearing a tasteful, loose-fitting sand-colored dress. She was sitting alone and immobile in front of a martini. If she seemed vaguely familiar to him, it was not because she matched his perception of Chekhov's heroine. "So that's how Russian literature gets twisted in the brains of American financial wizards. No dog in the world, not even a Newfoundland, would turn that woman into what Chekhov had in mind. My guess is she's a French film actress. In the past few years the Island has become one large studio."

"Well, I'm going to ask her for a dance, and you see if she doesn't dance with me, no matter who she is. I'm prepared to pay what it takes."

"What if she's richer than you?" asked Arseny Nikolaevich.

The very idea gave Baxter the best laugh he had had in ages. But soon they had forgotten about the "lady without a dog" and were on to French women in general, particularly in 1944, when they liberated Paris from the Nazis and made close friends with a number of liberated Parisiennes. No doubt about it: 1944 was the best year for Frenchwomen.

Be that as it may, the woman sitting alone at the table was not French at all; nor was she an actress; and if Baxter had known the actual state of her finances, he never would have laughed. For Tanya Lunina—and she was the lady in question—though the recipient (compliments of Comrade Sergeev) of the highest Soviet per diem, was scarcely able to make ends meet, so expensive was life in Yalta. She had taken the cheapest inside room at the Vasilyevsky Island Hotel and found a nearby Italian restaurant of the same category, but even if the room was nice and clean and air-conditioned, with carpets on the floor and aromatic blue water in the pink toilet bowl, even if the food at the restaurant could not be had in Moscow for love or money, still . . . all she had to do was to walk three blocks in the direction of the sea and she was in a world where people took luxury so much for granted that money ceased to exist. It made a brilliant comeback, of course, in the form of shopwindow prices along Tatar Quay, but that did not help Tatyana.

Just for the fun of it she had wondered on her own what it would be like to turn a trick with a dreamboat of a capitalist, but each time the thought entered her evil little head she would laugh it off by asking herself, And who would have me, with that surplus of pretty young things all over Bailey-Land Square? So all she could do was sit out the cocktail hour under the trees in a Simone Signoret pose, then take a stroll along Tatar Quay, glancing nonchalantly at the shopwindows, and then—again nonchalantly, like a tourist curious about a quaint back street—turn up the alleyway leading to the Vasilyevsky Island and dial Andrei's three numbers, only to receive the same answer every time: "Mr. Luchnikov is out of town. I'm sorry, Madame, but we have no information as to his whereabouts." She had run up an enormous telephone bill, and she was planning to throw all caution to the winds and stop in during the next day or two at the local office of Filmexport USSR—in other words, of Comrade Sergeev's colleagues—and present them with it. What do they take me for, anyway? I'm holding up my end of the bargain, and I expect you to do the same. As it is, I've gained a good five pounds on that pasta of yours, and there's no steak in sight. You bastards, you! You self-seeking, penny-pinching bastards!

Tanya had been vouchsafed the *ne plus ultra* of trust—a trip to Yalta on her own. All Soviet itineraries—for tourists, teams, or the multifarious delegations—gave Yalta a wide berth: the temptations of so cosmopolitan a haunt struck the Soviet authorities as too much for the rank-and-file to bear; for some reason, they considered Simferopol and its concentration of ultramodern architecture, fashionable Feodosia, skyscrapers of Sevastopol's multinational corporations, the sumptuous villas of Yevpatoria and Gurzuf, the minarets and baths of Bakhchisarai, the Yaki's sprawling suburbs of *nouveau riche* ranch houses, and the steel lacework of the freeways less likely to undermine ideological determination, less dangerous than ever-dancing, never-slumbering, multilingual Yalta, *the* hangout of the international film and literary "in" crowd. According to the wise men of Agitprop, the very atmosphere of

Yalta would exercise a corrosive influence on such sacred Soviet concepts as "the State borders," "the hammer-and-sickle passport," "vigilance," and "patriotic duty," causing the Soviet people to lose "a sense of their own worth, of their superiority over the bourgeoisie" and succumb to anarchic dreams of epicurean self-indulgence. In fact, these were but idle fantasies of the typical Agitprop mind; there was nothing particularly dangerous in Yalta for the all-conquering ideas of socialism. But since the Island of Crimea did not officially exist, it had been a constant thorn in Agitprop's side from the civil war (when the invincible Red Army suffered crushing defeat) to the flourishing present. Agitprop would have been much happier if the Island did not actually exist, but alas, somewhere beyond the scope of Agitprop, beyond its sphere of influence, the Island most definitely did exist and therefore provoked occasional vague reflections and plans. And since it was an official from that sphere beyond the scope of Agitprop who hatched the unquestionably attractive idea of developing contacts at the *present* stage of history, like it or not the Agitprop mind had to set to work and justify contacts with the Island. In protest, in a kind of Agitprop backlash, the Agitprop mind declared Yalta ideologically taboo.

To be sure, the cream of the bureaucracy and its offspring as well as the most deserving artists still came to Yalta for a good time, and now Tanya Lunina had been deemed worthy. Sending her on her way, Sergeev hinted broadly that the all-seeing eye would be following her every step, but considering that Luchnikov had given the slip to an entire office created in his name, she had reason to doubt its infallibility. Yes, now even those dizzy heights had their freeloaders, she thought as she sat there watching two elderly yet trim Englishmen sitting nearby (one of them looked familiar—an actor, probably), the climatic screens and their tantalizing, miragelike silhouette up on the crest of the Yalta range, the naked girls popping out of the sea and splashing everyone in their path as they raced back to their drinks, the handsome wandering Yaki waiters who treated their job of serving the swarming crowds like a baseball game, the wandering musicians and magicians, the bobbing masts of Turkish, Greek, Italian, Israeli, and Crimean boats, two white cruise ships, ocean-going yachts nosing in to shore, a pair of glass-bottomed helicopters with the inevitable

IT'S THE REAL THING sign in Coca-Cola script adapted to Cyrillic and to the mixed Yaki alphabet, and all the signs beginning to glow above the roofs of the second, skyscraper line of Yalta— watching all this and sipping her dry martini, which she would have tossed down long ago had she been in Moscow. For sipping away at her per diem helped her to forget about the all-seeing eye and Comrade Sergeev and the damn telephone bills.

If the truth be known, she had been to Yalta before, in secret, on one of the days when Andrei abducted her from the pension in Laspi where the team was staying. They had sped here in his crazy Peter Turbo, had dinner on the revolving roof of the Nevsky Prospect, and spent the night in the bridal suite there. She recalled how stunned she had been by Yalta at daybreak. Coming out of the hotel, she saw the nearby café in the tiny square filled with people of different shapes and colors, a girl in a pointed hat playing her flute almost inaudibly, and a few couples left over from the night before (and the past) whirling in a waltz on the terrace of the White Warrior's League restaurant. The mecca of world anarchism, eccentricity, and sin. Naughty Yalta.

As she learned from her talks with Sergeev, Tanya had underestimated her informers. All the romantic flights in the Peter Turbo had duly shown up in Comrade Sergeev's files. The same held for Andrei's quick *"piston"* trips to Paris, Tokyo, and San Diego. Without exerting the slightest bit of pressure, Comrade Sergeev had made it clear to her that the reason no action had been taken on the reports, the reason they had ended up in his files was that he had certain designs on her, designs of a professional nature: he had long had his eye on her as a creative partner.

Tanya realized the drunk scene with the Hub had meant a turning point in her relationship with Andrei. There was a time when he would fly thousands of miles for one little *pistonchik,* and now he had vanished, vanished in Russia, in Moscow, vanished from the face of the earth. What had happened to him? Surely he didn't attach any importance to the little tussle they'd had. He used to be so forgiving. His Moscow hooligan, he called her lovingly. And now he was angry with her. So I had a little more than I could hold. Who doesn't every now and then? And what makes him so high and mighty after all the girls who've passed through his hairy paws?

Only once after the incident did he phone her in Moscow. The connection was terrible. She hardly recognized his voice. Where are you? she asked—and froze. It was the most natural question in the world, yet in her new capacity it took on a new and shameful connotation: she was spying on him. In Ryazan, said Andrei. You know, Solzhenitsyn's birthplace. Whose birthplace? she asked, not catching the name. Solzhenitsyn's! Andrei repeated. Whose, whose? This time she did catch it, but it made no impression on her. Solzhenitsyn had completely gone out of her head after his exile, though he probably had not spent much time there before. It was a rather idiotic conversation. The Hub sat right there at the kitchen table, trying to look as though his mind was elsewhere or blank or completely taken up by the tiny portion of yogurt he was eating: after the dramatic incident in the First Division he had taken it into his head to go on a diet. I'm in Ryazan, and I'm going first to Kazan and then to Berezan. The connection was so bad she found it hard to gauge his mood, though he sounded chipper enough. When will I see you again? asked Tatyana. I'm running out of coins, shouted Andrei. When will I see you? Not for some time, I'm afraid, she pieced together. Cut the games, Andrei, she shouted. Come back, come back now. Forget Kazan, forget Berezan! I want to see you! I miss you! I need you! What? I'm running out of coins! Good-by! When are you leaving? Not for some time. I'm going back to the Island. When are you leaving? Not for some time. I'm running out of— Even though she knew they had been cut off, she went on about how she missed him. She made it clear she meant it in the physical sense. She did it to get through to the Hub, who since the Sergeev deal had refused to touch her. When she finally hung up and turned to look at him, she found him two open doors away with a raincoat over his shoulder and an Adidas bag in his right hand. Where are you going? she asked his back in a disgusted drawl. To Tsakhkadzor, it replied. And that was the end of the Hub.

The news of the idiotic telephone call distressed and angered Sergeev. Professional that he was, he was able to hide the distress, but the anger came bursting out. What a stupid, irresponsible way to act! Who does he think he's playing cat and mouse with? Doesn't he realize his every step . . . Tanya looked Sergeev straight in the face and smiled. Maybe he doesn't realize you know his every step. Maybe he hasn't guessed yet. He's terribly naïve, you know. I'll bet he's convinced he's shaken you, Comrade Sergeev. You know how they are in the West, always underestimating our governmental organs.

Now that she was alone, she spent more time with the children, got them ready for Pioneer Camp. She tried not to think about either of the men in her life and even managed to put Sergeev and Co. out of her mind.

And suddenly there was Sergeev knocking on her door all in a stew with a spanking new foreign passport, a letter of introduction from the Committee of Soviet Women, and a packet of White rubles that at the time seemed quite impressive. You leave immediately. For where? Wait till you hear: Yalta! Who's going with me? You're going alone. We trust you implicitly. What do you want me to do there? Spy on someone? I don't know how. I'd get myself thrown in jail! How can you even think such a thing, Tatyana? You know your duty, your simple, sacred duty. All you have to do is to be with Luchnikov, with your beloved. But why can't I meet him here first? He's here, isn't he? That's no concern of yours. Again the anger burst through. Your only concern now is to fly to Yalta, take a room at the Vasilyevsky Island, and phone Andrei Arsenievich daily at the *Courier,* at his penthouse, and at his father's estate, Kakhovka. The minute you make contact, let us know. But why can't I . . . Look, Sergeev broke in rudely, do you want to go to Yalta or don't you? Of course I do, and down deep she was rejoicing like a schoolgirl: Yalta, all alone, beautiful clothes, all expenses paid! Hurrah! And what was the upshot of it all, Madame? Loneliness and rage. Damn Andrei for disappearing as if she'd never existed!

Suddenly two red-white-and-blue vans, alarm lights swirling, sped across the embankment to the trees. Policemen wearing white helmets with transparent shields and carrying long white clubs piled out and formed two ranks. Though the Crimeans used the pre-Revolutionary word for policeman (which called up in Tanya's mind the paunchy, fat-headed boors in illustrations of nineteenth-century literature), the force itself was absolutely up-to-date.

The police vans were followed immediately by an open Land-Rover with the omnipresent press. Rows of telephoto lenses focused first on the police formation, then on the embankment, where the crowd had begun to act strangely. A few of the photographers hopped down from the Land-Rover and spread out through the tables in the square, clicking as they went. One of them happened on the two sprightly old gentlemen sitting not far from Tanya and began shooting them from all angles without so much as a please or a thank you until the one in jeans put on a pair of dark glasses and the other one pulled his Panama, flamboyant ribbon and all, over his eyes. Meanwhile, all service had come to a halt. The waiters assembled on a band platform and unfurled a bright-green flag with an outline of the Island and the word "YAKI" embroidered on it. They shouted a slogan and sang a song, both of which were incomprehensible but spirited. Three or four started playing trumpets, and the rest clapped and danced in accompaniment. The naked girls crowded up to the platform and applauded wildly.

Next came the silver vans of TVMig ("Up-to-the-Minute TV," the local on-the-spot news program) with their winged-eye emblems. The policemen, shields down, moved forward in slow formation. The crowd on Tatar Quay was now in utter chaos. Suddenly three explosions went off in quick succession. A column of burning gasoline swirled up into the evening sky.

Tanya climbed up on her chair and leaned against the edge of the umbrella. What she saw was a rough-and-tumble free-for-all with three distinguishable groups: boys in T-shirts patterned after the flag unfurled by the waiters, boys in T-shirts with a hammer and sickle emblazoned on the front, and boys in the oddest of raiments—kimonos or Circassian tunics—with wolf tails on the back. They all took the fight quite seriously, swinging baseball bats, hurling Molotov cocktails. . . .

"What's going on?" asked Baxter.

"The third generation of Islanders is going through an identity crisis," said Arseny Nikolaevich with a smile. "As far as I can make out, a Yaki rally is being broken up by elements of the extreme right and the extreme left, the Young Lupine Hordes versus the Red Front. As you can see, our waiters to a man back the Yakis. They *are* Yakis. But my grandson has also turned Yaki activist recently. More likely than not, he's in the thick of it right now, fighting for the idea of the new nation."

"Just what we needed to add a little spice to the evening," said Baxter. "I'm enjoying my stay here more and more."

"The only trouble is, they're turning into a pack of animals."

"So's everybody else. They're fighting in London, they're fighting in Paris." Following the example of the Frenchwoman, he clambered up on his chair and looked on, shading his eyes with his hand. "Things seem to be quieting down," he said after a while. "A couple of cars are in flames, a few windows broken. I see some laughing faces. The cops are pushing the kids back to the beach. Now they're all going in for a swim! Good for them!" He climbed down from the chair and headed for the Frenchwoman. Arseny Nikolaevich could not believe his eyes. Baxter was almost his age, and here he was going up to an elegant, sophisticated young lady and taking her by the elbow. Just like that! He'd always thought these Americans rather boorish. Taking her elbow as if she were a whore. Will he be surprised at her reaction! Will I have a good laugh!

Tanya jumped down from the chair to find the fashionably dressed elderly man from the nearby table towering over her—red furrowed face and spud nose. They sat down. Tanya raised her brows. The man took out an alligator-covered pad, then a gold Montblanc fountain pen, scribbled something fast and, smiling paternally, pushed it over to Tanya.

What she saw was a dollar squiggle, a one, three zeros, and a question mark. She looked up at his face. Baby-blue eyes.

"Ça va?" asked the old man.

"Ça ne va pas," said Tanya, and reaching out for the Montblanc, she crossed out the one and traced a thick three over it.

"Ça va!" shouted the dirty old man triumphantly.

She outlined the zeros a few more times (to make them as important as the three) and stood up.

"Which do you prefer," he asked, "the Oreanda"—he pointed in the direction of the hotel—"or the yacht?"—he pointed in the direction of the port.

"Your own yacht?" asked Tanya. She looked absolutely calm, her English was holding up well, she brushed the hair out of her eyes serenely, she was the Grand Duchess of Sex. But beneath the surface everything was aflutter: Well, well, Tanya old girl, I didn't know you had it in you.

Baxter assured her it was his own yacht, completely private, he'd sailed from one end of the Mediterranean to the other in it, it was a highly comfortable floating residence. He mimed to Arseny Nikolaevich that he would phone him later, took the beautiful Frenchwoman by the arm, and led her down to the port through the rubble left by the recent skirmish—bits and pieces of slogans and T-shirts, baseball bats and jagged bottles.

Arseny Nikolaevich looked after them with a feeling of vexation, even bitterness. Considering all he'd been through, he certainly should have been able to give up his idealized view of women by now, but here he was, vexed and bitter, and repulsed, yes, even slightly repulsed. How could a woman with such a fine face be so cheap as to go off on the spot with an old man she'd never seen before? Would she really do dirty old Bax's bidding? She didn't look like a professional. . . .

So deep was his disillusionment that he left enough to pay for the Uchan-Su, walked across the square to his old open Rolls, and drove to Artek, where the Nesselrodes' Friday at home would be in full swing.

I'll create a sensation, I suppose, he thought morosely as he crawled down the far right lane out of the sunset and into the dark-blue abyss, at the foot of the Ayu-Daga, where even at this early hour the lights of one of the oldest enclaves of the Island aristocracy were burning brightly. Luchnikov senior at a Nesselrode Friday! He had long since shunned provacuee salons with their claims to carry on the traditions of the Russian *haut monde*. For two or three decades he had scorned all the Wednesdays, Thursdays, and Fridays. Life on the Island had changed radically, yet the closed circle of provacuees clung to the style and spirit of Russia's "silver age." After a while they stopped inviting him, but his standoffish attitude still rankled in their minds: Luchnikov is so taken with the rest of the world he looks down on his own kind. It was actually quite a feat to resist turning cosmopolitan in the cosmopolitan atmosphere of the Island, and the mastodons, as Andrei called them, had to work hard to keep the spirit of old Russia alive from generation to generation.

Old Nesselrode, a monarchist representative to the Provisional Duma and co-owner of Savash Munitions, was a typical mastodon in this respect, and recently he had taken to pestering Luchnikov senior with invitations again. "I say, Arseny Nikolaevich, you've sulked long enough. You really must come round to one of our Fridays in Artek. Lidochka, our Lidochka, has brought in a marvelous group of young people, and your son is—well, he's their idol. Can't say I approve of his ideas, won't do the provisionally evacuated army any good, but one doesn't want to fall behind the times, does one?" Even now the mastodons refused to speak of "our country" or "our Island," preferring "our provisionally evacuated Russian army" and "our base of evacuation."

Whenever these invitations came up, Arseny Nikolaevich would mumble something noncommittal. If for no other reason than that the Nesselrode girl was rumored to have set her sights on Andrei, he had no intention of visiting the family.

Yet here he was, wending his melancholy way to Artek in protest against the contemporary code of ethics that allowed a cynical old moneybags to buy up an elegant lady with a few scratches of the pen. Vulgar. Disgusting. As fictive, as false as the Nesselrodes' salon was, it still stood for the Old World. . . .

The first thing Arseny Nikolaevich noticed in the Nesselrode living room was Madame Nesselrode playing the traditional Rachmaninoff études. Rachmaninoff had stayed with the Nesselrodes whenever he came to Crimea, and legend had it he enjoyed listening to Madame play his works and intersperse them with her memories and dreams. Now all the chairs were occupied by provacuee relics in uniform and mufti. He looked next door where the middle generation—the financiers and their ladies—was playing bridge, and out on the veranda where the young crowd stood chatting, cocktail-style, with drinks in hand and hors d'oeuvres within reach, the first sign of real life.

Although Arseny Nikolaevich's entrance did create a sensation, it was less of a sensation than he had expected. Mikhail Mikhailovich, elegant as ever in his dinner jacket, opened his arms to embrace him, and Varvara Alexandrovna stopped playing and offered him her exquisitely manicured hand for a kiss; but both looked slightly unsettled.

It turned out that beneath the calm of it all the Nesselrodes' Friday had been shaken in the most unforeseen manner: Kostya, their youngest son, had just come back from Yalta badly beaten and in tatters. And what tatters, too! Why, they're simply barbaric

—blue jeans and a cheap shirt with the insignia of those impossible Yakis!

In other words, Kostya took part in the free-for-all on the embankment. Yes, he did. Isn't it awful, Arseny Nikolaevich? Dragging a child from a good family into their street battles! But you couldn't have chosen a better day to come and visit us. And why is that, Varvara Alexandrovna? Surely you don't suspect me of— Not you, *cher* Arseny Nikolaevich, but unfortunately your grandson Anton—whom we all just adore, I assure you—was the one who lured our little Kostya into that uncivilized Yaki nationalist movement and dragged him along to the embankment debacle today. Street fighting, you understand, will not further the diplomatic career we envision for him. But more important, the boys were in mortal danger: the Lupine Hordes were involved!

"And the Red Guard hooligans," added Mikhail Mikhailovich with a frown, "both pro-Soviet and pro-Chinese. Why, every rabble-rousing element was present and accounted for, all except the Young Turks, who got there too late, I hear. In any case, I've spoken to Colonel Mamontov of OSVAG, and on Monday I shall bring up the issue in the Duma. These are but the buds of the Idea of a Common Fate; the fruits are still to come. Of course, SOS kept a low profile; in fact, it wasn't anywhere to be seen. But mark my words, SOS is at the bottom of all the political intrigue here on our Isl— I mean, in the Provisional Evacuation Zone."

"SOS?" said Arseny Nikolaevich uncomprehendingly.

"You mean your son hasn't told you about the new party he's founded?" asked a dandified provacuee type wearing a monocle, trying to sound nonchalant, and obviously an OSVAG man. OSVAG, the Island's Intelligence Agency, went back to Volunteer Army days, and all agents were provacuees in good standing.

"I haven't seen my son for several weeks," said Arseny Nikolaevich, "but he's due in tonight."

"From Moscow, I presume?" V. A. Vostokov was all smiles.

"From Stockholm, actually," Arseny Nikolaevich replied coolly and went out on the veranda. When first surveying the scene, he had noticed his own stretched-out, bony, slightly hunched body and longish nose there in the person of his much-loved grandson; now he watched him holding forth, the center of attention, waving his arms in excitement, playing the general to Kostya's wounded private with a pat on the back, and leaning picturesquely against the railing, highball in hand. Lidochka Nesselrode and her guests, all draped in Greek tunics (the theme for this Friday, it would seem), were watching and listening as raptly as Arseny Nikolaevich.

"*Yaki!*" shouted Anton, suddenly noticing his grandfather. "*Granati kaming, kabakhet,* surprise! *Sigim-sa-fuck!*" The tunicked guests repeated the wonderful Yaki expletive *sigim-sa-fuck* with great glee.

Arseny Nikolaevich put his arm around his grandson's shoulders and looked him up and down. He had a black eye, a bruised cheek, and a rip in his Yaki-flag T-shirt. Kostya Nesselrode, the hero of the hour, looked a good deal worse: his T-shirt was in shreds, his bandage wet with pus, his jaw swollen. But he wore a warrior's brave smile.

"Did we give it to them, Grandpa!" shouted Anton, switching to Russian. "The Reds and the Blacks—both falling like flies! What a bunch of sissies! You should have seen us! Yakis are real men. We fish for a living or pump gas. Some of us have even worked as mercenaries. Did we give it to them! You can see for yourself. TVMig should be on now."

On came the theme of the Island's most popular program. Its goal was twofold: to transmit live all important events on the Island and then to repeat them, cleaned up and edited, as docudramas.

Everyone had turned to the brilliant large screen in the corner of the veranda. Three sprightly commentators—speaking Russian, English, and Tatar, respectively—were telling the story of the skirmish on the Yalta embankment two hours before, freely cutting one another off and grinning from ear to ear the whole time. Suddenly a shot of Anton shinnying up a pillar flashed on the screen. "Who is this well-connected young man?" asked one of the commentators caustically. The next shot panned the white tables of the square to land on Arseny Nikolaevich and Fred Baxter sipping Uchan-Su. "Duma Representative Arseny Luchnikov might have seen what his energetic grandson was up to if he could have torn himself away from his Uchan-Su" (close-up plugging the drink) "and his friend American financier Fred Baxter, who is again honoring our shores with a visit." The bastards, they even included the Frenchwoman with her charming little derrière sticking out! Then a close-up of Baxter, his eyes shining. "Looks like his stocks are on the rise, wouldn't you say?" "The bastards," Anton cried out. "Not a word about what we stand for. The usual off-color clowning, that's all."

The next shots were highly effective. The Lupine Hordes on the attack, mouths wide open, sabers waving in the air. The sabers aren't sharp enough to kill anyone, but they could do a good job of maiming an enemy for life! The Red Guards on the attack. Racing frenzied through the crowd, leaping from hotel balconies. The Molotov cocktail is making a comeback! The camera pans the scuffle, zooming in on photogenic details. "What violence!" all three commentators exclaim at once.

"Look, there I am, there I am!" shouted Kostya Nesselrode, though he scarcely had anything to shout about: a Red guardsman had shoved him to a wall and was beating and kicking him with all his might. Next Anton came on again, handing out his father's Taiwan special and receiving a blunted saber blow across his cheek in exchange. And then Arseny Nikolaevich, putting on his dark glasses and Fred Baxter pulling his flamboyantly ribboned Panama over his eyes. "Please stop bothering us," said the Russian commentator sarcastically. "We're just out for a spot of Uchan-Su." Another quick plug. The police ranks, closing in like Roman cohorts from every side. Streams of water, tear gas. Flight. The abandoned embankment strewn with weapons, smoking cars, and broken windowpanes. The three commentators at their round table. They look at one another with ambiguous smiles. "Who came out on top? Who's the winner? As the Soviets say in these circumstances, 'The winner is . . . friendship!' "

The final shot was of the winding road down to Artek with Arseny Nikolaevich in the old open Rolls slowly taking one curve after the next. "Is that what Arseny Nikolaevich Luchnikov thinks about today's event? Oh, and by the way, Arseny Nikolaevich, where has your *Courier* editor son been keeping himself? Not you-know-where again?"

And on that note the program came to an end.

I will never come down to this bedlam again, thought Arseny Nikolaevich. I will stay up on my mountain and take pot shots at reporters.

"Who do they think they are, the bastards!" shouted Anton.

"Sneering at people, smearing people's private lives! Wait till we Yakis go after them! They won't know what hit them, that band of pseudointellectuals! Tearing our people apart for the sake of a few cheap smiles!"

"They won't know what hit them," Kostya Nesselrode exclaimed weakly but full of enthusiasm.

"Well, I'm for SOS," said Lidochka Nesselrode firmly and full of enthusiasm. She was standing at one end of the veranda against a background of the dark sea, her tunic catching the breeze and modeling the fine lines of her hips. Her light-brown hair streamed out behind her.

The rest of the Greeks left the television set with the cheap smiles Anton had in mind; they were quite impressed by the band of pseudointellectuals on TV. Now they turned their attention to the spectacle of Lidochka trying to ingratiate herself with son Antosha and father Arseny. A group of adolescent boys screaming their lungs out for a new nation was ridiculous but conceivable; a thirty-year-old provacuee socialite with a past making up her mind to snare the editor of the *Courier* and falling for the romantic Common Fate line—well, my dear, that was ridiculous and inconceivable! Imagine what would happen to poor Lidochka Nesselrode if her dream came true and she woke up one morning to find herself Lidochka Luchnikova. How would she fit in? Papa Nesselrode is a dyed-in-the-wool monarchist, and Lidochka worships him: he sired her, after all. Mama Nesselrode is for constitutional monarchy, and Lidochka is her spitting image. Her new father-in-law is one of the pillars of democracy as we know it on the Island and a staunch constitutional democrat. Her new husband is the creator of the Idea of a Common Fate and favors the Sovietization of Crimea. Her new stepson, as you can see with your own eyes, is a citizen of Yakiland. Poor Lidochka, how hopeful her face, how romantic her fluttering pose against the Pontus Euxinus! She seems to picture our monarch in the role of General Secretary of the Central Committee of the Communist Party of the Soviet Union, a Politburo approving a constitution proposed to it by the People's Freedom Party and a Yaki Autonomous People's Republic safe within the crimson womb of Mother Russia. . . .

Arseny Nikolaevich was called to the telephone. "Hello, Arsy," came the voice of the old reprobate through the receiver. "Looks like we don't have to be put out to pasture yet, the two of us."

"Congratulations," said Arseny Nikolaevich curtly, "but your prowess has nothing to do with me."

Baxter laughed awkwardly. "That isn't what I meant, Arsy old pal. I meant the goddamn mass media. Those sons of bitches are crazier here than in the goddamn States! Now the whole island knows you're at the Nesselrodes, and it'll soon know everything there is to know about my yacht. Some bastard on the pier has been busy taking pictures since we got here. What do they want from a pair of old has-beens, anyway?"

"Is that what you phoned to tell me?"

"Pipe down, old pal, pipe down! You'd think she was yours, the way you're reacting. She's a free agent, her own woman. I haven't stepped on anybody's toes. I'm sorry, Arsy, but I've been the perfect gentleman."

"Look, I'm sick of the whole thing." Arseny Nikolaevich purposely avoided referring by name to the party at the other end of the line because Vadim Vostokov was hovering not far off and listening in. "I'm going back to my mountain as soon as I fetch Andrei from the airport. Come up for a breath of fresh air if you feel like it." He paused. "Bring along anyone you please."

"I don't know if I told you, Arsy, but I'm flying to Moscow tonight. What do you say we meet at Aero-Simfi for an hour or so? There's something important I want to talk to you about. Is the Imperial Bar all right?"

Luchnikov senior hung up and went back to the veranda. He asked his grandson whether he wanted to go to the airport with him and unexpectedly received a positive, even enthusiastic response. Where's the old *atats* flying in from? Arseny Nikolaevich shrugged his shoulders. I thought he was in Moscow, but he's on a flight from Stockholm. You never know with Dad, said Anton. I wouldn't be surprised if he dropped down on us from outer space. Arseny Nikolaevich was glad to hear Anton talk so warmly about his father. He does love him after all. The only time he's hostile is when he comes back from Italy and his still embittered mother, now the Contessa Malcovanti, but in a few days he's over it, back to his good old self.

"May I come along?" asked Lidochka Nesselrode with pleading eyes. "I do so love the airport atmosphere. I feel I've been cooped up here in Crimea forever. And then it's so inspiring. I'm a bit of a poet, you know."

"A bit of a poet?" Anton looked amazed. "Tell me, Lidochka, what other secrets are you keeping from us? Are all those things people say about you true?"

"Quiet, you horrid little beast!" she cried, waving her fist at him. Then, glancing over at Arseny Nikolaevich, she added, "I'm old enough to be your mother."

In the end they had to take her along, tunic and all. They put her in the back seat and sat up front together, Anton behind the wheel.

All the way to the airport Anton babbled on about his new ideology, as if trying to convert his grandfather in the time allotted. Sixty percent of the population now considers itself Yaki. You old provacuees are totally divorced from modern life; you don't know what people think, what they want. Today's youth is morally obliged to foster Yaki national consciousness. The Russian element on the Island has had its day; the Tatar element is ancient history; as for the British influence—well, the less said the better. We can't leave the future to ghosts. We need new blood.

Arseny Nikolaevich agreed with the general tenor of his grandson's remarks, but felt them premature. A nation takes time to develop, a few generations at the very least. The Yakis have no culture of their own. They even lack a language.

Anton objected.

Not that jumble of mangled Russian, Tatar, and English with assorted Romance and Hellenic roots!

A Yaki grammar is in the works, and Yaki dictionaries and newspapers will follow. A television channel, too. There are interesting Yaki writers even now. Under a Yaki pseudonym, Ton Looch, I myself have dabbled a bit in . . .

"If your movement is to have any impact at all, it's got to tone down its demands. Its prime function should be educational and not—"

"If we tone down our demands, we'll lose our race against time." All at once Anton lowered his voice. "Maybe you're right, Granddad," he said thoughtfully. "Maybe we were born too early.

But if we hold off any longer, it will all be over in a flash. Either the Union of All Unions will swallow us up or we'll succumb to fascism, so when you come down to it . . ." He stopped there.

For the first time Arseny Nikolaevich took his grandson seriously. He realized he had been underestimating him. The boy had grown up, he was no longer a child.

Lidochka Nesselrode did not take part in male talk. She was all female, a self-styled romantic, and spent the ride leaning back in the soft leather seat gazing up at the stars, moon, and clouds.

Aero-Simfi lay to the north of the capital just beyond the mountains. It was an entire city in itself with microgroups of large and small brilliantly lit structures, a complex system of roads, sprawling parking lots, and, presiding over it all, a gigantic incandescent mushroom of a control tower.

Aero-Simfi's administration prided itself on running "the airport no one wants to leave." The passenger strolling on comfortable, springy carpeting through its endless lounges, corridors, and gift shops, its elegant boutiques and intimate all-night bars, lulled by barely audible yet pleasing music, aware of precisely articulated yet unobtrusive announcements preceded by a soft, velvet-on-velvet gong—the passenger feels he is in the safe and caring hands of today's humanistic civilization, and tends to forget why it was he so needed to fly away to the slushy nightmare that is Moscow or the city of eternal strikes—where his bags were likely to be thrown out into the street—Paris. Nor is there any real need to leave: our hypothetical passenger can live a full life here for weeks on end watching takeoffs and landings, sampling the wide variety of ethnic cuisines, chatting with high-spirited tourists, sleeping soundly in soundproof and fragrantly air-conditioned grand hotels—going nowhere, but enjoying all the excitement of travel.

The Imperial Bar was empty except for Fred Baxter and his lady friend.

"Tina," the reprobate said ceremoniously to his moll, "this is my old buddy Arsy. Arsy, I want you to meet Mademoiselle Tina from Finland. How's your Finnish, Arsy? Too bad. Anyway, Mademoiselle Tina understands English, German, some Russian, and even a teensy-weensy bit of French, n'est-ce pas?"

Tina (none other than Tanya, of course) gave her hand to Arseny Nikolaevich with an open, placid, and—or so it seemed to the elderly nobleman—somewhat contemptuous smile. They were sitting in a semicircular booth upholstered in morocco and illuminated by an old-fashioned lamp with a tasseled shade.

"I'd like to have a few words with you before my flight." Baxter looked disheartened and tired. "Perhaps Mademoiselle Tina would enjoy a chat with the young people at the bar."

"Yes, how would you like a drink?" said Anton, taking a lady on either arm. The handsome, slightly graying bartender (a walking advertisement for "Have a Smirnoff—it will take your breath away!") was glad for the company. Naturally he was—or considered himself—a Yaki, and Anton's battle-scarred T-shirt made him more than professionally attentive to their wishes. He turned on the television set behind the bar and switched from channel to channel until he came to a repeat of TVMig. Anton provided his own heated commentary while trying to fill Tina in on the movement with pidgin phrases in her various languages. An appeal to Lidochka for help went unheeded. She was off in a world of her own: the airport at night, a dimly lit, half-deserted bar, a young woman of noble blood awaiting the arrival of her noble husband-to-be, the convergence of two aristocratic souls in a world of plebeian passions.

Tanya pretended to understand almost none of the Russian—and almost all of the English. As usual in Crimea, the conversation went back and forth between the two with a liberal admixture of Tatar, Italian, and words of uncertain provenance.

"It's all so complicated, sir," said the bartender. "Take my case. My *atats* was a pure-blooded Cossack, my *anima* part Greek, part British. I married a Tatar girl, and our daughter has just married a Serb who is one-quarter Italian. A real cocktail of nationalities we've got here on the Island, sir."

"A cocktail we call Yaki," said Anton.

"That's it! A Yaki cocktail! I'll patent it!"

"And what do I get for the idea?" asked Anton, laughing.

"Yaki cocktails on the house whenever you like, sir!" replied the bartender with a grin.

"Are you here as a tourist, dear?" Lidochka asked Tanya. "*Ja? Wunderbar!* I am waiting for my fiancé. He is coming back after a long journey. *Nicht verstehen?* Damn, how do you say 'fiancé' in German, anyway?"

Meanwhile, the two men were having a serious conversation under the tasseled lamp. "Our days are numbered, Arsy, What do you say we get smashed? Just like in the good old days, okay?"

"I got drunk in the good old days, Bax. You're the one who got smashed."

"Well, maybe I did spend quite a bit on booze," said a sadder but wiser Baxter. "Booze and babes both. You're going to laugh, Arsy, but I'm in love again. Remember how you laughed at me in France? Every time I forked out a hundred francs for a whore I'd fall in love with her. But this is my last chance, Arsy. I . . . I'm like putty in her hands. . . . She's a miracle, Arsy, believe me. I've never had a woman like her before. She's so . . . sweet, so . . ."

"Shut up!" His face wrinkled up in disgust. "I have no desire to hear the confessions of a doddering idiot."

"I understand," said Baxter, laying his big boxer's paw, now splotched with old age, on Arseny Nikolaevich's well-groomed hand.

Thank God I've been spared that pigmentation problem, Arseny Nikolaevich caught himself thinking.

"Do you have any idea how few of the old gang are still alive?" asked Baxter.

Arseny Nikolaevich shrugged his shoulders. "I do my best not to think about it, Bax. As long as I'm up there on my mountain, they're all still alive for me."

"What I wouldn't give to live up there on your mountain," said Baxter. "With you and all the old gang . . ."

"You're halfway there right now," said Arseny Nikolaevich, looking down at his glass. "What's that you're drinking?"

" 'You're our Noah,' they tell me. 'Build us an ark.' 'Crap,' I tell them. 'I'm an old goat. Throw me overboard.' Believe me, Arsy, the only reason I'm here is to see my good old buddy." Leaning back into the morocco cushion, he took a long look at his friend, as if seeing him for the first time. "*You* are the real Noah! You, Arseny Luchnikov." He leaned forward again, resting on his elbows like a trucker. "You've heard of the Trilateral Commission, of course. Well, I sit in on a lot of their meetings. It's all for show. I make believe I know what's going on and approve of all their efforts to save mankind. Latter-day Shems, Hams, and Japheths trying to build a Noahless ark to guide them. Somehow they found out we were friends, and they began putting the screws on me to, well, talk with you. Do you want to know what the Trilateral Commission thinks about Crimea? Not that I really care. I mean, the only thing I care about is you and all our old friends. You're the real reason I came, but they asked me to ask you—"

"You really are going off the deep end, Bax," Arseny Nikolaevich broke in. He was getting annoyed.

"All right, I'll stick to the facts," said Baxter. He lit a Havana and embarked on a slow, precise exposition of the commission's position using the delivery that held the commission—or the board of directors of his bank—spellbound.

"The situation in and around the Island is becoming impossible. All the Soviet Union has to do to annex it is snap its fingers. After all, it lies naturally within the Soviet sphere of influence. The population has been demoralized by the turbulence of democracy, and the Idea of a Common Fate—that is, reunification with the Soviet Union—has captured the imaginations of the many. Adherents of the Idea are either unable or unwilling to imagine the consequences of this new Anschluss. And when it comes, it will come without the least strategic finesse. It will consist of a simple, unconscious, physiological act: the big swallowing the small. The only reason it hasn't happened yet is that certain highly influential forces are reluctant to make the move; furthermore, these forces reflect a widespread mood in the country, even if for ideological reasons it is not permitted to surface. They argue that the Soviet Union has no need for a new autonomous republic, that it will have great difficulty assimilating a population of five million with no previous experience in the Soviet way of life, and that Crimea's economic boom will end the day after reunification. At present, the rigid Soviet system has more or less made peace with the idea of a miniature, tinselly Russia on its underbelly, made peace with it ideologically, strategically, and most of all, economically. Confidential sources report that a full third of Russia's hard currency enters the country via Crimea. In other words, the status quo is being seriously threatened. Pro-Soviet, pan-Russian feeling on the Island is rampant. All opposing factions—Yakis, Chinese, Albanians, Lupine Hordes—are infantile fantasies with no political credibility. Strange as it may seem, the Soviet system is less governed by its leaders than the various Western systems; it is often wrenched one way or another by poorly studied elemental forces that are much like tectonic folds. The day when the USSR swallows the Island is not far off."

"No one here has any doubt about it," Arseny Nikolaevich put in.

"The thing is it will be *forced* into it; it will do it against its will. The Trilateral Commission has received clear indications to that effect direct from Moscow."

They sat there for a while looking at each other until Arseny Nikolaevich broke the silence and his vow by asking Baxter for a cigar. "And then?" he asked, fixing on the desperado's tough baby-blue eyes through the smoke.

"Then the imagination takes over," answered Baxter sardonically. "Why should the West have any interest in maintaining an independent Russian zone? Strategically, Crimea is of no use whatsoever. You have barely enough natural resources to keep yourselves going, and the Arabat Oil Company is slowly but surely moving into the Persian Gulf. What is your industry to us but one more competitor in a shrinking marketplace? The logical thing for us to do would be to sell you down the river or at least wash our hands of you, but no, the West—and, first and foremost, the Trilateral Commission—does in fact have an interest in maintaining an independent Crimea. In accordance with the contemporary state of the art of politics our interest in you is both moral and 'aesthetic.' We feel that in the totalitarian flood we must keep an aesthetically pleasing ark afloat, the OK *Special*. Well, what do you think?"

"Quite astute, actually."

"Aha!" exclaimed a triumphant Baxter. "So aristocratic romanticism isn't dead yet. You'll be happy to know that what we used to call old-fashioned Russian aristocratic sentimentality or the psychology of noble impulses is what futurologists currently consider the most positive and pragmatic position for all mankind."

"Which makes me Noah."

"Which makes you Noah." Baxter nodded. "You and you alone."

"And where is your Ararat?"

"The North Atlantic Treaty Organization. In return for a clearcut, decisive pro-Western, even pro-American orientation, we will back you militarily. Stability will be restored, and everyone will breathe more easily, especially in Moscow. Oh, they'll put on a rip-roaring propaganda campaign and throw fifteen or twenty dissidents in the clink, but it will all calm down in no time. The commission's Moscow sources are pretty much unanimous about the scenario. Even in Moscow there are people who understand we're all in it together. You've read Sakharov, haven't you? Well, the Kremlin reads him, too."

"I'm not your man," said Arseny Nikolaevich firmly. "I'm too old, Bax, I've seen too much grief, and I don't want to lose my mountain, I don't want to leave my mountain, Bax. I'm nearly eighty, Bax. If I'm young, it's only in comparison with my mountain. And one more thing: I don't want to compete with my son."

"I understand." Baxter nodded. "Look, Arsy, what do you say you take me with you to your mountain? I'm sick of the commission, sick of all the pragmatists and optimists, the Harry Kisselburgers who solve the world's problems with a scratch of the forehead. . . . No, I have a whole new way of looking at life. What if everything that really matters takes place beyond the bounds of human existence? I'm not kidding, Arsy old buddy, sell me a side of your mountain. I'd give up everything to be there with you, whiling away the evenings over cards. Just you and me and Tina . . ."

"You really think she'd stay?" asked Arseny Nikolaevich, putting a comforting arm around Baxter's shoulders.

Whenever a serious conversation ended in a stalemate, they would immediately drop it, make believe it had never happened. That was the way they made it clear to each other that friendship came first—before politics, the economy, everything.

"She could at least spend part of the year up there with me," he said, opening wide his baby-blue desperado eyes. "And if she needs some fresh flesh, I'll just pack her off to Nice or Miami for a while. I'll treat her like a daughter—well, most of the time. Actually, Arsy"—he leaned over and whispered in his ear—"I've made her a proposition along those lines. I've asked her to become my constant companion, my traveling companion. I'm positive prostitution is just a game to her. She's a very special woman, one of a kind, and you know the experience I've had. . . ."

At that moment they heard a gentle, velvet-on-velvet gong and a pleasant voice informing them that the SAS jumbo jet from Stockholm was ready to land, and a large screen to the left of the bar lit up to show the plane easing down on the runway, its landing lights blinking brightly against the dark sky. The brand-new, ultramodern system—Aero-Simfi had been chosen for its trial run—then switched on its in-flight cameras, and each of the four cavernous cabins succeeded one another on the screen, row after row of passengers whispering excitedly or attempting to assume a state of anabiosis. There was no sign of Andrei Luchnikov in first class, but in the back of tourist class a heavily stubbled version of his face flashed across the screen.

All at once Tina jumped off the barstool and ran off.

"Tina!" Baxter yelled and jumped up, holding out his hands to her.

She did not even turn her head.

What had happened was that while the two elderly gentlemen were off on their own talking politics, Tanya-Tina had finally put the pieces together. From the Russian snatches in Anton and Lidochka's conversation she was able to establish who was who and why they had all gathered here at Aero-Simfi. The tall boy, whose hand had just happened to brush over her back on several occasions, was Andrei's son, the silly girl with the romantic notions considered herself his fiancée, and the tall gray old man, the friend of her "client" (the word made her break out in a sweat), was none other than the famous Arseny Luchnikov. Still groggy from identifying them all, she could not absorb the shock of seeing Andrei's cocky face on the screen, and bolted.

For more than half an hour she wandered from corridor to corridor, rode the escalators up and down. The quiet music followed her everywhere, and now and again a smiling face would come up to her and ask whether she needed any help. Tanya's lips were trembling, she was afraid of bumping into a wall or climbing up one like a half-squashed fly. Only now was she beginning to see her "spur-of-the-moment adventure" for what it really was. She tried hard to push it out of her mind: how the old man had held her in his arms and then undressed her, exploring her entire body slowly and deliberately, how he had entered and taken her, taken her long and hard, muttering some American smut she luckily couldn't understand, and then—she tried not to think of it, it was all so shameful—then he began telling her—she couldn't believe it—how he loved her . . . loved a whore? . . . and then he had asked her for something else . . . maybe he'd had a monkey-gland transplant . . . and with a face disfigured by the terrible memories she could not push out of her mind she went into the open but empty Aero-Simfi branch of the Bank of Crimea and handed a timorous young clerk Baxter's check.

The check, it turned out, was for five thousand dollars instead of three. Generous old ape! Impressed by the ape's signature, the clerk respectfully counted out the amount in large, crisp notes with "Bank of the Armed Forces of South Russia" written boldly across them. She had never held so many tichas in her life. Now I can see my future—as a whore. Only who will ever pay me that price again? Soon I'll be standing outside train stations and locker rooms, the lowest of the low. Something must have snapped in me when I gave Sergeev my signature. Or maybe it goes back to the day the Hub cracked the bottle over Andrei's head. Everything takes its toll. Justify it any way you like, any way you can—you're still just a paid informer, a dirty whore. You're unworthy of Andrei; you've no right to sleep with your husband; you don't know what late-blooming flowers your friend the ape may have given you on his yacht, even if the crew treated you more like Grace Kelly than Seaside Sadie; and how can you face your children?

She looked up to see a security point manned by two armed guards. Their eyes were glued to a screen showing passengers from the Scandinavian airliner going through Crimean customs, but they graciously moved aside to give her a better view.

"*Française?*" asked one of them.

"Moscow," she said.

"How long since you defected?"

"Defected?" she said, peeved. "I'm here on official business."

"Good for you, Madame! I've never understood why people defect from the Soviet Union."

His partner offered Tanya a chair without a word.

She saw him immediately. He was striding along with an ugly green backpack over one shoulder. All his clothes were Soviet: flimsy imitation jeans that had obviously seen better days and bigger bottoms; a formless cotton hat with LENINGRAD written across the front and a plastic peak; and a short, wadded nylon jacket with an ugly open shirt sticking out from underneath. His striking red mustache was lost in the red-and-gray stubble that covered his face, but he was all smiles, holding out his arms to greet, off camera, his noble papa, his handsome son, his romantic fiancée, and, probably, that disgustingly rich American friend of the family with the monkey-gland transplant.

The second guard broke the rhythm of his gum chewing long enough to note that the man on the screen "could only be one of yours."

Luchnikov moved off camera.

Without acknowledging the guard's remark, Tanya jumped up, pushed back her chair, and started running down the corridor to the multilingual exit signs, the line of yellow Peter Ford taxis, and the deliverance or destruction of the black night beyond.

"What took you to Stockholm?" Arseny Nikolaevich asked his son. "We thought you were in Moscow."

"You can't imagine the adventures I've just had in the Historical Homeland!" said Luchnikov spiritedly as he hugged his father and son and gave the beaming Lidochka Nesselrode a pleasant if somewhat bewildered smile. "First I ditched my tail, bamboozled them left and right. Then I spent two weeks crisscrossing the central provinces without so much as a forged document. They said it couldn't be done, they said our mighty Russia was invincible. But I did it! And that's not the half of it! Believe it or not, I crossed the border illegally! I escaped, flew the coop! I defected! I've turned them into a bunch of clowns!"

Arseny Nikolaevich listened indulgently while his son spewed out his slang. Look at him, half gray, and still the little boy; look at him showing off, proud of how Soviet he is, proud of all that shopworn claptrap.

"No, really, our Russia is a wonderland," Luchnikov went on, telling the story of how he'd spent a whole week with a stark-raving-bonkers jazz musician paddling an Aleutian canoe to Lake Pukhu-Yarve in the wilds of Karelia, then another whole week by the lake eating only fish and berries, and how finally the jazz musician's Swedish friend flew in for them in his own tiny plane and, after the plane barely missed crashing in some pines, flew them back unimpeded over the border. Ben-Ivan, the Russian jazzman, had reason to believe that on that day all the border guards would be blotto—it was the day the latest supply of vodka and wine was due at the local general stores—and sure enough, there wasn't a sign of life all along the sacred strip. So much for the iron curtain. Now the Finns—that was a different matter: the Finns, those bastards, have an agreement with the Soviets about turning over escapees, so they had to bribe them, bribe them with a whole case of vodka. Anyway, then they flew over to Stockholm. "Ben-Ivan will stay on a few weeks and slip back in. He'll make it, too. He's into the occult. . . ."

"But what's the point of it all?" asked Arseny Nikolaevich, aghast at as much as he could follow. "You're *persona grata* there. Or have you changed your mind?"

Andrei Arsenicvich emptied a glass of Prince Golitsyn's Nouveau Monde with great relish, looked radiantly from one to the next, and said, somewhat pretentiously, "I have returned from Russia full of hope. For it is like a field, which shall never be barren!"

Wandering through Yalta, Tanya failed to notice its nocturnal beauty: the climatic screens adjusted at night to catch and reflect the moonlight, the play of lights over the mountain slopes, the spectacular glass giants of the "second line," the stone lions, eagles, naiads, and atlantes of the "first, historical line" along Tatar Quay. She was completely absorbed by her panic. Glancing at her face in a shopwindow, she failed to recognize it, so distorted was it by fear. She had ceased to feel her own presence in the pulsating city around her. Mechanically she entered a dazzling but empty supermarket and walked up and down the rows, picking up random items and putting them back. At the check-out counter she found a ridiculous-looking Bolivian hat left in her hand, paid for it, and walked out with it perched on her head. Soon she came upon a small square of old-fashioned houses: one with a globe on the roof and an eagle spreading its wings on the globe, another with lions guarding the entrance, a third with caryatids holding up the walls. She felt a bit calmer in these surroundings and suddenly realized she was hungry. I know what I want to do, she said to herself, thrilled at the discovery. Not drown, hang, or poison myself. I want to get a little food in my stomach.

Across the square she spied a brightly lit all-night café. On her way there she passed a large trailer with a West German numberplate nestled under a clump of tall cypresses waving in the sea breeze. All its doors were open, and she saw some people playing cards inside. A man with nothing on but his trunks sat smoking on the steps. When he noticed Tanya, he called out to her quite civilly and asked about her rates.

"Bastard!" she shouted back at him.

"*Verzeihung!*" he said apologetically, adding something like "There's no reason to get so upset."

The name of the café restored her good humor. With a little imagination Wilkinson's could be construed in Russian to mean "son of the fork," an apt name for a café, she thought. She went in through a revolving door and sat down at the counter, several stools away from a full-buttocked woman stuffing herself with strawberry cream pie. Tanya ordered shish kebab and was eagerly served by a pair of Yugoslav "guest workers" with nothing but sex on their minds. Within a very few minutes she was enjoying the deliciously prepared meat with a variety of condiments, a salad and pilaf on the side, and a bottle of mineral water.

"I bet it's nerves," said the cream-pie woman.

"What's nerves?" Tanya gave her a hostile look. She was sloppy as well as voluminous: her thighs bulged out of her shorts, her stomach hung down between her legs, her breasts rolled in and out of her blouse and were spotted with whipped cream, and her mouth was all shiny—either her lipstick had smeared or she had strawberry juice trickling down her chin.

"These nighttime"—she giggled—"binges. I never used to indulge like this, believe me. I was as slim as you are; slimmer. You should have heard the way they whistled at me along Tatar Quay. I was a real sexpot, everybody's favorite. Now I'm going through a bad period: stress. I sleep all day, eat pies all night. Seven a night. Pretty good, eh?" She looked over at Tanya to see whether the cabalistic number had made any impression on her, and seeing that it had not, she added almost sinisterly, "Or as many as a dozen. A baker's dozen! Pretty good, eh? And all because of men." She fixed her gaze on Tanya again.

Tanya could feel the insolent, wanton eyes boring into her. She was certain a lesbian proposition was in the offing. Now I see it, she thought. Now I see what makes capitalism so sickening and offensive. They've got everything they could possibly want and then some, but it's never enough, so they prostitute themselves for new delights. But it can't go on like this, and neither can I. I'm going to catch the first plane back to Moscow. Screw Luchnikov, screw Sergeev and Co. I'll take the kids out of the Pioneer Camp, have the car repaired, and drive down to Tsakhkadzor with them to visit the Hub. I'll go into training with him. He's the only one who really loves me, I'm his wife, he's my husband, he'll forgive me, and I'll go back to living in our world, my world, a world where you can't get anything you need and everybody's afraid of everything, the real world. I'll find a job selling fruits and vegetables and live a normal life of thievery. Meanwhile, she was stuffing food down her gullet and had twice spilled Thousand Island dressing on the elegant Muir and Merrilees dress Andrei had bought her in the spring.

At the other end of the semicircular counter sat a scrawny girl in a dark T-shirt. She looked like a half-plucked chicken, with bulging, terror-crazed eyes. At first Tanya thought she was seeing her own reflection, and her blood ran cold, but then she recalled how tastefully she was dressed and coiffed and that she had shish kebab in front of her and the girl had none. . . .

Suddenly the kitchen door flew open and out of the sparkling tile and aluminum stepped a man of forty-five or so in a chef's uniform. He immediately headed for the terror-stricken girl, leaning over the counter, smiling, making scabrous remarks. The girl tried to cover her face with her napkin, but her eyes kept darting about looking for a means of escape.

At that point a man wearing tinted glasses entered the café. He ordered a coffee and drank it standing up. Though he did not look directly at Tanya, he did keep glancing up at the mirrored ceiling that gave an unobstructed view of everything going on. So they've come to get me, thought Tanya. Sergeev in person, too. Same mannerisms, same glasses. True, the beard is a little on the operatic side, a Ramses beard, but pasting on a beard is the simplest thing in the world. Well, you won't get me. I'll never say die. I'll find a hideout where no one will call me spy or prostitute. . . .

"Ha! Ha! Ha!" the cream-pie woman guffawed. "You can't fool me! I can tell. I'm a real psychologist. I can tell a case of nerves when I see one."

"Leave me alone, will you! I'm hungry, that's all. I haven't had a bite to eat all day. Just because you're a mental case, it doesn't mean—"

"Gotcha!" the cream-pie woman shouted, grabbing one of the Yugoslavs behind the counter. Tanya's outraged tirade had obviously gone right past her. "Thought you could get away from me, eh?" she said, yanking him across the counter by his shirt. "No such luck! You'll be climbing my dunes before the night is through, so eat up, you traitor!" And she shoved a piece of pie into his mouth.

The man in the tinted glasses held his coffee cup up to his mouth and turned his head.

Tanya's elbow slipped. The plate, together with what was left of the shish kebab, went sailing off the counter and smashed into smithereens on the tile floor.

The man in the tinted glasses quickly went out the door and melted into the night.

The girl with the crazy eyes pressed the napkin to her mouth as if trying to block the scream of horror trying to escape.

The cook in the dazzling white apron made a cowboy-film leap over the counter and lifted her off the stool, forcing her pelvis against his groin.

The cream-pie woman pulled her captive the rest of the way across the counter, sat him on her knee, and went on force-feeding him.

Tanya heard herself screaming the scream the girl in the dark T-shirt was afraid to let out, but she could not quite bring herself to run: what if the black square held even more danger and insanity? Yet it was only a matter of time. She took out some tichas and determined where the cashier was sitting.

He was a dark, good-looking middle-aged man who seemed absolutely impervious to the goings on. All he did was puff away at his Dutch cigar and look over at the only other customers, two men in dark glasses. "Okay?" he asked them with his eyes across the room. They grinned and held up big thumbs.

Suddenly the girl with the crazy eyes made for the revolving door, the awful cook (Tanya noticed for the first time he had nothing on under his apron) hot on her heels. That was the last straw. Tanya jumped up, threw the tichas at the cashier, and pushed through the door before the cook, determined to calm the frightened girl down. She was too late: the girl had disappeared by the time she emerged.

Everything was calm. The fountain in the middle of the square gurgled peacefully, its two cupids frolicking in a bronze thicket. The lights in the Germans' camper shone brightly. Tanya turned towards the café. It looked peaceful, too. The sex maniac was peacefully wiggling his dimpled bottom back to the kitchen. The cream-pie woman was peacefully polishing off her pie. The boy behind the counter was peacefully wiping cups dry. The cashier was laughing with the two men in dark glasses, who had come out of their corner. Tanya felt as though she had fallen asleep and just now awoke from a nightmare.

She sat down at the edge of the fountain. The breeze that had rustled the cypresses before, now stronger, played with her hair. The eagle, the lions, the atlantes and caryatids all evoked a pleasant, peaceful past. She burst into soothing, childlike tears. She always enjoyed her tears; she remembered the comfort they brought her as a child.

Three narrow streets led into the square, and Tanya heard a purring sound coming from one of them. She looked up to see an open Land-Rover emerge and pull up to the camper. The driver leaned out and asked the Germans, in English, whether they knew a Nazi song they could sing for him. When the Germans protested they didn't know any Nazi songs and had never known any, the man from the Land-Rover said, "Don't tell me you've never heard of *Horst Wessel*. All you have to do is sing with your arms around your buddies' necks. You know, rocking back and forth. The way you always do it." He acted it out so vividly that Tanya picked up nearly everything.

"We're not going to sing that *Schweinerei!*" one of the Germans spat out.

"A hundred bucks, okay?" said the man from the Land-Rover.

"Just throw your arms around your buddies' shoulders and sing. The words don't matter. The main thing is to sway in time. Got it? Here's the dough."

The Land-Rover screeched into reverse and disappeared. The Germans linked arms over shoulders and began singing the first thing that came into their heads. All at once a trio of elephants came lumbering out of the three narrow streets, a spine-tingling scream rent the soft Mediterranean night, and from the bronze thicket, where a minute before the two cupids had been playing alone, rose the terror-stricken face of the girl from the café. Then Tanya heard her own scream. She gagged her mouth with her hand and stood rooted to the spot, trembling. The elephants were closing in on them, each with a bottomless sex maniac astride it. By now the Germans were getting into the swing of things, too, and even the words had started to come back.

"Cut!" an amplified voice thundered out over the square. "That's it for tonight. See you on Wednesday. Thank you!"

Lights flashed on in the old buildings, people flocked into the square, Land-Rovers piled high with equipment darted back and forth through the crowd. The girl with the crazy eyes was immediately lifted out of the fountain, bundled into a stunning alpaca wrap, and whisked over to a white Ferrari, which she drove off in, alone. Not until Tanya saw her behind the wheel did she remember having seen her on the screen as well.

A group of men came up to her and started talking and laughing. She was unable to catch even the drift of what they were saying. Then she noticed the man with the Ramses beard sitting nearby on the edge of the fountain and smiling at her. "They're telling you that your chance appearance on the set added a nice twist to the scene," he said. "You provided a reflection of the heroine's crisis. By way of gratitude they'd like to offer you a little something."

"Tell them they can keep their charity," said Tanya, completely worn out by the experience.

Ramses stayed with her after the film crew had dispersed. "Those wretched Hollywood loudmouths! Ever since they've 'discovered' the Island, they've been shooting the most preposterous nonsense here. . . . Allow me to introduce myself, Madame Lunina. My name is Vadim Vostokov. Colonel Vostokov. I am with OSVAG, the local intelligence agency, and I should very much like to have a talk with you."

"How alike you are," said Tanya. "You even dress alike."

"You have in mind our Moscow colleagues, I presume," Vostokov said with a smile, "and you are absolutely right. Nowadays intelligence is big business, big business on an international scale, so of course we, too, are subject to the general standardization process."

"Intelligence!" said Tanya mockingly. "You mean spying, bugging, tailing."

"Madame," he replied, not without remorse, "I am afraid that what you call spying, bugging, and tailing is not the most loathsome of our responsibilities."

"Is your beard real?"

"You may pull it, if you like," Vostokov said, smiling.

She gave a good, stiff tug. Vostokov did not blink an eye. A few gray hairs had come out in her fist, and she squeamishly brushed them away. Vostokov gently took her arm, and they set off together. Crossing Tatar Quay, they came to a small café on the beach, a series of private recesses with cane tables and an unsurpassed view of the port. Among the long motor launches lining the piers Tanya noticed the *Elyse*, the large ocean yacht on which just a few hours before she had, to use a current Moscow euphemism, "made a brilliant statement." Vostokov ordered a coffee and a gin fizz.

"A beautiful vessel, the *Elyse*," he said thoughtfully after the waiter brought the order. "Mr. Baxter has exquisite taste."

"All right, out with it," said Tanya. "Just remember, I don't scare easily." She downed her drink in one gulp and immediately felt calmer.

"I understand the reasons for your valor, Madame." He smiled.

The Crimean and Moscow "colleagues" did indeed share a number of mannerisms: barely perceptible, but *very* barely perceptible, smiles; dazzling candid remarks followed by elusive, but lucid, threats; and sudden bouts of ennui, of resignation—what can I do, it's my job, in any other circumstances we'd be the best of friends.

"I have no desire to dazzle you with my omniscience, Madame, nor do I claim it. Intelligence always exaggerates omniscience."

Well, that's one difference, thought Tanya wryly. The KGB would never confess to anything less than all the knowledge all the time.

"However," Vostokov went on, "I do know the reasons for your self-assurance. They are two. The first is Andrei Luchnikov, an extremely powerful figure on our Island, I grant you. The second is, of course, Colonel Sergeev"—Vostokov could not restrain himself and, pausing, glanced over at Tanya; all he got for his pains was a wry smile—"a highly competent specialist. By the way, please give him my best if you see him in the near future." He paused again, this time to give Tanya a chance to process the "dazzling information."

"Bravo," said Tanya. "You shouldn't run yourself down, you know, not with dazzling information like that. Really, Colonel Vostokov, you shouldn't run yourself down."

"Oh, I'm not running myself down, not in the least. You see, Tatyana Nikitichna, anyone can gather information nowadays. There's no trick to it at all. No, more to the point—and much more challenging—is the problem of how to project oneself into the psychology of the object under investigation. I find it extremely difficult, for example, to understand the motive for your hysterics in Wilkinson's just now. Having studied you for a number of years, I of course rule out all possibility of physical dysfunction. . . ."

Yes, Mr. Vostokov is a good several rungs higher than Comrade Sergeev.

". . . so I am forced to fall back on this." He took an elegant leather wallet from his jacket pocket and laid out several first-rate snapshots on the table: Tanya and Baxter smiling at each other over champagne in the soft light of the cabin; Tanya and Baxter shedding their clothes; naked Tanya in the old man's embrace; contorted faces with beads of sweat; Baxter writing out the check; Baxter's paternal grin.

Again her head was spinning, and a scream gathered force behind a membrane that tried to give but could not. The dark sea rolled a hundred feet away from them. All she had to do was to make a dash for it, vanish into it, turn into a sea creature with no thoughts or feelings. . . .

"As I pointed out back in the square," she heard Vostokov saying to her, "our responsibilities can be quite loathsome, actually, and alas, what I have to offer you now is blackmail. It has no other name. I can only assure you—though I understand it is scant compensation—that I engage in these unsavory affairs for ideological reasons. I am a Russian aristocrat, Tatyana Nikitichna. The Vostokovs can trace their line back to—"

"So you're a Russian aristocrat," said a hoarse, unearthly voice from within her. "If you're an aristocrat"—another Moscow expression came to mind—"I wouldn't want to shit next to an aristocrat!" And as she skimmed her hand across the table, the thickish, Polaroid-like prints soared up, a fluttering cloud, into the Black Sea blackness before falling on the pebbles below or flying off into the night of the capitalist jungle where the very air is pornographic. She squeezed her eyelids shut so as to see nothing and pressed her hands over her ears so as to find the world completely changed and the dawn of socialism rising over a warm and peaceful sea, and then she saw the Caucasus, a Pioneer Camp, her last virgin summer, the hour before the gymnastics coach—a broad-chested hulk like Colonel Vostokov, but minus the Egyptian beard —deflowered her. . . .

When at length she opened her eyes and ears, Colonel Vostokov had vanished. In his place sat a wiry ruffian with greasy, crow-wing hair and a slobbering mouth. He wore a cockeyed grin that prominently displayed a set of long, horsy teeth and sickly gums. "On your feet, you KGBitch!" he ordered. "We'll show you and your Kremlin flunky lover boy it's too soon to bring out the champagne! On your feet!"

Three figures wearing black leather jackets and hoods over their heads stood at the entrance to the recess, blocking out the sea with their impressive shoulders.

Tanya stood up, her mind racing. How could she keep from delivering herself to the thugs? Breaking away was out of the question. She'd have to submit for a while, wait till they let their defenses down, and then hurl herself down from a parapet or under a car or grab a knife or a gun away from one of them and . . . stick it in her own guts. . . .

"All right, get moving!" Horse Teeth commanded and pulled a hood over his head, too.

Tanya left the café surrounded by the four hooded brutes. Out of the corner of her eye she saw the owner and two waiters looking on in fear from behind the lighted bar. Out of the corner of her mind she thought how wonderful it would be to hear someone call out, "Cut! Thank you! That's it for tonight!" But unfortunately this was no film.

A huge black Russo-Balt with dark-tinted—and doubtless bulletproof—windows was waiting on Tatar Quay. They shoved Tanya into the back seat and tumbled in after her, except for Horse Teeth, who sat down next to the driver and took off his hood. The car slipped quietly along the embankment and was soon climbing the winding asphalt ribbon on its way either to the freeway or the back mountain roads of the town.

One of the thugs stuffed a thick piece of rubber in her mouth, the next tore open her dress and set to pawing and sucking her breasts, the third cut off her panties and thrust his hand inside her. They all worked in complete silence. The only sound came from the front, where Horse Teeth sat gurgling with pleasure. Tanya realized she had no chance of breaking away, she was in for it this time.

The limousine was barreling along a narrow street lined with sleepy houses when suddenly a military jeep shot out of an even narrower side street and stopped short in front of the Russo-Balt. As with all accidents, no one quite grasped what had happened at first. Because the Russo-Balt interior was so luxuriously upholstered, neither Tanya nor her back-seat companions suffered very much: they all simply bumped into the roof and fell back on the soft cushions. Horse Teeth, however, had knocked his head against the windshield and was half groaning, half weeping in pain; the driver, who had been rammed in the chest by the steering wheel, was unconscious. Three young men in battle dress jumped out of the jeep. Then another, identical, jeep sped up from behind with three more men. They were standing and held automatics. After a quick explosion the door of the Russo-Balt collapsed, and the soldiers quickly dragged the passengers out. In no time flat all the thugs were in handcuffs and stacked rather unceremoniously in the second jeep, the driver's unconscious body on top.

One of the soldiers went up to Tanya and placed his fingers for an instant on her temples. The oval rainbow on his beret was vaguely associated in her mind with the pre-Revolutionary Russian air force.

"Please accept our apologies, ma'am," said the soldier. "We were a little late. Your bag, ma'am. This way, please. Our jeep is unharmed. You have nothing to fear now. We'll take you back to your hotel."

Tanned face, white-toothed smile, strength, and calm. What world were they from, these six strapping lads, each more hale and hearty than the next? She gathered her torn dress around her and finally managed to form her trembling lips into words. "Who are those brutes?"

"I'm sorry, ma'am, we have no information about them as of yet."

"And who are you?"

"The air force, ma'am. A subdivision of the Kachinsky Special Operations Regiment. An emergency call. By the personal order of Colonel Chernok. Rest assured, ma'am, you are completely out of danger."

Tanya was not completely out of danger. No sooner had she closed the door of her comfortable room than she collapsed on the floor. Having caught her breath, she started crawling her way to the bathroom. She spent a long time trying to get around a soft red pouf that had strayed into the middle of the room, but her head got wedged under the telephone table and one leg was jammed by the bed. She whimpered for a while in that awkward position, then in a fit of rage attacked the pouf head-on and found to her surprise it could have been moved by a kitten. Finally reaching her goal, she turned on the taps full blast. To the roar of the water she pulled off her clothes and picked herself up in front of the full-length mirror. She looked as wild-eyed as the girl at Wilkinson's. She was eighteen, Tanya fantasized about the girl, a spy and a whore, she had just returned from a hard night on the town all battered and bruised, maybe even harboring a dose of the pox or the clap or a colony of crotch lice. Who could she sell herself to now? Who was low enough for her? The mirror was beginning to steam over from the hot water. No, that wasn't the filthy Wilkinson's girl there in the mirror, it was me, myself, a thirty-eight-year-old mother of two dearly loved children, wife of a former world champion, mistress of a world-renowned journalist—the flower of Russian womanhood. And she thought of the wives of the Decembrists following their husbands into Siberian exile. . . . She watched her contours blur in the steam of the mirror. Just as they disappeared entirely, the bath overflowed. Lacking the strength to move, she felt the water climb to her ankles, she saw it cover the soft, pliant carpeting of the main room, watched her slippers start floating next to the bedside table. Finally she tore herself away from the bathroom, went over to the table, took out a handful of capsules—sleeping pills, laxatives, relaxants—and broke them open, emptying the contents into an empty tumbler. It filled quickly. Now all I have to do is get it down, she thought with a nervous laugh. There's some Coke in the fridge I can use as a chaser. Better hurry. Don't want the fridge to drown. When the maid comes in, I'll be floating up near the ceiling. What a joke! Moscow will have a good laugh, a top-level laugh. What was that? Tangled in the chandelier? Ha! Ha! Ha! That's what I call style. . . . Whose style? What style?

In her left hand she held the tumbler, in her right a slightly smoking bottle of Coca-Cola. The water was up to her knees. Someone was pounding on the door. The phone had been ringing for some time without a letup. Black humor at its finest, she giggled, and they won't let me go through with it.

"Open up, Madame, open up!" shouted the maids on the other side of the door.

The door began to shake. She took the phone off the hook.

"There's a gentleman waiting for you in the lobby, Madame Lunina," said the porter in a gentle voice.

Another gentleman. Here everyone was a gentleman. But it was too late. No one could stop her now. A tilt of the head and the tumbler would be empty; a swallow of Coke, and its contents would swirl through the system. One last pleasure—the tingle of ice-cold Coke.

They broke down the door and immediately scattered with a squeal. Tanya, still giggling, teetered down the hall. The little balcony at the other end gave an unobstructed view of the lobby. Let me just catch a glimpse of my gentleman. Curiosity may or may not kill cats, but it certainly turns people into animals. Let me see what boar would come to visit this doddering old sow.

Down in the lobby, comfortably ensconced in an armchair and completely engrossed in the morning edition of the *Courier*, sat Andrei Arsenievich Luchnikov, impeccably shaved and scented and turned out in a white linen suit compliments of Yves Saint-Laurent. He was so absorbed in his reading that neither the maids' panic, nor the stream of water flowing downstairs into the lobby, nor the naked figure of Tanya staring down at him from the balcony could distract him.

"Andrei!" she cried out in desperation.

Both tumbler and bottle flew against the staircase wall and shattered. The soaking wet carpet eagerly drank up the pill powder.

In a flash Luchnikov grasped the entire situation, flew up the stairs, and pressed the flailing Tanya to his breast.

The perfectly trained porter and his assistant behind the reception desk maintained a perfectly professional detachment, but in fact they had followed everything closely.

"I say, Mukhtar-*aga*, they *are* sending us a new breed from Moscow these days."

"No doubt about it, Finch. Some serious changes must be afoot."

"Tell me, Mukhtar-*aga*, what do you think of the Idea of a Common Fate?"

"I am certain, Finch, that we have much to offer the great Soviet Union. Though not Russian myself, I take pride in its extraordinary achievements. The USSR is a multinational country, and many of my fellow Tatars live along the Volga. And you, Finch? What do you Anglo-Crimeans think of reunification?"

"I think we have a great deal to teach our Soviet comrades in matters of hotel management."

"Good for you, Finch. I am glad to be able to work with a man of such progressive views."

"Excuse me, gentlemen!" called Luchnikov from the head of the stairs. "Would you come and put Madame's bags in my car?"

A quarter of an hour later they were speeding along the freeway to the capital in Luchnikov's long, sleek Peter Turbo. Andrei kept turning and kissing Tanya on the cheek. "One of these pills will do you a lot more good than all of those," he said, holding out a pink tranquilizer. "It's all in the past now, Tanya, and it was all my fault. I got so bound up in my Russian adventure I completely neglected you. Do you want to know what happened to you?"

"No!" she cried. "I don't want to know a thing! Nothing happened at all!"

Then the pill took over, and she was all peace and joy. Every-thing around her lit up. A land of milk and honey flew by below the freeway's steel girders, while up ahead green hills stretched out at the base of the bright-gray stone foreheads and fangs of an ancient range. It was a country of bewitching but naïve roman-ticism, the White Guard's dream come true.

"Nothing happened or has happened since the day you left our flat. Life has been one long empty delirium. The only thing that's happened since then is your coming for me, that and nothing else."

Luchnikov smiled and gave her another peck on the cheek. "The thing is you were tracked down by the Lupine Hordes, the ultrarightist conspiratorial (though, given our system, any con-spiracy is a sham) branch of the League for the Rebirth of Homeland and Throne. Of course, they don't give a damn about the Homeland or Throne. In fact, they're nothing but a pack of fascists and common hoodlums speculating on the romanticism of the Whites. The 'lupine' part of their name, the wolf-tail symbol, comes straight from General Shkuro's cavalry, and the 'hordes' part is a complete misnomer: the group has few members and practically no influence on the population as a whole. What it has got is considerable financial backing—in other words, arms—and rabid fanaticism. To make matters worse, it's headed by a crack-pot by the name of Ignatyev-Ignatyev, a former classmate of mine, who has seen us as sworn enemies all our lives. He has some sort of complex, when it comes to me—more likely than not, homo-sexual in nature—and he's the one who organized this evening's escapade. His men have been following you for days and chose tonight to strike. They thought that by molesting you they'd get even with me on several counts. Fortunately, another of our classmates, Vadim Vostokov, discovered the plot—he's with our intelligence—and contacted yet another of our classmates, Sasha Chernok, an air force officer, and he called out his special opera-tions team. Your would-be kidnappers are spending the night in the Kachinsky Regiment guardhouse, and early tomorrow morning they'll be arraigned. That's it."

"That's it?"

"That's it." Another peck. "Double Ignatyev is a total degen-erate. All my other nineteen classmates from the Tsar Alexander II (Liberator) Classical School for Boys are friends and political colleagues, and we count for a great deal here on the Island. You're in complete safety, darling. How happy I am to have you at my side again! We'll be together forever."

By then they were circling above Simferopol, about to plunge into the tunnels of the Underground Knot. The city was at their feet.

"See that pencil sticking out in the middle of it all?" asked Luchnikov. "That's the Courier Building. And up at the very top, the point of the pencil, is where I have my pad. It's a great place. We'll spend a few days there and then a few days up at Suru-Kaya, my father's estate, so you can rest and give Antosha a chance to get to know his new stepmother."

"No!" she suddenly screamed. "We're not going anywhere! We're not going to live together! Send me back to Moscow, Andrei, please!"

"Time for another one of these," he said, holding out another pink pill. "Pull yourself together now, Tanya. You can do it. Just think of the whole thing as a gang attack. It happens all the time in the Soviet Union, you know. According to top secret statistics on unmotivated crime, *we* are the world champions. Don't worry, darling, you'll get over it."

Several minutes later they were in the express elevator speeding toward the pencil point. Though in fact merely one enormous barn of a room, Luchnikov's "pad" boasted the latest in playboy design: a number of unexpected levels and staircases, a wraparound indoor balcony, beds and hammocks galore, several wood-burning fireplaces, and, of course, a bathtub suspended from the ceiling. Tanya immediately made a little niche for herself between two protruding walls hung with tiger skins. Through the slanting glass roof above her she could see nothing but sky and stars. "This is where I want to be, Andrei, but don't touch me tonight, please, not tonight. Bundle me up in some nice blankets, bring me some milk, and turn on the TV. A sports program, if there is one. And don't touch me. I'll tell you when it's all right again."

He did everything she asked: he found his favorite Mexican and Scottish blankets and tucked her in like a child; he brought her a pitcher of hot milk and a plate of warm cakes; he switched on the twenty-four-hour sports channel.

". . . nothing short of a miracle of athletic longevity," the avuncular sports commentator was saying as he materialized on the screen. "A 1960 decathlon champion retraining for the coming games as a shot putter."

"There now," said Luchnikov, "everything okay?"

"Just fine," she whispered. "You go off to your classmates. . . ."

VIII

In the Glass Wigwam

Late summer in Crimea: the scent of woodworm in the east; the warm smell of high-quality wheat in the central regions; the spicy aromas of Tatar bazaars in Bakhchisarai, Karasu-Bazaar, and Shufut-Kala; and everywhere the tantalizing secretions of the subtropics.

Late summer was also the time to think about the traditional rally from Alushta to Sugdeya along the Old Roman Road. The road was used only for the breath-taking annual rally, which attracted the most daring drivers from all over the world. It seemed to have been built by the rulers of the Bosporan Empire expressly to enable the Roman legionnaires to conquer and destroy the empire. A hundred miles of dirt sparsely covered with gravel, ruts dating back centuries, slanting soft shoulders, and three hundred eighteen hairpin curves over yawning chasms. The surest way to popular acclaim was to win the Crimea Rally. Once, fifteen years ago, Andrei Luchnikov had come in first, outracing the world aces in his locally built, custom-built Peter Turbo, and it was that victory which marked the beginning of his phenomenal popularity.

You feel like a military pilot going into battle, he liked to tell his friends. It's like flying directly into an abyss. And you can't touch the brakes: the enemy is all around you. You have to be mighty aggressive if you want to make it through. I could never do it again.

Seven or eight of his classmates had come together that evening before the fire in Luchnikov's penthouse. They were eating shish kebab delivered sizzling hot from the *Courier*'s basement kitchens and drinking their favorite, Nouveau Monde, from Prince Golitsyn's cellars. Tanya looked down from her lair, the same niche she had picked the first night. She left it as rarely as possible. For several weeks now she had kept her television set tuned to the sports channel, watching basketball and soccer, interviews, and, especially, track and field events from all over the world. It seemed to relax her. From time to time the commentators gave reports from the Tsakhkadzor training camp. The Hub's resurrection did seem somewhat of a miracle. They showed him quite often—big, powerful, and white-toothed as ever—first thanking the Party for its role in the development of a healthy athletic program, then reporting on his own quickly developing progress. And a fantastic success story it was, too: forty years old, and he ran up to twenty-one meters. What could the Soviet coaches do? They'd thrown a youngster off the team and welcomed Gleb aboard.

Looking over the balcony, Tanya could not help noticing the ravages of time on the group: bald spots, gray streaks, limp curls. Yet they all acted as if people who weren't balding and gray didn't know what they were missing. The self-centered supermen, she thought. Scorn for the old when you're young and for the young when you're old—that's the true sign of a superman.

And in fact they happened to be talking about how best to humiliate the bright, aggressive young Yaki activists. In the middle of the discussion, Count Novosiltsev, Volodya to his friends, announced nonchalantly that he had decided to enter the rally again. Unlike Luchnikov, Count Novosiltsev was a professional race driver, and besides his European and American credits he had raced in no fewer than seven Crimea rallies and come in first three times. Instantly the room was silent and all eyes turned to the count, who, still sipping his champagne, peered back at his friends over the rim of the glass with the eyes of a wolf.

When Andrei introduced the count to Tanya as a close friend, she had to laugh. Count Close Friend looked her brazenly, shamelessly, in the eye as if there could be no doubt they would end up in bed together. He's a bit of a wolf, your friend the count, she told Andrei afterwards. He's a big bad wolf, said Andrei respectfully. You'd better keep an eye on him, she said. Don't worry, he smiled.

"Don't you think you're stretching things a bit?" Colonel Chernok asked cautiously. "Like it or not, at forty-six the reflexes aren't what they used to be."

"I'll mow them all down," the count said coldly. "Take my word for it. I'll mow those small fry down in a cheap little Zhiguli." And satisfied with the effect he had produced, he downed the rest of his champagne. In the process he took a quick glance up at Tanya's lair. That's right, he'd beat them all, local competition and foreign, and beat them in one of *our* (he stressed the word "our") Soviet Zhigulis. A Zhiguli 06. Of course he had customized it, put in the latest Peter engine, and (thank you, Sasha) incorporated the latest in aviation electronics. He had also completely rebuilt the chassis of the puny Italo-Soviet bastard (for a Zhiguli was basically a Fiat assembled in the Soviet Union) and fitted it with racing tires—you've never seen such fat tires, gentlemen!—with special spikes of his own invention.

"Three cheers for the count!" cried Timosha Meshkov, also known as Little Boy Bald, the richest of the classmates and owner of the mighty Arabat Oil Company. Little Timosha had been a fan of the count's since their early school years. "And they say the aristocracy is a dying breed!"

"The aristocracy shall never die," Count Novosiltsev moralized. "It arose in antiquity from among the strongest, bravest, and cleverest of warriors, and antiquity, gentlemen, is closer than we think."

"Tell me, what do you mean to prove by throwing down the gauntlet?" the rather corpulent Professor Fofanov inquired sedately. Professor Fofanov was an influential member of the Provisional Institute of Foreign Relations—that is, the Island's foreign office.

"It will have far-reaching consequences," said Luchnikov pensively.

"*Yaki!*" the count cried out. "Our leader knows whereof he speaks. For me it's a purely professional thing, my final escapade" —again he threw a casual glance up at Tanya's quarters—"but

Leader Boy over here is talking about the political ramifications. Don't you see that we have to win this year's rally? With Duma elections three months away and SOS on the line, we've got to knock those swaggering young Yaki nationalists out of the picture. The winner of the rally can write his own ticket. He can be king, consul, president, tsar—till next season, at least. Then, too, think how Soviet prestige will rise when a Zhiguli takes first place."

Silence. Someone sent another bottle around. Tanya turned up the volume on her set. She was watching a terribly boring European Cup soccer match between a namby-pamby team from Moscow and a pack of belligerent beer-fed Dutchmen.

"Have you made any trial runs yet?" Luchnikov asked the count.

"I could drive the Old Roman Road blindfolded. But if you think . . ." He paused. No one said a word. All eyes avoided Luchnikov.

"I'm entering, too," he blurted out.

Tanya switched off the set. All eyes turned to Luchnikov.

"Not in a Zhiguli, though." He smiled. "In my own Peter. It's a second childhood."

"But what for, Andryusha?" Count Novosiltsev asked softly.

"To be second, Volodya. Or first if you . . . if something happens to you."

The dead silence that followed was broken at last when one of them came out with "Martyrs of the Idea, both of you!" and they all started laughing and kidding one another about where the Bolshies would pack them off to when the guiding idea of their lives came to life and their pitiful but beautiful little snail of a birthright homeland merged with the great ugly leviathan their ancestral homeland had become.

They immediately set to work. The main question was whether they should take the risk of plastering SOS all over the racers. Although the whole Island was well aware of its existence—the newspapers and talk shows had made a national issue out of whether it was to be considered a new party or simply a private political association—it had not yet been formally constituted.

"In the light of our plans for the future," said Luchnikov, "it will make a perfect formal announcement of the party. You're not only a martyr, Volodya, you're a seer."

What plans for the future? wondered Tanya. What plans for the future has this band of egomaniacs cooked up? But immediately she checked her thoughts: they were, she realized with horror, the thoughts of a spy.

"I wonder what Madame Tatyana's opinion on the matter is," said Count Novosiltsev, training his yellow wolflike eyes on Tatyana's balcony again.

"It is Madame Tatyana's considered opinion that you're all on the road to suicide," she replied coldly. She expected laughter; she got an eerie silence. Her curiosity piqued, she leaned over the railing. What she saw was the pack of them staring up at her, and for the first time she found them all strikingly handsome and—bald spots, gray streaks, and all—as young and dashing as the Decembrists.

"You're not the first to express that opinion," said the count after a few awkward moments.

Andrei gave a forced laugh and said, "Just you watch. Now she'll tell us we're a pack of animals and don't know when we're well off."

"Well, you are a pack of animals," Tanya said, "and even if I don't understand all the ins and outs of your politics, I can tell you don't know when you're well off." And so saying, she turned up the volume again, disappeared into her lair, and picked up a pile of French fashion magazines. She had felt the necessity to suppress a feeling of irritation before, but for the first time she admitted to herself it was Andrei she found irritating. Her love was on the wane. Could that be? She felt herself sinking into depression, felt a gray film spread over the glossy pages of the magazine and the bright television screen, where the Muscovites had just scored a stupid goal and were making ready to go through the whole rigmarole again when they knew beyond a doubt that their opponents were stronger.

Andrei visited her every night, and she always welcomed him. They always came simultaneously and shared a few minutes of tenderness. And then he went off somewhere in the depths of his spacious wigwam, talked on the videophone with the *Courier* staff, made all kinds of long-distance calls, scribbled away at something or another, drank Scotch, splashed about in the bath, and she began to feel she had just been not with her lover but with a stranger who had what it took for a good fuck, a very good fuck, who had satisfied himself and her and was therefore of no more concern to her, just as she was of no more concern to him. She knew she had to tell him everything—about Sergeev and why she had accepted his proposition, about her anger, about Baxter, about Vostokov. Only by telling the whole truth could she rid herself of the alienation she felt, but how could she talk through all her troubles with a stranger? It was a vicious circle, and the feeling of alienation grew.

As a matter of fact, Tanya was by no means at the top of Luchnikov's priority list. After his return from the Soviet Union he found his paper in a less than satisfactory state. Business was booming, all right, and his readers were every bit as loyal, but it had lost the life that he and only he was able to give it. In his absence, the Idea of a Common Fate had appeared on every page, but that was the problem: it had merely put in an appearance, sat there, instead of pulsating like a live artery. Soviet features and all Soviet themes had grown stiff and formulaic, almost bureaucratic in style, and anyone who felt the need to view the Soviet Union from the standpoint of a free Crimean would have to buy the *Russian Sun* or even the reactionary *Russian Artilleryman*.

To remedy the situation, Luchnikov took to writing more of the paper himself. Soon the articles on his "Journey through Wonderland" began to appear. He talked about the poverty of contemporary Soviet life, the brain drain, the feeling of demoralization on the part of those left behind and the birth of a new spirit to combat it, the massive lie of the mass media, the utter torpor of the leadership class. Not a day passed but he was on the phone to Moscow, hounding Beklemishev for more and more critical materials. The secret inner circle of the still unofficial but very much active SOS was of the opinion that, given the historical significance of the vote facing the Island population, it had a right to know the whole truth about the country, the great power with which it would soon be called upon, as Russians, to merge.

When does he sleep? Tanya wondered, though never asked. Here in the penthouse of the gigantic aluminum-and-glass pencil he was lord and master; lord and master over her, too, she felt. It was the first time she had seen him in the role, and she did not much care for it. It made her neither friend nor lover; it made her a handy home sex machine.

Working late? she wondered after the guests had dispersed. Scanning the wigwam from her lair, she finally spotted him high above herself in what he called a "work cave," hunched over a typewriter, working on his latest *Courier* piece.

THE NONENTITY: ON THE HUNDREDTH ANNIVERSARY OF STALIN'S BIRTH

They all laughed at young Koba, the future Stalin, when he was in exile: Koba's forgotten to change his socks again; Koba sleeps in his socks; Koba's feet smell like ripe Brie. Needless to say, everyone who laughed at him then in Turukhansk was done away with, but at that time, pockmarked little Iosif just sat there, torturing himself over his dilemma: if he took off his socks and washed them, he would be admitting defeat; if he kept them on and continued to smell, he would be even more of a laughingstock. He decided to keep them on, keep stinking, with the pigheaded scowl of a true nonentity.

It is our opinion that an important psychobiological aspect of the Great Russian Revolution remains insufficiently elucidated: the gradual but eventually overpowering takeover by incompetents and nonentities.

The Revolution has made its mark in the genetic code of the Russian people by favoring raging mediocrity (whose name is always and everywhere the majority over the free-and-easy, feckless, and, in the end, insolent behavior of any elite, whether we call it the nobility, the intellectuals, the artists, the *nouveau riche*, the West).

By restating a highly complex issue in these terms, we do not in the least mean to sweep any of man's social, political, or economic outrages under the carpet; we simply wish to highlight a new aspect of the issue, what we have termed its psychobiological aspect. Moreover, given the subsequent development of events, we shall go so far as to call it the decisive aspect. But why focus on it here in these pages at a time when our Ancestral Homeland is preparing to celebrate so important an occasion? Because we may be certain that when the actual date of the anniversary arrives, the official Soviet press will mark it with no more than a medium-sized article observing all the parameters of the day: though an outstanding Communist, it will say, he committed certain "errors" by overstepping the bounds of power allotted to him as an individual.

Yet the people themselves, as we have had occasion to observe, are planning an unofficial celebration, a celebration meant to honor an exceptional mediocrity as a great man. More than half the long-distance trucks whizzing by us, for example, displayed portraits of the Generalissimo in his barbaric uniform—and this not only in the south, not only in Georgia, but throughout the central regions as well.

The aim of our modest essay is to show this Communist for what he was: a rank-and-file representative of what we call the psychobiological shift, a nonentity virtually thrust to the top. The Bolshevik Revolution had its share of talented leaders—Lenin, Trotsky, Bukharin, Mironov, Tukhachevsky, and the like—who led the outraged masses according to Marxist theory. But they did now know they were doomed; they did not see that the main force of the Revolution lay in its psychobiological shift, a shift that would eventually destroy the personal and glorify the impersonal, a shift that would provide an incompetent, a nonentity to step forth and assume power.

"Revolutions devour their offspring" says a well-known adage. We protest. Revolutions devour the offspring of others. Trotsky, Bukharin, Blücher, Tukhachevsky are not offspring of the Revolution; true, they surfaced in its stream, but only to be sucked under. The Revolution's true offspring are the Molotovs, the Kalinins, the Voroshilovs, the Zhdanovs, who rose from the depths to the crest of the psychobiological wave.

We often laugh and poke fun at the films made at the height of Stalin's reign by such masterful Soviet directors as Romm, Kozintsev, Trauberg (all of whom returned to the classics during the thaw to become "great artists" and even "liberals"), the various and sundry rehashings of *Maxim's Childhood* and *Man with a Gun*. We are wrong to do so. Though prostituting themselves in the process, these and other leaders of the intelligentsia were fulfilling what was called at the time their "social duty," which is to say, they had discerned, quite astutely in fact, the wants and desires of the reign of grayness and incompetence then in full bloom. If a brazenly dull-witted, thick-skulled, bandy-legged individual took center stage in Soviet art, it was merely a reflection of Soviet life, for in life, too, this faceless figure, the expression of a vast collective brazen incompetence, had emerged as the center of attention. Any figure standing out from the mass of nonentities, *any* such figure—not only intellectuals, but men of the people: a bright sailor, a flashy anarchist, an enterprising peasant or kulak—became an object of scorn and derision for this art, which, after laughing its full, would preach his dissolution in the mass of mediocrity or his outright destruction.

Once more, art, the servile art of the times, was merely a reflection of the psychobiological tendency in life. Any head daring to stand out over the multimillion-headed flock was doomed to savage destruction. Savage and unnatural death was also the lot of popular revolutionary heroes like Sorokin, Mironov, and even Makhno, who actually saved Bolshevik Moscow by delivering the Voluntary Army a devastating blow from the rear. In their stead, the psychobiological process advanced incompetents of the caliber of Voroshilov, Timoshenko, and Kalinin, until finally it produced the biggest incompetent of all, the biggest nonentity of all, Iosif Stalin. The sword or, rather, the saw of the psychobiological revolution had done its deed: it had sliced off the all too prominent heads of Trotsky, Bukharin, and Tukhachevsky, and made the rounds of every village and town, its only criterion being flashes of talent, a gift of some kind. Thus did the lowest of the low, the nonentity to end all nonentities, consolidate his power.

Everything, but everything, Stalin undertook was tainted by his mind-boggling incompetence. Repealing Lenin's New Economic Policy, he hurled the country back into misery and starvation. Claiming to organize agriculture, he annihilated millions of able-bodied peasants and set up a system of supreme incompetence: the collective farm, or kolkhoz, as a direct result of which many millions died of hunger in the Ukraine, the Volga region, all over the country, and thousands upon thousands were forcibly relocated. Then, perceiving a rising tide of dissatisfaction within the Party and fearing a certain feisty Kirov, whose head had begun peering out over the flock, he again took the path of least resistance. Kirov's murder, the primitive show trials, and mass terror—these were perhaps the high point of his incompetence. Unfortunately for the country, they took place at the time the psychobiological shift was reaching its peak, and were therefore inevitable.

As World War II approached with its own inevitability, Stalin began searching wildly for a kindred spirit or, rather, a closely related biostructure. He found it, naturally enough, in Hitler. Hordes of stultified Germans and hordes of stultified Russians divided up Eastern Europe between them. No one could have exhibited more incompetence in preparing for war than did Stalin. First he exterminated all his qualified commanders, completely ignoring the geopolitical (and therefore complex) aspect of day-to-day events and relying on his psychobiological similarities with nonentity number two, Adolf Hitler. Then, when Hitler betrayed him, he retreated in great panic, setting whole towns on fire and leaving millions of our people to death or slavery. But

Hitler, nonentity that he was, prevented Germany from winning a quick and easy victory. Think how criminal a nonentity it took to take on the entire world without ever imagining (a complete lack of imagination was yet another bond between the two ringleaders) that people might stand up and fight back.

Now while the two numskulls were choking each other (or rather, while Adolf was choking Iosif), the Anglo-Saxons had a chance to do a little maneuvering and come to a decision about which beast happened at the time to be more dangerous. Talk about your weak, decrepit Western democracies! Stalin, scared to death (he had taken to his heels and quit Moscow by then), was of course thrilled to accept Allied aid. At least that required neither wit nor talent.

The war proved the greatness of our country: after a decade devoted to the destruction of anyone with the least bit of talent or originality, it was able to rise to the occasion—the prospect of national annihilation—and put together a team of topnotch commanders and military engineers, daring pilots and tank officers.

The war proved the mediocrity of our psychobiological leadership: Russia, officially one of the victors, lost three times as many lives as the loser, a Germany burnt to charcoal by Allied bombers.

Postwar reconstruction was rivaled only by the prewar construction. Generalissimo Stalin proved incapable of masterminding the least new project, the least reform. Instead, he created a slave army twenty million strong. Not to be outdone by the most heartless of Pharaohs, he set up the famous GULag to drain off any bit of talent and creativity the relative freedom of the war years might have prompted. Again the nonentities feasted and caroused, never thinking that the day of reckoning might be at hand. But of course their power peaked together with the biological death of their idol. From then on, things began to go downhill. The mysterious process of human development, paying Marx's incompetent analysis no heed, had entered a new phase.

No, Stalin did not die in 1953. He is alive today. His presence is felt in a propaganda machine of unprecedented scope, in the sessions of the so-called Supreme Soviet, in the sham elections, in the rigidity of the contemporary Soviet leadership (or at least the group carrying on the legacy of Kalinin and Zhdanov and its aversion to reform), in the breakdown of human economy (food, clothing, services—all areas of *human* existence are stymied by Stalinist dementia) and the growth of inhuman economy (tanks, rockets, bombs—all means of destruction loom like a phantom of syphilitic delirium), in the rejection of all iconoclasm and the imposition of a stale, dated ideological boiler plate on a nationwide scale, in the spread of what is known as "mature socialism" (and is in fact social and spiritual stagnation of the worst kind) beyond Soviet borders.

And yet the psychobiological shift *has* peaked. Stalin is losing ground. Recovery has begun.

The GULag is no more, today's counterpart being a mere shadow of its former self. If iconoclasm is anathema, still—or therefore—iconoclasm exists. New writers, directors, artists, and composers have appeared on the scene. The borders are easier to cross. The most important sign of recovery is that people with a desire to overcome Stalinism's global inertia have made their way into the inner circle of power. True, it is still more advantageous, less dangerous to be a Stalinist; anti-Stalinists have a hard time of it in the upper reaches and are forced to hide behind the phraseology of the official lie. But at least they are trying to use their brains, trying to rescue Russia from the pit she has been digging for herself all these years. They cannot yet speak out about reforms, but they ruminate on them. And when they lie, the thirst for truth is on their faces. Yesterday's Stalinist Russia rested on blood, today's rests on lies. Providence has seen fit to lead our Homeland from the great blood bath to the great lie. We cannot believe, we refuse to believe that all the decades spent under the heel of the nonentity that was Stalin have gone to waste. Stalin is dead. The sacred cow he left behind him is dying. Lies are better than blood. People in high places have begun to think for themselves. Surely we are moving in the right direction. What will the next period be like? They cannot hide truth seekers in insane asylums forever. More and more people in Russia will come to see the separation of truth from falsehood as a simple, natural process. Despite the "constant intensification in and expansion of all forms of ideological pressure," the concrete blocks of Communism are beginning to soften. People are looking for "highs," by which silly little word they simply mean a different kind of life, still hazy, perhaps, but coveted.

Cross over to the eastern part of our tiny Black Sea and take a stroll along the embankment of Sochi, the "national sanatorium." Under an endless stream of the slogans of "mature socialism" (the latest chef-d'oeuvre being THE HEALTH OF EACH IS THE HEALTH OF ALL), you will see crowds of Soviet citizens staring hungrily at one another, registering who has what jeans, glasses, swimsuits, as long as they are foreign, Western. People may be surrounded by the hammers and sickles and cogwheels of the thirties, but they are decked out in stars and stripes and advertising slogans. You can even see the two-headed tsarist eagle on the occasional Smirnoff T-shirt.

The peak of the revolutionary psychobiological shift is behind us. Stalin is on his way out. Our country stands on the brink of a new and perhaps more mysterious historical adventure than the Revolution. Shall we therefore dismiss Stalin the nonentity? No, we shall not, for even dead and buried he can conquer.

To our mind, present-day Russia is a battlefield of two powerful forces. If Stalin wins, then unbridled totalitarianism will reign. It will reign in the form of thick-skulled sheep who, ignorant of their own Stalinist incompetence for having forgotten Stalin, will spread havoc throughout the land. If Stalin loses, then Russia has an opportunity to blossom into a great creative community of people communicating directly with God, yet always mindful of its own sufferings and the sufferings of others, always harboring the memory of its nonentities, of blood and lies, of Stalinism.

Every aspect of life in Russia today must be examined in the light of these two forces. Let us take one of the most noteworthy of recent events as an example. We have in mind the emigration of the Jews and, under the same aegis, the flight of an intelligentsia wasted and worn after decades of public ostracism. On the one hand, their departure dealt Stalinism a significant blow. Who would have dreamed as recently as ten years ago that Soviet citizens would be permitted to leave the "stronghold of socialism" and settle in the country of their choice? On the other hand, it gave Stalinism a significant boost. What will be the effect of a mass exodus of thinking people, the very people who have been willing to stand out, stand in the way of the psychobiological process? Will they be permitted to return, to leave and return again? Will we finally overcome our xenophobia, join the family of man, and cease beating ideologies into one another's heads?

It would be difficult to imagine a more crucial, more dramatic moment for the future of our enigmatic society. The hundredth anniversary of the birth of that society's greatest nonentity gives us ample food for thought. Will our people find the strength to rebury his putrid remains, thus preventing an epidemic and providing fertilizer for a democracy to come?

A harmonious society needs both a majority and a minority; it needs them as much socially as biologically. The regular loss of a minority could prove fatal to the idea of a new Russia. Can a new, strong group keep from dissolving in the gruel of "mature socialism" and become the ferment of new, life-giving, anti-Stalinist processes?

Lord, give us strength!

IX

Out of Steam

Back in the bathhouse-behind-the-seven-locks outside Moscow the issue of the *Courier* containing the "Nonentity" article was making the rounds. It could not be read aloud because, as each of those present knew instinctively, to read something of that nature aloud was pure sacrilege. The thin, bluish pages of the overseas edition, retrieved from behind closed doors especially for the meeting here, fairly crackled in their hands. High-quality stuff! If we had newspapers like this, you wouldn't hear a peep about the lack of toilet paper. One of them grunted while reading it; another faintly sniggered; most of them, however, including the Important Personage, held their tongues: history, thank God, had forged them nerves of steel.

Wrapped in a thick towel he had bought in Sweden and leaning back with a bottle of Löwenbräu, Marlen Mikhailovich still kept close tabs on the faces of the entire crew, whose tacit bond of bawdy, locker-room camaraderie, unthinkable in their Moscow offices, held firm even in the presence of the Important Personage. The Important Personage received more than his share of attention, of course, and Marlen Mikhailovich had to hand it to him: that mask of his was impenetrable.

Needless to say, Kuzenkov knew the text of the Luchnikov piece by heart. The *Courier* it appeared in was two days old, and he had had plenty of time to prepare himself psychologically for today's steam session. He was even looking forward to his colleagues' questions. Who was there to ask, after all, if not the head of the Crimea desk and Luchnikov's "personal friend"?

"Well now, Marlusha, what do you make of all this?" the Important Personage finally deigned to ask.

As usual, he gave not a hint of what he himself thought. Marlen Mikhailovich turned to him, ready to start his reply, but was in no particular hurry. He knew that the Important Personage, by producing the slightest sound, would willy-nilly break the others' silence, and their remarks would provide him with some idea, some fleeting clue, of what the general mood was.

Which is exactly what happened. They'd had some vodka by then, after all, with a nice beer chaser, and the pores did open up after a dose of that dry steam.

"A complete about face?" ventured Ivan Mitrofanovich in the form of a half question.

"Some dialectician!" muttered Fyodor Sergeevich, clearly furious with the author.

"Drags God into it, too." Aktin Filimonovich smiled.

"So the Revolution devours the offspring of others," smirked Artur Lukich.

"That's the only thing I'm willing to concede," said Oleg Stepanov with his usual fervor. Within the past few weeks he had become one of the gang.

The one or two others mumbled and grumbled one or two other remarks, but the Important Personage was no longer listening. He had trained his eyes on Marlen Mikhailovich, and the glimmer of a smile the latter caught there assured him that his tactical pause had been appreciated. Marlen Mikhailovich knew that of the five or six supposedly casual, off-the-cuff remarks, the only one that counted for the Important Personage was "a complete about face."

The Luchnikov issue had been causing Marlen Mikhailovich no end of worries. In all his memoranda and oral presentations he had portrayed Andrei as a complex, contradictory individual, who, though not yet completely convinced by the Doctrine, was a true and selfless friend of the Soviet Union and a firm, even passionate backer of Crimean reunification with Russia. In other words, he was "almost" one of us.

It was as such, as an extremely important "almost," that Luchnikov had been accepted into the holy tabernacle—that is, the friendly hermitage of the steam bath. The fact that he had not appeared to value their trust might be put down to the vagaries of his Western outlook or aristocratic upbringing. But the capers that followed? The disappearance? The flight into the hinterlands? The cat-and-mouse tactics with the appropriate government organs? And finally the unthinkable—the uncanny, unheard of, and as yet unexplained slip over the border (where? when? how in the world?) and reappearance in Crimea! Granted, some of the capers —some, not all—could be explained away to the leadership as a final wild-oats escapade, or puerile adventurism, or that aristocratic upbringing rearing its ugly head again, but . . .

But the main worry was that after he showed up in Crimea, the *Courier* had undergone an abrupt shift in politics: from a clear-cut pro-Soviet—that is, progressive—line it had turned to an unadulterated dissident one. It began printing all kinds of unnecessary and totally one-sided items—articles, features, fillers, commentaries—with an ironic, sardonic, and sometimes simply snide tone to them. And now this. The "Nonentity"! This time he'd gone too far. Only someone completely foreign to our way of life—an offspring of the White Guard or a moral degenerate—would deal so basely with our history, with a man whose name for generations of Soviets has meant victory, order, power. And if it has meant violence and even obscurantism as well, then at least they were majestic and grandiose. Defaming the men who have made our history (and the men making our history today, for that matter) was a hostile, elitist maneuver, aimed at undermining both national and class solidarity. What had happened to Luchnikov? the Comrades rightfully wanted to know. Had he sold out to the CIA? Had he given up the Idea of a Common Fate?

Marlen Mikhailovich calmly picked up the weighty *Courier* (to be frank, he loved the *Courier* with all his heart) and shuffled quickly through its pages. The "Nonentity" article was on the other side of a full-page announcement of the upcoming Crimea Rally. "Let me just read the concluding paragraph, friends. Listen care-

fully now. 'Can a new, strong group keep from dissolving . . . !
Hmm, then comes that unfortunate metaphor . . . 'and become the
ferment of new . . .' Hmm, yes, uh . . . 'processes?' "

"Well, what of it?" said Fatyan Ivanovich. "Then he calls to
God for help. A regular fanatic. No wonder he wore that cross."

"Just a minute, Fatyan Ivanovich," Marlen Mikhailovich
snapped impatiently (it was all right to snap at Fatyan Ivanovich).
"There's an important message hidden here, friends."

Marlen Mikhailovich never quite knew how to address his steam-
room companions. The official "Comrades" was out of the question, and he could not bring himself to use the familiar "boys," to
say nothing of its folksy equivalents. For want of anything better,
he had come up with "friends" and stuck to it even though it
sounded slightly unnatural and was never picked up by the others.

"From these words I conclude beyond a shadow of a doubt that
Luchnikov has not modified his position one jot, that in fact he is
actively carrying out the program of the SOS, the Common Fate
League, as established by him and his powerful clique of classmates."

Another constrained silence. In the first place, not everyone had
grasped his point, and in the second place, the Important Personage had not yet made his feelings on the matter known.

"What the fuck" (the Important Personage used obscenity for
the simple purpose of easing the tension, reminding the others they
were in a *bathhouse* and not at a plenum or meeting) "is this
Luchnikov trying to prove with his Common Fate? Tell me, boys,
what's he trying to prove"—he flicked the *Courier* away disdain-
fully—"with ideas like these?"

It worked: they all smiled. What the fuck is he trying to prove,
shitting on the Revolution and Stalin and all we hold holy? You
know, he was on the barricades in Hungary, boys, shooting down
our soldiers. Who the fuck does he think he is, the bloody little
aristocrat, and what the hell does he expect to get out of a Soviet
Crimea?

"That's just it, friends. Not a thing! It's his topsy-turvy nonclass-
oriented psychology. Hysterical materialism, what the fuck!"

Oh, how out of place was Marlen Mikhailovich's obscenity,
both in this specific instance and in the context as a whole. What

on the Important Personage's tongue was a concentrated burst of folk energy was a further proof of distance, remoteness on Marlen Mikhailovich's.

"Let me ask you something, Marlusha," said Oleg Stepanov, taking him by the shoulder and looking him straight in the eye. Marlen Mikhailovich knew that the newcomer had every right to call him Marlusha, grab him by the shoulder, and even look him in the eye. In the past few weeks Oleg Stepanov had become the director of an ideological institute and a member of the Bureau of the Municipal Committee.

"Let me ask you something, Marlusha," he repeated. "The 'new, strong group' of people he talks about—is that the population of Crimea after it joins us?"

"It is." Marlen Mikhailovich could not help himself: he freed his shoulder from Stepanov's hand, knowing full well it was an unpolitic, even harmful thing to do. The Important Personage would scarcely countenance an overbearing attitude towards his new favorite.

"A fifth column five million strong, isn't that it?" Marlen Mikhailovich could not free himself so easily from Stepanov's burning eyes. "He wants to blow us up from the inside, that's what he wants, your Luchnikov, like Tito and his Haiduks trying to ride into the Kremlin."

"There's no need to muddy an already complicated, complex issue, Stepanov," said Kuzenkov with a frown. "You're smart enough to know that."

"Who taught you how to hedge like that?" asked Stepanov with a smile. "Your mother, Anna Markovna, perhaps?"

So that was it. Out of the blue and *bam!* right in the solar plexus. So they do know everything about me. Always have. Know about my poor mother, who's afraid to phone too often from Sverdlovsk on account of her barely noticeable Yiddish intonation, about all my relatives from that side of the family. Well, I suppose I'll have to take the bull by the horns.

"My mother," he said, standing up and throwing down his fluffy towel, that is, stripping himself bare, "My mother, Anna *Makarovna* Syskina—"

"*Siskind,*" Stepanov inserted with a giggle, though it was clear he had lost his nerve and was terrified at the thought of being slapped and failing to respond, not knowing how to react. "Anna *Markovna Siskind*. How can you . . . I mean . . ."

"My mother didn't teach me to hedge. She taught me to stand up to swollen-headed smart alecks like you, to the spiritual descendants of the Black Hordes. . . ."

A fearless hand was raised, a trembling cheek covered by an elbow, in other words, the slap took place without, fortunately, quite taking place, because at the crucial moment the Important Personage's lazy bass voice boomed out, "Go fuck yourselves, the two of you! That's what you get for reading White Guard shit here in the steam room. Forget those cock-suckers and their cock-sucking newspapers, you hear, Oleg, my boy? You hear?" He shook his finger gently, almost playfully at Stepanov, as if Stepanov had been the one who brought the "White Guard" newspaper into the bathhouse and not Kuzenkov at the request of the Important Personage himself. "You know what, Marlusha?" he said, turning to Marlen Mikhailovich not quite so amicably, but amicably enough. "Why don't you bring the latest issue of *Stud* next time? We'll have a good look at their meat, see how it compares with ours. . . ."

Stud was the Russian variant of *Playboy*. It was published on the Island by Hugh Hefner Associates in conjunction with Courier Publications. Luchnikov had thought up the title himself. Once before, Marlen Mikhailovich, whose safes contained *Stud*s together with all the rest of his Island-related material, had brought a *Stud* to the Finnish bath and caused whoops of prurient glee. Now there's a magazine for you! There's a real magazine! Why not have one of our own? Oh, not for the masses, of course, they mustn't be distracted, but the upper echelons could profit a lot from it. Whereupon they all guffawed, very satisfied with themselves. The conflict, now smoothed over, had still taken place, and smoothed-over conflicts that had nonetheless taken place were an important stimulus to meditation and speculation.

By the time the laughter died down, the Important Personage had completely closed up, withdrawn into himself. He stood up and moved towards the door, thereby putting an end to the discussion and leaving everyone at a loss.

There was nothing for them to do but pick themselves up and take themselves home. The meeting had run out of steam.

X

Compatriots

One morning the telephone rang in the *Courier* penthouse, and for the first time since moving in Tanya answered it. When Andrei was away, she preferred cutting off all ties with the outside world, though Andrei was not too happy about it; he wanted to be able to keep in touch, find out how she was getting along.

That morning she had forgotten to turn off the system, and when the phone rang, she picked it up mechanically, as if at home in Moscow. And what did she hear coming out of the receiver but an unsettlingly familiar voice saying, "Tatyana Nikitichna? Hello! *Privet!*"

"Is that you, Mr. Vostokov?" she muttered with hostility.

"Aha, so you've met Vostokov, have you? Congratulations! Good show."

"Who is this, anyway?" Tanya barked, though by now she could have no doubt.

"Why, Sergei, of course, Tanyusha," Colonel Sergeev said, as friendly as could be. Yes, that was his name, Sergei Sergeev. "It's been a long time, old girl."

"Lay off the 'old girl' crap, will you?"

"You're impossible, Tanya." Sergeev laughed. "A real minx."

"The minx crap, too."

"All right, all right. I just wondered how you're getting along. Oh, by the way, I ran into Gleb in Tsakhkadzor not too long ago. He's really something, you know? Blackjack or better every time."

"Blackjack?" she asked in spite of herself.

"Twenty-one. He puts the shot farther than twenty-one meters. What about you? Having a good time for yourself?"

"True confessions weren't part of the bargain."

"Brrr! I can feel that cold shoulder right through the wire. Where are you anyway? Crimea or Spitsbergen?"

"And where are you? Moscow?" The prospect that he was in Moscow brightened her mood a little.

"White-stoned Moscow." Sergeev sighed. "No expense is too great among friends. I wanted to remind you I exist."

"How could I forget you?"

"Just make sure you don't," he said, like a father scolding a naughty child. "Well, that's all. Shall I give Gleb your regards?"

"Yes, do." She was surprised at how easily, even sweetly, it came out.

Click. For the first minute or two she surprised herself again by thinking of the Hub. The mere mention of his name had sent a sensual spasm through her loins and up her spinal cord. She lit a cigarette and flopped down in the middle of the hateful glass wigwam.

Vostokov knows Sergeev and seems to respect him. Sergeev knows Vostokov and seems to think highly of him. But Sergeev speaks openly about Vostokov over the phone from Moscow. Since he must realize that OSVAG has Luchnikov's phones tapped, he can only be doing one thing—purposely blowing Tanya's disguise, making it absolutely clear who is pulling the strings. Maybe . . . But there was no end to the maybes. Maybe—ideally—it hadn't been Sergeev on the phone at all. Maybe it was an OSVAG man imitating him. Or the Americans. Or maybe Sergeev isn't afraid of Vostokov. Maybe he can talk so openly because he and Vostokov are in cahoots over Luchnikov. Or maybe Sergeev has to sacrifice her to the enemy for some reason. Or maybe . . . But was there any point in going on? The thing to do was to lay her cards on the table, tell Andrei everything, today, this evening. He'd understand. He would see that the only reason she'd "sold herself to the devil" was to be with the man she loved, the only reason she'd agreed to play this silly, dangerous game was to warn him of the danger in advance, share it with him, save him from it. Then why did she keep putting it off? Why did opening up to him seem more and more . . . impossible? What if she simply poured it out tonight? Oh, the relief! He'd believe her, he'd trust her when she told him she had no ulterior motives whatsoever, none, no matter how deep he dug.

But why didn't he ever ask me about anything? He never even asked how I happened to turn up in Yalta. He knew perfectly well I couldn't have got here without either defecting or receiving *special* permission. Maybe he had inside information and didn't need my confessions; maybe he knew what was going on and was keeping it to himself, the bastard! No, that wasn't it. He didn't ask for the simple reason that he never asked me about anything. She suddenly felt a sharp, piercing, self-willed antipathy to Luchnikov. He never asked her about anything, she thought for the first time, full of pity for herself and resentment against him. He never asked about her past or her parents, for example, or her profession, or her children. He never even asked about Sasha, who might well be his son. All he did was screw, screw and crack a few jokes. She never heard a serious word out of him. She never. He always. The always-or-never business was a recent, post-Simfi development. He used to ask her about all kinds of things.

Now he was completely absorbed in his own life. He was a master at that. All his friends were. They had no trouble doing the sort of things normal, everyday people could never dream of. Supermen, the lot of them, and Andrei more than the rest. He thinks he's infallible, he has no doubts about himself, he's fearless, he doesn't seem to care that secret agents by the score are casting their nets for him, recording his every word, filming his every move, that they may well have planted her in his bed, that even the sky-blue helicopter flying that ridiculous ALFUZOFF / ALL DIRT OFF soap ad past the penthouse day in and day out may be equipped with a telephoto lens capable of picking up every object in the wigwam, every paper on his desk, the used condom he had so breezily tossed out of the hanging bathtub after they had made love the night before. There wasn't a wall in the place, just a maze of moving panels. You had to be an engineer to keep the buttons straight. Who would ever want to live in a place like this? All sham, all show!

Having at last given her pent-up frustrations free rein, she felt a bit calmer, and having finished her cigarette and defied the helicopter with the traditional Russian "fig"—the thumb thrust between the first two fingers of the fist—she went out to do her shopping.

Even now she got a kick out of making the rounds of the shops; it cheered her when she was down. She found that pushing a shopping cart through Yeliseev and Fauchon, the gourmet supermarket, calmed her nerves like nothing else—row after row of tastefully displayed and packaged gastronomic wonders: fifty or so varieties of ham, an unbelievable assortment of fish caught hours before, Hawaiian macadamia nuts. . . . A Moscow housewife would pass out and a woman from the provinces—well, there was no telling what might happen.

Tatyana had begun making trips to the West many years ago and had therefore thought herself immune to the catatonic state first-timers experienced. In the pre-Andrei years, supermarkets had even come to annoy her. What good was it all when she had no access to it? A few jars of shrimp cocktail could cost as much as a Lacoste tennis shirt. But now they really turned her on. She didn't need to think of money, didn't even need to carry any. All she had to do was to hand the ever-smiling check-out girl her plastic perforated Simfi Card. The girl would stick it into the computer and give it back, and she was free to go across the street to the Anichkov Bridge Café and give the officers there a thrill. Defense Headquarters was right next door, and the Crimean officers (or "Russian officers," as they called themselves) would often stop for an apéritif. They were the most gallant of gentlemen and apparently untouched by the wave of homosexuality sweeping the Island.

The check-out girl handed her back her card (Tanya always chose her because she liked the Chanel No. 5 she wore), nodded pleasantly when Tanya asked her to have the bags delivered, and then said in Yaki, "*Khanam,* someone *zhdyot* you *na Anichkov Most.*"

"Who?" she asked. She had picked up quite a bit of the language. "Who is waiting for me? That's impossible."

The check-out girl gave her an insolent smile, an insider's smile.

"Friend," she said. *"Bolshoi* trouble, *khanam.* Friend-*aga, kaderle, yaki."*

Crossing the street under the blinding sun, under the falling leaves, Tanya decided that whoever had been on the phone that morning would be the "friend" waiting for her at the café. Vostokov, most likely, though it could be one of the Film Export people . . . She never dreamed that in the corner under a framed photograph of Anichkov Bridge (the actual Leningrad bridge the café was named after) she would find Colonel Sergeev himself.

It took her some time to recognize him. He looked like the most ordinary businessman: gray flannel suit, Oxford shirt with narrow stripes, knitted tie, designer eyeglasses. He was calmly reading the *International Herald Tribune*—the stockmarket report—as if he calmly read it there every day. The *Courier* and *Le Figaro* were waiting their turn next to his Campari-and-soda. A pencil-thin Dutch cigar finished off the picture of quiet contentment (Tanya had the feeling it was no show—he really was content). Since it was too early for apéritifs, there were no officers yet. In fact, the only other customers were a powerful-looking American black and his chubby German friend cooing together in another corner.

"Sorry for the little game this morning," Sergeev said sincerely and openly. "I thought I'd better give you a little psychological warning. . . ."

"Another miscalculation on your part," said Tanya coldly.

Without waiting for her to order, the owner brought Tanya some Martell and a cup of Brazilian coffee, flashed a friendly smile, and disappeared.

"Aren't you afraid to sit here? With Defense Headquarters right next door, I mean."

Sergeev's smile showed how much he enjoyed her naïveté. "This is my favorite spot in Simfi. I come here first thing whenever I fly in from Toronto."

"Toronto," she said sarcastically, but then noticed a TWA Toronto–Simfi tag on his attaché case.

Sergeev, noticing that she had noticed, was now completely and utterly content. "We've been so worried about you at the office," he said, lowering his voice slightly, though it seemed an unnecessary precaution for a Russian-speaking Toronto businessman having a drink at his favorite Simfi café.

"I'm touched. What sensitive people you work with."

"Not a bad group, actually. After Ig-Ignatyev tried his little kidnap caper on you, there was talk of retribution in kind. By the way, you're lucky Vostokov kept an eye on you that night. You can't beat that man's intuition. Efficient, too. Warning Chernok to send out his special operations unit." Sergeev was showing off how well informed he was.

"But why did he call on Chernok? Why didn't he use his own men?"

"Ask him yourself." All at once there were overtones of mystery in Sergeev's voice. "You see him all the time. With the other classmates."

"He's not in the inner circle. He was a year behind them."

"Is that so?" Sergeev covered his eyes for an instant.

Tanya realized she had given him an important piece of information. "Happy?" she asked. "Something you can use?"

"Thank you, Tanya," he said simply. "And please drop that venomous tone. I fail to see what purpose it serves, especially here, abroad."

"So here you and I are compatriots?" she asked with increased venom.

"Yes, here you and I are compatriots," he said, suddenly stern, "true compatriots. We have a common cause, you and I."

"A common cause?"

"Andrei's safety. Believe me, Tanya, trust me. I have other interests, too, of course; it would be senseless for me to deny it. You're nobody's fool. But as far as Andrei is concerned, Tanya, our goals coincide a hundred percent, I swear."

"What do you want to know?" she asked casually, making a sign to the owner to bring her another Martell.

The owner was there in a flash with a new snifter on his tray. Sergeev did not even look up as he approached.

"I want to know what the classmates talk about when they're alone together," he said calmly. "They're meeting more and more often these days. What is their mood like? What are their plans?"

"All they talk about is racing. The rally. Count Novosiltsev and Andrei are both planning to enter, the maniacs."

"That's not what I had in mind," said Sergeev brusquely.

"Well, that's all they talk about. Peters, Ferraris, Maseratis.

You'll never believe it, but Novosiltsev is entering a Zhiguli! Cylinders, valves, brakes, fuel—that's all they talk about."

"Don't think you can fool me with that drivel!" For the first time there was the hint of a threat in his voice. "First think why you're here, then think a little harder about their talks."

"Look, why don't you ask Vostokov?" She caught her taunting grin in the mirror and decided to tone things down a bit. "He does drop by now and then. They consider him a friend."

Sergeev immediately took advantage of her retreat to give that mocking, superior grin of his own. "Vostokov? Don't make me laugh! You want me to ask Vostokov? Vostokov is the competition!" The grin vanished with the same professional abruptness with which it had appeared. "Of course, we know all there is to know about him. About you, too, for that matter. And don't you forget it."

"You mean Vostokov's Polaroids," she sputtered in indignation.

Nothing stirred in Sergeev's face, yet Tanya could tell he was taken aback. Maybe he didn't know about the pictures or the *Elyse.*

"Right, the Polaroids," he said in a monotone.

"Well, I just want you to know they don't mean this much to me," she said, pointing to the tip of a long, finely groomed nail. "You don't suppose Andrei and I have any secrets between us, do you, Sergeev?"

This time he was clearly taken aback—and furious. "You don't mean to tell me, I hope, that Luchnikov is privy to our relationship," he said, fairly hissing with rage.

"That is exactly what I mean," she riposted bravely.

"Really now—" and he exhaled a large puff of Dutch smoke to screen the bewilderment in his eyes—"really now . . . Trying to have it both ways? Or change sides? It's a dangerous game you're playing. . . ."

Just then the café filled with noise, laughter, and spirited voices: a group of officers, five air force and three navy, had come in from next door. They took their places at the circular bar and were soon turning and saluting Tanya with their glasses. "Tatyana Nikitichna, want to hear the latest joke from Moscow?" one of them called out to her. She picked up her glass and went over to the bar. She looked smashing in the mirror—a handsome woman, elegantly dressed, surrounded by eight handsome men in uniform. The mirror also showed Sergeev paying for his drink, tucking the bill away in his attaché case (for reimbursement), and withdrawing. Evidently military secrets lay outside his purview.

XI

Up in the Stratosphere

The week after the bathhouse altercation, Marlen Mikhailovich was down with a stiff case of what could only be called nerves. He was under a constant barrage of indirect glances. Clearly something or other had leaked out. The telephones rang much more rarely, and the upper floor was as still as death. Not that there were no calls at all. His "neighbors" rang up quite often. Together they decided to send the highest-ranking member of the Luchnikov staff to the Island. Sergeev, the man in question, was perfectly willing, of course. Marlen Mikhailovich understood him well. No matter how distasteful the job to be done there, the Island always seemed to give him a lift. Perhaps it heightened his class sensitivity, or excited him with its petty, everyday capitalist pleasures, or—most likely—cleared his head: that sun, that heady breeze . . . Squinting slightly, Marlen Mikhailovich could picture himself on the Sevastopol embankment or Lapsi Pass. The phone rang and, still squinting, he picked up the receiver. It was the call he had been waiting for all week. Very formally, as if they had never steamed together, the Important Personage told him to prepare for a meeting on a level that took his breath away. Tomorrow at this hour he was to report to a section of the building where even people of his stature needed a special pass. You will have forty to fifty minutes—no more, no less—to discuss the current situation on the Island.

Immediately Kuzenkov called all his staff members together and told them he would have to keep them late this evening and ask them to come in an hour earlier in the morning. He himself would spend the night at the office (his rank entitled him to his own private lounge and lavatory adjacent to the room where he worked). They had been asked to put together a concise but extensive report, complete with statistics, on the present state of politics, the military, industry, trade, and finances in the Eastern Mediterranean Region, Crimea-Russia, the Provisional Evacuation Zone of the Armed Forces of South Russia, OK, or "that viper's nest of White Guard offspring," depending on the mood of the stratosphere. Then everyone got down to work: telephones jangled, secretaries ran to and fro, and Marlen Mikhailovich riffled through mounting piles of paper, though he could not help wondering what purpose all the documentation served if the only reason for the meeting was to remove him from his post for incompetence and either demote him or, if he was lucky, shunt him off to the side.

When he saw the next day who was taking part in the meeting, he realized things were more complicated than he had thought—or at least not so clear-cut. The Important Personage was by no means top dog. True, he occupied an extremely advantageous position: he was at the same table and on the same side of the same table as three Most Important Personages—though two chairs removed (just to make it ethical). The three assistants of the Most Important Personages together with the Important Personage's assistant occupied analogous positions at a table in the corner of the vast office. The Important Personage's assistant gave Marlen Mikhailovich a friendly smile. He was Marlen's ally, an intellectual prodigy with impeccable academic qualifications. All those present shook hands with Marlen Mikhailovich, whereupon he was shown to his place at the main table opposite the Most Important Personages, the "portraits."

After taking his seat and centering his file in front of him, Marlen Mikhailovich looked up at the portraits. They glowered back, stern and businesslike. Every year they showed more traces of fatigue and age despite the ever-increasing successes of the

System and the Doctrine on a world scale. Marlen Mikhailovich's demeanor fully reflected the unwritten code of ethics by which the institution conducted its affairs: suitably businesslike and severe, it also displayed the awe that comes of adoration. Practicality had always to be tempered by a minute admixture of involuntary awe.

The awe came naturally to Marlen Mikhailovich. He did not need to pretend or force himself to feel it. Face to face with the portraits, he found it as instinctive as breathing. Because the portraits represented the Party and the Party meant more to him than life itself. It gave him a sense of belonging, and no matter what happened to him today, he knew he belonged here. He was a soldier of the Party wherever it saw fit to use him, even in the lowly district committee.

Yes, they could all feel his sincerity, they valued it highly. Look, a paternal gleam in one of the portraits' eyes, a sincere and deep-felt token of esteem. It all went to prove that the portraits thought of their subordinates as symbols of the great, mighty, and eternal —eternal as the Siberian taiga—concept of the Party.

But in a flash the ever-so-subtle yet heartwarming exchange of emotion was over, and the practicalities began.

"Let's see now, Comrade Kuzenkov, it seems we're here to have a little chat about your little Island," said one of the portraits in a decidedly folksy accent. "It's been a real thorn in our side, that little Island. For years now. I can't tell you how many letters the Central Committee gets from the working class saying it's high time to do something about it."

Marlen Mikhailovich drank in every word, nodding vigorously to show, first, that he fully appreciated the significance of personages of such magnitude gathering to decide the fate of the modest object of his concern; second, that he fully grasped their predicament; and last, that he was fully prepared to deliver an exhaustive report on all major issues confronting "the little Island." As soon as the portrait finished, Marlen Mikhailovich opened his folder and cleared his throat.

But the moment for the report had not yet come. The second portrait, who had a face that seemed to project a strong character, but in fact was merely battling with a set of inordinately heavy jowls, began to push some pads along the table with his stubby fingers and grunt out scraps of sentences to the effect that the problem had been blown out of proportion, that there wasn't any problem at all, that there were other, more important problems, that the time was historically ripe for . . . At this point he discovered his pads had traveled so far down the table that if he gave them one more push he would have to explain why he was pushing them—an annoying prospect—so he drummed his stubby fingers on the edge of the table as if trying to recapture his train of thought, then stretched a resolute hand across the green cloth covering, and retrieved the pads. He immediately started pushing them again.

Take away the principles he embodies, thought Kuzenkov, and what an extraordinarily unpleasant person he is. He was amazed and ashamed at himself for thinking such a thing. In the pause that arose, he tried to show by a contrite smile and a quick fiddling of papers that he fully understood how insignificant his own little Island was in comparison with the world at large and the social progress of all mankind, and that he was fully prepared to deliver a slightly abridged version of what was anyway quite a concise report.

But then the Extraordinarily Unpleasant Personage, completely ignoring Kuzenkov, turned his head slightly towards the official whom we have been calling the Important Personage, but who for him was no more than a junior colleague, and asked straight out whether the solution of the so-called Crimea problem would require any more than General X's landing force.

Horrified, Marlen Mikhailovich gave a start. Everyone noticed, everyone's eyes were on him. The Decidedly Folksy Personage stared at him, impassive, fishlike, through his thick glasses; the Important Personage, in a slightly lopsided (but completely relaxed) pose, fixed him with an expectant left eye; and even the Extraordinarily Unpleasant Personage threw a quick, sidelong glance in his direction, though accompanying it with a grimace and keeping his head turned towards the Important Personage in anticipation of his response. The only person in the room who did not look over at Kuzenkov was the third portrait, who from the start had been rather reserved—that is, completely engrossed in a monumental doodle.

"Well, what do you say, Marlen Mikhailovich?" asked the Important Personage. "Would that solve the problem?"

"Militarily?" Marlen Mikhailovich asked cautiously.

"How else?" said the Extraordinarily Unpleasant Personage to the Important Personage, ignoring Marlen Mikhailovich once more. "It might be a good occasion to try out our new air-cushion military craft."

"Militarily, General X's landing force is not at all sufficient to solve the problem posed by the Island of Crimea," Kuzenkov said in a voice so firm he surprised even himself. "The Island's armed forces are not to be taken lightly," he said even more firmly. "May I remind you of the recent victory over Turkey, clear proof of battle-readiness."

"Are we Turks then?" The Extraordinarily Unpleasant Personage chuckled.

Naturally, they laughed with him. The assistants turned and laughed at one another. Pealing bells of laughter came from the Decidedly Folksy Personage: "No, that's too much! Turks!" The Important Personage laughed, too, but only *pro forma*: he was taking a surprisingly independent stance. Only the Rather Reserved Personage, still doodling, made not a sound. Only he and Marlen Mikhailovich.

"*They*," said Kuzenkov with a new feeling of absolute calm, "*they* are not Turks."

Silence. Stupor. Stupefaction. Kuzenkov had dared to spoil a portrait's joke! Cut his argument to pieces with a clever comeback! Everyone immediately began fumbling with papers, leaving Marlen Mikhailovich on his own with the Extraordinarily Unpleasant Personage. The Extraordinarily Unpleasant Personage sat there bullishly, staring at his stiff fingers. His face hung down in all but indecent bags.

And suddenly, after only a brief pause, a fresh laugh rang out. It was the Important Personage, shaking his head and looking over approvingly, almost conspiratorially at Kuzenkov. "You know, he's got something there, Comrades. They're *not* Turks, they're Russians, and Russians always beat the hell out of Turks!"

The eyes of the Decidedly Folksy Personage showed a new glimmer. The Rather Reserved Personage doodled away. The Extraordinarily Unpleasant Personage refused to meet the Important Personage's gaze.

So the Important Personage and the Extraordinarily Unpleasant Personage are rivals, thought Marlen Mikhailovich.

"What is your point?" the Extraordinarily Unpleasant Personage asked the Important Personage, though the question was meant for Marlen Mikhailovich. "Are you putting those puny Whites on a par with us? Are you questioning the success of a military solution to the problem?" His voice grew more ominous with every word. "America trembles before our might, but not these bastards, is that it? Why, our fathers chased them across the steppes almost weaponless, chased them across the steppes like rabbits! But no. 'The Island's armed forces are not to be taken lightly.'"

Marlen Mikhailovich felt sure he saw the Important Personage give him a private wink, but with or without external support he was now ready to rise to the occasion. He was no longer frightened of the Extraordinarily Unpleasant Personage and cared only about making his point—namely, that the situation was much more complex, ambiguous, than they made it out to be.

"Let me explain what I mean," he said. "The Crimean army is extremely well trained and equipped. If General X's landing force were made up of Turks (or, say, Americans), the Crimeans would rout it for certain. But"—noticing the Extraordinarily Unpleasant Personage about to open his mouth, he forged on—"I can state without a shadow of a doubt that never, *never* will a Crimean soldier open fire on a Soviet soldier. I am not talking about military tactics now, I am talking about the prevailing mentality. A number of influential Crimean officers regard their armed forces as part of the Soviet army. In principle, our Ministry of Defense could be sending them its daily memos."

"Nonsense!" shouted the Extraordinarily Unpleasant Personage. "They're White, aren't they?"

"They *were* White," Marlen Mikhailovich objected, appalled at how uninformed a leader could be. "Their grandfathers were White, Comrade."

"But what about all those parties of theirs?" He screwed up his face in disgust. "The Cadets, the Octobrists . . ."

"Crimea has more than forty registered parties, including the two you mention," Marlen Mikhailovich said dryly.

The insolence implied in the curt reply so stunned the Extraordinarily Unpleasant Personage that his mouth fell open, though he was perhaps equally stunned by the idea of so sacred a concept as *party* broken up into forty all-but-powerless units. Kuzenkov saw a flicker of genuine curiosity behind the Decidedly Folksy Personage's thick lenses, and the Important Personage was almost beaming. "Don't forget to mention the Common Fate League," he prompted.

"Yes, of course. The most important recent event in the political life of the Island is the appearance of a Common Fate League headed by influential middle-generation representatives of the Russian population."

"Sounds earthshaking," said the Extraordinarily Unpleasant Personage ironically and, leaning back in his chair, turned to face Kuzenkov for the first time. "Well, what do they want, this Common Fate League?" he grumbled coarsely.

"The reunification of Crimea with Russia," Marlen Mikhailovich replied plainly and precisely.

"You mean the progressive forces on the Island," the Extraordinarily Unpleasant Personage said with a crooked smile.

"It would be a grave mistake on our part to identify the Common Fate League with what we call progressive forces."

"Whoa! Hold on a minute," shouted the Decidedly Folksy Personage. "Isn't this reunification business going to be more trouble than it's worth? Where will we put them all, anyway? Forty parties and nearly as many different nations. Besides the native Tatars they've got their Russian population and their Greeks, their Arabs and Jews, some Italians. . . . I even hear they've got an English colony."

"The Party has amassed a good deal of experience in these matters," said the Extraordinarily Unpleasant Personage. "The multiparty system, of course, can be done away with in days. The nationality issue is more complicated, though as I see it, the Greeks belong in Greece, the Italians in Italy, the Russians in Russia, and so forth."

All the assistants, Marlen Mikhailovich, and even the Important Personage kept a reverent silence. It was time for the portraits to speak among themselves.

"Whoa, there! You mean exile?" asked the Decidedly Folksy Personage. "Haven't we had enough of that?"

"Not exile. Just a little well-balanced resettlement. Oh, not the way we used to go about it. No, upholding the highest humanitarian ideals. All nonnative groups will be repatriated, and the native population, the Crimean Tatars, will receive autonomy under the protection of, say, Georgia."

"The way you tell it, it all sounds fine and dandy," said the Decidedly Folksy Personage, scratching the back of his neck, "but I bet it won't turn out like that. First the Americans will stick their noses into it—"

"We know how to deal with them," said the Extraordinarily Unpleasant Personage with a haughty smile. "I didn't say it would be easy, but there's no point in making it seem impossible. Ideologically, we have everything to gain by liquidating the remains of the *other* Russia."

"And economically?" countered the Decidedly Folksy Personage. "Think of all the hard currency we get from the Island now, the electronic hard- and software. . . ."

"Ideology is not an area to economize in," said the Extraordinarily Unpleasant Personage.

"Your proposals?" the Rather Reserved Personage put in abruptly, setting aside a completed doodle and looking up at Marlen Mikhailovich with calm, hostile eyes.

A burst of adrenaline shot through Marlen Mikhailovich, and for a moment he lost his orientation. But lowering his eyes and clenching his fists under the table, he pulled himself together. Thank you, tennis, for teaching me to make a comeback, he said to himself.

"First of all, Comrades, let me stress that I always do my utmost to accomplish the will of the Party. No matter what decision the Party takes, I vow to pursue it as the only correct and possible one."

He paused.

"If we thought you'd do otherwise, you wouldn't be sitting here," sneered the Extraordinarily Unpleasant Personage.

What a cruel, inhuman sneer, thought Marlen Mikhailovich. I've never seen anything like it.

No one intervened. The reaction to the "declaration of love" was seemingly nil. But then the Important Personage's assistant half-closed his eyes and half-smiled, and Marlen Mikhailovich understood it had been a good gamble.

"As for my own proposals—and I might point out here that I

have devoted twenty years of my life to the Island—I would warn against any definitive action at this point. The political situation on the Island is extremely involved. There are signs of a new pan-Crimean consciousness, for example. The fourth generation of Russians, the Russian youth of the Island, is very much taken with the idea of combining the various ethnic groups into a single new nation they call Yaki. This spirited but undisciplined movement represents no real threat to the Common Fate League, which despite its unofficial status has quickly become the guiding mentality, the mind set of the rest of the Island. Sympathy toward the Soviet Union and even the desire to merge with us are rampant. Naturally, the numerous left-wing and communist parties support the Common Fate idea, but they spend most of their time squabbling. The Chinese influence is weak, but quite in evidence. Groups of anarchists appear, disappear, and reappear quite regularly. We must also take into account the political institutions of Old Russia embodied in the administrative apparatus of the ruling elite—the provisional evacuees, or, as they are known, provacuees. Nor should we forget the Tatar nationalists, though Yaki influence is growing fast within their ranks: they see it as a viable alternative to the Russia idea. Finally, there is the ultraright, a semicriminal—and therefore potentially dangerous—band called the Young Lupine Hordes. The West, by the way, does not particularly care about Crimea. NATO pays it little attention in its strategic plans, and the various intelligence agencies keep track of it only because it is historically a potential hot spot. But let me get back to the Island itself. If a referendum were to take place tomorrow, no less than seventy percent of the population would vote for merging with the USSR. I am certain of it. Of course that does leave thirty percent. In other words, great care must be taken in wiring the connection: one false move could short it and cause a terrible conflagration. Elections are only three months away. They are sure to clarify the picture somewhat. We must use every minute of those three months to intensify our observation and increase our influence by expanding contacts and stepping up propaganda, especially in the form of political literature. But although it is naturally in our interest for the Common Fate League to emerge victorious, we must, I feel, refrain from backing it directly. SOS, as the League is commonly called, is a highly complex phenomenon. It is headed by a close-knit band of influential public figures known as 'the classmates' and including Andrei Luchnikov, the publisher of the *Russian Courier*; Colonel Chernok, an ace pilot; Count Novosiltsev, a popular athlete; and Timofei Meshkov, one of the Island's richest industrialists. Hard as it may be to believe in this day and age, Comrades, these men are totally free of outside influences; they are pure idealists. Their movement rests on an idealistic concept, what they term their guilt complex, the guilt they feel vis-à-vis their Historical Homeland, Russia. They realize that if their cause—the cause of their lives—is successful, they stand to lose all their privileges and bring ruin upon the provacuees and their class as a whole. It's enough to bring a smile to the lips of any politician, I know, but there it is—and it's spreading fast. Finding a truly scientific—that is, Marxist—explanation for it all is difficult but not impossible. Since it would require a long and detailed analysis, however, I cannot go into it here. Theory can wait; we have practical matters to attend to. SOS requires our constant, closest attention. Like any idealistic movement, it is highly sensitive to the emotional ups and downs of its leaders. Indeed, it is currently going through a phase that at first glance may seem a total transformation, an about face."

Pausing to turn a page, Marlen Mikhailovich sensed something strange in the air and looked up. He was astounded by what he saw. Suddenly everyone in the room was frozen in rapt attention, everyone's eyes were glued to him. Even the Extraordinarily Unpleasant Personage looked human, the outline of his former face showing through the bags. In a flash Marlen Mikhailovich realized what the meeting was for. They were upset by the about face, concerned that the Island of Crimea would float out of their reach, that they would be robbed of what they had long considered their due. Sorry, gentlemen, he said to himself triumphantly, you won't get us that easily!

Later, of course, Marlen Mikhailovich put himself through hell for that "us," for dropping Party vigilance and identifying with the "idealists," but at that moment he was triumphant. The first thing you think of is a military solution. Quick! Mow them down! You can't see farther than your nose, you know that? Some leader you are! Another Pharaoh. And under it all you're terrified, shaking like a leaf. You're even afraid of your neighbor two chairs away. In fact, you may be more afraid of him than of anything on earth.

The Extraordinarily Unpleasant Personage could tell he had been found out. He quickly pasted the haughty sneer back on his face, leaned back in his chair, and began drumming his fingers again. He even gave a little yawn and glanced at his watch. But it was all an act, and he knew the others knew it.

"In fact," Marlen Mikhailovich continued, "there is no about face at all. A passing fancy for the silly ideas of our dissidents or the new emigration, perhaps, a typical idealistic reflex. Luchnikov may be fearless when it comes to the bullets of the Lupine Hordes, but he's scared to death of being snubbed by a jazz musician or an artist, the Moscow friends of his youth. That's the reason for the shift in the *Courier*'s Soviet coverage."

He made one more pause before plunging into his peroration. It had seemed dangerous enough to him yesterday before his run-in with the Extraordinarily Unpleasant Personage. Now it seemed doubly so.

"I am deeply convinced that in these tense preelection times the classmates, not wishing to be accused of treachery, are bending over backwards to show the population what they regard as the truth about the Soviet way of life. They want their people, who have one of the highest standards of living in the world and are used to the so-called freedoms of bourgeois pseudodemocracy, to know what they can expect when they cast their votes for reunification with the great Soviet Union. Our country's name no longer appears without the epithet 'great' on the lips of Crimea's masses.

"Considering the complexity of the situation as I have just outlined it, I respectfully repeat my original proposal: that instead of taking an irrevocable decision at this time, we keep our finger firmly on the pulse of the Island."

Marlen Mikhailovich closed his folder and sat silently looking down at the imitation-alligator cover with xxv stamped in the corner. Would the Twenty-fifth Party Congress be his last?

"Are there any questions for Marlen Mikhailovich?" asked the Important Personage.

"Are there any questions!" bellowed the Decidedly Folksy Personage. "We'd be here all night if we asked all our questions."

"Marlen Mikhailovich," the Extraordinarily Unpleasant Personage said gently.

Marlen Mikhailovich shuddered ever so slightly as he looked up. The Extraordinarily Unpleasant Personage was smiling an engaging, almost friendly smile. It was a smile that said, Now I see what you're up to, now I understand your game, and now that I know you're not one of us, I might just as well be civil.

"As you are doubtless aware, Marlen Mikhailovich," he said civilly, "I have many questions for you. A great many questions. An endless supply of all different kinds of"—pause—"questions. But surely that comes to you as no surprise."

"I am ready and willing to answer any questions you may have, and again let me stress that, as far as I am concerned, the Party's decision is paramount. History has shown that experts make mistakes. The Party never makes mistakes."

The blank face of the Important Personage's assistant told him that this time he had gone a bit too far, but by now he was past caring.

Suddenly the Rather Reserved Personage spoke up. "The consensus seems to be that Marlen Mikhailovich Kuzenkov should be given a long-term assignment with the Institute for the Study of the Eastern Mediterranean Region. As a general consultant there, he would be able to study at close range the problems facing our island territory." He gave Marlen Mikhailovich a niggardly smile. "You will be our finger on the pulse of the Island. You will be directly responsible to Comrade [here he gave the name of the Important Personage]." Then he thanked them all for their participation in the meeting and stood up.

The meeting was over.

Marlen Mikhailovich went out into the corridor, his head spinning, his body shuddering from the sudden release of tension. Thank you, tennis, he thought again, for teaching me to relax. And all at once he was overcome by a transport of joy: a long-term assignment on the Island! Who could ask for anything more! Even if it was a kind of demotion or exile, he thanked his lucky stars for it. Things could have ended a lot worse. He could have been sent off as an ambassador to a place like Chad or Mali. No, it was actually quite a victory: his old job had gone to the Important Personage, and the whole Island issue had been moved one level higher.

The Important Personage took his arm, whispered, "Satisfied, you fucker?" and poked him in the ribs.

"What can I tell you?" said Marlen Mikhailovich. "It's a smart decision. I'll be much more useful on the spot. And Vera . . . There are so many things she can help me with. . . ."

"What do you mean?" said the Important Personage with a wink. "You'll have the pick of the crop down there. I must say I envy you a little. If I can get away for a week, we'll have a ball!"

Looking into the eyes of his new immediate superior, he saw there was no sense in trying to argue Vera Pavlovna and the children into the package. The decision had been made at a higher level: Marlen Mikhailovich would leave his "anchors" at home. Oh, well, after the Shevchenko defection he could understand their prudence even in the highest echelons.

"We'll have a ball, I guarantee it," said Marlen Mikhailovich in the bathhouse spirit.

"Wait a second. It won't work," said the Important Personage, suddenly and sincerely depressed. "I'm too well known. You can't even hide in a bathhouse there, can you?"

"No, those video-tape cameras sneak in everywhere."

"Well, then you be careful, you hear?"

"Don't worry."

Having come to the end of the corridor and the green runner, they faced a white wall and a bust of Lenin done rather disconcertingly in black stone. The Important Personage put his hand on Marlen Mikhailovich's shoulder and said, "By the way, there's no reason in the world to hide Anna *Makarovna* away like that. How many Comintern delegates are still alive and kicking, after all?"

Marlen Mikhailovich thanked his patron with a wan smile.

XII

The Old Roman Road

The starting shot for the Crimea Rally was traditionally fired in Simferopol at the entrance to the Southwest Freeway, but the racers had a choice of how to get from there to the Old Roman Road. They could take either the eight-lane freeway past spectacular Mount Chatyr-Dag or any of the ten exits and try their luck along the convoluted asphalt roads below. The point was to get an early start on the Old Roman Road because its serpentine course made every attempt to pass a gamble with death. Fifty miles of straight freeway may seem like a gift—touch the pedal and off you sail— but in fact, the jockeying for position was so cutthroat that many of the participants never even made it to the Old Roman Road; they rammed either into the crash barriers or else into one another. As a result, several drivers preferred the asphalt labyrinth that wound through Mashut-Sultan, Angara, and Tamak; they preferred the edge it gave them over the roaring pack in Alushta, the chance to slip onto the road at Demerdzhi and be the first to wag a tail of gravel dust in the face of the competition.

Luchnikov and Novosiltsev had worked out a clever plan. The count would slip off at the first exit ramp and disappear from sight, while Andrei took care of slowing down the main stream of freeway cars by darting in front of the leaders, changing lanes, and braking unexpectedly. If the count reached the Old Roman Road first, he would not have to worry about Billy Hunt or Conde Portago, to say nothing of the local aspirants.

As always, the rally had attracted the best racers in the world —ten or so superstars, two dozen stars, and any number of asterisks, all full of ambition and raring to go. Ninety-nine cars qualified altogether. "100 −1" said all the T-shirts, jackets, matchboxes, and other promotional paraphernalia. Cars of all makes and color combinations were firing their engines and testing their brakes in the gigantic parking lot beside the freeway. Little by little they began taking their places along the starting line, anxious to pour out onto the course.

The ebullient crowd numbered several thousand, but the cream was concentrated in the stands near the lieutenant's statue. TV helicopters hovered overhead, and newsmen and *paparazzi* swarmed through the square. The Crimea Rally was an unofficial national holiday. It brought everyone together but at the same time heightened the rivalry among ethnic groups: Tatars backed Tatars, Anglo-Crimeans put their money on the local English, provacuees all had Russian favorites, and so on. During the last few years, however, the winner had been one or another of the international champions of the Billy Hunt or Conde Portago caliber.

Billy Hunt, white of tooth and of skin (he was from South Africa), called his cars, naturally enough, Hunters. It was all but impossible to tell what today's monster had been to begin with. The body was decorated with the trademarks of various manufacturers: Alfa-Romeo for the transmission, Porsche for the brakes, Ford Mustang for the carburetor. . . . Each company paid him royally for the right to advertise on his flanks, but money meant nothing to him. He was a true fanatic, putting together a totally new Hunter for every race and ordering each part to his own specifications. Life off the course was like a series of mirages to him. The most beautiful women in the world were at his feet, and though he deigned to pick one up from time to time, the scandal sheets would no sooner fete their honeymoon than a separation was in the offing; none of the women could keep up with his giddy pace, for one thing, and then, they all knew he would swap the lot of them for one good spark plug. He was totally ruthless. He called his cars Hunters not only because of his name but because in every race he would chose a victim—the potential leader—hound him mercilessly, ride his tail, and finally "bag" him and cross the finish line victorious.

Conde Portago was the lean and haughty type, and looked much younger than his thirty-six years. His style was the antithesis of Hunt's: he kept aloof. He and his silver-gray Hispano-Suiza Flamenco seemed to be battling against time and time alone; all he cared about was speed. When someone "got under his feet," he would show no more emotion than a curl of a paper-thin Castilian lip. At several recent races El Conde had ended up Hunt's booty, but he paid Hunt no heed and never commented on his defeats. Needless to say, El Conde's private life was a riddle to the press.

Sitting at the wheel of his Peter Turbo, Luchnikov looked on, unconcerned, as the reporters flitted about the Hunter and the Flamenco. Not that he was exactly ignored by the mass media himself. The fact that the forty-six-year-old publisher had entered the race was great human-interest material, and the fact that his Peter Turbo was covered with SOS! JOIN SOS! SOS! added a hot political twist. But as soon as the reporters began barraging him with questions and sticking microphones through his window, he pushed them away and lit up a cigarette. And smiled enigmatically. The main thing was to smile enigmatically.

The strategy was to funnel all publicity to number eighty-seven, Count Novosiltsev's exotically named Zhiguli-Kamchatka, and it worked. The minute he pulled up, the reporters were all over him. Nothing from the Volga Auto Works seemed to be left but the tin box, the emblem, and the first half of the name. All the rest was pure Kamchatka—that is, the count's imagination. The result was an open single-seater stripped down to allot as much space as possible to the huge modified engine and extended fire wall. It featured a custom lighting bar that shone through all gravel dust and greatly enhanced the grille; a specially designed frame; wide, road-hugging, heavily lugged tires; massive, brightly painted rubber bumpers and flared sides; a jet-nozzle exhaust pipe; and a uniquely rigged system of mirrors enabling the count to see far into the distance and down under the wheels. Novosiltsev had kept it a secret even from the classmates. Luchnikov could not help smiling to himself. Volodya had been called Kamchatka all through school because he always sat in the back row, which teachers traditionally called Kamchatka after the far-off Siberian peninsula. Volodya was always up to something back there: copying homework, or chewing spitballs to shoot at the class goody-goody, Timosha Meshkov, or wrestling with the boys on either side of him, or playing by and with himself. Then one summer he went to visit his aunt in San Francisco, and that was the end of Kamchatka. During those few months the pimple-ridden troublemaker had turned into a sleek, athletic young superman. From then on it was boxing, karate, high jumping, and racing, racing, racing. Soon a new nickname caught on: Novo-Sila, meaning "new strength." The classmates still used it.

Luchnikov found Volodya's return to Kamchatka touching and somehow fitting. He waved his gloves at him, but Novosiltsev could not see, surrounded as he was by the gentlemen of the press. He was enjoying posing for the photographers in his favorite headgear, an outlandish contraption similar to the winged helmet of ancient Gaul. Luchnikov looked on in a nearby TVMig monitor, as Novo-Sila demonstrated his famous three-hundred-sixty-degree turn. It really was something to see—a seemingly clumsy hulk of metal literally swinging round on its axis. Luchnikov looked over at Billy Hunt, who was eying the car carefully, sizing it up. El Conde, needless to say, sat examining his nails and whistling, totally oblivious to the goings on.

"Hey, *chellow!*" Luchnikov suddenly heard from the crowd. He looked up to see his son bounding towards him, waving a YAKI cap and smiling. Luchnikov was glad to see him, yet ashamed as well: I don't think about my family any more; I don't think about my son, or my father, or Anton's mother languishing in Rome, or my future wife, for that matter, whose binoculars are probably trained on me this minute. I've freaked out on politics, that's my trouble; I've let this damn reunification thing go to my head. Petya Sabashnikov's right: I've turned into a real ratfink. "Hey, *chellow!*" his son called out as if running into an old friend unexpectedly.

The word *"chellow"* had become so much a part of Island lingo that even the most inveterate anti-Yaki provacuees caught themselves using it. It was a hybrid form made up of the Russian (provacuee) *"chelovek"* and the English (Anglo-Crimean) "fellow." (During the fifties the Americans at the army base tended to add their energetic "man" to it—oh, how Andrei and his pals had loved that word—but when the base was dismantled, the "man" disappeared.)

Luchnikov opened the door and Anton scrambled in, rattling off something in Yaki, more for the medium, his new linguistic skill, than the message. Although most of what he said was lost on Luchnikov, he did make out that he, the *atats*, was great, that the Crimea Rally was *yaki* and a real *holituy* ("holiday" plus "*saban-tuy*," a Tatar word for "holiday"), but that he'd better not expect to win, because Masta Fa, the Yaki choice (who was exactly half his age, Luchnikov noted), was going to take the race hands down.

"How about switching to Russian now?" Luchnikov suggested, mussing up his son's hair. "Or are you getting rusty?"

Hiding his relief, Anton went on in the language of his fore-fathers. "You know, it's funny, Dad, but we seem to have become political opponents."

"What do you mean? We're not opponents."

"So you think we're completely powerless. You think we have no future."

"It's too early to say," said Andrei, not without a touch of sorrow in his voice. "Give it another two or three generations. If the Island's still around, that is."

"It's not going to sink, is it?"

"No, but the mainland calls. . . ."

"You know what all my friends think? We think your Idea sucks," Anton said matter-of-factly and without the slightest rancor. "You have no right to call the Island Russian. That's imperialism. Less than half the population is Russian by blood."

"The same holds for the Soviet Union."

A thundering voice announced through the PA system, "Five minutes, everyone. Five minutes! Will all participants please approach the starting line."

Luchnikov switched on the engine and began observing the in-strument panel. Out of the corner of his eye he could see his son looking over at him with respect. "Is Granddad giving his recep-tion tonight?"

"Of course, Dad. It's going to be what the Americans call a swell party. The drivers are coming and all kinds of neat people. By the way, is your lady friend planning to make the scene? I think I know who she is. Her name is Tina, isn't it?"

"Tanya."

"Tanya, not Tina?"

"Tanya! Where did you get that Tina from?"

"*Yaki, atats*! See you tonight! And don't bother to put yourself out. Masta Fa's going to win anyway. Watch for the orange Eagle!"

"*Yaki, chellow*! said Luchnikov with a wave.

With a minute and a half to go, he turned on his CB radio and said hello to Tanya.

"How are things going?" she asked.

"Nothing special," he said. "Go and find Brook and hitch a ride to Sugdeya in the *Courier* helicopter."

"But that's not the way we planned it."

"Find Brook and fly to the finish with him," he repeated coldly. "Roger. Over and out." She had been rather obstreperous of late, he thought as the seconds ticked past, and today she had even wanted to stay at home. They had almost had a fight.

"Go!"

The rockets flew up, and the cars surged forward.

The Crimea Rally guidelines placed no limitations whatever on engine or car size. You could race a gigantic Russo-Balt, the ultimate in modern comfort, or a tiny shoelike Midgit. In principle, the terrifying blue sharks and yellow dragons stalking the sound barrier on the salt flats were also welcome, but they would be hopeless when it came to the curves of the Old Roman Road.

Luchnikov had not gone in for any customizing; he had not altered a part. Of course, his Peter Turbo was practically one of a kind anyway, the pride and joy of the Peter plant in Dzhankoy. It was one of a limited edition of about fifty sent around the world in advance of the initial advertising campaign. The engine had been so carefully sealed that the oil did not need changing until after the first fifty thousand miles. Ten or twenty years ago he would have crawled into its belly no matter what, but now, he had to admit it to himself, he had no interest in the race at all. If it hadn't been for the SOS, he couldn't have paid it the least bit of attention. He had changed: he thought of his former self as of another person; the exhilaration he had felt last spring in Koktebel was gone, never to return. How much had he lost, and what was he gaining in its place—power, prestige, authority? What were they worth in comparison with a single second of that old-time exhilaration?

Yaki, he said to himself, watching the mighty silhouette of the Chatyr-Dag come into sight against the blue and gold of the sky. *Yaki*, five minutes down, and I haven't given a thought to preparing the way for Volodya, my only aim today, my only goal.

About fifty feet up ahead three cars were running together. Billy Hunt had been trying to get into the draft of the flying torpedo, Conde Portago, but a bright-orange car with green feathers painted all over it had sneaked in front of him and blocked him off. It was none other than the Yakis' "invincible" Masta Fa in his Eagle. Well, what do you know! thought Luchnikov. He's giving Billy quite a scare.

Let's see now. It's too late for me to slow El Conde down. He'll get to the Old Roman Road first, no matter what I do. But Billy, for all his hunting instincts, is still vulnerable. All I need is a little help from Masta Fa. And if El Conde is all by himself, Novo-Sila will be able to handle him just fine.

For a while Masta Fa kept Hunt from passing and sitting on El Conde's tail. Then Billy began to hang back a bit and try sitting on the Eagle's tail instead, but Luchnikov shot forward and beat him to it. He could almost see Billy's white teeth gnashing. The only way Hunt could reach his immediate goal now was to brake so much that he risked falling back into the main pack of cars. So he took an entirely new tack: he veered off to the left and pushed his Hunter to the hilt, hoping to spurt at least a few feet ahead of Masta Fa. Billy Boy's redlining it for sure, thought Luchnikov, and I've got rpm's to burn. So he zipped into the gap between the Hunter and the Eagle.

For a few seconds the three of them were running neck and neck. Luchnikov stole a quick look to the left and saw Hunt bent low over the wheel, fuming; a quick look to the right and he saw the inspired, flaming eyes of a young Tatar. Mustafa—that's his real name, thought Luchnikov. He's no Yaki; he's a genuine Crimean Tatar, with maybe a drop of Greek blood. They were all changing their names these days—my Ton Looch and this Masta Fa—as if that were all it took to make a nation.

Just as Luchnikov was thinking it was time for him to burst

ahead, Billy decided to shake him up a little and swerved to the right, grazing the Hunter bumper against the Peter Turbo. The air filled with the smell of burnt rubber and the roar of a powerful engine, and the Peter Turbo left the Hunter behind. Luchnikov watched Billy in his rear-view mirror. He was hanging back again, trying to cut diagonally across the freeway and start tailbiting his real booty, El Conde, who was still far in the lead. He won't make it! Those ravenous Ferraris, Mazdas, Spitfires, and Peters were closing in on him. Another second or two and the Hunter would be swallowed up by the pack. Half of Luchnikov's mission was accomplished: he had gained no less than a minute for the count.

Passing Masta Fa with ease, Luchnikov could not resist glancing over the edge of the freeway for a bird's-eye view of the surrounding countryside, and sure enough, he saw a bright spot winding along the road below. Not only that. TVMig's helicopter was hovering directly above it: the director must have guessed their plan.

For curiosity's sake Luchnikov slammed on the brakes. He watched the unexperienced Yaki cringe in terror. But the distance between them remained constant: Masta Fa had good reflexes. Several seconds passed. The pack started catching up. Masta Fa turned sharply to the right, but Luchnikov stood firm, and the pack panicked; some braked, others tried to shoot ahead, but the majority soon brought them back into line. A few seconds later, when order had more or less been restored, Luchnikov disoriented them all again by switching to the far right-hand lane, where he seemed to be chasing El Conde, a hundred feet in front of him, but actually was catching another glimpse of Count Novosiltsev flying through the green wilds of the gorge to the tortuous road leading up to Angara Pass. The few other smart alecks who had chosen the lower road were way behind him.

For a while there were no new developments. Each time a car tried to stray out of the pack, Luchnikov's bright-red Peter Turbo would jump in front of it, and the unfortunate upstart would be forced to change lanes or slow down. Luchnikov seemed to be playing the honor guard to El Conde's victory car. During one of his lane-changing expeditions Luchnikov noticed the giant *Courier* helicopter flying next to him over the chasm the freeway was crossing at the time. Through the open doors he saw a few familiar faces grinning at him and pointing their thumbs in the air. *Yaki!*

Then he heard a click in the car and Tanya's worried voice. "We're with you, Andrei. Be careful. Don't take any chances."

"Get off the line, please, and don't call again."

Suddenly the Hunter disengaged itself from the left flank, and this time its target, the big game, was Luchnikov, not El Conde. So Billy, too, had guessed what was what, and Billy was not easy to shake. Luchnikov gave the wheel a few jerks and followed Billy's razor-sharp reactions with a smile. Billy was back in the race, back in his stride. Luckily there were only a few more miles of freeway left, and all he had to do was hang in there. Soon the enormous silver bow of the Alushta off-ramp came into sight, and the racers began steadying themselves for the vertiginous turn that would spit them out onto the Old Roman Road.

The ramp was three times narrower than the freeway, and Luchnikov just managed to slip in before the Hunter. El Conde hit the gravel first, sending up a huge train of reddish dust. Then out of nowhere, like a jack-in-the-box, Count Novosiltsev flew into the fray and up the sinuous road. The classmates' plan had worked: Novosiltsev was on Portago like a shot, and Luchnikov was sheltering the Zhiguli-Kamchatka from the Hunter. The minute before Luchnikov's tires screeched into the gravel, Hunt turned on his blinding headlights. When the dust had died down and his eyes adjusted to the light, Luchnikov saw the silhouette of the Kamchatka and of the count's broad shoulders and winged helmet up ahead. The count raised his right arm for a moment and waved at Andrei.

The hairpin curves began almost immediately. Up and up the cars climbed, deep drops first on one side, then on the other. To the left along the slopes and in the fertile green valleys lay the sumptuous villas and hotels of Demerdzhi; to the right lay the sea, rocky bays alternating with miniature fishing villages, yachts and a Yalta-bound luxury liner. Here and there some rickety stakes marked the most dangerous curves, but more often there was no protection whatsoever. The racers sped past other dangers as well: badly eroded shoulders, broad fissures, and the remains of landslides. But then, it was the deplorable condition of the road that made this race *the* race. For want of time—or was it for a lark?—Luchnikov had not bothered to go over the course beforehand. But

Volodya had been through it at least fifteen times in the past month and knew every crack. So onward and upward with SOS! The count was safely in Portago's draft and saw no need to pick him off just yet, and Luchnikov kept Hunt guessing by meandering as much as the road would allow. In other words, the race was on.

It all looked rather innocent from on high: a leisurely caravan spread out over several miles, clouds of dust pierced by colorful arrows and sun-glazed mirrors, and if from time to time the pieces changed places, they seemed to have agreed to do so in advance. In fact, of course, the race was more cutthroat than ever. The Flamenco and the Kamchatka were a good quarter of a mile ahead of Luchnikov and Hunt. And if Luchnikov's meandering looked quite harmless from above, Tanya was beside herself whenever the television set in the *Courier* helicopter showed the two cars nose to tail or—through the dusky, dusty glass—the drivers' faces, teeth bared and features flattened with tension. After each of Luchnikov's maneuvers she watched Brook, Meshkov, Fofanov, Sabashnikov, Vostokov, Beklemishev, Nulin, Karetnikov, Denikin—everyone in the helicopter with her—wipe the sweat from their foreheads and look at one another. They were all in a state of extreme agitation, and the rat-a-tat-tat of the TV commentator did nothing to calm them.

"Yes, Andrei Luchnikov and Billy Hunt are locked in a nerveracking battle, ladies and gentlemen. Who would have thought that the publisher of our very own *Courier* would make such a brilliant comeback after all these years and with none other than the worldrenowned Hunter from the white tribe of Africa as his nemesis? The cars are now headed down to Tuak. They're picking up speed. Here comes a curve. Hunt veers off to the left, trying to pass the Peter Turbo by hugging the edge and, as you notice, damaging some overhanging shrubs in the process. Luchnikov follows suit; then, outguessing the Hunter, swerves back to the right. There's a short straight stretch coming up here now. Luchnikov spurts forward to lead the Hunter by one and a half lengths. Meanwhile, the leaders are keeping up their dizzy speed, Count Novosiltsev still on El Conde's tail, and both men breaking all records. Will you look at that traffic! Traffic on the freeways leading to Kuchuk-Uzen,

Tuak, and Kapsikhor is at a standstill. People have abandoned their cars and stand bewitched at the sight of car after car whipping down the Old Roman Road, the road of the Roman legions. Watch carefully now! There's a fourteen-degree downhill curve coming up! Conde Portago and Count Novosiltsev take it in their stride. Now watch again as Luchnikov's Peter Turbo comes blazing into the curve. He seems to be taking off over the sea. And how does Hunt react? My God, he's cutting him off, pulling past on the outside. He's literally leaped over the stones on the shoulder of the road, leaped over the precipice, and leaped ahead of Luchnikov! A perfect example of the daredevil stunts that have earned the White Hunter his world-wide reputation! He *feels* the road, feels it in every inch of his wheels, of his skin! Out in front El Conde still has his lead, with Count Novosiltsev holding a constant gap and Hunt coming up fast. Luchnikov is doing what he can to save face, but his chances are almost nil. What brings these two veterans out of retirement, anyway? Could it be more politics than sports? I'm sure you've noticed the SOS slogans on the cars. . . . But to get back to the race, the leaders are halfway through the snakings now and the rosy terraces of Kapsikhor are in view. . . ."

Luchnikov had no time to admire Billy Hunt's feel for the road. He was terribly thrown by the sight of Hunt's monster tearing out of the sky and landing in front of him, blocking his passage. The Hunter had howled off after Novosiltsev, and his rpm's were way down. The count raised his hand again to show Andrei he had taken in the whole scene and would act accordingly. He was on his own now. He would have to overtake the Flamenco immediately and let Spain and South Africa pull each other back.

In the meantime, Luchnikov downshifted and gave the accelerator three swift jabs. The turbine kicked in, and the Peter redlined and shot forward. Three pitiful white posts signaled the bright-blue sea ahead and the blind curve to the left. The squeal of the brakes, the stench of the tires. One more curve safely rounded and a new drop on the way. The gap between Hunt and Novosiltsev was narrowing. Luchnikov had a clear view: it must have rained here recently, and the dust was less of a problem. He could even see the gaping crack in the clay-and-rock inside shoulder of the upcoming curve, the count's first chance to squeeze past the Flamenco. I'd risk it, thought Luchnikov a split second before he saw Novo-Sila risk it—and the ground break from under him.

A good twenty cars had made it to the Old Roman Road, and a good twenty drivers witnessed the tragedy—they, the passengers and pilots of a whole flock of helicopters, and millions of people in front of their television sets.

Having lost the ground from under its wheels, the Kamchatka flew into a sharp boulder jutting out of the chasm and flipped over in the air. The blow was so powerful that the safety belts snapped and Count Novosiltsev's body was catapulted out of the car. In an instant both body and car disappeared in the depths of the chasm. No one heard the gas tank explode.

Later all the racers testified to the shock they felt at witnessing the catastrophe. Even Conde Portago braked; even Billy Hunt lost a few seconds. Only Andrei Luchnikov forged ahead without hesitation, and it was that push which enabled him to pass them both and take the lead. After it was all over, he admitted to himself that from the evening Volodya declared his intention of entering the race he had had a premonition of the outcome, and from the very beginning he knew he would not brake or lose a single second: the real winner was to be neither Novosiltsev nor Luchnikov but the SOS.

Speeding down the steep slope to the village of Paradiso, he caught sight of its hilltop Greek church and was about to cross himself when he decided it would cost him a fraction of a second, and whispered instead, "May he rest in peace! Rest in peace, Volodya! Rest in peace, Kamchatka, Novo-Sila, true friend!"

"Rest in peace!" he bellowed, watching in his mirror as Portago and Hunt flew, oddly splayed, over the curve he had just completed. Suddenly he was boiling with rage and inspiration: he realized he had won.

When the TV screens showed the knight in winged helmet lying prostrate on the rocks, everyone in the *Courier* helicopter crossed himself. Tanya crossed herself for the first time in her life. They all had tears in their eyes, and Timosha Meshkov was sobbing like a child.

Trying to come to grips with the meaning of the gesture she had just made, Tanya gazed down into the abyss from the other side of the helicopter. Immediately her eye was drawn to a white van perched on a hilltop: there was a man with a gun sprawled out on its roof. She grabbed Vostokov by the shoulder and pointed, unable to say a word. Vostokov promptly activated his two-way radio. "On your guard, Sasha! There's a white Ford van on the first hill past Paradiso with a sniper on the roof!"

A jet Thrush instantly swooped down out of the flock of helicopters, and no sooner did its shadow touch the white van than the sniper's shoulder twitched: he had fired. The cars had just begun turning behind the giant rocks hiding the descent into Novy Svet. The *Courier* pilot wrenched his craft seaward, and everyone rushed to the other side for a view of the caravan. When they saw the bright-red Peter Turbo still streaming out in front, they let out a collective sigh of joy.

"The Lord God Himself guided your eye, Madame," whispered Professor Fofanov, and kissed Tanya's hand.

Luchnikov, of course, had noticed neither shot nor sniper. Nor could he have seen the three stalwarts who jumped from Chernok's helicopter onto the roof of the van to capture the culprit. Luchnikov generally preferred to ignore the safety measures taken by his friends on his behalf, though he knew full well that Chernok's emergency squad was always on the alert. He would not see the bullet hole just above the left rear wheel until much later. Now he was sailing into pseudo-Genoese Sugdeya, exultant Sugdeya, for the glorious finish.

That evening at Kakhovka, Andrei, the classmates, and Tanya slipped up to Andrei's room in the Guest Tower to watch the sniper being interrogated on TVMig. Thirty, thin, and crew-cut, he reminded everyone of Lee Harvey Oswald. His Russian was pure, un-Yakified, so he could only have been a provacuee. Yet no one was able to identify him. It was presumed he came from the northwest part of the Island, where in the region of Karadzhi and Novy Chuvash there was an isolated colony of Guard Cossacks that traditionally provided recruits for the Lupine Hordes.

Slouching in a chair with his legs crossed, the sniper grinned into the camera. His face showed a combination of brash defiance, hidden fear, and self-satisfaction. He had never had so much attention in all his life.

"Your name, sir?" a Security man asked him courteously.

"Ivan Schmidt," he said with a smile, "but you can call me Vanya, boys." He categorically denied all connection with the plot to murder the new champion, pooh-poohing the patent evidence as circumstantial. The camera gave several close-ups of the gun with its sniperscope. "You've got me all wrong, boys," said Ivan Schmidt, still smiling. "I never dreamed of firing the thing. I was just watching the race, squinting through the sight to get a better view. Really, I don't even think of the thing as a weapon. It's more like a telescope, the way I use it. That's right, a telescope. Whenever I can't find my binoculars, I grab this contraption."

"So it's just a telescope, Mr. Schmidt?" said the Security man, pointing to the evidence.

"That's right," said "Mr. Schmidt."

"Then will you tell us why it has a rifle on the other end?"

"Well, you see . . ." He lowered his eyes and then, looking up with a sullen smile, began talking very fast. "You see, it's like this. Sometimes, when I can't find a gun, I do use this telescope for a rifle, but believe me, I wouldn't ever dream of shooting a Russian and a champion, even if he was Comrade Luchnikov. I'm a patriot, a Russian patriot. Come to think of it, what gives you the right to manhandle me like this, ask me all these questions? The constitution says that— Wait a second! You're not from the KGB, are you?"

With that, live coverage of the interrogation came to an end, and tapes of the rally flickered back onto the screen. They would be repeated over and over until every bar on the Island had studied each incident along the circuit down to the last detail.

"Tomorrow the blackguard will be out on bail," said Professor Fofanov, "and by the time all the preliminary investigations and other judicial red tape are done with, he'll be safe and sound somewhere in Greece or Latin America."

"You mean he won't go to jail?" Tanya asked indignantly. "Is that true, Vostokov?"

"Yes, more likely than not, our Mr. Schmidt will wriggle out of it," said Vostokov. "Such are the vagaries of bourgeois democracy, Madame," he added with a meaningful smile.

Just then the winners' line-up flashed on the screen.

"The real winner of today's race is Count Vladimir Novosiltsev," said Luchnikov from the screen, looking grief-stricken and exhausted.

"One bad break after another. I've never had such a run of bad luck," muttered Billy Hunt, through his teeth.

"Next year I'll be first!" said Masta Fa with a broad smile.

"I deeply mourn the loss of my friend and relative, Count Novosiltsev," said Conde Portago, his eyes turned away from the camera.

"You mean they're related?" asked Madame Meshkova in amazement. "Didn't you know?" said Madame Denikina. "They're somethings-in-law. I don't know how you say it in Russian. Volodya's daughter married a nephew of Portago's last year, Baron Lenz." "No one ever tells me anything!" Madame Fofanova complained. "Well? Is it a good marriage? Is Katya happy?"

The TVMig team took over again. In the gathering dusk three men in handcuffs were being escorted to a police van surrounded by a milling crowd of reporters and curious passers-by. The TVMig commentator swirled to face the camera and began chattering in English into the microphone. "The police have arrested three more suspects in the Paradiso region. All three were armed with sniper weapons. It looks as though one of the racers had a pretty penny on his head and quite a few young gallants hoped to claim it. . . ."

They all sat and watched, all but Andrei, who lay in a corner looking out the window at the sun dispersing the last heat of the day over the Valley of the Bible. It was almost dark by the time they left. For the first time he and Tanya were alone in his Tower, in his father's house. They said nothing for a while, a zone of gloom and emptiness growing up between them.

"Tanya," Andrei finally called over to her, "can you give it to me? Now?" His voice quivered slightly.

Something is wrong, thought Tanya, but stopped there. In this room, in the darkening shadows, his call sounded uncommonly urgent. Although she did not turn to him at once, her body immediately responded, opened up to him. She slipped the straps from her shoulders, and her dress fell to the floor like a tunic. Then she took off her panties and bra and went up to the man lying on the rug trembling. His eyes shone, his throat made pitiful cackling noises. What are those noises? she wondered as she lowered herself on her elbows and knees next to him. Is that the way he cries? She gave a shudder of recognition: abomination and lust had come together again in her life. He entered her, and for the first time he seemed to be tearing her apart inside and out from genitals to breasts, growing stranger, larger, more stupefying with every thrust. Like the Hub.

"So you saved me, you saved me, you saved me?" he asked, squeezing her thighs in his hands.

She bit her lips, trying not to groan. Bastard, she thought. Pitiful little snotnose. Paper superman, she thought, rocking in the rhythm of his movements.

"Did your duty, eh?" he said, his face covered with tears and sweat, but his body still ripping away. "Did your bosses' bidding. Kept alive a valuable catch for them. Answer me, you bitch! Tanya, Tanechka! Answer me!"

"I can't speak," she gasped hoarsely, certain his eruption was gathering.

But he went on and on, purposely dragging it out. His wet hand touching her nipples was weak, but his red-hot rod rammed home again and again. At last she let go and moaned.

"So we can't talk, can we?" he said, choking on his tears. "We have to keep our professional secrets, eh, Comrade? But saving my life is part of the deal. My life, but not Volodya's. Why couldn't you have saved Volodya, you dirty cunt, you! You dirty fucking whore!"

It was then the eruption finally started, and it all came pouring out of him—his weakness, worthlessness, fear. She responded to his fountain with bursts of loathsome pity and protection.

For several minutes they lay side by side on the rug.

"Forgive me," he said, breaking the silence. "Just after the race a well-wisher filled me in on all the details. Why didn't *you* ever tell me? No, I should have asked you myself. I knew there was something fishy going on. You couldn't just turn up like that, not without *them*. I don't know why I never asked. Forgive me, Tanya. . . ." He stretched out his hand and touched her breasts. She wrenched herself away in horror and whispered, "Filthy bastard!"

He stood and opened the door to the bathroom. A band of light cut across her leg. She wrenched her leg away.

"Your room is to the left along the balcony," he said. "You have your own bath. Don't be too long about it. The reception starts in half an hour. You're right, Tanya. I feel I've been purged of some disgusting filth. Forgive me." The next thing she knew he was sniggering, laughing as he always laughed, as if nothing had happened, as if he hadn't just torn through the corpse of his mistress and used her as a slop bucket for his cowardly slime.

"We'll talk things over later," he said in his usual condescending conqueror tone. "Up you go, Tanya baby."

"Lay off the 'baby' crap, will you?" she wheezed, without stirring. He shut the door behind him. She heard the water running.

For a while she lay there immobile, feeling as though life were seeping out of her and she were losing weight and fury and disgust and all the charm she used to have at her command, and only skin and bones and grief were left, a grief so heavy it made up for all the weight she'd lost. Slowly she realized they'd had their last time together: beyond that door there was nothing left for them.

When at last she'd picked herself up, gathered her clothes, and looked in the mirror, she noted indifferently that her charm was still intact. Then she stepped out on the balcony, turned left, and went into her room to wash and get dressed for the party. At the other end of the balcony she noticed a girl in a dark sweater leaning against a pillar and smoking. The girl did not look up at Tanya.

The rally receptions of Feodosia's Marshal of the Nobility were by now a Crimean ritual. Though the race drivers were the guests of honor, a large part of the attendance consisted of members of the Provisional Government, leaders of the White Warriors' League, select representatives of the diplomatic corps (from the officially nonexistent embassies), local barons of industry, the upper echelons of the armed forces, heads of various national and religious groups, including the Crimean khan's court—in sum, a Who's Who of Crimean society, and all quite honored to be included in Luchnikov senior's guest list. Those not included also flocked to the reception. The giant mountainside estate was, in fact, open to all, and the throngs pushed in all night.

Provisional Prime Minister Kublitsky-Piottukh had arrived at Kakhovka early that morning for a confidential talk with Arseny

Nikolaevich. He had once been Arseny Nikolaevich's student in Russian history and soon advanced from disciple to world authority on early Russian Christianity. He ended up prime minister as a compromise of various inter- and intraparty intrigues rather than through any effort of his own. Once in office, however—poor, modest intellectual that he was—he resolved that it was meant to be, it was his life, he had been chosen, and he set about fulfilling his obligations with a strong sense of duty tempered only by a growing sense of absent-mindedness.

The prime minister was told that his mentor was at morning exercises, but the servant who led him into the park behind the house had to direct his head upward before he could locate him. For there in the crisp Koktebel air old man Luchnikov was scrambling up a steep rock with the aid of a rope. Observing ascent and descent from below, Kublitsky-Piottukh felt certain that he had come to the right place, that Luchnikov was his man, *the* man predestined by God for the task he had in mind, and when he learned that Arseny Nikolaevich had chosen the exercise to combat vertigo, he felt even more certain. As for Arseny Nikolaevich, the moment he spotted the figure of the prime minister down in the park, he knew that history had come to sound its clarion call again, and deeply depressed, he made up his mind to send history packing. He spent the whole day running from Vitya, as he called the P.M., claiming preoccupation with the reception, and Kublitsky-Piottukh wandered through the park under Pushkin's rock-hewn profile or lay on a chaise longue staring out at sea and wondering whether there mightn't be a spiritual or eventually even a political cure for absent-mindedness. Meanwhile, the government muddled through perfectly well with no leadership.

Towards evening the prime minister's personal secretary delivered his navy-blue Pierre Cardin suit with the Order of Vladimir in the buttonhole. After changing, he stood in Luchnikov senior's office watching the Mercedeses, Rolls-Royces, Lincoln Continentals, and Russo-Balts glide past and giving himself up to a series of historical meanderings that reached their peak when a Soviet Zil unloaded the delegation from the Institute for the Study of the Eastern Mediterranean Region.

Before the awards ceremony there was a minute of silence in memory of Count Novosiltsev, a "most worthy compatriot and the pride of Russian sportsmen," as the Provisional prime minister put it. After so daring a formulation Kublitsky-Piottukh could not help glancing over at the Soviet comrades. The director's fleshy face showed no expression whatever, but Kuzenkov, back for another stint, this time as a "general consultant" for the Institute, gave him a pleasant bow of the head.

Count Novosiltsev's body had been removed to Saint Vladimir's Cathedral on Cape Kherson. After the reception all the classmates would be driving there for the funeral service. But now the winners were standing next to the prime minister, their cups, medals, and checks awaiting them on an antique inlaid table. Microphones hung down or jutted up from everywhere, and TV lights flashed on and off.

Of the four winners Andrei was the oldest, most elegant, and most austere. Tanya, standing in a special section with the "ladies of honor," could not bear to look at him. How could she connect this image of self-assurance and determination with her whining, whimpering, puling torturer? It's over, she thought, I'm through. Tomorrow we'll argue and split for good. I'll never let him touch me again. I don't love him. Did I ever love him? Maybe not since that night ten years ago in the elevator.

Everyone seemed to be looking at her. The publisher-editor of the *Courier* and winner of the Crimea Rally has chosen this evening to introduce his future wife to society. Several times she felt the eyes of Luchnikov senior resting on her. Even from his place, as he stood with the dignitaries, he had recognized her as that odd bird from Aero-Simfi, yet he seemed to be smiling quite pleasantly at her. He's a hundred times better than his son, she thought. He doesn't try to force his ideas on people. He probably doesn't even think about politics. Honor—that's his main concern. And for the first time in her life she herself began to think about honor. It was an old, silver, tarnished word, but tarnished only up to a point. She lifted her chin proudly and stood looking straight ahead in all her splendor (enhanced, not diminished, by the sexual excesses she had been through).

While Kublitsky-Piottukh droned on, Luchnikov looked over the audience. His eyes first lit on his friends' mournful faces, then sought out Tanya. What's she got to look so high and mighty about? Who do you think you are? A Moscow pleb turned KGB queen. My Fair Comrade. And don't think you're the belle of the ball, either. Not with high-fashion model Margot Fitzgerald just in from Florida to celebrate Billy Hunt's nonvictory. And don't forget you're here by the grace of an organization a lot less innocent than *Vogue*. Yes, I know you saved my life. Thank you very much. But I can't stand to look at you any more.

Suddenly he picked out Marlen Kuzenkov among the Soviets. Well, well! To what do we owe this pleasure? Nothing ever "just happens" with that crowd. Of course. The election's coming up. He caught Marlen Mikhailovich's eye, and they exchanged smiles.

Will wonders never cease! Octopus and Vitaly Gangut. I'd recognize those ironic smiles anywhere. So the Soviet Fellini is Soviet no more. I suppose I'll have to make it up with him. Friends are friends, after all.

Next he caught sight of his spiritual leader, Father Leonid. His first reaction was one of joy, but then he thought, It's nearly two years since we talked together, sat together in silence. My spirit is weak, Father Leonid. I need you. Why is it written that "the very hairs of thy head are numbered"?

Luchnikov also sensed the presence of a pair of eyes on him; he could not pinpoint them, but he felt them beyond a doubt. Way at the back of the room he saw his son standing on the window sill. He was wearing a jacket and tie and had his arm around a raving beauty. But those eyes, they were still trained on him. Where were they hiding? Then he noticed a woman in a white blouse and black sweater standing in the doorway. Her hair was pulled together in a bun, her eyes hidden behind a pair of oversized tinted glasses. That was what had made her eyes so hard to locate—the tinted lenses. Who was she? But just then the prime minister handed him his cup, medal, and a check inserted in a fine leather folder.

Applause. Kublitsky-Piottukh's soft cheek. Cup in hand, he stepped up to the microphone. "Ladies and gentlemen," he intoned and, with the merest trace of a smile, added, "dear Comrades, let me repeat what I have said before: the true winner of today's race is my late friend, Count Vladimir Novosiltsev. He was the one who suggested that we enter the rally after so many years. I wish to pay tribute to his sportsmanship and fidelity to the ideals of our youth. He was a man of honor and vision, a Russian knight in shining armor.

"Throwing down the gauntlet to our talented Island youth, to say nothing of the great racers of our time, men like Billy Hunt and Conde Portago, Novosiltsev took a great risk. He did so for one reason only: to display the initials of our newly founded political society, SOS, and thus bring it to the attention of the public.

"It was my firm hope that Count Novosiltsev would announce the formation of SOS, the Common Fate League, at this evening's awards ceremony. Now I must take his place.

"SOS is not a political party. We welcome all Islanders, no matter what their political beliefs. What holds our adherents together is the feeling of a bond with our Historical Homeland, a desire to move beyond insular isolation, for all its euphoria, towards the great spiritual development of mankind in which the country called Russia by us since childhood but in fact called the Union of Soviet Socialist Republics has been assigned a cardinal role. We call upon you to consider our proposal carefully and to join in our struggle for the definitive reunification of Crimea and Russia. Ours is a daring yet noble attempt to share the fate of two hundred and fifty million of our brethren who, through decades of gloom and untold suffering, relieved by only an occasional glimmer of hope, have carried on the unique moral and mystic mission of Mother Russia and the nations that have chosen to follow her path. Who can say? Perhaps Crimea will provide the spark to ignite the Russian engine in the world rally of History.

"It therefore gives me great pleasure on this festive occasion to announce the formation of the Common Fate League and its intention to take part in the upcoming Duma elections. Rather than put forward our own candidates, we shall support those candidates in currently existing parties who share our philosophy of history. The people must decide. The people must decide knowingly, consciously. The *Courier* and other media publications supporting SOS have made a special effort to provide an accurate picture of contemporary Soviet life; they have held nothing back. I give you my word of honor. Yes, a vote for SOS is a vote for sacrifice, and we can only guess at the extent of the sacrifice involved. Yet the choice we place before the electorate is a choice between comfortable stagnation in the backwaters of civilization and active participation in Russia's messianic future—that is, in the spiritual development of our time.

"You know me. You knew our hero Count Novosiltsev. You know my friends Chernok, Meshkov, Fofanov, Sabashnikov, and Beklemishev—all potent forces on the Island and in the world. They join me in asking for your support. Cast your vote for the candidates who believe in SOS! SOS—the Island of tomorrow! Lord, give us strength!"

The moment Luchnikov's cup touched the table, all hell broke loose. Who would have thought that the cream of society could create such a furor? Applause, catcalls, shouts of devotion and profanation. But then he raised his hand, and the hall fell silent in an instant. The idol's power is beginning to take effect, he thought, as he launched into a paean of gratitude to the organizers, the government, sports manufacturers, and numerous athletic clubs that had made the rally possible; to the foreign participants and guests; and last but not least, "to the fair sex honoring us tonight with such rare beauty."

Just as he thought. The cameras immediately turned to the ladies of honor, first panning the group and then returning for close-ups of Tatyana Lunina, Margot Fitzgerald, and Lucia Clark. Lucia, of course, waved hysterically at the cameras, screaming "SOS! SOS!" Good old Lucia. She never missed a chance to ride the crest of a wave.

Father's reserved face. Anton whistling jubilantly with two fingers. His golden girl laughing and trying to imitate the whistle. Now I recognize her! She's one of the girls he brought home that time. Tatyana's haughty, distant eyes, making it absolutely plain she has disassociated herself from the proceedings. The Soviet Institute people whispering excitedly among themselves. Marlen taking in the exuberant crowd.

After the SOS sensation the ceremony was a terrible anticlimax, but Kublitsky-Piottukh stumbled through it as best he could. Billy Hunt was furious: even without a running translation he could tell that no one was talking about cars any more and that he had been drawn into something against his will. Masta Fa tried to put in a word for the Yaki movement, but having no experience on the podium, he kept slipping out of the new language into Tatar, Russian, or English, and soon everyone was tittering.

The disconcerting eyes behind the tinted lenses followed Luchnikov all the way to the southwest lawn, where he was to hold a press conference. This time he caught a bit more of her. She was wearing a black sweater and white slacks and had quite a nice figure, though she was most likely one of those boring American academic types with a Ph.D. in Russian literature. He asked Brook whether he happened to know who she was. Brook happened to know everything: she'd come from New York to attend an international board meeting of Amnesty International, and her name was Parsley or Thyme or . . . Sage! That's it, boss, Sage! Whereupon Luchnikov completely forgot about her.

While the press conference got under way, the rest of the lawns, all the terraces, and the grand ballroom turned into one huge cocktail party, with more than enough hors d'oeuvres to keep everybody—for nearly everybody stayed—content. Without Andrei, Tanya was completely alone. She was furious with him for dropping her in the midst of all these doddering idiots. She asked him for a martini and took it upstairs to the solarium, where she thought there would be fewer people. No, there, too, everyone gaped at her with undue familiarity. One group of snobs sneered so brazenly at her that she walked up to the ringleader, a shopwindow dummy draped with jewels, and said, "What's the matter, you bitch? Are your eyes stuck out on their stalks?" The woman gave a start and mumbled something in French, but the art of Moscow repartee was not lost on the rest of the company.

From the corner of the terrace Tanya stared out at the bay and the gliding lights of sloops and yachts, at the play of lights up and down the coast, and at the cluster of winking and blinking lights huddled together in the Koktebel foothills. She stared into the distance so as not to notice the nearby floodlit lawn covered with cross-legged reporters listening with rapt attention as the classmates went on about SOS. Andrei looked fantastic in his navy-blue suit, there was no getting around it. From where she stood he seemed the same slim, sprightly Looch she had fallen in love with at that party ten years before. But the bubble was not long in bursting. Looch clipped a pince-nez to his nose à la Chekhov and read out a statement. It was the pince-nez that did it. Why can't he wear glasses like everybody else? The snob. Why must he always show off, make himself out to be strong and determined? She knew better now, she had seen him tremble, heard him whine. He couldn't fool her. It was a put-on, a dirty put-on. Just to make a splash, he was willing to drag millions of happy people after him into a deep, dark pit.

O tempora! O mores! and *oh là là!* They're so hooked on publicity, these politicos, they leave their lady loves to pine and admire the landscape. It's enough to drive a girl into the arms of another. Am I right or am I right? Tanya turned to see two nattily bearded playboys holding out their cards with broad smiles. I'm *Stud*, Madame. And I'm the *New Tatler*. We'd like to get to know you. They walked up very close to her, and Stud laid his hand on her thigh. Are you satisfied with your lover, Madame? No, no, we have no reason to doubt it, it's just that our readers would like some details. Do your "intersections" take place spontaneously, or do you follow a schedule, like a production schedule? What is the official line of Soviet sexology? Your preferred birth control technique? Have you heard that your legal spouse is now the Soviet shot-put champion? Does he keep a mistress? How many lovers have you had in your life? Have you ever thought of the male element in the Idea of a Common Fate? I mean the yearning of something hot and hard to plunge into boundless female flesh.

The *paparazzi* were on them like flies by now, snapping away, and Tanya had still not been able to get a word in edgewise. At last she brushed Stud's hand off her thigh and gave him a punch in the nose. Both men's jaws dropped.

"Now let *me* ask *you* something, fellows," she said in a lazy, insolent voice. "What's your stand on the Idea of a Common Fate?"

"One hundred percent pro!" said Stud immediately.

"With it all the way!" confirmed Tatler.

She burst out laughing.

"And why the laughter, Madame?" asked Tatler immediately.

"All laughter is masturbation," affirmed Stud.

"I was just picturing you in your new Agitprop jobs," she said.

Another group of snobs clapped and laughed. She knows how to give it to those whippersnappers! Good show, Madame Lunina! Good show! Now there's something we could do with here—that brassy democratic way the Soviets have about them. One must have an enormous sense of power behind one to put that canaille from the yellow press in its place. Have you heard what one of them did to Princess Veshko-Vershkovskaya? Reduced her to tears, he did. . . .

No one had any idea that Tanya was about to scream. She was certain she could not bear another minute of it when who should come up to her but the evening's host and—could it be?—Fred Baxter. From one minute to the next she was calm: the two old gents made her feel absolutely safe. Both were smiling at her, and Baxter—she couldn't believe her eyes—even looked a bit sheepish. They started a friendly, informal kind of conversation, as if they were old friends and had no secrets from her. Arseny Nikolaevich told her that Baxter was trying to buy up part of his mountain, but the greedy hand of American imperialism would not make it to the valley past the northern slope because the valley past the northern slope was heaven on earth. Have you been there yet, Tatyana? Then let's all go tomorrow. You won't mind if we make it into a hike, will you? Oh, of course not, I forget. You're quite the athlete, aren't you? We'll have lunch on my subsistence farm. Just think, Tatyana: no electricity, no gas, and certainly no atomic energy. Everything is just as it was in the eighteenth century. And wait till you see how beautiful it all is, how well organized. If only mankind could have stopped there!

Having said his piece, which both charmed Tanya to the core and showed the snobs how one treats family guests, Arseny Nikolaevich apologized for having to run off, and left her alone with Baxter.

Wonder of wonders, the old desperado was downright nervous. Tanya smiled and asked him whether he knew all there was to know about her. "Oh, yes, darling," he said with a sad smile, "of course I do. I got a full report that night on the plane to Moscow. My business manager had a full file ready. Where that bastard gets his information the devil only knows. It's a shitty, crazy, mixed-up world, darling. CIAKGBMI5OSVAGETCETC—they're all one big crock, let me tell you. I've traveled all over the world since I left you, and the details keep rolling in. Why am I back? Well, the *Elyse* was still in Yalta, and I thought . . . Actually, darling, I'm here because I had to see you. Please hear me out. It will only take a minute. I know you did what you did that night out of desperation, or spite, or some other negative impulse. I just want you to know that old Bax has put it all out of his mind. It never happened. What? Noble, you say? Go ahead, smile your sarcastic smile. Call it noble if you like. I call it old-fashioned. Tanya, I worship you."

"What does 'worship' mean?" she asked. She was severely limited by the fact that her English vocabulary consisted almost exclusively of sports terminology.

"It means I revere you."

Although the explanation did not help at all, she could guess from his eyes that it was something men did not usually say to whores. And suddenly she cried out, "Save me, Bax! Take me away from here, anywhere!"

His eyes were riveted on her. For a moment she thought he was her father.

"Nothing could be simpler," he said. "I can take you wherever you want to go, whenever you want to go. I can give you anything your heart desires, or at least absolute comfort and absolute security. Are you laughing at me, Tanya?"

"If you only knew how confused I am."

"I know everything."

"Not quite everything."

"Everything but Andrei."

"That's what I mean."

"Well?" asked his faded blue eyes.

He really does love me, thought Tanya. He really is old-fashioned. She stared back, trying to make him understand everything with her eyes alone: there was no more Andrei, it was all over.

"Okay," said Baxter. "Now where do you want to live?"

"New Zealand."

"Fine." He nodded. "New Zealand it is. I know some beautiful spots there, and it's not at all as boring as they say."

"Good . . . Yes . . . New Zealand," she said. "Where it's not at all as boring as they say." She had suddenly begun to shiver. A shadow flitted by, pausing the length of a shutter click.

"Get a hold of yourself, Tanya," said Baxter. "There's nothing to worry about. All the pictures will be destroyed. Look, we can fly out tonight if you like. Just give the word. London? Paris? New York? Or straight to New Zealand. Or maybe spend the night on the *Elyse*, out at sea. And if you'd rather be alone or take along my private secretary for company, be my guest. . . . Maybe I've lost all my marbles, but there's one thing I know for sure. You are my queen for the rest of my life. I may have picked it up from an old song, but I mean it."

Now, too, his eyes more than his words told her she was saved. There was a light at the end of the tunnel; it even had a name: New Zealand. Then everything went dark again. "It won't work, Bax. I'm sure your people have told you I have two children. I can't just leave them in Moscow, and *they* will never let them out of the country. They never let a defector's family out to see him."

"No problem," said Baxter. "One quick call to Alexei and it will be all settled."

"Alexei?"

"Kosygin, of course," he said. "He'll do anything for me. We're old fishing buddies."

She laughed. How simple life could be! Fred Baxter calls Alyosha Kosygin and—no problem! A little fishing here, a little golf there, and the green hills of New Zealand.

"Let's go, Bax. No, not a word to Andrei. We don't want to spoil his evening. One sensation an evening is enough. His SOS might even suffer. We can wait. We'll phone him from somewhere. Where? Let's see. How about the yacht, far out at sea? Yes, let's get away from the Island today, from its problems, its chains. No more OK for me. There's one thing I want to do first, though, and that is pay a visit to Saint Vladimir's Cathedral on Cape Kherson and light a candle there. Let's go now, Bax dear. The classmates will be arriving at dawn, and I'd prefer not to meet them there."

Not until after the press conference, which lasted a good two hours, was Luchnikov able to attack the champagne, and attack it he did, glass after glass.

"Hi there, Mr. Marlboro," said a soft voice beside him. He turned and saw the mousy American girl, Ms. Sage, from Amnesty International.

"I'm sorry, but . . ." He began, then suddenly realized who she was. "Krystyna!"

It had taken him a long time to connect this timid, awkward professor type with the freewheeling sex bomb, international call girl, wandering nympho of his fantasies—if he fantasized about her at all any more. She had been no more than a carefree one-night stand to him, one of many. Still, it was unusual her name had come back to him. As soon as he heard that voice, that trace of a Polish accent, that Marlboro come-on, suddenly he remembered every detail: how she'd stolen into his bed, challenged his sexual supremacy, and then capitulated oh so sweetly. He smiled. She blushed. Her whole face turned bright red; then a drop of sweat formed on her brow.

"You've changed, baby," he said ironically. "You've been a real riddle to me all evening. Who's that trying to hypnotize me? I wondered. The idea of a terrorist attack actually crossed my mind. No, really, I can't get over it. You've changed your style completely. What is it? A new stage in women's lib? Or is that old hat by now? No, of course, now you're into Amnesty. A gay divorcee with a hefty alimony, is that it? Sorry for all the questions, baby. It's an occupational hazard, you know. By the way, that blush looked stunning on you. Is it part of the new look, too? A return to the classics?"

"If only you knew how glad I am to see you, Andrei," she said softly, reaching out and touching his elbow with her fingertips.

Well, well, he thought. She's got a real current flowing from her. Don't tell me she's in love with me! Yes, that's it. Unbelievable. She's made a romantic image out of me. Women! Will I ever learn?

He scanned the crowd for Tanya. She was nowhere to be seen. He told Krystyna he was ravenously hungry and asked her to join him in a delayed midnight snack of scampi poached in Nouveau Monde champagne. She accepted. He asked Hua to lay the table on the south balcony, which had direct access to the Guest Tower.

They sat together on the balcony overlooking the valley, now quiet, and the dying embers of a pleasantly hungover Koktebel. Kakhovka, however, was still very much alive; the respectable crowd had left, and the younger generation had taken over. The lawn where first Kublitsky-Piottukh, then the cross-legged reporters had sat was now a dance floor, and the discreet spotlights in the grass showed several pairs of legs executing the latest steps.

During the late-night collation, Andrei learned an important bit of news: Krystyna's friend Pamela and Anton had gotten married last spring, and Pamela was now pregnant; in other words, the champion of the Crimea Rally was soon to be a grandfather. Not bad, said Luchnikov to himself, everything at once, though he was not quite sure what he meant by "everything."

Though Krystyna had not become pregnant, she had not been lying fallow either. After realizing the vanity of her youthful delusions—first leftism, then feminism—she had decided to devote herself to freeing prisoners of conscience throughout the world. "And you were a big influence in my change of heart, you know that, Mr. Marlboro?"

"I'm sorry, Krystyna, but ashamed as I am to admit it, the fate of all those Chileans and Argentinians seems rather removed from our reality. Russian prisoners—now that touches us to the quick. We're up to our necks in home-grown Russian problems."

"Actually, it was Russia that got me involved," Krystyna said sadly (she was a new person). "I wanted to find out more about you. Maybe my Slavic genes were to blame. You know, our sentimentality? Anyway, what started as a roll in the hay kept coming back to haunt me. I decided to exorcise you by deromanticizing you, studying you. I did some serious research on your Idea, and what happened? You won me over. The articles I read called it a typical manifestation of Russian Sadomasochism, but I saw it as something much deeper, more important than that. It may even have a religious tinge to it, I don't know. In any case, I started feeling disgusted with myself for leading the silly, dissolute life I led, and decided to donate half my money and all my time to Amnesty. And believe it or not, I haven't had another man since you."

Amazing, he thought, but why such asceticism? He looked over at her pleasant oval face, and her long, graceful neck. She did have a kind of monastic freshness about her. The discovery stirred his imagination; she reminded him more and more of Old Russia, this American, of well-bred young ladies and "diamond-studded skies...."

"How old are you, Krystyna?"

"Thirty-one."

"And Pamela?"

"Twenty-two."

Three years older than Antoshka, he thought.

Suddenly an uninvited guest appeared at the end of the balcony.

Luchnikov quickly drew his miniature pistol. Calm down, the man mimed by holding up one hand, and with the other he set a small box on the floor, pulled out a long strip of metal from it, and pressed a button. On came TVMig, and the man disappeared.

"What was that all about?" asked Krystyna, frightened.

"Just a joke," answered Luchnikov with a malevolent smile, putting the pistol back in his shoulder holster.

"Those of you who are still awake," the intrusive voice of the announcer was saying, "are going to be treated to a peek at the secret life of the mighty few. The footage you are about to see was shot twenty minutes ago. Watch carefully now. Explanations will follow."

The screen showed Cape Kherson: the dark outlines of Saint Vladimir's Cathedral and the surrounding hills, with here and there a ruin—some marble columns, the fragments of a capital or mosaic—glistening in the lights of the Sevastopol port.

A Russo-Balt purring slowly up to the Cathedral. A woman stepping out. White dress, tanned shoulders. She is followed by a lanky figure. A middle-aged man. The two of them walk up to the entrance. The doors creak open before them. Only a few candles are burning; the vaults and side aisles are in total darkness. A massive coffin stands in front of the choir. The body of Count Novosiltsev. The angle changes abruptly. A blasphemous TVMig cameraman has slipped behind the altar. The tall old man remains standing in the doorway while the woman approaches. Now there can be no doubt: the woman is Tanya.

Luchnikov watched as she stood over the head of his friend with a candle in her hand. The ultrafast lens picked her exhausted and almost spiteful face out of the shadows and locked it on the screen. Little by little the spite drained out of it; only the exhaustion was left.

He looked at that face long and hard.

"Are you saying good-by?" he heard Krystyna's voice ask from far away.

He turned off the vile box.

XIII

The Third Administrative District

Marlen Mikhailovich made a new friend in Simferopol. His name was Mr. Mercator, the owner of a small spice-and-tea shop and a broad-beamed optimist who, though he had no discernible nationality of his own, proudly traced his family tree back to the Mercator projection.

Marlen Mikhailovich enjoyed ducking in under the striped awning of his establishment on Sinopsky Boulevard and entering its cool, cozy world of superabundance. For Mercator's tiny concern was stocked with item after item that he could never have found in the special-privilege cafeteria at work or even in the Kremlin's Granovsky Street "Special Section" shops. He appreciated the very dimensions of the shop, so unlike the gigantic Simfi supermarkets, which, crammed as they were with food unavailable in Moscow, retained an elusive connection with their empty Soviet counterparts. Perhaps it was that these vast emporia were what the Soviet man in the street envisioned as the future of communism.

Mr. Mercator's store was free of the slightest whiff of communism. The select teas and spices plus a few fine cheeses and hams were redolent of old-style capitalism at its height. Moreover,

Mr. Mercator's prices were more than reasonable, and after he and Marlen Mikhailovich became friends, they dwindled to pure symbolism.

It was, in fact, to save money that Marlen Mikhailovich had taken to buying his own food. He soon calculated that eating at home came to about one-third as much as eating in restaurants. Everyone working at the Institute earned high hard-currency salaries (and as general consultant Kuzenkov received the maximum, the same as the director—i.e., the ambassador), yet they all saved every possible "White ruble" for more capital expenditures than so evanescent a commodity as food—for example, the gifts they had to take back to Moscow for wives, children, relatives. . . .

Mr. Mercator had a fluent, though less than literate, command of a good twenty languages, Hebrew included, and could spot people's nationalities at a glance. When Marlen Mikhailovich first came in, he immediately stood him a cup of coffee: he had a soft spot for Soviets. When a few days later he saw Kuzenkov on television, he began preening himself on his important new customer. He was extremely flattered by the attention Marlen Mikhailovich paid him, by the interest he seemed to take in everything he had to say. As soon as Kuzenkov stepped in the door, Mr. Mercator would leave the business at hand to his two young assistants, inquire ceremoniously whether Mr. Kuzenkov had time for a cup of coffee, and usher him into his private office, where, ensconced in cool, soft leather armchairs, they would chat for an hour or more.

"I wonder if you can tell me," Marlen Mikhailovich would say, fixing Mr. Mercator with his best Party squint, "I wonder if you can tell me why a small businessman like you should be so in favor of the Idea of a Common Fate."

Mr. Mercator would raise his eyebrows, open his arms, then press his hands to his breast. Dear Mr. Kuzenkov had no need to worry on that score. Like all thinking Crimeans (and he took the liberty of including himself in that category, business being only part of his life), he, Vladko Mercator, supported the Idea of a Common Fate implicitly and had every intention of voting for its candidates.

Yes, but did Mr. Mercator realize that a victory for SOS could bring about the merger of Crimea and the USSR in deed as well as name?

"Dear Marlen Mikhailovich (if you allow me to be so bold), it is hard for me to believe that an event of such magnitude will take place during the life span of our generation, but should it in fact take place, I can't tell you how thrilled I shall be to witness a turning point in history. What's that you say? 'Happy is he who meets the world in its most fateful works and days'? May I note that down? Alexander Blok, you say?"

Mr. Mercator took out a heavy leather ledger and copied out the two lines of Russian poetry in it. "I just adore all things Russian! And not in the least because I am one sixty-fourth Russian, like Nicholas II, may he rest in peace; no, *all* of us here on the Island, even the Tatars, feel a special affinity to Russian culture. Our leaders, the provacuees, have always shown a certain lenience when it comes to minority groups, and we Mediterranean peoples, we especially appreciate tolerance and grace in matters of national origin. I, for example, have a cousin who is an influential lawyer in Venice and an aunt who owns a tea company in Tel Aviv. There are Mercators on Malta and Sardinia, in Marseilles and Barcelona. *Homo mediterraneus* is a man of peace, Mr. Kuzenkov."

Marlen Mikhailovich groaned.

"Is your stomach bothering you, Marlen Mikhailovich? May I offer you a spot of Benedictine? By the way, it's the genuine article. I order it direct from the monastery. My customers appreciate it. But to get back to the provacuees. Think of what they have to offer to the great Soviet Union! You may take my word for it, they're the cream of the Russian nation, the Russian nation at its most brilliant, its most noble. Oh, I know they used to be reactionary. They even put up quite a fight against the great Trotsky and Lenin. But how long is it since then, I ask you? Ages and ages! True, not all of them are as progressive as our remarkable Andrei, but surely the Soviet Union has grown powerful enough by now to allow a certain exchange of opinions among its citizens."

Marlen Mikhailovich groaned again. He was terribly depressed by the shopkeeper's twaddle. "Why is it you refuse to understand that if our two countries merge you will no longer own your fine little shop?"

"*Yaki!*" cried Mr. Mercator, beaming. "Then I'll be the manager, the socialist manager, isn't that what you call it? How could the great Soviet Union decline to accept my experience, my Mediterranean connections?"

"But even if it does accept them, you won't have any English tea to sell, or Italian prosciutto, or French cheese, or American cigarettes, or Scotch whisky. You won't have any kiwi fruit from New Zealand. You won't have any—"

"Ha! Ha! Ha!" laughed Mr. Mercator. "This isn't the first time I've noticed your penchant for black humor. Ha! Ha! Ha! I'm a great fan of black humor."

Marlen Mikhailovich groaned yet again. "Even your diminished stock will be constantly plagued with shortages. You'll have to put certain items under the counter. You'll have to serve endless queues of smelly people. How about copying this into your beautiful ledger? 'Capitalism is the unequal distribution of wealth; socialism, the equal distribution of misery.' Winston Churchill."

"I can't tell you what a pleasure it is to talk with an educated man. I give you my word, Marlen Mikhailovich, that we, the businessmen of Crimea, will do our best to turn socialist poverty, in Churchill's words, into socialist wealth. It will be child's play, actually. A bit of energy, initiative. What is human civilization but the equal distribution of the good things in life, material and spiritual? That's what Jesus taught us."

"That's what Jesus taught us, true. But we haven't been very diligent disciples. Besides, life makes its little emendations, and by now even Churchill's aphorism needs updating. Might I suggest, Mr. Mercator, that you copy it down in a slightly modified form, namely: 'Socialism is the *un*equal distribution of misery.' "

"And whose idea is that, Mr. Kuzenkov?"

"Excuse me, but I must be going. Much obliged for the chat."

Mr. Mercator always saw his honored guest to the door and even went outside with him. He wanted his neighbors and competitors up and down Sinopsky Boulevard to see him with his Soviet Comrades, that is, his big shot. The Yaki assistants Khasan and Albert put Kuzenkov's purchases in his car, a decidedly second-hand Peugeot. They themselves drove fancy Peters, but they were highly impressed by the all-powerful Comrade's discretion and put it down to the general modesty of the great Soviet Union.

More than once Mr. Mercator had hinted that he would be happy to invite Marlen Mikhailovich to his flat in town or his dacha in Karachel—they would all be happy, his wife and children. But each time the subject came up, Marlen Mikhailovich gently changed it, and Mr. Mercator would make it clear he understood and all but apologize for having been so forward: who was he to invite so high an official to his house? Once Marlen Mikhailovich lost his temper and said straight out, "I'm afraid you don't understand me at all. The reason I can't visit you is not that I'm conceited; it's that I'm followed. I'm under constant surveillance, and every new contact I make can lead to unforeseen complications."

Mr. Mercator was highly indignant. The nerve of OSVAG hounding an important man like Mr. Kuzenkov! He would sit down and write a letter to the *Courier* and bring the whole affair out into the open! I hate to say it, Mr. Mercator, but you've got it all wrong again. It's not your men who are tailing me; it's mine, my Comrades. They're just itching to write a denunciation. It's actually rather a widespread phenomenon in our milieu; call them what you will—reports, memoranda, briefings—they're an unfortunate part of Stalin's legacy. Mr. Mercator was terribly depressed when Marlen Mikhailovich left that day, but the next time he returned, he found Mr. Mercator his usual radiant self. He'd given a great deal of thought to the denunciation issue and came to the conclusion that it had its roots partly in a healthy perfectionism and partly in a strong sense of community, of family: all brothers felt they could take their complaints to Mother. Why, that was just what we needed here on the Island and in the badly fragmented West as a whole. Yes, Mr. Mercator you're absolutely right. The West does need a sense of community.

They're incurable, he thought as he attended rallies, scanned campaign posters, watched television programs, read newspapers, and sounded out people at diplomatic receptions, aristocratic salons, openings, exhibits, and endless sports events. Day by day the old values suffered further setbacks. Delegates of practically every stripe, even the monarchists, opened their speeches with vows of fidelity to SOS. Rejecting the Idea of a Common Fate was tantamount to conceding the election in advance. Only extremist groups with no hope for a seat in the Duma allowed themselves to attack the Luchnikov brethren—Yaki nationalism, for example, which was losing ground fast and now seemed no more than a naïve and innocent youth movement.

All this time Moscow had been sending Marlen Mikhailovich coded messages by the score, inquiring whether he had his finger on the pulse of events, whether he had been able to regulate the pulse, direct the events. Direct them? What factions did they want me to infiltrate, what action did they want me to take when everyone but everyone was bursting with love for the great USSR? Revolutionary theory and practice suggest, Moscow responded, that in complex situations like these the surest support comes from the working class, the vanguard of the proletariat. You must find a suitable excuse to visit the Arabat industrial zone, establish contact with labor union leaders and local Social Democrats. Beware of the party calling itself the Communist Oilmen. We have it on good authority that they are in direct contact with Belgrade. Give the Central Committee a detailed report on the state of affairs and general mood in the Arabat zone.

What kind of nonsense is this? What in the world do they think I'm going to find there? Can't they see what an infinitesimal part the working class plays in the political life of Crimea? Don't they realize that the "working class" is made up of beer-guzzling, steak-gobbling nabobs? Have they no idea that a full sixty percent of the working population is foreign—Turkish, Greek, and Arab—because the Crimeans don't like dirtying their hands? How can they cling to such antiquated dogmas? How can they concoct the most improbable "historical facts" to validate them? How can they refuse to let Marxism develop?

Marlen Mikhailovich was beginning to fear his own ideas. It was not so long ago that he, too, thought of Arabat as a citadel of class consciousness. Now he would wake up in the middle of the night, get out of bed, light a cigarette, look out at the empty boulevard—dark but for a few shop fronts and the all-night artists' clubs, whose lights glimmered through the naked trees—and think that at that moment, in that Crimean winter's night, he, Marlen Mikhailovich Kuzenkov, member of the Communist Party of the Soviet Union, was the most reactionary person in the country, that no one so opposed merging this tiny country with the vast mainland as he.

How did the Island find its way into what was nearly the middle of the Black Sea? What forces of Providence separated it from the mainland and to what end? Could it possibly have been to set our generation of Russians this torturous task? And his thoughts turned to the Chongar Straits and the twentieth of January, 1920, one of the best-kept secrets in Soviet history, the day now cele-brated annually on the Island as Lieutenant Bailey-Land Day. For it was on that day that a foolish acne-prone young Englishman stood up against the avalanche of the Revolution and single-handedly defeated the victorious proletarian army. He stood and conquered. To this day no one in the Soviet Union besides Marlen Mikhailovich and a handful of specialists had the right to know about that day, let alone discuss it. The only people left to know and discuss it were a pitiful band of renegades and moral misfits, the two or three million members of the "critically thinking intel-ligentsia"—in other words, a band of second-rate citizens.

Marlen Mikhailovich had first gained access to the secret ar-chives twenty years ago, during the Khrushchev years, when the department dealing with the Eastern Mediterranean Region began operation. How well he remembered his initial shock. It came not so much from the defeat of the Red Army's crack southern divi-sions as from the damage to his faith in Marxism. For suddenly the young scholar glimpsed a new, unsightly view of one of its cardinal teachings, the role of the individual in history, and suddenly his inner harmony was lost. Kuzenkov later returned to the secret archives again and again. He became obsessed with Lieutenant Bailey-Land Day. Though it took place nine years before his birth, he began fantasizing he had witnessed it himself.

The twentieth of January. Twenty degrees below zero. Every-thing favored the logic of the class struggle: completely demoral-ized and disorganized, the Volunteer Army had panicked and was boarding a string of decrepit ships in Sevastopol, Yalta, Feodosia, Kerch, and Yevpatoria; the last battle-ready divisions—led by Mamontov, Markov, and Drozdovsky—were fighting a group of Tatar saber detachments that had swept down the mountain gorges; the Cossack regiments were completely unnerved by Bol-shevik propagandists, ditto for the crews of the mighty British squadron summoned to guard the northern coast. In a spectacular show of class solidarity with the Russian proletariat, British sailors and marines had abandoned their ships, which were frozen into Alma-Tarkhana harbor, and were holding rallies under red flags up and down the ice- and wind-swept embankment and amidst the stands, huts, and minarets of the bazaar. In an even more spectacular show of class solidarity, the forty-mile Chongar Straits had frozen over for the first time in a century, and the ice was so thick that columns of thousands of men, artillery and all, could cross it. And in the most spectacular show of class solidarity, the armies of Frunze and Mironov were actually crossing the glittering ice under the glittering icy sun. The ice was slippery and the horses' hoofs skidded now and then, but the flags were flying in the pale winter sky, the bands playing "This Is Our Last and Most Important Battle," and the Red Army men cursing gaily at not finding a trace of resistance at the class enemy's final refuge.

The only sin against the logic of the class struggle came from twenty-two-year-old Lieutenant Richard Bailey-Land, turret captain on the battleship. Perhaps because he was slightly in his cups, he armed himself with a carbine and ordered his gunners to remain on board; then he had them aim the turret in the direction of the advancing columns; then he had them open fire on the columns with their gigantic sixteen-inch shells. How accurate they were was immaterial; the shells broke the ice, the vanguard drowned in the icy water, the rear guard broke ranks, and panic took over. The whole thing was visible from the Alma-Tarkhana embankment with a pair of second-rate binoculars and at times with nothing but the naked eye. Telegraph machines started clicking all over the Island: British fleet resists Reds. The White Army was seized by a flurry of activity. From the Sary-Bulat airstrip dilapidated old Farmans, Nieuports, and Vityazes with rainbow insignia on their wings began taking to the air in threes and dropping explosives on the ice. Commander-in-Chief Baron Wrangel ordered all his forces out to the northern banks, and for the first time in a month they obeyed. The Drozdovsky Division advanced to assault position. Shkuro's Lupine Hordes abandoned the warm gorges and their sportive massacre of the local Tatar population for the icy steppes. The remains of the Russian fleet in Balaklava Bay set aside their political bickering and raised both steam and its Saint Andrew banners. The British crews returned to their posts. Odd as it may seem, class antagonism gradually gave way to the temptation for military victory. The British government refused to forgive the rebels after the war was over, and most of the sailors preferred settling on the Island to serving the harsh sentences the Ruler of the Seas meted out to recalcitrants. Like the white convict colonies in Australia, they formed the basis of a permanent settlement, and were the antecedents of today's Anglo-Crimean community.

In the twenty-four hours following the ice-breaking episode, the Red Army suffered untold losses. Marlen Mikhailovich remembered bursting into tears at the lists of casualties in the ranks of the heroic Second Cavalry, the Inzensky and Simbirsky infantry regiments, the armored battalions, the horse artillery. They all fought desperately; they all sought new routes to the Crimean shores. But the Chongar froze only at the neck; to the east and to the west it was still water. As the Red Army men drowned by the thousands, the Volunteer Army was reborn. Hotheads among them called for a new campaign on Moscow, but reason prevailed. Several days after the Island had rebuffed the attack, a powerful southeaster came up and the Chongar Straits were hit by a terrible storm. The battle's hero was at length discovered in the Sary-Bulat officers' club, where for two days and nights he had been playing cards with Russian pilots.

Marlen Mikhailovich examined the lieutenant's portrait carefully. Protruding ears, a ridiculously arrogant gaze, slicked-down hair. The retoucher had done a good job of hiding the pimples but could not hide the fact that they belonged there. The lieutenant did not even look his age; he was more like a grammar school boy forced to repeat his last year, the poor relative of an already impoverished aristocratic line that had traditionally provided officers to the Royal Navy. How monstrously absurd—a mangy little snot-nose changing the course of history, the mighty, the symphonic course of history! Marlen Mikhailovich was particularly upset by the fact that Dick Bailey-Land brushed aside all praise—the dithyrambs, the eulogies, the talk of David's slingshot and personal heroics. "I simply wondered what would happen," he told reporters. "Believe me, gentlemen, I had no intention whatsoever to defend Crimea or the Russian Empire or anyone's constitution or democracy or what have you. I swear. I was simply curious about the ice, the attack, the guns, the mutiny—I thought it would be a jolly good show to mix them all together. I suppose I was most interested to see how the guns worked. You must admit it was a perfectly killing state of affairs." At which point he would begin sniggering into his embroidered handkerchief and the reporters would scribble enraptured purple passages about British humor —and David's slingshot.

How could it be? the young Marlen Mikhailovich would ask himself, bewildered. Without a drop of class consciousness, without a trace of hatred for the victorious masses, with no more than a morbid sense of curiosity, this ratty little aristocrat changed the course of world history. He must have been crazy, out of his mind. Or no, he was just putting up a front with all that swagger; deep down he knew that the victory of the Donbass miners and the Petrograd metalworkers was the beginning of the end for lawn tennis in Essex. But no matter how Marlen Mikhailovich tried to explain the facts away, deep down he knew that Bailey-Land *did* lack all hatred, all class prejudice; that he *had* no more than "wondered what would happen."

Recalling the lieutenant, Marlen Mikhailovich recalled other historical trouble spots, dead ends, where Marxist theory lost its fundamental validity. There were even those terrible times when the music of the Revolution began to sound like a cacophony, which, if it did occasionally include strains of true melody, did so only by chance and only to drown them again in the depressing delirium of the fundamental score.

Marlen Mikhailovich winced at the flood of heretical ideas and started shuffling through the various guidelines, reports, and instructions he had received from the Important Personage. Suddenly he pushed all the papers away, sighed deeply and freely, as if a load had been taken off his mind, and burst into tears of devotion to his own secret, desperate love—Crimea.

I love this island; I love its memory of the old Russia and the dream of a new one; I love its rich and dissolute democracy, the ports of its rocky south open to the entire world, the energy of historically doomed but eternally resilient Russian capitalism; I love the girls of Yalta and its bohemian atmosphere; I love Simfi's architectural turbulence; I love the well-fed flocks in the eastern pastureland and the sweeping wheat fields in the west; I love even its supple seallike contour. After all the years I have devoted to this miracle of nature and of history, how can I stand by and watch as it crumbles at the whim of some Extraordinarily Unpleasant Personage? Its fall can help no one, not even our country, and the rest of our leadership has formed no set opinion on the matter. O God, I won't survive it! O God, I must prevent it! Thus did Marlen Mikhailovich Kuzenkov, general consultant to the Institute for the Study of the Eastern Mediterranean Region, call out to the Deity.

For the time being, however, Marlen Mikhailovich had to carry out the Central Committee's directives and prepare for his trip. He had a car sent over from the Institute, threw his toilet articles and a pair of pajamas in his attaché case, and set off for the Arabat industrial zone to visit his natural ally and drink from the source of class consciousness.

Looking down from the freeway at the farms of the rich Germans (who not only supplied the whole Island with all the milk products it needed, the bastards, they also managed to export cheese and ham to Europe), Marlen Mikhailovich thought over the report he would send to the Important Personage—how much truth to how much demagogy—and the speech he would give to the Friendship Society and the ways he would dodge the Communist Oilmen. In short, he was on the job as if nothing had happened.

"Oh, what farms! What herds!" sighed his driver, Feofan Lopatov by name.

Marlen Mikhailovich stole a quick glance at the man's fat face. What did he mean by that? Was he trying to provoke a response or had it just slipped out?

"Hmmm," said Marlen Mikhailovich.

Now it was the driver's turn to glance over at him.

For a minute or so they drove on in silence.

"What would our people think if they could see this land!" said Lopatov, looking Marlen Mikhailovich straight in the eye. "Some soil, eh, Comrade Kuzenkov? Some soil!"

There were no rules against waxing enthusiastic over Crimea's natural wealth and beauty. Why, then, was Marlen Mikhailovich afraid of his driver and his driver afraid of him?

"Keep your eye on the road, Lopatov," he said dryly, pointing straight ahead. "Keep your eye on the road." And to himself he said, A year after reunification the Crimeans will be as scared of one another as we are. Luchnikov thinks the Russians will learn guts from Crimea, but no, Crimea will learn to cringe and fawn from us. . . . If only I had the guts to give all this up and go on television with a declaration of war against the SOS, open these fools' eyes for them, appeal to the West. . . .

"Here we are, Ak-Mechet," cried Lopatov as they started down towards the Sea of Azov.

The Tongue of Arabat was visible from the freeway. It was a strange natural phenomenon, a sandy spit about a mile wide and seventy miles long. The eastern coast of the spit was lined with beautiful beaches washed by the waves of the crystal clear Sea of Azov, the western coast with the putrid, shallow, stagnant Savash, a valuable reservoir of oil, natural gas, and a myriad of other sources of energy. Everything on the spit was organized accordingly. The western edge and the entire Savash were covered with oil rigs, distilleries, refineries, reservoirs, and overpasses—an industrial jungle; running down the middle was a six-lane motorway with all that went with it: telephones every few miles, service stations, coin-operated machines with cigarettes, soft drinks, tea, coffee, chewing gum, and snacks, plus several well-appointed bars. The eastern edge, so near and yet so far from the jungle, was dotted with piers for yachts and other private boats and with towns and villages providing ultramodern housing for both workers and executives and all kinds of amusements for all kinds of tastes. The main centers on the Tongue were the towns of Ak-Mechet, Bem-Major, and the Third Administrative District. It was the latter Kuzenkov was bound for, because it was there the Arabat Oil Company had its executive offices and labor union headquarters. At the northernmost tip of the spit was a small town called Bem-Minor-and-a-Kopeck that had a little of the Wild West in it and was the object of the most contradictory reports on the Island: people said either that it was deadly dull or that it was the chance of a lifetime. Apart from loading docks and piping, it boasted twenty or so bordellos catering to the most varied preferences.

Just as the colorful conglomeration of the Third Administrative District's skyscrapers came into view, Marlen Mikhailovich made up his mind to ditch Lopatov and spend his time here alone.

What's his rank? No less than a major. He glanced over at him again. What a face! A real Nero. You couldn't find a more decadent proletarian.

Marlen Mikhailovich waited until they were inside the hotel to make his offer. "Listen, Lopatov, I won't be going anywhere for the next three days. Why not go and have a look at Bem-Minor-and-a-Kopeck? I've heard some mighty wild stories about the place, and this may be your only chance."

Lopatov's eyes lit up with a wild fire. At least he had an imagination.

"But what about . . . I mean . . . you, Comrade Kuzenkov . . . here . . ."

"There's one thing you don't understand, Lopatov." said Marlen Mikhailovich with a subtle smile. "We're all human under the skin."

"Oh, I agree, I agree," Feofan Lopatov cried out, beaming. I couldn't have put it better myself, he thought. We're all human under the skin, and we all like a good time. Even this big shot, this secret general consultant. He knows they told me to keep close tabs on him, but he's human, too; he wants his own little fling. Immediately a doubt niggled at his brain: with his many years of experience, he knew that if the comrades caught him at Bem-Minor-and-a-Kopeck it would mean the end of his career and he'd be forced to spend the rest of his life back home. Even so . . . Lopatov passed a gloomy eye over the empty hotel lobby with its springy carpet, fancy lamps, and bored bartender, peered out the glass wall at the glimmering waves of the Sea of Azov, and once more sighed to himself, We're all human. He had made up his mind. If this isn't worth the risk, damn it, I don't know what is. I'd be crazy to pass it up. Three days with the whores of Bem-Minor-and-a-Kopeck! Three days of nonstop orgy! Let them throw me out of the Party if they want to. I'll see more in my three days with the whores and homos than the Comrades see in a lifetime of mass meetings. . . . The dreary years of service as a chauffeur-spy flashed before his eyes. Soon OK will be shot to hell, and I'll have nothing to show for those years, nothing to reminisce about.

Reading these thoughts in Lopatov's fleshy face, Marlen Mikhailovich was again surprised at how "the people," our people, had changed in the past few years. A minute later Lopatov was gone, speeding in the embassy car to the fleshpots of Bem-Minor-and-a-Kopeck.

With a sigh of relief Marlen Mikhailovich began making himself at home in his magnificent two-room sea-view suite. He looked out of the floor-length windows lined with juniper bushes at the spotless little streets leading down to the beach. Every once in a while a car drove past or a young boy ambled along, his bright plastic anorak fluttering in the breeze. Marlen Mikhailovich suddenly felt cozy, completely at ease, completely cut off from all the confounded problems and ludicrous directives that had been assailing him. I'll spend three days here in perfect solitude, phone nobody, meet nobody, and throw together my report at the last minute. What can I possibly accomplish here? I can neither postpone nor hasten the catastrophe for a minute. I'll spend three days in front of the television set, chasing TVMig around the dial and following the latest campaign developments. I'll go out for walks, read the papers, watch television . . . and try to determine where to go from here—where, with whom, and for what purpose. When the time is up, I'll put a call through to Moscow from a local bar and tell Vera to call me back from her sister's. Maybe she's not bugged all the time. Vera will understand everything immediately. I'll ask her to go and persuade the Important Personage to keep them from making any catastrophic decisions.

He turned on the set. The channel it was tuned to was showing a silly French situation comedy, the next channel an American jazz group, the next a rerun of the Soviet hockey championship. . . . TVMig was on Channel Six. The machine-gun patter of the commentator ruined his sunny mood and brought him back into the real, crepuscular world. What he saw, live from Yevpatoria, was an amazing event: a Lupine Hordes convention pledging its support for the Common Fate League. Some relic of a colonel (he must have been Shkuro's last living cavalryman) was going into raptures over a recent trip he had taken to Moscow. He had been particularly impressed by a Red Square military parade. Not once did he mention communism. It was all Russia, power, imperial boundaries, the flag flying over all latitudes. The twenty-first century belonged to Russia! Marlen Mikhailovich noticed Professor Fofanov, a classmate, on the podium. A week ago a liberal pinko like him would have been beaten to a pulp at a meeting of this

314

ultrarightist group, and now, a week before the election, he was its honored guest and speaker.

The telephone rang. Marlen Mikhailovich gave a start. Who could it be? Who knows I'm here? The people whose business it is to know, in the person of William Ivanovich Kokkinaki. Kokkinaki was Sergeev's latest code name on the Island. A distinguished professor of archaeology from California, he had come to Feodosia on a privately sponsored research trip. In slightly outdated Russian the archaeologist invited his old friend and Crimea-lover Marlen Mikhailovich to pay him a visit in Feodosia. Any time you feel overburdened with work or *unwanted guests,* just come and see me. I've rented a gem of a house by the sea. It will be just like the good old days. We'll argue about the third layer of the Tepsen funeral mound or the origins of prehistoric reservoirs on the Leginer slopes. Unwanted guests? said Marlen Mikhailovich. I'm not expecting any guests. . . . Of course. I understand. I like my privacy, too. Why, only yesterday I was plagued all day by a terrible bore of a coin collector with the curious name of Ignatyev-Ignatyev. I advise you to leave all such visitors to your—ha! ha!—driver or to me personally. And if any ancient Egyptians happen to call, just give me a ring, will you? Here's my number.

Trying to make sense out of "Kokkinaki's" gobbledygook, Marlen Mikhailovich stared at TVMig with unseeing eyes, until suddenly he realized he was watching another one of those amazing events. It was a press conference in Bakhchisarai. The khan's court press attaché was delivering a statement. His Highness the Islamic Leader of Crimea's Tatar Nation calls upon the faithful to vote in favor of the Common Fate League. He is confident that, as an integral part of the great Soviet Union, Crimea will be able to make a greater contribution to the cause of nonaligned nations everywhere and to the anti-imperialist front of all brothers in Islam.

The phone rang again. This time it was the reception clerk. In the most engaging tone and the purest of Russian he wondered whether the gentleman wouldn't like supper in his room.

Next to appear on the screen was Andrei jumping out of a helicopter at a military base in Kacha, with his new woman, Krystyna Sage, close on his heels. She looked quite attractive in her jeans and leather jacket, but she couldn't hold a candle to our Tanya. No, Andrei, you're a fool, a complete and utter fool. They were met by Chernok and three hundred cheering young pilots.

Supper? Yes, yes, please. Oh, just something light and simple. Yes, that sounds fine, and could you add . . . and a side portion of . . . Oh, yes, and a bottle of Scotch . . . No, no, that's right. A bottle. Black and White will do. . . .

Luchnikov mounted the platform, raised his hand for silence, and said, "Friends! The Spaniards sent their caravels out to sea not knowing what each mile would bring. They plowed the Atlantic in darkness and in gloom. They found America, of course, but it might just as well have eluded them, they might just as well have been swallowed up in that darkness and gloom. Yet what is man's fate if not to push on to new shores? Shall we find Russia, our dream, our destiny? As pilots aiding us in our search, you must be aware that our darkness and gloom are much blacker, much bleaker than anything the caravels had to face."

A strapping young man with lieutenant's stripes jumped up waving his cap and said, "We fly in all weather, Andrei!"

The rest of the pilots burst into cheers. Colonel Chernok lit a cigarillo. Andrei smiled sadly. His lady love gazed devotedly at her lord and master.

The wily beast, thought Kuzenkov furiously. Reverse psychology propaganda! He frightens them with "darkness and gloom," and they react with derring-do. What is the matter with these people? Again and again Solzhenitsyn warns them to stop and take heed; he screams it at them from their TV screens. They all listen reverentially and come to the staggering conclusion that only a great nation could give rise to so powerful a personality, only the great Soviet Union!

Perhaps there is a stage in a man's life when he is particularly likely to hatch brilliant, harebrained schemes. How else can Luchnikov's uncanny insight into the Islanders' psychology be explained? If Kuzenkov hadn't known better, he would have thought the KGB had a hand in it, but he knew for a fact that the top brass had no desire to see Crimea under Soviet domination; the Sovietization of Crimea would mean the loss of a fertile field of operations. No, there was no getting round it; it was all Andrei's idea, it came from within, from within the very best.

As was its wont, TVMig ended with a close-up still of Luchnikov's face. It was a strange combination of predatory smile and sad, almost mournful eyes.

"You degenerate!" said Kuzenkov, holding up his fist to his former friend. "Ignoring your family, abandoning your mistress, avoiding your old friend all these months! You're obsessed by that sadomasochistic Idea, that snobbish guilt gone berserk!"

"I couldn't agree with you more, Marlen Mikhailovich," said a slightly scratchy voice behind him.

Kuzenkov jumped away from the television set. A man was pushing a cart into the room, a cart laden with trays and silver-lidded dishes—his modest repast—and a bottle of Black and White. The man was a bony type in his late forties. He had a smile that revealed a pair of diseased gums, and a gray forelock that hung over his eyes. "You've hit the nail on the head," said the waiter. "Andrei Luchnikov is a moral degenerate. I've known him since we were children. We went to the Tsar Alexander II (Liberator) Classical School for Boys together."

Staring at the waiter, Kuzenkov realized in a flash that he was no waiter at all, that it hadn't been very bright of him to let Lopatov go, that they'd been waiting for him, that he'd better call Professor Kokkinaki and fast.

The would-be waiter bowed his head and clicked his heels. "Allow me to introduce myself. Yury Ignatyev-Ignatyev. I do hope you'll forgive me, but this was the only way I could manage to see you, and see you I must." He flicked back his tails in a nineteenth-century gesture, but since the chair he chose was the brazen contemporary type that engulfs its victim, his attempt at elegance failed miserably. Righting himself after the debacle, he decided to try a more appropriate gesture and crossed his legs casually.

The concatenation of periods and styles struck Marlen Mikhailovich as so preposterous that, despite the tension he was under, the edges of his mouth turned up. Nonetheless he barked out, "Ignatyev-Ignatyev of the Lupine Hordes? I am quite well informed about you."

"About my past, Marlen Mikhailovich," said Ignatyev-Ignatyev, giving his nails a quick inspection and again looking more false than casual. "I have recently been purged from the ranks of the Lupine Hordes, and I am proud to say the event took place several days before they sold out to SOS. I am currently a member of the Communist Oilmen party."

"Congratulations," said Marlen Mikhailovich. "From the frying pan into the fire. Good show. And now would you please leave me alone. I'm not quite—"

"Furthermore, I am a member of the Central Committee of the Party and wish to speak to you as such." He stretched his hand out tentatively towards the bottle.

"Don't you touch that bottle!" Kuzenkov snapped with a coarseness that surprised even himself.

By now Luchnikov had disappeared from the screen and a commentator was jabbering away about a scandal at the Yalta Majestic: Lucia Clark, world-renowned film star, had found her present flame, producer Jack Halloway, in bed with local provacuee Lidochka Nesselrode, while . . . and so on and so forth. Among those interviewed in connection with the affair was the recent Soviet émigré director Vitaly Gangut. Gangut categorically denied any part in the hanky-panky, stating that Lucia Clark could go (quick blip) herself, and Lidochka Nesselrode was just a (long series of blips). Neither of them was good enough for good old Octopus, the best producer alive today. There could be no doubt that the interviewee was on the road from tipsy to plastered. When the interviewer asked him whether it was true that he and Halloway were in Crimea to brainstorm a blockbuster, Gangut gave him a sly smile and shook his finger at him.

"You appear to know that scoundrel as well, Comrade Kuzenkov," said Ignatyev-Ignatyev, nodding at the screen.

"You are no comrade of mine," growled Marlen Mikhailovich. He poured himself a full glass of Scotch and put down the bottle unambiguously out of reach of the uninvited guest.

"By the way, I know him very well," said Ignatyev-Ignatyev with a broad smile. "Vitya Gangut is not only a moral degenerate, he's an alcoholic to boot. Oh, and there's another thing he has in common with his friend and our hero Andrei: they're both traitors to their country."

After a few gulps of Scotch everything seemed bright and humorous. "Might I ask you to leave the room, O patron of the Russian Land?" Kuzenkov said to Ignatyev-Ignatyev, showing him the door. He held out his hand in the archetypal Lenin pose.

Gangut's face was back on the screen. In response to a question about SOS, he frowned, as if he had just slapped a mosquito on his neck, and muttered, "It's an abomination." Close-up still of Gangut's frown.

Next came the world news. TVMig gallivanted throughout the world with ease: oil, depraved sheiks and revolutionary leaders, terrorists, playboys, scientists, athletes, models, and whores.

"Yes, I am a patron of the Russian Land," said Ignatyev-Ignatyev, puffing out his meager chest with pride and reaching for the bottle again. Marlen Mikhailovich moved it away again. "And the better to thwart its foes—bastards like Luchnikov, that is—I was willing to sell my soul to the Communist Oilmen."

"Tell me, what exactly do you mean by the Russian Land?"

Ignatyev-Ignatyev's eyes lit up with joy. So he's not going to throw me out! So we are going to have a dialogue! "First and foremost, my concept is diametrically opposed to Luchnikov's," he said quickly, jumbling his words together.

"Is that all you can come up with?" asked Marlen Mikhailovich. He sounded disappointed. "What a bore, Ig-Ig. You don't care about Russia. All you care about is Luchnikov. It's a fixation."

Ignatyev-Ignatyev hung his head, and Marlen Mikhailovich heard a muffled but desperate mumbling coming from his mouth. At last he made out the words "Scotch. Pour me a Scotch."

"Why should I? I didn't invite you. You are of no interest to me."

Ignatyev-Ignatyev pulled himself together. He smoothed back his forelock, struggled out of the chair, and began pacing the room. "You're wrong to treat me like this, Marlen Mikhailovich," he said. "I represent the only force on the Island capable of resisting the SOS epidemic. The West, as usual, has proved morally bankrupt, so we have gone to Belgrade for support and are currently making overtures to Beijing. Our coalition of leftist parties is the last hope of all who despise SOS."

"And you think I support you?" Marlen Mikhailovich smiled. "You think a Soviet diplomat supports you? Curious."

"You are a strong potential supporter," said Ignatyev-Ignatyev. "You have inside information to the effect that the upper echelons do not favor reunification. In fact, you represent them."

"Who told you that, Mr. Communist Oilman?" Marlen

Mikhailovich shifted the Scotch to his left hand and shook Ignatyev-Ignatyev by the shoulder with his right. "Come on, tell me! Where did you get it from?"

Ignatyev-Ignatyev said nothing, his head bobbing up and down helplessly.

"He got it from me," said a smooth, unruffled voice. Marlen Mikhailovich looked over to the door to see a man with a Ramses beard who could be none other than OSVAG Colonel Vadim Vostokov. Bowing elegantly, the Colonel crossed the room and placed a silver bucket with a bottle of iced champagne in it on the table. "Forgive me, Marlen Mikhailovich," he said, with an apologetic shrug of the shoulders, "but I was in fact imprudent enough to make a suggestion to that effect during one of my discussions with—or should I say, interrogations of—the criminal you see before you."

"To what do I owe the honor, Mr. Vostokov?" asked Marlen Mikhailovich almost gaily. The Black and White had done its duty. Everything seemed so simple now, so one or the other. It was like television of the good old sixties, precolor, pure illusion.

"I'm flattered you know my name." He uncorked the champagne with great skill. "Can you hear the northeaster howling? We're in for a storm. The perfect time for a cozy game of political poker."

Champagne after whiskey was like a silvery piano entrance after the orchestra's chords. "I just want you to know," he said, toppling into a chair, "that I'm being covered by Major Lopatov next door."

TVMig had now come round to what it poetically called the "cod-liver oil of Leningrad's river lamps" and illustrated with the wavy needle of the Peter and Paul Fortress against the red stripes of a dying sunset. At last the camera zoomed in on three self-conscious young men wearing black knit scarfs and heavy overcoats with turned-up collars.

"The adjoining room is empty," said Vostokov amiably. "Major Lopatov is at this very moment in the Bangkok Massage Parlor."

"Ladies and gentlemen," said the voice of the commentator, "we are broadcasting direct from the cradle of the Proletarian Revolution." The commentator himself appeared on the screen wearing a trench coat with a turned-up collar and a fedora with a turned-down brim. "Since we do not have the authorities' permission to film the interview you are about to see, we apologize in advance for any technical difficulties we may encounter." He turned to the three young men. "And now let me introduce you to Igor, Slava, and Valera. All three are members of what they call the New Right."

One of them pulled a sheet of copybook paper out of his coat and, having cleared his throat, began to read: "In the name of the New Right of Krestovsky Island, St. Petersburg, we appeal to the Russian government on the Island of Crimea, to the commander-in-chief of the armed forces of South Russia, and to the head of Security to take Andrei Luchnikov, editor of the pro-Soviet *Russian Courier*, into custody. Soviet youth and its vanguard, the New Right of Krestovsky Island, consider Andrei Luchnikov a renegade and a traitor to our cause—"

At this point the camera started jumping crazily and the screen filled with fuzzy splashes of light and dark. Unperturbed, the commentator explained that the interview had been disrupted by the People's Militia, but that the interviewees had escaped in time on a motorcycle.

"There!" Ignatyev-Ignatyev shouted jubilantly. "Did you hear that? They want Luchnikov in custody! Soviet youth has spoken!"

"Yes, but they're a rightist group," said Marlen Mikhailovich, bubbling over with laughter, "and you represent the ultraleftist standpoint now."

"What difference does that make!" Ignatyev-Ignatyev blustered, spraying saliva across the room. "The important thing is they want Luchnikov arrested. The main culprit! Before it's too late!"

"There's passion for you," said Vostokov with a sympathetic nod in Ignatyev-Ignatyev's direction. "He's worshiped Andrei since childhood. We recently got our hands on his diary. Imagine, nearly a thousand pages of passion, hatred, love, and rage. He fantasizes being Luchnikov's wife."

"It's a forgery, a fraud!" screamed Ignatyev-Ignatyev, his eyes glistening. He was in the transports of delight a young man feels when the object of his love—ardently desired, no matter how unfaithful or base—is being discussed in his presence. "Let me have a little of your Scotch, Marlen Mikhailovich," he begged. "Just a drop."

"Go and get a couple of bottles from the bar," said Vostokov sternly. "You can put it on the Security account."

"At your service," said Ignatyev-Ignatyev and disappeared.

Vostokov turned off the television set, and the wail of the northeaster rushed to fill the void. The beam of a spotlight lit up the wave-pitted horizon.

"I've been looking forward to a chat with you, Marlen Mikhailovich."

Kuzenkov laughed. He felt the temerity of youth: the certainty that he knew in advance all the moves they would make—these people caught in their own devices—that he saw through the absurdity of their fun and games; he, Marlen Mikhailovich, knew the fundamental reason, the Why and Wherefore of the whole mess, and with the temerity of youth he denounced that Why and Wherefore as base nonsense.

Vostokov sighed. "Everything is so hideously confused. Be honest with me now, Marlen Mikhailovich. Do you understand what's going on? You're one of the leading figures in it all."

"Whether I understand or not is completely beside the point. All that matters is that I, unlike you, Comrade White Guard, have the upbringing and education to see the Why and Wherefore."

Just then the Communist Oilman reappeared, his nose and upper lip locked in the painful grip of "Professor Kokkinaki." "One moment, gentlemen. Our friend here has brought along a special neuroparalytic bomb to try out on you," said Kokkinaki-Sergeev, releasing Ignatyev-Ignatyev with a shove. He sat down, opened his attaché case, and pulled out three bottles of Siberian vodka.

"Give me back my diary, Kokkinaki," Ignatyev-Ignatyev whined. "Give me back that filthy forgery."

"Well, well," said Marlen Mikhailovich, surveying the gathering. "Looks like a family reunion."

Sergeev smiled. "Not quite, but we do swap some information. Intelligence work would be impossible otherwise. Isn't that so, Mr. Vostokov?"

Vostokov showed no sign of playing along with Sergeev and, in fact, ignored him entirely. "I wonder if you would care to complete your thought, Marlen Mikhailovich," he said. "You were saying you knew the Why and Wherefore?"

"That's right," said Marlen Mikhailovich, pouring one-third Scotch, one-third champagne, and one-third vodka into his glass. "The Why and Wherefore spins us all in its whirlpool, turning work into a senseless waste of time and money, turning life itself into an absurdity. Marxists and monarchists, CIA and KGB—it spins us all in its whirlpool, while it swims on, sleek and powerful, inexorable, a shark if there ever was one!"

There was an awkward pause.

"Quite impressive," muttered Vostokov.

The awkward pause resumed, accentuated by the quiet gurgle of Ignatyev-Ignatyev swilling vodka.

"I have a proposal to make," said Professor Kokkinaki. "A man-to-man proposal." He looked over at Ignatyev-Ignatyev. "Well, call it what you like. In any case, I propose that we all get rip-roaring drunk in honor of the northeaster and then take a trip down the road to the ladies of Bem-Minor. By the way, Lopatov's had his head cracked open with a bottle at the Bangkok."

"Sometimes we have no choice," said Vostokov.

"The more I think of that sleek bitch," said Marlen Mikhailovich, "the more I think a cracked skull is a viable alternative. Any of you phony James Bonds want to try my cocktail? I'm beginning to feel a bit queasy. Say, what are those blinking lights out at sea? Is it starting?"

"We'll know when it starts," said Sergeev. "The Crimean fleet goes out on maneuvers, then our men in Novorossiisk follow suit, and the Americans fly in and take pictures. Who the hell needs it all?"

"The shark knows," said Marlen Mikhailovich, imitating the motions of a large fish and smiling quizzically.

The phone rang. It was none other than Andrei Luchnikov. "Listen closely, Marlen. I've just given the TVMig people the slip, and I have to talk to you. I'm about five hundred yards away, directly on the beach, the Trident Bar."

"But I have company," said Marlen Mikhailovich. "We're having a grand time talking over the Why and Wherefore."

"I know who's there," said Luchnikov quickly. "Give them any excuse. It's urgent."

"*Très bien, très bien,*" Marlen Mikhailovich said, laughing slyly. "My honored guests are highly intrigued. Why don't you come and see for yourself? We can have a game of political poker and listen to the roar of the northeaster. Remember the song that goes, 'With a northeaster on its way and solid ice,/It's hard to build a communistic paradise . . .'?" Whereupon he hung up and gave his "guests" a broad smile. They gave their most professional non-committal response. The poor devils, thought Marlen Mikhailovich, certain they know everything, certain they've set the course, and they more than anyone are at the beck and call, at the mercy, of the shark, the bitch, the Why and Wherefore.

"That was Luchnikov."

Again neither of the intelligence officers moved a muscle, but the Communist Oilman, who until then had sat slumped over his vodka, leaped up, knocking over the glass and quivering like a damsel in distress.

"He's downstairs in the bar," said Marlen Mikhailovich. "I'll bring him up."

"I'll never survive it," Ignatyev-Ignatyev muttered to himself.

"Is the Sage woman with him?" Vostokov asked quickly.

"He's alone."

On the way out Marlen Mikhailovich locked the door from the outside. We'll be long gone by the time they find a way out, he thought. Gone where? Seaward?

Down in the lobby he went up to the policeman on duty, flashed his passport, and complained that a band of drunkards had burst unannounced into his room and refused to leave. The policeman immediately ran out to his car to call for reinforcements. How dare they disturb a Soviet diplomat, a Comrade!

Marlen Mikhailovich raced past the quivering juniper bushes and along the deserted street down to the beach, where giant whitecaps were tumbling over the breakwater in rapid succession. Feeling a sudden stab of cold, he realized he had run out in his shirt sleeves. He looked left and right. The waves had left the beach covered with foam, the fires in the sky were doing their wild dance. Running his hand through his tangled wet hair, he thought joyously, This night may solve all my problems. It was then he noticed three bright, warm windows in the basement of a beach-front building—the Trident Bar. The moment he stepped inside, the treacherous night disappeared. It was warm, it smelled of strong coffee and rich tobacco, and a warm, rich bass voice was singing:

> Gonna take a sentimental journey,
> Gonna set my mind at ease,
> Gonna make a sentimental journey,
> To renew old memories. . . .

The owner was watching the USSR-Canada hockey match on television. A gigantic Alsatian dog with a black stripe down its back gave Marlen Mikhailovich a friendly show of teeth as he came in. Luchnikov and Krystyna Sage were sitting in a corner booth.

"God, look at you!" Andrei laughed. "Soaked and soused. You know, I've never seen you drunk before. Look at him, Christie. He's blotto."

Ms. Sage, prim and proper in her buttoned-up leather jacket, gave Kuzenkov a friendly smile. Thanks to TVMig the whole Island knew that she carried two pistols, one in each pocket.

"Nikolai," Luchnikov called over to the owner, "give my friend here a sweater and a hot toddy, will you?"

"Nikolai," Luchnikov called over to the owner five minutes later, "give us some sou'westers, will you? We're going out for a breath of the northeaster."

With a flick of the wrist he stopped Krystyna's attempt to follow them. They went out into the roaring night and walked slowly along the narrow strip of shells still left between the masonry of the Third Administrative District's embankment and the billows rolling in from the dark.

"Marlen!" Luchnikov shouted in Kuzenkov's ear. "The deed is done! We're assured of victory! The latest poll shows that SOS will win over ninety percent of the votes next week!"

"I hope you're satisfied!" Marlen Mikhailovich shouted back.

"I'm terribly depressed!" answered Luchnikov.

"And well you might be!" shouted Marlen Mikhailovich. "You're nothing but a pitiful pilot fish for a gigantic, sleek, and senseless shark!"

325

"What are you talking about?" Luchnikov asked, momentarily dismayed.

Instead of answering, Marlen Mikhailovich pointed out to sea and smiled another of his quizzical smiles.

But Luchnikov had completely retreated into himself. Striding along, soaking wet, in the borrowed sou'wester, iridescent from the flashes of fire in the sky, he was both buried in thought and oddly young and heroic, the people's choice, a champion to the core.

"Next week, after the election, the Duma will formally request that the Soviet government accept Crimea as a republic of the USSR. Can you guarantee that nothing untoward will happen, nothing barbaric? It's utterly uncalled-for in our case, utterly unnecessary. The Czechs—they're a different nationality, they wanted to break away; we're Russians, and we want to be part of you. Violence is of no use. Tact and deliberation will go so much further. . . . The Soviet constitution gives each republic a number of rights, including the right to maintain its own armed forces. But our military *wants* to join forces with yours; we don't need coercion. The changeover to socialism must be undertaken gradually. We can be a source of hard currency for a long time to come. I don't care if they ship me or the classmates off to the wastes of Kulunda or to Vladimir Central Prison, I don't care if they stand us up against the wall; I just want to make sure they handle the island gently or at least without recourse to barbaric acts. Otherwise it will be a shattering experience for you as well as us and could lead to . . . might even lead to . . . well, war. . . . I've tried to go to the top with my requests for reassurance. As usual they make believe we don't exist. In the end, though, *you're* the one who carries out the policies, Marlen. That's why I've avoided you all these months. If TVMig had caught us together, we would have lost our credibility, both of us. But time is short now, and I've got to know. Have they got brains enough to keep from going off the deep end?"

Not once during his tirade did Luchnikov turn in Kuzenkov's direction. When he did look over at him, he was appalled. Normally the picture of placid stability, Marlen Mikhailovich was wildly disheveled and staring wild-eyed into the rumbling darkness of the Sea of Azov.

"Brains?" he screamed, and burst out laughing. "They've got all the brains they need. We prefer our brains in small doses."

"What's the matter, Marlen? Look, let's go back to the Trident." After a good deal of pushing and pulling, Luchnikov was able to deflect his friend's powerful body from its wayward course. But a few steps later Marlen Mikhailovich tore away and pressed up against the concrete slabs of the Third Administrative District's dike, his arms open wide, his eyes bulging out at the storm, his mouth distorted by caustic laughter.

The thundering whitecaps rolled on. Luchnikov thought he detected an increase in their intensity. Though they still broke about fifty feet away, the foam traveled much farther. He gave them an hour to work their way up to the dike and skim over it, as they now skimmed over the sea.

"So that's your scheme, Looch! First you preach moderation, then you offer yourself up as a sacrifice. You want to save everybody, right? Messianism? A passage to the stars? The road to Golgotha? Can't you see that it doesn't make one bit of difference how wise our wise men are or how much you're willing to sacrifice? Can't you see *it*? Can't you see it sleek and shining? Can't you see it whirling us round and round?"

Terrified, Luchnikov tried shaking Marlen Mikhailovich out of it, then gave him a hard slap across the face. "You're having a breakdown, Marlen! Get a hold of yourself! What are you babbling about?"

"The Why and Wherefore." He laughed loudly. "What else?"

"You can't expect me to take your Marxist ravings seriously." Luchnikov laughed hesitantly. "I'm no Marxist."

"Ha! Ha! Ha!" Kuzenkov's laugh had grown to a satanic roar. "You don't need to be a Marxist to see *it*! Believe in your God if you like, but look at reality too! Look at *its* giant sleek body!" He leaped over the dike and ran, arms outstretched, towards the sea. A moment later a wave rolled over him, submerging his whole body. Luchnikov rushed after him. When the wave receded, they were both up to their waists in seething white foam, surrounded here and there by whirlpools of spinning driftwood, bottles, Styrofoam, foam rubber, and scraps of bright-orange oilskin. Luchnikov gauged he was twenty or thirty feet from Kuzenkov and could reach him before the next wave, but before he could set off he was blinded by an intense light from the dike. The first thing he saw after regaining his orientation was another white hull racing towards them with a new cargo of flotsam.

"Stop, Marlen! Stop!" he cried in desperation.

Like a child overcome with delight at the prospect of a swim, the general consultant turned a jubilant face to Luchnikov and called out, "The shark! The shark!"

The wave engulfed him, then tossed him up on its crest. The light showed a massive board ramming into his head. A second later the water covered Luchnikov as well, but he swam towards Kuzenkov with all his might.

By the time he had dragged the lifeless body out of the water, the dike and surrounding sand were full of people. He made out Krystyna, up to her waist in water, several OSVAG men running up to him, Sergeev, Vostokov, and even Ignatyev-Ignatyev. It was as light as day: TVMig was covering it live.

XIV

Spring

In the middle of spring—that is, towards the end of April—the slopes of the Kara-Dag, Suru-Kaya, and Holly Mountain are covered with mountain tulips and poppies, a joy and inspiration to the eye, and wormwood, savory, and lavender fill the air with a fleeting but unforgettable olfactory poetry. No one misses an instant of the string of brief instants when they are in bloom: windows stay open at night, mountain walks are the order of the day. I hope this slope blooms thousands and thousands of times after I'm gone, thought Arseny Nikolaevich. The way it's bloomed for Max these fifty years. And when the earth turns cold and the sun turns cold, another slope just like this one will in all probability appear elsewhere in the universe, it, too, to be covered once a year with tulips and poppies, lavender, wormwood, and savory. . . . And with a smile he went on to think that the theory of probability might also account for another, identical old man amidst the vegetation in those unknown parts, but he suppressed the smile with a short laugh. Still fit, and kinder than ever, the tall old man in the old white alpaca sweater and hiking shoes was eminently worth reproduction—by the theory of probability or any other.

Arseny Nikolaevich was accompanied one day on his morning walk by Lieutenant Colonel Filip Stepanovich Boboryko, Ret., a friend and coeval, who had fought in the Ice Campaign alongside him. Unlike Arseny Nikolaevich, however, Filip Stepanovich was flabby and short of breath, and in fact had been forced to retire in 1937 for reasons of health. Moaning and groaning his way through the intervening decades, he had managed to found, develop, and pass on to his children a small but quite profitable ship-repairing business, and had circled the globe many times over. Now, huffing between the groans, he first upbraided Arseny Nikolaevich for dragging him along on this trek—an absurd undertaking, really, for two Methuselahs like ourselves—then told the story of the trip he had taken to Moscow the previous year and the pleasure he had felt at hearing the Soviet Army Band in concert.

"They gave a capital performance, *mon vieux*, believe me! I'll be damned if they didn't sound Russian, genuinely Russian. It was just like the old days. They even had a drum major with a baton. And the banners and flags! They might just as well have belonged to the Semyonovsky or Preobrazhensky regiments. The trumpeters, too. They were all so broad-chested and mustachioed. Now there's imperial power for you! Do you know what I think when I look at our troops? Forgive me, Arsyusha, I know you won't like this, but I think they have more in common with those pushy Jew boys in the Tel Aviv commandos than with a Russian army. Oh, and the songs they played—imagine: 'King of the Seas,' 'Totleben,' 'The Slav Maiden,' and even one of ours. You'll never guess. They played the 'March of the Drozdovsky Regiment'! Without words, of course, but I sang along, Arsyusha, I sang along in Soviet Moscow, I sang and wept. . . ." And forcing his unwieldy body up on a rock, he sang, hand on heart and not without inspiration:

> See our foes take flight before us;
> We're Drozdovsky's Volunteers.
> With Russia's colors flying o'er us,
> On paths of glory we've no peers.

As he reached the end, he lost his breath and began coughing and wheezing, and delicately turned away to hawk up some phlegm into a bush.

"Good old Boboryko," Arseny Nikolaevich said with a smile. (Even as a boy the lieutenant colonel was called simply Boboryko, his slightly ridiculous surname doubling as a nickname.) "I'm sorry to have to disillusion you. Your broad-chested trumpeters have never even heard of Drozdovsky. They've got their own words:

> As we march, one main idea
> Gives us courage and support:
> To take the Island of Crimea,
> The doomed White Army's last resort.

They've done a bit better with the text, don't you think?"

Two months had passed since the Provisional State Duma had formally petitioned the Supreme Soviet for admission into the Soviet Union as the sixteenth republic. So far they had not only received no response, they had received no reaction whatever, as if the whole idea were a childish whim and OK unworthy of the Eurasian giant's attention.

"Say what you like, Arsyusha. They *do* honor Russian traditions in the armed forces. Imagine, one day I went to Lefortovo to look for my military school and, imagine, I found it with no trouble. The same red walls and white columns—almost nothing has changed. The building now houses the Artillery Academy, so of course there was an officer on duty at the gate, a well-built lad, well strapped and belted; one of us, Arsyusha, a genuine Russian officer. I went up to him and told him I had studied there as a cadet. Imagine, he didn't turn on me, not in the least; he was friendly, respectful. . . ."

"What are you getting at, Boboryko?" asked Arseny Nikolaevich gently. "Come now, out with it."

"All I'm getting at is that while the world goes on about Soviet militarism, it's also true that we Russians have always loved war and—" Filip Stepanovich broke off, extremely agitated. His hands trembled, his breathing was irregular.

"Let's take a seat, shall we?" He sat his old friend on a large rock warmed by the sun. The enormous basin of Koktebel harbor and its sailboats and motorboats, the helicopter-speckled sky, the terraced houses, and the gracefully winding freeway lay beneath them. It was quiet here on the slope. They could hear a bird trilling nearby.

"Tell me what it is," said Arseny Nikolaevich. "Get it off your chest."

"All right," said Filip Stepanovich, breathing normally again. The grass had a heady fragrance to it. "We're a dying breed, dying off day by day. We couldn't even put together a battalion. The few of us left want your opinion. We know, everyone knows, that *they* will soon be here. What do you think? Have we the right, as the last of the Volunteer Army, have we the right to look upon them as *our* army?"

Arseny Nikolaevich did not hesitate for a minute. "No," he said. "They are *not* our army."

One warm May evening on the terrace of the Nabokov, Anton Luchnikov got the urge to serenade his pregnant wife. Hey, J.J., he said to one of the musicians, let me have your horn for one number, okay? I want to play for my wife. She's very pregnant. They were all old friends, all good Yakis, and J. J. Brill, saxophonist extraordinary, was glad to lend him his golden treasure as long as he promised not to ruin the reed with his slobber. And so the idol of the Châtelet *correspondance* lit into his own metro retro rendition of "Sentimental Journey." He had dug the music out of his father's archives and was sure he would wow them all with its age, but the Nabokov clientele seemed to know it well—to say nothing of the musicians, who immediately joined him, doing their best not to smile when he played a bum note or two. Then the band's black vocalist, Zaira of the long legs, wound her black dress tightly round her body and, looking for all the world like one of her own svelte legs, stood up next to Tony and sang:

> Gonna take a sentimental journey,
> Gonna set my mind at ease,
> Gonna make a sentimental journey,
> To renew old memories. . . .

As he played, Anton looked straight at his wife, his eyes brimming over with love. She'd be delivering any day now. I'll have a child, my own flesh and blood. And now that Mother's gone, that child will fill what we call by that awful term "the void," the black hole in space she left behind her. After his mother's recent death he had felt a change come over him. Perhaps he had matured, perhaps it was something else, but the change was a fundamental one. Every man has his cosmos, but mine is too open, too empty. Mother's gone, and Father doesn't even know about it; his orbit is receding, moving farther and farther away from me, from Granddad, revolving in cold rings around base fame. How lucky I am to have a warm and loving wife. Look at her. Even in that loose-fitting burnoose you can't hide it. My baby, my child . . .

Time to renew old memories myself. The day I saw those two American girls in the shopping district of Istanbul, could I have dreamed that one of them would be my wife? It's all Granddad's doing, actually; he told me in so many words, She's the one. Granddad, not Dad, though maybe he thought it that night at the Calypso when he looked at us so strangely. Anyway, he's got other things on his mind, he's too busy making history. History, politics —what a load of bull! If only I could play the sax like J.J.!

When he finished playing, he bowed formally and gave the saxophone back to its owner.

"Not bad, not bad," said Brill seriously. "Do you want to work on it with me some?"

"Do I! We can start tomorrow."

"The sooner the better, with the Reds on their way."

"They play the sax there. I learned all I know about the sax in Moscow. Ever heard of Dim Shebeko?"

"Of course." Brill nodded respectfully. "I always forget he's from there."

Anton went back to his table and the presiding golden goddess. Next to her sat his best friend, the rally finalist Masta Fa, and several other representatives of the First National Yaki Congress. Unfortunately, no sooner had the Congress come into existence than it broke up into a number of groups, the groups into cliques, and the cliques into individuals. Granddad was right, thought Anton. The Yaki idea was born before its time. It needed at least another generation to amount to something. Maybe the creature currently stretching Pamela's womb out of shape would make a true Yaki if not for . . . if not for this sad and beautiful spring when our whole Island, every crag and bay, is transfixed in expectation of the inevitable, hypnotized by the mysterious silence of the North. Though what do I care? I'm not going to follow in my father's footsteps, I'm not going to swap my freedom for a political idea, one is more foul than the next, I don't need that kind of fix, I'd rather play my sax, I'd rather go off to Malibu with Pamela, forget about being Russian or Yaki, forget about the Island and Crimea, I've had enough. . . . Over and over again he recalled the tumble-down *palazzo* on the outskirts of Rome, the peeling wallpaper, the creaking floorboards, the smell of decay and inescapable disaster. . . . Feeling Pamela's worried look on him, he gave his head a good shake. "Well, how did you like it, sweetheart?" He smiled.

"Pretty good." She smiled back. "I always thought the saxophone was all talk with you, but you really can blow that thing after all."

"J.J.'s going to give me lessons. In a year I'll be as good as he is."

"Great!" she said, stroking his head. The larger her stomach grew, the more maternal she was with her Russian lover boy. "I'm going to write home tomorrow and tell Mom I was wrong: I thought I was marrying the next prime minister, and I married a sax player."

"Who gives a fuck about prime ministers?" mumbled Anton, embarrassed. "Jazz is a free and independent country. It doesn't need any of that politics crap."

"Well, well, aren't we apolitical all of a sudden?" Masta Fa put in. "You've come back from Italy a changed man, Tony. What is it? You didn't let the Red Brigades brainwash you, now, did you?"

Everyone laughed but Anton and Pamela. He had told no one but Pamela the reason for the trip, nor would he ever. Who else had the right to know about the pots of black vomit, the cracks in the *palazzo* walls, his mother's death rattle, her eyes dimmed with narcotics, his lonely prayer breaking off in a spasm? Not Father. No, Father less than anyone. He turned away from Masta Fa without a word. So I've lost all my friends. Masta Fa is no more than a political ally if I don't feel I can talk to him about what is closest to me. What about Grandfather Arseny on his mountain? I wonder. . . . Of course. He's different, he'll understand. I'll tell him all about her. Yes, Pam and I will go to Koktebel tomorrow.

"Well?" asked Masta Fa, his eyes drilling furiously into Anton's. "That's it, isn't it? You were scared shitless by the Red Brigades."

"Who gives a fuck about the Red Brigades?" mumbled Anton, gulping down his cognac and lighting a cigarette.

"I knew it!" shouted Masta Fa. "We're all scared shitless! We're not Yakis, we're a pack of shits!"

After taking part in the Crimea Rally, Masta Fa had been snubbed by the Bakhchisarai aristocracy: a Muslim is not allowed to participate in the giaours' barbaric entertainments. Then his father, a millionaire plantation owner, threw him out of the house with the words "Go back to your Russians!" Now he was planning to take revenge on them all by going off on his own to nurse his wounds.

Masta Fa's words had the desired effect: everyone at the table forgot about jazz and the charms of late spring, about affairs of the heart and marijuana, and began debating the hopeless Yaki issue. Although he had vowed never to let himself get sucked in again, Anton was soon leaning across the table, pounding his fist, brushing the hair out of his eyes, and arguing with Masta Fa in the worst Russian style, hardly able to keep his tears back. "But can't you see, Masta Fa, can't you see, all of you, we haven't got a nation yet! Much as I hate to say it, there is no Yaki nation! The only time our rallies got anywhere was when we had to defend ourselves with our fists. All our discussions were a joke, and the Yaki language—we made fun of it ourselves."

Masta Fa jumped up and grabbed Anton's pounding fist. "You made fun of it, you Russians! You're all a pack of masochists, that's what you are! For three hundred years the Golden Horde did damn well what it pleased with you, and you didn't make a peep. And Stalin? Screwed you raw for forty years, and you call him the Father of Nations. Now you're turning bare-assed to the Reds and begging them to fuck you and the Island out of existence. Well, you can have your Russian masochism, damn you! I want no part of it!" He pushed Anton back into his seat and leaped over the terrace railing in the direction of his green Bakhchi-Maserati. In a few seconds it had roared out of sight.

"Well, there's a Yaki for you," Anton said sadly with a shrug of the shoulders. "The whole Yaki 'nation,' actually. Calling us Russians! What's Russian about me? I'm just as much Italian."

"Italian?" asked Zaira, who had joined them. "A cute little blond like you?"

"So you think all Italians are dark and surly?" asked Pamela, rising over her stomach in a huff. The nerve of that Zaira, trying to lure a man away from his pregnant wife for a night.

"Hair color, skin color—that's primitive racism," said Anton. He was despondent over Masta Fa's malicious outburst. "You know why we're quarreling over trivia?" he said after a moment's thought. "Because we're worried about whether the Reds are coming."

"Don't worry. They're coming," said a voice Anton could not quite place. It was a Russian voice, but Anton detected a Soviet intonation. Yes, there was no doubt. He looked over and saw a short young man sitting sideways at the far end of the table. He had a beard that went up to his eyes and wore a soldier's shirt embroidered with lilies; in short, he was the model of a Soviet hippie. "You're from Russia, aren't you?" he asked.

"Yes, just in," the hippie answered mysteriously.

Anton turned back to his friends and went on with his idea. "Whether the Reds come or not, it is the duty of all Crimean youth to further the cause and ensure that the Yaki seed lives on. We must organize multiethnic agricultural communes, perfect our language and culture . . ." Suddenly he felt the ironic gaze of the new Soviet arrival resting on him again. He quickly turned to meet the gaze. Sure enough, the boy was laughing. "And what are you laughing at, may I ask?"

"I'd just like to see what kind of multiethnic communes you set up in the Crimean Autonomous Soviet Socialist Republic," he said. "Nobody here understands what Bolshevism is all about. Even you Yakis who are against reunification, you have no idea how quickly they'll do away with you."

"Who are you anyway?" they asked him. "Are you from Moscow?"

"I left Moscow a week ago."

"What are you? A tourist? No, they cut off tours after the Duma made its request. Part of the Jewish emigration? No, they never come here."

"I'm just a runaway," he said modestly.

The whole table burst out laughing. What a place to run to!

"I don't care where I go. I can escape from anywhere to anywhere."

"A regular Houdini," said Anton.

"Yes, something like that," said the boy with the utmost simplicity. "My name is Benjamin Ivanov, but my friends call me Ben-Ivan. I'm into the occult. Every year I find more signs of freedom in myself. Just ask your father, Tony. Last summer we crossed the Soviet-Finnish border together. I put a whole outpost out of commission, messed up their radar, too, and at a good distance."

"So you're the one!" said Anton.

"At your service." He stood up and bowed, walked over to the railing of the terrace, and disappeared among the branches of an overhanging plane tree.

Anton shook his head in amazement. When he looked back at the table, there was Ben-Ivan again, smiling at him. Before he could recover, he felt Zaira's soft lips against his ear. How about a dance, sexy?

"Sexy will dance with me," said Pamela angrily, though she could scarcely have heard Zaira's unuttered invitation. "We'd so like to hear your rendition of 'Sentimental Journey' again," she added, immediately at peace with her.

Zaira was an easygoing soul herself, and she went straight up to the platform, grabbing the new rearrival on her way. As it turned out, he had a trombone with him and did some professional-sounding solo work with Zaira, whom he appeared to know well, well enough to tickle her springy posterior with his slide. Everyone on the terrace was dancing, dancing and smiling. Leaning against his wife's enormous stomach, Anton felt the baby's heartbeat coincide with his own. He looked around at his friends, the unconstituted new nation of the Island of Crimea, and thought, Hey, *chellows*, you're the best-looking nation I've ever seen. Everyone on the terrace was dancing to a thirty-five-year-old song, dancing and smiling. A sweet cloud of marijuana hovered over their heads, and a harmless swarm of high-as-a-kite midges; beyond, a golden sunset was dissolving the sky. Inside the Nabokov, through the crystal-clear glass, the elegant clientele was still drinking its martinis, but the spirit that had pervaded the restaurant until recently—when hardly an evening passed without a reception for visiting émigrés

—that spirit was gone. Here and there a laughing mouth, here and there a prophet's furrowed brow, a drunkard's crooked lips; here and there a nose stuck in the air by a secondhand lady with a pout for good measure; and looking down on them all from oak-paneled walls, the portraits of Turgenev, Merezhkovsky, Bunin, Akhmatova, Brodsky, Voznesensky, Akhmadulina, and many others. WRITERS ARE THE MAINSTAY OF THE PARTY, Anton recalled seeing at the Moscow Writers' Club. Here at the Nabokov the lack of reality flowed rather from the smoke enveloping them all—the mild and today, for some reason, mildly depressant narcotic. Then a sudden twist in the dance opened up a pathway through the trees, and in a flash the vast golden sky, the cubes, spires, sphere, squares, and terraces of the Simfi skyline, the sparkling *Courier* skyscraper brought Anton back to reality. The bright light burning at the point of the *Courier* pencil made it look like a lighthouse. His father was in tonight. Why did he need that ridiculous light? Who needed a lighthouse on a golden night when everything far into the future was so clear?

The invasion began that very day, though of course tradition required that it wait until dark. In the short interval between sunset and dawn an endless stream of turbojets wailed over Simfi.

The head and mastermind of SOS, publisher and editor of the *Russian Courier*, Andrei Luchnikov, heard the wail and understood: the deed was done. He switched off all the inside lights, and he and the classmates stared out at the lights amassing in the sky. They belonged to Soviet Anteyas, gigantic airborne landing craft, circling above Simfi, waiting their turn to land.

As always, TVMig was on hand. Anyone who happened to be up at that hour have watched the first whale of the naval landing force open its jaws and belch out jeep after Blue Beret–crammed jeep—though the program came to an end rather suddenly when a small band of Blue Berets ran towards the camera with rifle butts raised.

"There, you see?" Beklemishev said calmly. "They've done it again. Lied in their teeth. They can't help lying."

"But I didn't negotiate with these rookies," shouted Luchnikov. "I negotiated with the State Planning Committee! With Comecon and the State Planning Committee. Do they know what's going on?"

Two days before, the penthouse had been the scene of great rejoicing: Moscow had broken its ominous three-month silence, and Luchnikov was put in touch with important governmental figures. The consensus seemed to be that it was time to begin coordinating the two economies. Luchnikov, exultant, put the Moscow comrades in touch with the corresponding Simferopol governmental, commercial, and financial agencies. In other words, things were proceeding just as the classmates had predicted: the pragmatists had ruled the day; unification would take place in careful, tactically planned stages; and there was no possibility whatever of an invasion. The mere thought of an invasion was absurd—how could a country invade a country that had joined it of its own free will? Crimea was no Estonia, Latvia, or Lithuania, after all.

Everything seemed to be going well but for one ominous detail: the golden-green luminescence of recent sunsets over the entire territory of the Island had filled the classmates with a growing but inexplicable anxiety and kept them up at night in Luchnikov's penthouse, unwilling to disperse.

The videophone indicator flashed, and Colonel Chernok came on the screen. He spoke softly but clearly. "Naval landing craft of a new, air-cushion variety are approaching from all sides. Tank columns are disembarking on the beaches, marine forces in the bays. Aero-Simfi is glutted with Anteyas. Our radar installations report approaching fighter aircraft. I presume their mission is to blockade our bases."

"Why should they want to blockade our bases?" cried Meshkov. "Don't they realize that our bases are theirs?"

Laying his hand on Meshkov's trembling shoulder, Luchnikov said to Chernok, "Try to get through to General Staff and ask what has caused the invasion."

"Invasion??" Chernok smiled. "What invasion?"

"What are you talking about?" shouted Sabashnikov without a trace of his former buffoonery.

"Turn on the Moscow channel."

Fofanov found Moscow on the television set. What they saw,

instead of the color grid normally shown late at night, was Arbenin, the broad-faced newscaster, in his usual baggy jacket, droning his way through a TASS communiqué that from the tone of it perhaps was of greater importance than a report from the Central Statistics Bureau but surely of less importance than Comrade Kapitonov's speech on the occasion of the presentation of the Order of the October Revolution to the town of Kineshma. "As is well known," (to whom and on what basis was unclear, since the Soviet population had been kept totally in the dark) "broad segments of the originally Russian territory" (not a word about the State Duma; it might just as well not exist) "of the Eastern Mediterranean Region" (even in this context the name Crimea was out of the question) "have appealed to the Supreme Soviet of the Union of Soviet Socialist Republics for inclusion in one of the Republics." (Another little fib, an off-white lie; that was not quite how the request was worded). "Yesterday at a meeting of the Presidium of the Supreme Soviet the appeal was approved in principle. It must now gain the confirmation of the Supreme Soviet as a whole.

"To celebrate the reunification of the peoples of the Eastern Mediterranean Region with our great socialist commonwealth, the Committee for Physical Culture and Sports of the Soviet of Ministers, together with the Ministry of Defense and the All-Union Voluntary Society for Assistance to the Army, Air Force, and Navy, have decided to carry out a series of war games in the Black Sea area under the general name of Spring. The games are scheduled to begin on the [previous day] of May. We will keep our viewers informed of the course of the games on Central Television's Second Program."

"That's enough," said Chernok from his screen. "You can turn it off."

The classmates watched as the officer of the day handed Chernok a radiogram. The colonel smiled again, this time a bit sarcastically. "Our American friends inform us that a squadron headed by the aircraft carrier *Kiev* has just left Odessa and a squadron headed by the aircraft carrier *Minsk* has just left Novorossiisk, both bound for our shores."

"Our sources confirm the report," Vostokov injected with faultless composure.

"That's it for now," said Chernok. "I'm going to have a look round in my helicopter. As far as I can tell, I'm no longer in charge here. I simply want to satisfy my curiosity and see how they're going about it."

A few seconds after the videophone went blank, the classmates saw a large green helicopter with Soviet markings fly up to the penthouse. It stopped just short of the glass walls, its open door jammed with soldiers trying to peer through the reflective glass.

"Do you think they've come for us?" Luchnikov asked Vostokov.

Vostokov did not respond.

"Where's Sergeev?" asked Luchnikov. "When are they supposed to come for us?"

Vostokov did not respond.

Suddenly a bright light from the helicopter pierced the glass, and for a few seconds they felt like insects under a microscope. Then from somewhere above them a series of shots rang out. They looked up to see Krystyna Sage with two pistols in her hands. The helicopter immediately extinguished its light and backed off.

"So you plan to defend yourself to the bitter end," Vostokov sneered. "Like Salvador Allende, eh?"

"Put down those guns!" Luchnikov shouted to Krystyna.

She immediately did as she was told.

"Who told you to shoot?"

She sank to the floor and sobbed, her head in her lap.

"What do you propose we do now?" Sabashnikov asked the assembled company. He was a new man, dead serious. "Shall we sit and wait for the KGB like Dubček and his cronies?"

There was a long pause. Luchnikov was the first to speak. "Petya's right. Let's at least give the comrades a run for their money. And while we're at it, we can take one last look at our favorite haunts, at our Island."

They all stood without a word.

Several minutes later a number of cars rolled out of the underground garage and slowly, with the utmost dignity, drove off their separate ways—Meshkov's Russo-Balt, Beklemishev's BMW, Fofanov's Mercedes, Sabashnikov's Jaguar and all the rest, with Luchnikov's famous Peter Turbo, the symbol of the Idea, taking up the rear.

"The next time we met," said Sabasha just before they disbanded, "may be in the Potma glassworks like the Decembrists." And so as not to cry, he laughed. . . .

It was growing lighter by the minute, and Vostokov, who had remained behind to have a better look at a constellation of helicopters that had appeared with the sun, was able to make out Colonel Sergeev at quite a distance. He was in full dress, and Vostokov could not help thinking how preposterous it looked on him.

"Have they all left?" he asked Vostokov from a distance. The buzz of the approaching helicopters was still no louder than the buzz of a swarm of bumblebees, and Sergeev's low voice echoed, brittle, off the bright tiles and through the dormant kinetic sculpture of Courier Square.

Vostokov was sitting at the foot of the sculpture, which, according to its maker, embodied *Stability in Fragility*. With legs crossed and arms folded, he watched Sergeev's approach. I wonder. Will he shoot me himself or leave it to the helicopters?

Sergeev stopped in front of him.

"Why didn't you arrest them in time? You had your orders." Sergeev's voice had the same "I wonder" quality to it that Vostokov noticed in himself and in all members of the profession at even the most critical junctures.

"Why do you think?" he asked Sergeev arrogantly. "Can't you guess?"

"You're a good man, Vostokov," the Moscow colonel blurted out, almost giving his colleague a pat on the back. "I knew it all along. Listen, hop into your jalopy and make yourself scarce while you can. It's your best chance, believe me."

"What if I decided to carry out my orders?" Vostokov caught himself wondering again. An indestructible impulse.

"Then it will be your only chance."

"*Yaki*," said Colonel Vostokov. "You're a good man, too, Sergeev."

A good ten minutes before the special KGB commando piled out of the first helicopter on Courier Square, Vostokov's maroon Volkswagen had disappeared into the Underground Knot.

The Azerbaijani officer in charge of the operation was crestfallen. He thought back with nostalgia to his stint in Czechoslovakia, when he'd lined the whole government up against the wall, hands up. Apparently the Comrades here in Simferopol were less politically aware.

Up and down the skyscrapers lining the Boulevard of the Twentieth of January the first rays of the sun were joined by red flags and tricolors. The higher the sun rose over Simfi's main thoroughfare, the more the crowd grew along either side. The cafés and espresso bars opened several hours earlier than usual, and the mood was one of joyous excitement. Young people were hanging signs from the trees, signs that read WELCOME, MOSCOW! and SOVIET ISLAND WELCOMES SOVIET MAINLAND! and CRIMEA + KREMLIN = TRUE LOVE, and the most original of all: MAY AN INVIOLABLE FRIENDSHIP FLOURISH AMONG PEOPLES OF THE USSR FOREVER! Streams of cars were dammed in both directions, and the police were running their legs off trying to clear the street for a parade of several units of what was now their own Soviet army. For the time being, not a single Soviet soldier was to be seen in the center of town. The enormous screens in the bars and the tiny transistorized screens in the hands of the public showed TVMig from various other parts of the Island. For once, however, TVMig did not appear to be on top of things: reporting was muddled, and reports kept being cut off. The rather forward TV crew upset the modest Soviet recruits, and whenever a camera moved in for a close-up, the Soviets' faces would darken, the screens go blank. Yet the grandiose scale of the war games was unmistakable. The Moscow channel, meanwhile, was running yesterday's evening news, "Time," which featured the spring sowing campaign, the speech given by the temporary chargé d'affaires of the Republic of Mozambique on the occasion of his country's national holiday, and a presentation of awards to veterans of the coal industry. . . . Champagne had begun to flow along the Boulevard, and the mood was more and more boisterous: Who cares about television anyway, everything's going to be just fine, soon we'll see what it's like with our own eyes, Brezhnev himself may be flying in tonight.

All at once a siren began to wail and a powerful, obviously Soviet voice came through the PA system repeating, "All vehicles and pedestrians are to clear the roadway immediately! All vehicles and pedestrians are to clear the roadway immediately!" With the aid of the announcement, the Simfi police managed to chase off some of the cars and direct the rest onto the sidewalks—under the trees or up against the buildings.

At last, half a dozen amphibious armored cars sped down the center of the road, their headlights glaring red and sirens going full blast. All that was visible out of the top was a cluster of blue berets and shaved necks. The cheers of the crowd never reached the soldiers as they rushed past.

A foreigner in the Café Champs de Mars suggested they might be off to "take" the Council of Ministers. He was laughed down. But several minutes later TVMig gave a report from Senate Square with the impressive colonnade of the Council of Ministers in the background and armored units rolling in from all directions. Once more the screen went blank just as things started to get interesting. TVMig was definitely having a bad day.

Meanwhile, the Peter Turbo that won the Crimea Rally was stuck in an immense traffic jam on Baron Square. Under any other conditions it would naturally have been the center of attention, but now the crowds were craning their necks to catch the first glimpse of the Soviet columns.

Krystyna had quickly shed the image of the lithe and silent lover-bodyguard tagging after the leader of the Idea. Her face was swollen from crying, and there was fear in her eyes. "Please, Andrei, listen to me, please! We've got to get out of this car. Everybody knows this goddamn car. They'll find you right off the bat. Here, put on this wig and let's get out of here. They'll be after you any minute."

"I'm not hiding from anyone," said Luchnikov contemptuously, his television smile never leaving his lips. Black sweater, blue shirt, red ascot, cigarillo hanging from the corner of his mouth—his supersophisticate look. "If they issue out an order for my arrest, I'll submit to it. If they try any funny business, I'll put up a fight."

Suddenly she burst into uncontrollable sobs. Luchnikov was furious. What a sissy this "woman of iron" had turned out! Tanya would never have stooped to such sniveling. But Luchnikov was also trembling violently inside, and it did him good to take his own fears out on Krystyna. He even took her by the neck and gave her a good shaking. "Wipe your nose, you bitch!"

"At least think of me," she said, still sobbing loudly. "What will I do without you? Let's get out of here, Andrei! Think of somebody else for once in your life! Think of me for a second, you lousy bastard. Think of somebody else!"

"So I'm a megalomaniac, is that it?" he raged. "You think I did this all for myself, made this hell for myself?"

"Hell" was now inundated with thundering band music from loudspeakers, decked with flags of all the political parties of Crimea and with the red Soviet flag, filled with laughing faces.

Luchnikov lowered his head and pressed his palms against his temples, his fingers against his closed eyelids—anything to stop the cloud of gloom descending over him. Maybe Christie is right, in her feminine way. She's reminded me about my father, whom I'd forgotten, about my son, whom I'd forgotten, about my grandchild, who will be along any day now and whom I've forgotten before he's even born, and now she's reminding me about herself, whom I don't know enough to forget. I've forgotten Tanya, forgot her back in Moscow, that's why she went off, and this new one, this Christie, I don't even know well enough to forget. And yet, no, in the end she's not right. Forgive me, O Lord, I may have to pay for being so callous, but I *didn't* think of myself the whole time, I thought of Russia, of her sacred path, of Your path, of redemption.

As they left the *Courier* skyscraper earlier that morning, Krystyna had reminded him about his father, and he had stopped and phoned Kakhovka from the first booth. The call was taken by the new librarian, former Prime Minister Kublitsky-Piottukh. No, Arseny Nikolaevich wasn't in; he'd left in the middle of the night without a word to anyone and driven his faithful servant Hua and the Rolls to Simferopol; he, Kublitsky-Piottukh, couldn't help suspecting Arseny Nikolaevich's sudden departure had something to do with the events of the day, about which Andrei Arsenievich was naturally better informed than most, and though he himself, that is, Kublitsky-Piottukh, owed him a true debt of gratitude for all his family had done for him, still, he felt it his duty to register his dissat—

Alone at the Simferopol flat, Hua wept into the receiver when he heard Andrei's voice. Andlusa, somesing tellible happen. . . . Ahseny he leave flat in old army coat and take from basement old lusty gun. . . .

Now, caught in traffic, he realized he was completely cut off from his immediate family, and suddenly he thought, Life isn't worth living without them, or without Pamela of the Golden West, or his future grandchild, or Tanya's Sasha, or Tanya herself, or without this Christie, who seemed to love him so much. Suddenly all history, philosophy, and politics went up in smoke, and he felt like a blob of protoplasm, a pitiful barely living organism, a mere receptacle for something quivering, thirsting for protection. He had felt that way only once before in his life—after the Crimea Rally.

"Attention!" a powerful loudspeaker voice boomed over Baron Square. "All vehicles and pedestrians along the Boulevard of the Twentieth of January, Sinopsky Boulevard, and Preobrazhenskaya are to clear the roadway immediately!"

Luchnikov pulled his sun roof back and stood up in the car. He could see the first column of tanks advancing along Sinopsky Boulevard, guns raised and lights burning. Then he saw some TVMig cameramen in their silver blazers running to the baron's statue instead of to the tanks. What was going on? Buses, police wagons, and the TV crew itself blocked his view. "What's going on there?" he asked into the void.

Krystyna was now sitting motionless. She had on a man's hat, dark glasses, and a bandanna over her mouth and nose.

"Here, have a look at the screen, Mr. Luchnikov," came a pleasant voice from the neighboring Cadillac. It, too, had a sun roof, and its owner, a stockbroker by the looks of him, was following events half through the roof and half on the screen of a built-in TV set. "It's a historic moment, Mr. Luchnikov, one the Bolsheviks have been looking forward to for sixty years: the definitive capitulation of the Volunteer Army."

Luchnikov shuddered in horror. It was all absolutely clear on the screen. At the pedestal of the baron's statue stood several hundred old men—nearly enough for a battalion—in military formation and dress: decrepit overcoats falling apart at the seams but with Volunteer Army chevrons on the sleeves and stripes on the shoulders. They all had weapons of sorts: rusty rifles, carbines, Mausers, even sabers. The television cameras first panned the trembling formation, then zoomed in on individual faces covered with pigmentation, on cobwebs of sclerotic veins, on watery or glassy eyes peering out over many-layered bags; on hunched backs, vast paunches, extremities racked with arthritis; on the wheelchairs some of the men had reported in.

"What kind of nonsense is this, Mr. Luchnikov?" asked the stockbroker. "What is this farce supposed to prove?"

As the cameras ran along the formation, Luchnikov had the most peculiar reaction—namely, that it actually was an army and these relics were soldiers, that the casualties inflicted by time on their bodies and ammunition only reinforced the feeling they gave of being an army. Then Luchnikov saw the man he knew he would see sooner or later in that formation: his father. Arseny Nikolaevich stood in the first rank, which was reserved for the best-preserved and most jaunty-looking. Some of them, trying to puff out their medal-studded chests and make a great display of high spirits, looked ridiculous. Luchnikov senior, simple and dignified in his Cadet coat and colonel's insignia, stood leaning on his gun in the pose he and his fellows-in-arms must have assumed between attacks at Kakhovka. He made a strange contrast with the reporter beside him, all dapper and self-assured in his silver blazer and TVMig emblem. Far in the background, behind a sea of heads, flowers, flags, and signs, the headlights of a column of tanks moved slowly forward.

"The presidium of the White Warriors' League firmly rejected the proposal of the Provisional State Duma," Luchnikov heard his father saying calmly. "True to its vow, the subunit of the armed forces of South Russia present here today opposes the invading Soviet forces."

"But Professor Luchnikov . . . ," said the reporter, flashing an ironic grin at the camera.

"Colonel," Arseny Nikolaevich inserted gently.

"Excuse me, *Colonel*. The General Staff and all the men in our own armed forces have welcomed the heroic army of the great Soviet Union with open arms. . . ."

"Yes, but we're the Volunteer Army," bellowed a broad-chested old codger next to Arseny Nikolaevich. "We're the Russian army!"

"And does the Russian army plan to fight?" asked the reporter.

"No, we plan to capitulate," said Arseny Nikolaevich. "The Volunteer Army plans to capitulate in view of the enemy's superior strength." A faint smile appeared on his face, and he added, "Capitulation sounds a good deal more sane than—"

The all-powerful PA voice drowned out the "insane" word. "Clear the roadway immediately! Tanks will be passing through in five minutes!"

Hundreds, thousands of cars, one on top of the other, separated Andrei from Arseny. There was no way he could get to his father, no way he could save him. Chaos had set in. Then above the bazaarlike cacophony a single voice rang out: "Right dress! Attention! Forward march!"

The formation pulled itself together and set itself in motion. The last Andrei Luchnikov saw of his father he was moving the silver blazer out of his way with an energetic thrust.

The next shot was an aerial one, revealing an asphalt lake between the tanks and the old men's unit, the perfect space for a historic capitulation. Had TVMig engineered the space, the better to set off its "tragicomedy"? The candid camera of TVMig's maniacs knew no emotion, no fear, but was perhaps less candid than it appeared.

A large, striking white flag of capitulation unfurled above the Volunteers while the front rank carried the Russian tricolor and several company banners. The young helmeted faces of the Soviet tank crews looked imperturbable except for a gaping halfwit here and there. The tanks had not yet begun to move, the only battle so far taking place between the tanks' headlights and the camera's spotlights.

Meanwhile, an off-screen English-language commentator reported the scene as if it were the last minute of a World Cup match. "Yes, it's a gripping event we're witnessing here, gripping and symbolic. Six decades after the fact, the White Army is laying down its arms before the Red Army. The doddering old men you see on your screens were once the inspired young heroes of the Ice Campaign. How many are left? Have they passed on their traditions? Who are they now and who are their conquerors?"

Rank by rank, the old men threw down their rusty arms before the tanks and marched off to the side with bowed heads and hands behind their backs.

Suddenly everything changed. The faces of the tank crews vanished down the hatches. The commentator broke off in midsentence. A group of Blue Berets with machine guns on their shoulders had materialized from among the tanks and, pushing the last ranks of the Volunteers out of their way, were running up to the TVMig platforms. The image on the screen began to jump. For a second or two Luchnikov could make out two soldiers twisting a silver blazer's arms behind his back, then a rifle butt into the camera lens put an end even to that, but a moment later three new silver blazers appeared, with soldiers in hot pursuit.

"The landing force is engaged in a peculiar operation," wheezed the famous newscaster Bob Kolenko, shielding himself with his elbow. Though blood was pouring down his face and a supremely unruffled Blue Beret behind him had the barrel of his rifle against his neck, Bob Kolenko saw the camera's red eye shining on him and forged on valiantly. "Yes, an odd game they're playing. A full-scale imitation attack on the mass media. As you can see on your screens, this young soldier is trying to strangle me with the barrel of his carbine. I must say he's taking the game a bit too seriously. . . ."

Eventually live transmission was cut off altogether, and the winged-eye emblem took its place on the screen.

The Cadillac owner, obviously upset, looked over at Luchnikov and said, "These TVMig smart alecks are being terribly antagonistic to *our* new troops, don't you think?" He turned the dial to Moscow, where crowds in various parts of the Island were shown rejoicing in the streets. One shot caught a group of parachutists descending in the form of the letters USSR.

When Luchnikov looked up again, the tanks had begun to advance. "My father's life is at stake," he said to Krystyna. "You take the wheel. I'm going to find him."

She responded by lunging, grabbing at him like an animal. He suddenly felt a wave of aversion to her, but before he could act on it he noticed a group of drunken men in the door of a trailer pointing at him and laughing. They looked familiar, but were far enough away that he had a hard time placing them. Of course. Jack the Octopus Halloway and his Hollywood buddies plus—the drunkest, rudest, lewdest of them all—his former Moscow friend Vitaly Gangut. *He* was the one pointing at Luchnikov, *he* was the one snorting foully, and once he felt Luchnikov's eyes on him, he screamed something out at him, then pointed at the Soviet tanks surrounding the baron's statue, then doubled up with laughter. Finally he took out a little blue booklet and waved it over his head triumphantly. So he's managed to wangle an American passport, Luchnikov realized. He thinks he's untouchable, free, a citizen of the world, and I'm a serf of Mother Russia. He turned away from the Hollywood crowd as if he had never seen them, and, throwing off Krystyna's hat, began stroking her hair, kissing her, calming her.

"Take it easy, girl. Take it easy, easy, easy. I need you. I love you."

Slowly her fingers loosened their grip and slid down his chest. She even smiled.

At that moment a shadow fell on them. Someone had just made a tiger leap over the front of the Cadillac. "On your feet, Luchnikov! I'm going to punch your head in!"

Luchnikov looked up to see a handsome young man in a striped shirt and white jeans with a dark, sharply chiseled face—a real Yaki. He parried the blow, and peered into his assailant's angry, spiteful features. Where have I seen him before? Then he lowered his fists. "Masta Fa! Is it you?"

With demonstrative disgust the young man wiped off his hand on his jeans. "I'm Mustafa, not Masta Fa," he said in a rage. "To hell with the Yakis! Fuck the Russians! You're all a pack of degenerates! I'm a Tatar!" Then he spat at Luchnikov's feet and added, "If I don't spit in your face, it's only out of respect for your age. But age is all I do respect in you. Otherwise you are beneath contempt!"

"Tell me, Mustafa," Luchnikov said softly. "Where is Anton?"

"Isn't it a little late in the game to think of your son?" Mustafa said maliciously. "You deserve each other, you Russian swine! Just wait till the next Holy War!"

"Please tell me. Has Pamela had her child yet?"

The tanks had moved on to the Boulevard of the Twentieth of January, and the traffic jam began to loosen up. Someone honked at them from behind.

"I beg you, Mustafa."

A note of pity sounded in the voice of the fierce though newly fledged Islamic warrior. "During the night they went to Koktebel, to Suru-Kaya. As far as I know she hasn't had the child yet. But I advise the lot of you to get off our island. Reds and Whites."

"Thank you, Mustafa. And calm down, pipe down. Our old way of life is over. Everything's starting from scratch."

By now a dozen or two cars were honking at them, and Luchnikov sat behind the wheel. He was about to turn on the ignition when he felt the boy looking at him with more puppylike wistfulness than spite or anger. "Hop in the back," he shouted. Suddenly a space cleared in front of them, and the Peter Turbo roared off in grand old style.

When they reached the baron's statue, the monument to Baron Wrangel, they saw signs of a terrible massacre: glass, blazers, a whole van decimated by a tank. A group of confused policemen were standing at the base of the monument looking down long, straight Sinopsky Boulevard, where the lights of a new tank column had appeared. Luchnikov slowed down and asked one of them what had happened to the provacuees.

"Oh, they've been sent to various hospitals," the policeman answered quite lackadaisically. Then he recognized Luchnikov and came to attention. "They took a real beating, sir. There were some bad injuries. Your father, sir . . ."

"What about him?" cried Luchnikov in horror.

"No, no, don't get upset. It's nothing worse than a broken arm, I think. Some friends of his took him off. That's right. Yes, two ritzy ladies in a Russo-Balt. Don't worry, sir. Everything's just fine and *yaki* with your father."

"Listen, sergeant, would you do me a favor?"

"Anything you say, sir. It'll be a pleasure." His face broke out in a good-natured smile.

"Dial this number, and tell Mr. Hua everything you know about my father. Then ask him to locate him and go to Koktebel with him at once. I'll be there."

"Yes, sir!" said the sergeant and started off for the nearest café.

Luchnikov had to circle the baron several times before he could duck into a tunnel of the Underground Knot. As he circled, he kept thinking he had something left to do in the square, something important. . . . Cross himself, he remembered at last, and just as he

351

began to descend into the tunnel, he caught a glimpse of the shining cupola of the Church of All Saints Radiant in the Russian Land and made the sign of the cross.

In the orange glow of the endless headlights everything seemed normal again: another normal day in Crimea's normal supercivilization.

"Why don't you hunt down your father yourself?" Krystyna shouted to Luchnikov over the roar of the cars. She, too, seemed back to normal. She had even lit a cigarette.

"Father's had his day; Anton hasn't," he shouted back. "We've got to stop him from doing something foolish."

"A wise move," came a voice from the back.

Luchnikov turned his head and saw Mustafa curled up on the back seat. He reached back and felt a hard, wet cheek under his palm.

"Forgive me, Andrei-*aga*," said Mustafa. "It was all nerves."

Luchnikov gave him a pat on the cheek and went back to the wheel. Krystyna covered the other cheek with kisses.

Before long they were whizzing along the Eastern Freeway, following the majestic war games from on high. As in the boring days of independence, the freeway was unencumbered by military vehicles. Perhaps the generals in charge of strategy thought its massive steel trestlework too flimsy. Down below, however, the roads were packed with tanks, armored cars, and military vehicles. Movement was by fits and starts. Vehicles bumped into one another, then stood for long periods, ugly herds of gray-green beasts crowding about the trough. The numerous helicopters hovering or flying back and forth above them seemed to be in charge of coordinating the columns, but they did not seem to be doing very well: the gray-green herds made scarcely any progress and were growing steadily. Though there were bottlenecks on several of the freeway off-ramps, the freeway itself was relatively free, and Luchnikov had no trouble keeping his Peter Turbo at a cruising speed of seventy-five miles per hour. From time to time the frightening whistle of a pair of twin-tailed Mig-26's would zoom out of the sun, cross over the freeway, and disappear into the blue. To the south, in the region of Baksan or Tam-Dair, a dark cloud of aircraft hung in the sky. It was there the parachutists were landing.

During one of the jet patrol's routine flights an unpleasant incident took place: the number two Mig brushed a wing against one of the helicopters, and although what happened to the Mig is hard to say—it disappeared instantly—the helicopter burst into flames and crashed into one of the "herds." In the confusion a number of tanks and armored cars opened fire. Fortunately, the Peter Turbo passed the danger zone without untoward consequences.

Karachel, Bakhchi-Eli, Saly, Mama-Russkaya . . . Now they were approaching the Otuzy off-ramp, which was only ten miles from Kakhovka.

"If Anton and Pamela are still there, I'll drive back down to Simfi for Arseny at once," said Luchnikov, thinking aloud. "Then by evening we'll all be together on the mountain and can decide what to do next."

"That means we'll be on our way tonight!" Krystyna exclaimed.

"Where to?" asked Mustafa.

"It's a big world," she cried triumphantly, ecstatically. This might be the most exciting day in her life. "You have no idea how big the world is. We can go anywhere we please. Isn't that right, Andrei? What? No response? So you're not coming with us? You'd rather stay faithful to your Idea? The Russian martyr can't come with us, Mustafa. Isn't that a pity? And I hoped the three of us would have our fun together. Looks like we'll have to go it alone."

Watching out of the side of his eye as Krystyna leaned back over the seat and showered Mustafa with kisses, Luchnikov sighed and thought to himself that he'd always preferred whores to their respectable sisters and liked Krystyna more as she was now than in her puritan guise.

Just then a red light flashed on the instrument panel: the reserve tank had just gone into use. Half a mile ahead was an uncrowded off-ramp leading to a mountainside hotel, with its own little shopping center, café, and Esso station. True, the station was jammed, but they had no choice. "We'll have to get off here and tank up," said Luchnikov. "I'll fill the jerry can, too. Who knows when or if we'll have another chance."

The idea of having to wait for service at a service station was so novel that people smiled at one another and shrugged their shoulders as if to say, It's a historic event, after all. We can queue up for once in our lives.

Luchnikov's car was twenty-fifth or thirtieth, and Krystyna, who had perked up considerably, sent the boys off to the café and took over at the wheel. Yes, it was a new age, gentlemen. Now the woman decided what suited her fancy and humored the man—not vice versa.

Looking back at her from the entrance to the café, Luchnikov wondered whether she was liable to go into hysterics again. No, she looked perfectly normal. Ms. Sage (someday he'd have to ask her about Mr. Sage) was sitting calmly in the driver's seat, her sweet brown hair flowing alluringly over her shoulders.

The café was crowded, and the two espresso machines worked nonstop. Voices rose animatedly over the jukebox and two television sets. The Moscow channel was pontificating about the lives and labors of living laborers, while TVMig, back on the screen after its recent rout, showed Soviet soldiers arresting the staff and searching the editorial offices of the *Russian Artilleryman*. Everyone in the café agreed that the temporary (of course it was only temporary) detention of all representatives of the mass media and political leaders was absolutely essential, given the monumental nature of the spring war games. Gentlemen—I mean, Comrades— we are entering a new, more advanced stage of social development, proclaimed one of the German farmers to a crowd of nodding beach bums. And I must say, gentlemen—I mean, Comrades—that the Soviet high command is handling the changeover very cautiously, tactfully. Remember the sacrifices that accompanied the changeover in Russia herself.

Luchnikov ordered a Campari-and-soda, Mustafa the new Yaki cocktail—for old times' sake. "Don't be angry with me," said Mustafa.

"Or you with me," said Luchnikov.

"Tell me, Andrei, is this how you pictured it?"

"I didn't think the scale would be so grand."

Three Soviet soldiers suddenly appeared at the door, three Blue Berets with submachine guns over their shoulders and daggers in their belts. Since they had never been in a Western café before, they stood there for a while, lost. They had begun poking each other in preparation for a quick getaway when the jolly bearded owner ran up to them with outstretched arms. "Friends! Brothers! Countrymen! What can I get for you?"

Everyone turned and welcomed the new arrivals with such

warmth that their heads started spinning. "Drink," said one of the soldiers, a tow-headed boy. "You give us vodka?" Red-faced, he tried to show the elegant Westerners what he craved, but the submachine gun kept getting in the way of his gestures.

"You look thirsty to me, boys," said the café owner. "How about some nice cold Löwenbräu?"

The soldiers exchanged glances of fear and amazement. A table was quickly cleared for them, and soon three unbelievably fancy bottles of beer were flowing golden into chilled mugs, and a basket of long, crisp bread sticks, a plate of finely cured ham, and a huge wooden platter with at least twenty kinds of cheese appeared as if by magic. The whole café looked on, delighted at the owner's hospitality.

For a minute the soldiers merely sat there, stunned and salivating, but then the towhead said, "Man, what a feast!" and the three of them went at it with great gusto. Someone gave them each a glass of Metaxa, and in no time they were high as a kite.

"I hope everything is as you like it," said the owner.

The soldiers' mouths fell open. Only now did they realize that the man was speaking Russian. "So you know Russian?" said the tow-headed soldier.

"We *are* Russian!" cried the owner. "Everything here is Russian. We do everything just the way you do."

The soldiers glanced around the café and laughed. "This isn't the way we do things. Not at all."

Before long they had taught everyone a war song about Kaluga and Kostroma, the towns they came from, and soon everyone was singing along with them and giving them watches, lighters, pens, and rings as souvenirs.

Mustafa looked on from the bar in disgust. "Those Russian soldiers are the scum of the earth."

"That's not true," said Luchnikov, putting his hand on Mustafa's shoulder.

"I know your arguments, *aga*. I've read your speeches. And when I think of your ideas in the abstract, you know what I see instead of the man of the world everyone looks up to? I see a spiteful little hunchback in one of Dostoevsky's underground flats."

"My back may be starting to hunch, Mustafa, but I haven't an ounce of spite in me. Tell me, what clan do you belong to?"

"Ahmed-Giray," he said nonchalantly.

"Well now! The proud clan of Ahmed-Giray?"

"All our pride belongs to the past," said Mustafa. "My father is a speculator in stocks and bonds. He's lucky. He's in Athens at the moment. Or do you think he ought to come back? Maybe they'll make him secretary of the regional committee. There are precedents, after all. Prince Souphanouvong, for instance . . ."

While they sat there drinking, Krystyna kept moving closer to the pump—and to disaster. Just when her turn was about to come, a gigantic Chrysler pulled up out of nowhere. Its monstrous shark-like fins, a rusty symbol of the golden fifties, reminded Krystyna of her childhood in Chicago, where she and her parents had settled after escaping from Poland. She remembered how those mighty cars had impressed her when she first saw them as a girl. By now they'd become collector's items. The driver was certain to be a snob.

A snob to beat all snobs, as it turned out: a tall stooped man wearing a leather jacket, jodhpurs, and gaiters! The rusty shark dated from the middle of the century; its driver seemed to hark back to its beginnings. He raced out to the pump and grabbed the hose before Krystyna. Krystyna smiled and held out her hand, assuming he would hand it to her.

"Fuck you!" said the man, shoving the hose into the womb of his own car.

"It's my turn, sir," she said and smiled again, though a bit nonplused. She did not understand what the man had said to her, but his actions spoke plainly enough.

"Fuck you," he repeated, staring at her as he filled his tank. A greasy gray forelock hung over his eyes, and his odd smile revealed a pair of diseased gums. What an unattractive man, she thought. One of the cars waiting behind them called out something in Russian to the effect that that was no way to treat a lady, whereupon the unattractive man straightened up and screamed at his antagonist, "I've had all I can take of these foreign whores! They're everywhere, everywhere! I'm sick of them! Sick of the bitches! Now that our Russian troops have come, it's time to kick them out, every last one of them!" Then he pulled the hose out of the car and aimed its powerful stream straight at Krystyna.

She was so stunned she could not move. Stunned, too, the people in their cars looked on, mute, as the liquid drenched her from head to foot. A slapstick scene from a silent film: squirting hose, static poses, gaping faces.

After dousing Krystyna, the unattractive man doused all the seats of Luchnikov's Peter Turbo, threw down the hose, and with a hideous giggle hopped into his car. Then he started the motor, lit a cigarette, tossed the match out the window in Krystyna's direction, and drove off.

At just that moment the door of the café opened and out came Luchnikov and Mustafa. What they saw was a gracefully spinning, fabulously beautiful Krystyna with flames sprouting out of her shoulders and thighs. Luchnikov always reacted instantaneously in such situations. Young Mustafa stood stock-still while Luchnikov, snatching a tablecloth off an outside table, set off immediately after Krystyna.

Krystyna was experiencing a euphoria of pain. Laughing wildly, she dodged both Luchnikov and her other pursuers. All she seemed to understand was that she was fabulously beautiful, that the flames sprouting out of her shoulders and thighs made her fabulously beautiful. The world had been suddenly refashioned by a bright, blazing dream, and these men chasing after her with rags wanted to deprive her of that dream.

Even so, she was nearly saved: Luchnikov caught up with her from behind, and Mustafa, who had at last come to life, was bearing down on her in front. Then she caught sight of the fence that marked the end of the asphalt surface and the start of an incline, an ineffably beautiful slope of tulips and rocks. She jumped over the fence and hurtled down the slope, immediately colliding with a rock and losing consciousness, then rolling along farther in a flaming ball.

The sun shone brightly the whole day, the sky sparkled over the whole of the Island, and Cape Kherson seemed afloat in the radiance of sun, sky, and sea. The day was at its height when Andrei arrived at Saint Vladimir's with Krystyna's body. The open parking area just before the cathedral gate—which offered a view of the sea, the ruins, and the crosses of the Orthodox cemetery—was empty except for an old green Volkswagen: Father Leonid had arrived. Andrei lifted the body carefully, as if not wishing to disturb it. Mustafa stood silently at his side.

Andrei turned to Mustafa. There was nothing tragic about his face. "Now Father Leonid will say the service and bury her here in his cemetery," he said quite matter-of-factly. "It is one of the most unusual, one of the most beautiful cemeteries I've ever seen."

"Then let's go, Andrei," said Mustafa, cautiously pulling at his sleeve. "Let's go into the church."

"Can a Muslim appreciate how smoothly Hellas blends into Byzantium and Byzantium into Russia here?" Andrei asked Mustafa with a smile. He walked up to the gate and stopped at the first column, completely oblivious to the weight of the dead body in his arms.

At that moment a mountain of gray-green metal, the aircraft carrier *Kiev*, was slowly, noiselessly gliding past Cape Kherson to Sevastopol harbor, the tanned figures on deck clearly visible from where Andrei and Mustafa stood. The radar antennas were turning, and a bomber was rising from the bowels of the ship.

"An impressive sight, eh, Mustafa?" said Luchnikov, squinting into the sun. He laid Krystyna's body on the ancient pattern of the mosaic floor. Heavily bandaged as it was, it looked something like a tailor's mannequin. Luchnikov lit a cigarette. "Quite a sight. A mountain of steel floating past ancient ruins. Nicely planned, eh?"

"Let's go, Andrei," said Mustafa, alarmed. "Let's go into the church."

"And look at that amazing missile carrier rising up on deck. The state of the art. Vertical takeoff. See how perfectly everything fits together. Even the helicopters, buzzing about like flies . . ."

"Isn't that one of ours over there?" said Mustafa, looking into the sky. "See where I mean? Up above the others. The blue one with the rainbow insignia."

"Yes, the loner." Luchnikov laughed. "Don't you see? The script calls for a lone hero."

As the aircraft carrier passed the tip of the Cape, it seemed to be rising up out of the sea in competition with the cathedral, which was built at the turn of the century to mark the spot where Prince Vladimir had accepted Christianity.

Suddenly the aircraft carrier said in a dull, booming voice,

"Popov and Yerofeev detachments to the third deck for a meeting with the local population. Attention. The commander welcomes all new sailors on board. . . ." Then the ship veered slightly and the voice faded away.

"Now do you understand what's going on?" Luchnikov asked with a smile.

The young man gave his head a shake in an effort to reposition the kaleidoscope of images it contained: the deserted Cape, the ruins, the cemetery, the heavy Byzantine-Russian cathedral, the gigantic Soviet cathedral of steel plowing into Sevastopol, the bandaged corpse of the woman on the mosaic floor, her hysterical lover falling apart before his eyes . . . He turned and ran towards the church.

"It's all a film!" He laughed, not noticing that Mustafa had disappeared. "It's all one big location! You've got to hand it to those Americans. Bravo, Octopus! *The Longest Day, Apocalypse Now*—they pall in comparison! Gangut's directing, isn't he? Good for Vitasya! It's brilliant, brilliant! Everything about it. Those ships, those planes—it must have cost a fortune! And I bet you're all having a good laugh at my expense! I bet you're shooting me at this very moment. A mad scene among the ruins. Remember asking me to do the script in Paris? Well, now I'm one of your actors instead. True, you have me to thank for Christie's death, though maybe it was one of your assistants who threw the match at her. Maybe it's a new school—*cinéma*-happening. Of course! Why has it taken me so long to see? Everything, absolutely everything comes from Halloway's bag of tricks. That's why you were making fun of me down there in the square. . . . Go on with your shooting, then. I'll keep laughing. That's what you want, isn't it? Nothing matters any more, so why not? Ha! Ha! Ha! It's a pity Krystyna can't laugh for you, too. Christie, how about a laugh for the gentlemen? She's got perfect teeth. One last laugh, okay? No go. I'm all alone now. How's the loner doing up there? Ha! Ha! Ha! The lone hero! All by himself in a flock of red locusts! Smashing!"

As it happened, the "lone hero" in the sky was none other than his close friend Colonel Chernok, who felt no resemblance whatsoever to the Hollywood type in question. He had spent the whole day circling over landing points of absurdly overmanned, overarmed contingents. From what he could see, the scope of the spring war games greatly surpassed the scope of fraternal aid to Czechoslovakia.

Chernok was flying a Thrush, the latest in helicopter technology, designed and manufactured by Sikorsky-Crimea. At present he was sitting in front with the pilot, but in a split second he could swing round to his videophone screen and talk to the commander of any regiment. He also had two young officers with him collecting and processing information from on-board computer terminals.

All the upper echelons of the armed forces (or nearly all) were members of SOS, and though the officers had been through countless variants of operation Reunification, no one had come up with the variant initiated the night before and proceeding apace, catastrophically growing in magnitude.

Early in the day Chernok began to have doubts about the strategic wisdom of the Moscow marshals and the tactical skill of the Soviet generals. The computers only confirmed what he could see with his own eyes—that the overblown military formations were holding things up or bringing things to a complete standstill. The result was unwonted and unwanted accumulations of men and technology at several locations on the Island. The concept underlying the operation was not altogether clear to Chernok. If there was one at all, it was not particularly "elegant." Soviet military theory is still far behind Soviet chess theory, thought the colonel, and pictured himself giving a paper—his personal contribution to Russian military vigilance—at the General Staff Academy in Moscow, an exposé of all the blunders he had observed. Wait a minute. They won't listen to me. In fact, they'll probably send me off to the back of beyond to work as a mechanic. One thing was clear, in any case: the invasion forces were trying to surround all army, navy, and air bases. Chernok had covered practically all the strategic spots from Sary-Bulat to Kerch and talked by videophone to the commanders. To a man, they were in high spirits and looking forward to meeting their Soviet counterparts. They were all flying Soviet flags. Several times Soviet officers—majors and major generals—came to the videophones and invited him to come and visit them. Since they invariably asked him for his whereabouts, he soon came to the realization that they were unable to cope with Crimean technology themselves and had no one to help them with it, because . . . because . . . Well, there's no point in deceiving ourselves. They're confining our commanding officers. Don't they see the consequences? Don't they know it could lead to internecine conflict?

He thought with alarm of Colonel Bonafede, the commander of a missile base not far from Sevastopol and the only high-ranking officer true to White traditions. Igor Bonafede was too much his own man to submit to arrest without a fight. The *Kiev* was on its way to Sevastopol. With all those bombers on board it was a perfect target for Bonafede's missiles!

Chernok ordered his pilot to head for Sevastopol and made immediate video contact with Bonafede's base. To his utter amazement, he found the colonel with a bottle of whiskey and a Soviet colonel. Breaking off a clearly jovial conversation, both colonels turned to the screen.

"Greetings, Comrade Commander, retired," said Bonafede.

"I see you have company, Igor," said Chernok.

"My name is Sergeev," said the Soviet officer politely. "Military Intelligence."

"Pleased to meet you," said Chernok. "Igor, can you see the *Kiev*?"

Bonafede laughed a tipsy laugh. "Not only can I see it, I can hear the crew talking. Listen, Sasha, Colonel Sergeev and I have been having an argument. I maintain I could have knocked out his *Kiev* with a single volley from a site a hundred miles away, and this shithead here won't believe me."

"Here's what I think of you, Igor," said the Soviet officer, bringing his right arm into the crook of his left elbow.

"And here's what I think of you, Sergei," said Bonafede, imitating the gesture.

"A serious argument," said Chernok curtly, cutting off the connection. Then he turned to his pilot and told him to reduce altitude.

"Reduce altitude, sir?" asked the pilot.

"That's what I said, wasn't it? And head for Bonafede's base."

They moved seawards and began a slow descent. The gigantic aircraft carrier came into view, maneuvering through warships and transports that stretched as far as the eye could see. Dozens of helicopters were landing up and down the coast. Columns of armed vehicles crept from the harbor to the center of town.

A hundred-eighty-degree turn in his chair and Chernok was back in his operations room—what a design!—face to face with Ensigns Cronin and Lyashko, his operational research team. For a while the three of them sat there, silent.

"Have they gone out of their minds, sir?" Cronin asked at last.

Chernok asked Lyashko to give him a full glass of Chivas Regal, neat.

"The odd thing is, sir—" Cronin began.

"We're under attack by a Mig-25, sir," interrupted the pilot.

Chernok downed half the glass and looked over his shoulder just in time to see the vapor trail of the passing destroyer. "What was that you were saying, Cronin?"

"A heretical idea, sir." The young man smiled.

"I'm sure you've had it, too, sir," said Lyashko in English. The men did their best to speak Russian, but were more comfortable with English.

"What's the bomber up to?" Chernok asked the pilot.

"Starting its second circle of attack, sir. I can see the base now, sir. There's an armored unit moving towards it."

"Keep descending in that direction then." Chernok finished off his drink and lit a cigarillo. "Yes, lads, I have had that idea, and what's more, I don't find it heretical in the least. I am all but certain that our troops—"

"Yes," Cronin cried out. "If it had been the enemy, if it had been an invasion, we'd have pushed them back into the sea!"

"Or annihilated them on the spot," said Lyashko with a cold smile. "Look, sir." A map of Crimea, complete with electronic pointer, lit up in the depths of the cabin. "Karachel is clogged with technology, Balaklava is one big traffic jam, Bakhchisarai is a tank park without a drop of petrol."

"Cronin, what would you have done?" asked Chernok, leaning back in his chair. "Let's play war."

"Missile volley, sir," the pilot managed to spit out before an explosion destroyed the Thrush and its four men.

Although Luchnikov must have seen the flash in the sky, he did not pay much attention to it. As far as he was concerned, it was merely another of the film crew's vile special effects. Look what they'd done to Krystyna. How immoral: put it all down on film, put it all up on the screen, just so long as the human tragedy looks real. And in the name of what? There are no goals any more. . . .

Poor girl, he thought. What made you come to Crimea and my bed? What made it all turn out like this? He picked up her body and headed slowly for the cathedral. Three figures came running up to meet him along the shell path: first Father Leonid, then Pyotr Sabashnikov in monastic garb, and finally Mustafa.

"Take her, Father Leonid," said Luchnikov, handing over Krystyna's body. "She was born a Catholic, but intended to convert to Orthodoxy. She loved me very much. Catholicism, Orthodoxy—what difference does it make? All Christians must band together when the world is plagued by evil like this blockbuster they're shooting."

"Blockbuster, Andrei?" said Sabashnikov, putting his arm around his friend. "Shooting, yes, but in the literal sense."

"If even you haven't guessed by now"—Luchnikov laughed—"what must other people think? Imagine the psychological trauma! Who gave Halloway permission to mock us on such an an unprecedented scale?"

"Come into the sanctuary, my children," said Father Leonid. "There we can be together. Many will come tonight, I can feel it. You come with us, Mustafa. You will not offend Islam by staying with us for this day."

"I'm a Buddhist," muttered the young man.

Father Leonid walked with vigorous strides, and Krystyna's white legs hung limply from the bend in his arm. Seeing them dangle, Luchnikov burst into tears.

"Console yourself, Andrei," said Father Leonid, turning his head. "An hour ago I baptized your grandson, Arseny."

Cape Kherson presents a stony face of cliffs to the sea, but along its base runs a thin strip of pebbly beach. There, in one of the many tiny bays, two couples—Benjamin Ivanov with his black Tatar, Zaira, and Anton Luchnikov with his lawful wedded WASP, Pamela—were planning their escape. Actually, there were five of them: the newborn Arseny was in on it as well. The bay had yielded up a tumble-down but still seaworthy motorboat and a jerry can of fuel, enough to get them to the Turkish coast.

Anton and Pamela, exhausted by the events of the last twenty-four hours, sat huddled together against the none-too-firm Island of Crimea. Arseny, sleeping, lay with his head in his father's lap and his bottom on his mother's thigh. The last few broadcasts of the now definitively silenced TVMig contained a confirmed report of Arseny senior's death and rumors of Andrei's arrest, or, as the terrified reporters put it, "temporary confinement." The emotions raging inside Anton were so strong that in the end he had sunk into a kind of lethargy. His wife, still weak from her labor and worried about the baby and their flight, was in no state to buck him up.

Luckily, Ben-Ivan had enough energy for the five of them. He was in his element: escapes were his specialty, or as he put it, Escape is my creative act. I am an escape artist in the true sense of the word. I am always grateful to my arresting officer, because he gives me another chance to escape. I will be very disappointed when Russia opens her border.

With the aid of his ever-dancing, ever-cheerful friend Zaira, Ben-Ivan had knocked the boat into shape, then "surfaced" long enough to buy the necessary blankets, oilskins, provisions—even a CB radio. He laughed as he told how "our guys," by which he meant Soviet soldiers, were welcomed with open arms in the Yeliseev and Hughes supermarket, and how they stuffed themselves with After Eight biscuits and roasted almonds, practically swooning with delight.

"Do we wait for night, Ben-Ivan?" asked Anton.

"Absolutely not," said the escape artist. "At night they'll crisscross the sea with lights, send up flares. If they find us at night, we're done for."

"And if they find us now?" asked Zaira, still full of good cheer.

"Things are different now, *kara kizim*. The sun is sinking into the horizon after a historic day. Twilight is a time of slits, rents, and tears, a time of gleams and glints into the world of the occult, a time when equilibrium wavers and the crystal vaults of heaven give way. You dig?"

Seaman First Class Gulyai of the aircraft carrier *Kiev* went up to the officer of the watch Lieutenant Pluzhnikov and said, "Comrade Lieutenant," but then started hemming and hawing as if sorry he had said anything at all.

"Well, what is it, Gulyai?" frowned Lieutenant Pluzhnikov, who was counting the minutes to the end of the watch and dreaming of shore leave. "Is anything wrong?" He was beginning to feel he was in for a show of "initiative," and although the initiator seemed to regret what he was about to do, he could not quite stop himself. Pluzhnikov gave him one last chance. "Got to take a leak, eh?"

"Well, you see, Comrade Lieutenant," said Gulyai with undisguised remorse, "we've picked up an object on the screen."

Why, you bastard, Gulyai! thought Pluzhnikov, looking at the shiny little flea in the corner of the screen. What the hell did you have to come and tell me for? What's that flea to you? What if a raft *is* bobbing in the waves? What if a few of our own *are* trying to make it to Turkey? Now I have to tell it to the captain, or you'll turn me in. He gave the seaman first class a good hard look. No he won't turn me in, not with that pure, strong face. But then he thought, No, that's just the type, and went and reported to the captain that an object had been sighted floating away from shore and into neutral waters in fucking sector –X and 3X. . . .

Captain Zubov was furious with the lieutenant. What do I care if a few of their natives grab a fishing boat and run for it? You can't teach class consciousness in one day. Let them go. We'll have fewer mouths to feed, that's all. I'll give Pluzhnikov a commendation to keep him quiet.

But then he noticed his assistant Grankin trying hard to pretend he had not heard anything, yet betraying the slightest trace of a smile as he gazed nonchalantly over the neon signs of Sevastopol. The prick. Making a psychological test case out of it. Well, two can play that game.

"Report the affair to the commanding officer," Zubov ordered, thinking that Grankin would get cold feet and be caught in his own trap. But Grankin immediately switched on the ship's radio and reported the incident down to the last detail with one eye on Zubov as if to say, Listen closely, you fucker, I picked up every word.

The commanding officer of the aircraft carrier, Rear Admiral Blintsov, had retired to his private cabin to put through a call to his wife, whom he knew he could reach at their Peredelkino dacha. He had to go over the list of things to buy in Sevastopol while it was still capitalist and, even more important, find out by means of their own private code whether their younger son Slava had slept at home or stayed out all night again with his Tsvetnoy Boulevard hippie girl. And now this unpleasant young Grankin was making a show of initiative with a report about some flea on the screen. We couldn't get along without bastards like him, of course, but that doesn't mean we have to like them. Zubov, now, he always looks as though he doesn't give a damn, but he's a good man—he can hold his vodka and he knows his field inside and out. . . .

Thus it was that fifteen minutes after Seaman First Class Gulyai's report, a helicopter manned by First Lieutenants Komarov and Makarov flew out over the boundless waters in search of a flea.

"Look, Tolya," said Komarov. "Isn't that Greece over there to the left? You know . . . Mythology . . ."

It was deserted Cape Kherson floating by them to the left.

The motorboat moved along at a swift pace, thumped now and then by friendly waves from the south. The sun was setting behind the Sevastopol hills, and both sky and sea glowed with a wondrous light. Then down flew the ominous dragonfly and hovered over the refugees. Can this be the end? thought Anton, hugging Pamela's shoulders. Are we all doomed, all of us here and all the Luchnikovs? His wife was trembling and crying. Zaira had raised her arms to the helicopter and was screaming, "Don't shoot, please! For the love of God, have pity on us!"

"Attention, everybody," said Ben-Ivan matter-of-factly, "I am about to make a cross." And stumbling back to the stern, he lay on his back, spread out his arms, and stared up at the helicopter cabin, wishing it away with all his might. The tension made his head and one of his legs twitch.

The two Soviet supermen looked on from above. "They look like nice guys, don't you think?" said First Lieutenant Komarov.

First Lieutenant Makarov nodded.

"And those girls—hot stuff!" said Komarov. "And look, a tiny kid, too!"

Makarov nodded again.

"Hey, Tolya! They're crossing themselves," said Komarov.

"They haven't got a single weapon on board. That's why they're doing it. They're using the cross as a defense against us! Okay, Tolya, time for the strike."

"How about over there?" said Makarov, pointing into the gathering dusk off to the southeast.

"But as far away as possible," said Komarov. "Those things are dangerous."

He turned the helicopter in the direction of Makarov's finger, and when they were a safe distance away, Makarov pulled the lever.

"Calling thirty-nine," Komarov drawled into the microphone. "Mission accomplished."

"Roger, over and out," answered Seaman First Class Gulyai, though he could see quite plainly on his screen that the mission had been botched.

Night had fallen on Kherson when the coffin containing the body of Krystyna Sage emerged from Saint Vladimir's Cathedral. It was accompanied by Father Leonid, Pyotr Sabashnikov, Mustafa Ahmed-Giray, and Andrei Luchnikov.

The sky was full of stars, and since the artificial glow of Sevastopol was blocked off by the massive bulk of the cathedral, they shone bright and clear over the hill, the white marble pillars of Hellas, and the black marble tombstones of Christianity.

The shells crunched discreetly under the feet of the small procession. Father Leonid swung the censer and read from Matthew, as if asking himself the questions. "What went ye out into the wilderness to see? A reed shaken with the wind? What went ye out for to see? A prophet?"

"Father Leonid," asked Luchnikov, "why is it written, 'The very hairs of your head are all numbered'?" His voice shook feverishly.

The priest turned his face to him. It was white in the darkness. "The light of the body is the eye. If therefore thine eye be single, thy whole body shall be full of light." Then he pressed Luchnikov's head between his hands.

"Why is it written that even the hairs of my head are numbered and that though two sparrows are sold for a farthing not one of them shall fall on the ground without our Father's will?"

Father Leonid dropped his hands and, turning his face to the sky, spoke into the void. "Strait is the gate, and narrow is the way, which leadeth unto life, and few there be that find it."

"Why all our strivings then? Why is it written that He has need of trials, yet woe unto them on whom His trials are visited? How are we to escape them, Father Leonid?"

The priest did not turn to Luchnikov, he seemed to be talking to himself, but his resonant voice filled the air. "Wheresoever the carcass is, there will the eagles be gathered together. . . . And many false prophets shall rise, and shall deceive many. . . . But he that shall endure unto the end, the same shall be saved. . . . Watch, therefore, for ye know not what hour your Lord doth come. . . ."

The gravediggers rested the coffin on the edge of the grave. Everyone stood still. His eyes riveted on Krystyna's calm, childlike face, Luchnikov mechanically repeated after Father Leonid the words of the prayer for the repose of the soul. The coffin was lowered, and the dry Crimean earth began to fall on it. Luchnikov stooped down to gather a handful and noticed another new grave: a black marble cross with the name TATYANA LUNINA inscribed on it. "So she's here, too. Tanya and Christie together." He smiled. "Things got out of control, you know what I mean?"

Sabashnikov put his arm around him, and Mustafa said softly, "Anton and Pamela are calling you on your CB in the Peter Turbo. They're out at sea, on their way to Turkey. I have their call sign. They'll be in range for another half-hour. What shall I tell them?"

"Send them my love," said Luchnikov, "with a special hug for the little one. And tell them I'm busy—busy burying my loved ones. . . ."

Sabashnikov squeezed his shoulder tightly and said, "Repeat after Father Leonid." And the three of them recited in strong, clear voices, "Thou shalt love the Lord thy God with all thy heart, with all thy soul, and with all thy might!"

The stars blazed in the sky, and fireworks shot up behind the cathedral in honor of the day.

Nearby, Colonel Sergeev stood hidden behind the ruin of a marble pillar, waiting for the end of the funeral service. God, what a life I lead, he thought. What have I been doing all my life?

Tormented, in great anguish, he glanced over and over at the illuminated dial of his watch. Suddenly something happened to the mechanism, and the second, minute, and hour hands began spinning with great speed, senselessly racing after one another, and the days of the week in their little window began pushing one another out of the way: Monday, Tuesday, Wednesday, Thursday, Friday, Saturday, Sunday, Monday, Tuesday, Wednesday, Thursday . . .

1977-79

About the Author

VASSILY PAVLOVICH AKSYONOV, who is generally acknowledged as the leading Soviet writer of his generation, was born in Kazan in 1932. His father was a Communist Party official. His mother, Eugenia Ginzburg, a historian, won international fame as the author of the memoirs *Journey into the Whirlwind* and *Within the Whirlwind,* in which she recounted her experiences of nearly two decades in Stalin's camps.

Aksyonov spent part of his childhood with his mother in exile in Magadan, Siberia, "farther from Moscow than from California," as he puts it. He was later educated as a doctor, graduating from the First Medical Institute of Leningrad in 1956. His first novel, *The Colleagues,* published in 1960, was followed in 1961 by *Half-way to the Moon,* which attracted the attention of the world press and established his reputation as the representative of a new, Western-oriented, questioning generation of Soviet youth.

Aksyonov's prodigious activity as a novelist, short-story writer, dramatist, and screenwriter soon earned him a place at the forefront of Soviet cultural life. Although frequent clashes with government authorities made it increasingly difficult for him to publish at home, he was one of a few writers permitted to travel abroad. In 1975 he was a visiting lecturer at the University of California at Los Angeles.

In 1979 he spearheaded the effort to create a literary anthology free of censorship, *Metropol,* and resigned from the Writers' Union after two of his fellow editors were expelled. Forced to emigrate from the Soviet Union in 1980 when his explosive novel, *The Burn,* was published in Italy, he now lives in Washington, D.C., with his wife, Maya. He has been a Fellow of the Kennan Institute for Advanced Russian Studies there and is currently writer in residence at Goucher College in Maryland.

Aksyonov's work is now published throughout the Western world. A collection of short stories, *The Steel Bird and Other Stories,* appeared in translation in 1979. *The Burn,* a novel about life in Moscow in the years of the thaw, will be published in the United States in 1984.

About the Translator

MICHAEL HENRY HEIM is associate professor of Russian and Czech literature at the University of California at Los Angeles. He has also translated novels by Milan Kundera and letters and plays of Chekhov.

Aksyonov, Vassily
    The island of Crimea